THE
WAY
AHEAD

— Book 4 —

THE WAY AHEAD

— Book 4 —

Kaleb England

aka NorskDaedalus

Podium

Podium

THE
WAY
AHEAD

— Book 4 —

CHAPTER 1

Tablet Monitor

As they drew closer to the city, Edwin began to notice more and more side roads connecting to their main path. Then again, it wasn't all that surprising on further reflection. There was no way the single, unswerving main road managed to connect every minor settlement in the area, and the supplementary paths weren't quite as straight as the cobbled street he and his companions were on, instead curving to gradually join in with their current direction of travel.

It seemed likely that they were built in such a way that it would be relatively easy to get from Sheraith to wherever the roads led or vice versa, but they were *very* much optimized for travel to or from the nearest large city.

Rather clever, all told.

Of course, the increased road quantity also increased the amount of traffic Edwin and his group encountered. Sure, there were still the daily couriers running back and forth and travelers making long-distance treks, but now they were joined by local farmers hauling in their harvests to the city, small groups of individuals on their way to and from laden with more manufactured goods . . . there was apparently a market of some form going on.

The density of nearby buildings increased as well. Here, Edwin saw way more wooden structures than stone ones, and that led to significantly different architecture than he'd grown used to. Back in Vinstead, the city he'd visited most often since landing on Joriah, nearly every building was built out of stone, with wood only being used for internals and a *bit* of structure. In Sheraith, by contrast, stone made up nearly all of every building.

"Oh yeah, what was up with the lack of wood in Vinstead?" Edwin asked Lefi. "There was a massive forest right there; why did everyone choose to use stone as their building material? Was there a fire at some point or something?"

"What do you know of the Verdant, and of Rhothos in general?" the Adventurer replied, voice as boisterous as always.

Edwin shrugged. "Not a whole lot. I know that Vinstead is *ancient*, though, like predating-the-Empire old. And the Verdant is this big magical forest with lots of crazy stuff when you go farther in, lots of great magical plants, slumbering ancient fey . . ." He cast a glance back toward Inion. The ancient fey, for her part, pretended to not really notice as she floated along, unsuccessfully trying to get Yathal to open up.

"I see!" Lefi's eyes brightened, oblivious to Edwin's additional musings. "Well, the Verdant is the nigh-literal heart of the southern half of the continent. It overflows with life and magic, only kept from encroaching upon and swallowing much of the continent in impenetrable woodlands by a mighty magical boundary. It took centuries to drive back the trees as far as they are now, and none wish to invite them back!"

Edwin frowned. "So . . . what, there's a superstition that if people use wood in construction, it'll weaken the boundaries of the Verdant's containment? Not to insult anyone, but that seems . . . kind of stupid. Stone has to be *way* harder to get and work with than wood."

Lefi shook his head. "It is no mere superstition, my friend. It has happened thrice over in history that whereupon too much wood was used in Vinstead, the Verdant leaked and caused a multitude of wild creatures to be birthed within the city."

"Wait, *what*? Like . . . it just summoned bears or whatever?"

"The houses sprouted limbs and began to grow a canopy, birds claimed their roosts in those branches, and beasts and monsters began their hunt in the streets. Thus, wooden buildings are strictly prohibited," Lefi explained.

"You think they'd have learned after the second time," Edwin remarked.

"Ah, but why would they pay heed to such a baseless superstition?" The Adventurer winked back at him, forcing Edwin to nod in concession.

"How do you know all this stuff, anyway?" Edwin had to ask. "I thought you ran away from home when you were Yathal's age or whatever. How'd you learn so much history?"

"Ah, you are mistaken in a pair of ways, you see? While I was still an Exceptional youth, my parents saw within me the greatness I was destined for and always encouraged me to fully realize myself—once it was clear that I was already free of the Management and wouldn't be able to rejoin regardless of what efforts they might endeavor to undertake.

"Alas, one day bandits set upon my village and burned it to the ground. I escaped the destruction on account of my exceptionalism yet swore my revenge upon the perpetrators. To this day, I continue to stalk the land in search of their leader in the hopes of getting my revenge."

"Wait, really? I'm so sorry, I had no . . ." Edwin immediately felt bad, though a part of him still whispered, *protagonist syndrome.*

"Ha! No, I merely proved far too Exceptional for my peers and thus the village head deemed that I was too much of a disturbance. He drove me out and my true calling as an Adventurer began!"

"Are you messing with me again?"

"Not in this case, no. That is . . . near enough to my history as to be sufficiently enlightening, however! Though in truth I was as eager to leave as they were to get rid of me—I was off on a treasure hunt, you see."

"Treasure hunt?"

"There was a great bounty to be found and I sought to claim it. Powerful magical beasts may maraud the country at times, and if you can kill them before the Enforcer is called out, their hides and meat can fetch truly wondrous prices!"

"That's . . . interesting, and it's strange that they would allow that sort of behavior to happen. Doesn't that kill lots of people?"

Lefi said, "I do not know that they care. Such activities are seen as exceptionally reckless and, that said, deaths would be inevitable so it matters not whether they die by a manticore's venom or an oversized hole in the ground."

"Is that in reference to something specific?"

"Manticore venom? Truly nasty stuff, it is! Completely incurable and it's more potent the more Skills you have—particularly those meant to resist its effects. Never fought one and I hope I never have to; one scratch and you're as good as dead."

"No, I meant the . . . oh, never mind. How do you know all this stuff anyway? Like some of it I'd understand, you just picked up a random bit of trivia here and there in your years of travel, but the thing about Vinstead? How'd you learn that?"

"Historical Recall! Such a marvelous evolution of the simple recall Skill, as it allows me to recall things I had never learned, akin to Common Knowledge. The two function together marvelously, I shall say. Beyond that, traveling and seeing all that there is to see does wonders for expanding one's mind."

"You really do have a Skill for everything, don't you?"

"Every little thing!"

"Other than Stamina Manipulation," Edwin teased. They may have only traveled together for a few months, all told, but he'd never seen the deceptively-young-looking man anywhere near as jealous as when Edwin had, through a combination of his magic, alchemy, and sheer persistence, unlocked a Skill to manually control the energy the System called "Stamina." He hadn't taken it yet, but it was definitely on his list for future Skills to grab.

"Oh, you little . . . ! You'll pay for that!"

Edwin managed to dodge the good-natured cuff, his training sessions with Lefi not wholly worthless, but found himself suddenly drenched in cold water.

"Hey!" he yelled at Inion, who had snuck up behind him with a bucket. "I thought you were talking to Yathal!"

"Gotta watch out for danger from everywhere! No safety!" she called back. "Also, he loved it!"

Edwin narrowed his eyes. Oh, if she wanted a tussle, he could *provide*.

* * *

Edwin lay pleasantly tired next to Inion atop his wagon. She had won, of course. Even discounting the fact it was a predominantly water-based fight against a water mage and *naiad*, Edwin couldn't win a fight if . . .

Oy! Snap out of it.

It had been a fun diversion as they approached Sheraith. Curiously, unlike Vinstead, the main road didn't run straight to the city's gate, but ran to the side of it. Connecting them was a road that split off, quite wide and in almost as good of condition as the primary thoroughfare. There was a bit of a backup while they waited for the guards to clear their wagon, made even slower by the apparent presence of a market and correspondingly large amounts of merchants. If it had just been Edwin, he could have joined the rest of the walkers, but thanks to his new carriage, he was stuck in an absolutely *massive* traffic jam.

In any case, it gave them enough time to figure out what to do with Inion, which turned out to be a more involved conversation than Edwin had really anticipated.

"You know, I think we probably could get you in," he said to Inion as he turned to Lefi. "Common Knowledge or whatever doesn't say she's a fey, right?"

"Not Common Knowledge itself," the Adventurer replied. "Though Identify Threat is a common Skill among guards, and that would identify her as such, if they thought to look."

"But would they be likely to?"

"Not particularly, no."

"Okay, so then you should be fine!"

"Hmm . . . nah. I don't wanna risk it!"

"What is it with you and cities? Do you just not like being around so many people away from nature or whatever?"

"No! No, of course not," Inion said. "Cities are fine. Remember when I tried to get into Vinstead with you? I like cities. I just don't like the guards is all, ya? Ya. It'll be fine! You go do your stuff and then we'll get me in later."

"Are you . . . scared of the guards after that one threw you down the street like a rag doll?" Edwin realized. "Ha!"

Inion glared at him. "No. Of course not. They caught me off guard is all. Had I known what they could do I wouldn't have been so much as budged!"

"Sure . . ." Edwin teased her. "So then what is it?"

"Look, you go in and do your stuff, I'll go commune with the river for a while, and I can give you new knowledge about the rivers here tomorrow when you sneak me in!"

"I'd be more likely to believe you if you ever actually provided any *actual* information other than how much fun you had. All the functional difference here is that I'll be sneaking you in . . . You just want to sneak in, don't you?" Edwin sighed. "You don't actually care about whether or not you'd be allowed in normally, you just want to do things a different way?"

She didn't respond so Edwin continued, "So what, should I meet you out here tomorrow? What are you going to actually be doing? Please don't let it be something that can be traced back to me."

"Oh, you're not going to tell me to not get in trouble?" she wisecracked.

"No. If I asked you to do that, you'd make sure to get in trouble just because you could."

"And you're not worried about that now?"

"I hope that it would at the very least be more trouble than it's worth."

"We'll see . . ." She stroked her chin in pretend thought. "We'll see . . ."

The spread of buildings outside of Sheraith's walls was significantly less sprawling than at Vinstead. Farmland dominated most of the landscape, with the few accompanying structures being very nice farmhouses and the like. For a while, Edwin was really confused by the presence of enormous fields of what *looked* like wheat, but only the stalks. Any grains that might have been growing were totally gone.

He didn't have to wonder about what might have caused them for long, though. One field was being harvested as they passed, and Edwin watched in awe as a single man hefted what looked like a combination of bucket and scythe, swinging it in a massive arc at approximately waist height.

There was a *blur* of silver and the massive flash of what Skillful Assessment interpreted as a greenish-brown Skill.

In a single motion, a huge swath of the field was cut just short of the head, the stalks bobbing back and forth from the sudden motion and accompanying gust of wind. Edwin could even see the farmer empty a truly staggering amount of wheat heads from the bucket mounted on his "scythe" into a sack sitting on the ground next to him. The sack didn't seem to fill up at all from what must have been enough grain to feed a small town for a month, and the farmer barely seemed weighed down as he picked up the bag and started walking to another section of the massive field.

Nobody else commented about the utterly absurd stunt, so Edwin just quietly shook his head and carried on.

As the line slowly progressed, a few more buildings started popping up. A couple inn-looking places with stables off to the side, a couple of dedicated stables, and then at last a ring of buildings built right outside of the walls, a miniature town unto itself.

Most people on foot were allowed free passage through the gate, the logic being that anyone without a pack was local enough to not need questioning, but anyone with so much as a backpack was pulled off to one of the sides of the gate.

The gateway's arch itself was massive and imposing. The stone seemed to be a single enormous monolith but thanks to Outsider's Almanac, and its ability to tag individual items, Edwin was able to tell that secretly at least seventeen different stones were involved. They were just held together with such precision that their seams were utterly invisible. Honestly, it was in some ways *more* impressive than just carving it all from a single rock, discounting the effects of Skills. After all, a single large mass didn't play nice with most object-based Skills like Rock Sculpting, meaning only the highest-leveled, and thus most expensive, sculptors and masons would be able to work with enormous stone blocks.

The gateway depicted a pair of blue rainbows cascading from a massive thundercloud. Or maybe they were waterfalls? They were probably waterfalls, actually. With that concept in mind Edwin was very easily able to pick out the stylizations of flowing water and he almost felt stupid for thinking they were a *blue rainbow* of all things. Well, whatever. He was the only one who knew about that little mistake.

. . . he'd still be obsessing over it for the next five years though. Edwin never found himself reminiscing about his stupidity from back home, but did he *ever* have a "greatest hits" of every stupid thing he'd done in the last nearly two years.

The gate itself was thick, solid wood made from some kind of tree they didn't have on Earth but he had hesitantly called "ironwood," and although he could only see the interior of the door, it was reinforced in as much a decorative manner as a structural one depicting some very abstract and stylized picture Edwin wasn't quite able to parse. Behind the gate there was a small hallway before opening into the streets of Sheraith itself.

He wasn't quite able to access the city itself yet. First, his group had to get past the three armored figures conducting the inspection of any group with a beast of burden or cart.

Junior City Guard
City Guardian
Experienced Lirasian Gatekeeper

The Gatekeeper looked at them—Identify flickering in concert with a couple of other Skills—and nodded. The one who seemed to be in charge of their inspection turned to Lefi, currently showing as an Adventurer-Mage. He made some gestures on a tablet—a *literal* tablet, not a computer, just a slab of granite with some carvings on it—and started in with a set of questions.

"Place of birth?"

"Riverbend"—there was a hint of a laugh in Lefi's voice, but the guard didn't seem amused—"Rhothos," he finished, and the Gatekeeper nodded.

"Current Registrar?"

"Rizzali of Vinstead."

"Reason and date for leaving?"

"Desire to travel, visiting a friend, and providing mentorship. Been on the road for two months or so."

"Most recent stop?"

"Ashglen."

"Family and given name?"

"Lefi Forolova."

There was a crack in the guard's otherwise stoic facade and Edwin could have sworn the man scowled at Lefi a bit behind his glimmer of recognition. "Right. Reason and duration of visit?"

"Visiting a friend, possibly a month or two. The kid needs a helping hand and she can provide."

The guard pointed at Yathal. "He yours, then?"

"As far as it matters."

"Good enough. Planned location of stay?"

"Rented room, or also possible with friend."

"Who's this friend?"

"Adventurer Rillah."

That got the guard to finally look up from his tablet. "The *daywasr*?"

Polyglot didn't translate the word, but given the man's tone it didn't sound complimentary, so Edwin didn't poke at it. He had a good enough idea, he felt.

"Yes, her. Is that a problem?"

The man snorted. "Not one of mine. Seven or twelve."

"Me and the kid or just me?"

"Both, but not the alchemist. We deal with traders separate."

"*Twelve?*"

"Twelve. You're free to go elsewhere, Adventurer."

"Twelve," Lefi agreed with a sigh and pulled out a small handful of silver. He dropped a number—Numeracy let Edwin cheat and instantly count twelve—into the guard's waiting palm. A curt nod later, the two spear wielders withdrew and allowed Lefi, Yathal, and Kyni through. They slipped into the crowd, but Edwin saw a string of two Skills play—namely, Whispering and Yelling—as they passed through and whispered into his ear with Lefi's voice.

"We'll be nearby and find you once you get through."

Fortunately, he knew basically what to do. It was the job of the Gatekeeper to ensure that only productive individuals would be let into the city; they assessed the potential value and risks travelers brought with them and set an entry price accordingly. Those who were sick or known troublemakers were usually refused outright, but Adventurers would usually get away with just a ridiculously high entry fee. Edwin wasn't entirely sure why the man had listed *two* prices, but no real matter. He was hopeful he'd be able to escape without one regardless.

"Place of birth?" the Gatekeeper asked once again.

"I, uh . . . think I'm supposed to just show this in response? I don't think I should say much more than that," Edwin replied, pulling out a small token—his Adventurer license, which had apparently at some point been updated to show his Ally of the Empire status according to Lefi. How the Adventurer knew that . . . Edwin didn't know.

No, "he has everything" or "he has all the Skills" don't count as explanations.

At first the Gatekeeper didn't seem to pay too much to him, finishing up some sort of Skill-based interaction with his tablet before finally looking to study the small trinket. "If you think that's supposed to . . . Oh, now that is interesting. Step to the side, my lieutenant will be with you shortly."

"What about my stuff?"

"It will go with you. Now, move."

"All right, all right."

At least the wait wasn't too long, and Edwin was able to entertain himself like he usually did—Prototyping and Sapper's Apparatus both made for *amazing* fidgets, enabling him to create massive physics simulations and let them play in his mind, or create crystal trinkets for more tactile toying, to say nothing of his ability for nigh-literal self-reflection.

An avior joined him after about ten minutes. The humanoid bird was slightly taller than Edwin and was armored in significantly more than the chain shirt and helmet of the normal city guards. A quick Identify confirmed his higher status.

Junior Provincial Defense Overseer

Edwin was out of practice examining avior expressions—not that he was ever *that* good, all told—but he still got the sense that the lieutenant wasn't in the best mood. "You're the one?" he asked.

"Edwin Maxlin," he confirmed with a nod. "That's me."

"Good. Now, do you want to explain that"—he pointed at the license—"to me and why it gets you out of normal questioning?"

Edwin shrugged. "I've been officially advised by T— Enforcer Lisana of Rhothos and Emperor Xares that I not divulge parts of my past and history."

"Nothing can ever be simple with Adventurers, can it?" the avior accused.

"Well, I think my companions had a pretty simple entry," Edwin countered, but he saw his reply didn't land well as the piercing eyes of the black-feathered hawk bore straight into his skull.

"Perhaps. But they aren't here right now.

"Now, Ally or not, it is my duty to ensure the safety of my city. Thus, you are to answer my questions honestly and fully. Or you're back out on the road, understand?"

"I guess? Can I answer that something is an Imperial secret?"

"I will check with every single thing you claim that for, and know that if that is a lie, you will find your life becoming very unpleasant very quickly.

"Now, first. Current Registrar?"

"What are you bringing into the city?" he finally asked. The interrogation wasn't *too* bad, but it did take a little while and Edwin was glad that it seemed to be coming to a close.

"Personal alchemy supplies," he readily answered. "Most of it is self-created, some of it I got in Panastalis."

"And the . . . many, many weapons we found lying on the inside?"

"Wait, what?" Edwin was confused, why were . . .

"Oh, that little . . ." He trailed off, unsure of the right word to express his frustration. He got his emotions under control quickly enough and breathed out. "Those would belong to my traveling partner, Lefi Forolova. I believe he's just inside the gate if you need to speak with him. I . . . actually forgot those were in there."

"What man needs more than one halberd?"

Edwin gave him a blank look. "You'll have to ask him."

"Very well." The avior set his tablet down on a nearby shelf. "Twenty-four."

Edwin flinched a bit at the price, but he still fished out the required coins from his pouch, dropping them in the avior's waiting hand.

"Your *friend's* weapons will be kept in the Weapon's Check; reclaim them when you depart. I'll be keeping an eye on you, Adventurer. Now begone. Blow away, I have other things I was attending to before this."

It had been some time since Edwin had been in a "real" city—Panastalis didn't count, it was basically just a town with an alchemy guild—and the last time he had been there, Skillful Assessment wasn't nearly as powerful as it currently was nor was he as adept at utilizing it.

Now that he had it on at basically all times, a thousand almost-invisible Skill uses caught his attention. A young boy was using Identify on pretty much everyone he could see as he walked hand in hand with his mother, a sky-blue gnome tiredly talked to a merchant as he wrote something in midair, and a farmer was using Packing to heft a massive, spatially expanded barrel over his shoulder.

Avior swooped from the sky and landed gracefully next to an uncovered stall, buying something, then took off once more. A pair of humans navigated around the stream of people while carrying a stone cube that was a bit over four meters a side. A seemingly empty stretch of road that was lit up with Skills lifted momentarily to let out a halfling and an avior locked in intense discussion.

"Are all cities this rife with Skill usage all the time and I've just been blind before now, or is Sheraith special in that regard?" he asked Lefi.

The man chuckled. "You look like Yathal, head darting every which way. Sheraith is perhaps more open with Skill usage than other places, but not by that much."

Did he *really* have to make the comparison to Yathal? Well, Edwin did *like* that he knew better now, but it still made him feel somewhat self-conscious. The boy was looking at a bunch of fall-themed decorations covering every surface, his head indeed darting every which way, and Edwin tried to keep his gawking impulses in check.

As they continued their journey farther and farther into the city, Edwin started noticing a few buildings made predominantly of stone blocks. The architecture quality seemed to improve proportionally, and it was obvious that they were heading to the nicer part of the city.

"How do you know where we're going, exactly?" Edwin couldn't help but ask. It was weird just blindly following Lefi. "And are you sure this is the right way? This all just seems so . . . nice, for an Adventurer."

"I know everything! And worry not, this is indeed the right way we must venture. We are nearly there, you see. Just around the corner. Furthermore, there are many Adventurers who have fabulous wealth to call upon!"

"Okay . . ." Edwin mundanely replied. "It's just that a lot of people are looking at us funny."

"Worry not of their opinions, they are merely envious of our freedom!"

He didn't really have a good comeback to that so he fell silent. After a quick check on Bill, the pony pulling his cart—fine as always—Edwin's attention drifted to their surroundings once again. The architecture in this nicer section of the city was . . . really, really impressive.

While they were all slightly different, of course, it was pretty clear that the architectural styles in favor included very, very few straight lines. Domes and arches were abundant, rounded walls more the rule than the exception. Very few of the buildings were grand and towering, though, instead leaning more toward short and wide—though "short" still meant three stories in some cases. It was more about the proportions than the actual size, accompanied with a distinct lack of towers and spires he might have normally associated with fantasy mansions.

Then there were the flatly magical features, sprinkled around from place to place—an intricate stone archway held up by posts no thicker than a pencil, floating steps leading to an entrance on the second story of a building, stone shimmering with almost holographic blues and golds.

Among it all, though, a single building broke the architectural standards to a flatly insane degree, and as they drew closer, it seemed more and more likely that it was their destination. The base looked like a natural jut of rock, sticking at least twenty feet out of the ground, but one that had been carved out into an almost mansionlike appearance, painted in all manner of colors but predominantly blue. Around the rock was a small grassy lawn and accompanying gardens, flourishing with life.

The most impressive feature by far, though, had to be the massive stone tower the rock smoothly transitioned into, rising at least a hundred feet into the air. Or . . . make that two hundred. Three hundred? Even as they got closer and closer to the base, the top continued to be out of range from Numeracy and Identify alike.

"Is . . . is that a wizard's tower?"

"Something like it," Lefi agreed, apparently distracted by the sight.

"And that's where we're *going*?"

"Indeed!"

"Why are we going to a wizard tower?"

"Where else would we go?"

"Are you saying that's where . . . Rillah is?"

"Rillah, yes."

"How?"

"Come along, Edwin! Further into adventure!"

"Are you sure we're allowed? Those guys don't look very happy with us," he noted, indicating a pair of City Guards—well, one was a Senior City Guard, but close enough.

"It shall be perfectly fine, I assure you!"

"I don't . . . oh, never mind."

"You there!" the Senior confronted Lefi. Why was it always Lefi that they thought was the leader? Edwin looked older than him and was the one driving the carriage anyway. Was it the hair? It was probably the hair, wasn't it? *He'd* certainly assume the guy with golden hair that glowed and flickered like it was literal fire to be the leader. Or maybe it was the Class? "What are you doing?"

"Well, my friend! I am attempting to enter the current home of my other friend! Now, would you happen to know the method by which we might obtain entrance?"

"I would, yeah."

"Marvelous! Might you enlighten us to that method?"

"You know what?"—the guard leaned forward—"I don't think so. Your lot doesn't get in."

"I assure you, I am perfectly respectable."

"Yeah, well, we don't want you lot in here; how'd you even get in?"

"My presence was requested by Adventurer Rillah."

"Ha! Now there's a joke. Let me tell you what, you scram right now and we won't haul you in for attempting to disturb the peace. You got it?" The man's voice rose and carried a hint of mockery with it.

Lefi took in a breath, but before he could say anything, a halfling woman—an Honored Senior Mundanity Assistant—was at the gate. "What is the disturbance?" she demanded of the guard. "The lady wishes to not be disturbed."

"Ah! Much obliged, my fair lady."

"These ruffians are attempting to force their way into the Spire's property, honored lady," the same guard spoke up. "We're just going to remove them before they bother—"

"Too late for that, and don't cut off your betters," she snapped, leaving the guard spluttering. "You, Adventurer. What are you doing here?"

"I was sent for by Lady Rillah, you see!" Lefi's fingers pulled out a small green stone from one of his pouches, and after a quick Identify, coupled with something Edwin recognized as Common Knowledge, and a few other Skills he *didn't* recognize, on the halfling's part, she nodded.

"Very well. Come in, let me close the gate."

"Much obliged, my fair lady."

"Your cart and horse can go in the stables around back. Come on, come on!"

That galvanized them into action, and Edwin quickly prompted Bill to enter the opened, very fancy gates.

"If you do get in with the *daywasr*, lemme know what it's like, eh?" the non-Senior guard spoke up for the first time as they departed, and his partner gave out a rough laugh.

Lefi did *not* take the statement well, and in the blink of an eye he had drawn his sword and held the guard at swordpoint.

"Oh, so you *do* want me to—" The Senior was cut off by the halfling's cough.

"Knock it off! Get in here, Adventurer. And you, shoo! Go bother someone else," the woman scolded, and she shut down the quarrel entirely.

"You'll pay for that, Adventurer," the guard promised, but Lefi didn't seem concerned.

"What was that?" Edwin quietly asked as they were led into the estate's grounds.

"Well, they insulted—"

"No, not that—though I may want an explanation at some point about that—but the little stone you showed her." He nodded in the direction of the halfling.

Lefi held out the plaque in presentation before withdrawing it. "Ah, apologies. I forgot you do not possess Common Knowledge. If Identified, it identifies my person as one who is allowed entry to see Adventurer Rillah."

"When did you get that?" Edwin hadn't seen any messages arriving for Lefi that might have carried the object with them.

"Oh, some time ago. We have known each other for many years, but this I received alongside my message as to her whereabouts."

That didn't answer all his questions, but Edwin found himself busy with stowing Bill away in the small stables they had on the property. Caring for such a large animal was . . . a very different experience, but Lefi had helped him learn a lot more about it. That conversation also revealed that Bill probably had Skills to make him easier to care for as well, which Edwin was able to spot once he knew what to look for. Pristine Coat, Eating, and Prime Health were all Skills that the Empire's Trainers knew how to unlock for horses, and all were standard fare.

Bill would have other Skills, of course. Unlike the Companion Skill Kynigos had for Yathal, Trainers couldn't perfectly control the Status of their subordinates. Thus, like most animals, the pony likely had a moderately sized grouping of Skills at a decently high level, but no evolutions.

In any case, Edwin was glad it didn't take too long and he didn't have to leave Lefi and Yathal standing around waiting for him.

The notes of a flute floated toward them, melodic and beautiful. It tickled Edwin's memory in some regard, though he couldn't remember why exactly. He nodded to Lefi as he rejoined his companions, speaking about something with the woman.

"So," he asked as they entered the tower's base, "onward and upward, I suppose?"

"Upward?"

"That's bound to be a *lot* of stairs ahead of us if we're going to the top."

"Ha!" Lefi clapped Edwin's back, sending him staggering as the Assistant opened the door for them, the faint musical notes spilling out as she did so. "Indeed! Onward and upward, my friend! Onward and upward!"

CHAPTER 2

Looking Up

The interior of the tower was every bit as impressive as the exterior. That it was bigger on the inside may not have been a surprise at this point, but the sheer scale of the expansion still awed Edwin. The entry hall alone looked like it was larger than the massive stone was in its entirety, the ceiling stretching beyond his Identify range, and there were very clearly some wings off to the side, circular doors shut tight. Across the arched roof and walls, a colorful mural of some kind depicted some massive scene that heavily incorporated weather alongside a host of individuals, avior and human alike.

It was also oddly silent despite a lack of architectural features to dampen the sounds of walking. In fact, the only noise he could hear was the flute melody floating from seemingly all around them.

At the far end of the hall a massive spiral staircase rose to the ceiling, supported by nothing and distinctly lacking handrails. It was simply a set of wooden slats floating in midair. That they bobbed up and down when pressed upon didn't do too much to help Edwin feel reassured about their stability, but Yathal had no such restraint and thought they were the coolest thing ever.

"Will the dog be accompanying you upstairs to meet the lady?" the halfling assistant asked, voice neutral.

Lefi glanced over at Kyni, circling anxiously around Yathal as he climbed over the stairs. "He will."

"Of course. The lady is at the top. Go at your leisure."

The stairs stretched on *forever*, or so it felt. After they climbed past the entry hall, the steps were magically fastened to the walls and so no longer bobbed up and down, but there was still a sizable gap in the middle of the spiral staircase and gave Edwin a sense of vertigo every time he looked down. While it didn't seem to bother his companions, Edwin had to fight off the knee-jerk reaction he had to potentially falling all the way to the ground. To try and help, Edwin didn't actually put any weight on the steps. Instead, he tethered Flight to the stone wall—covered with paintings and stone reliefs reminiscent of the main room below, but with a slightly different style to them.

Every so often, the style would suddenly shift, but there seemed to be a consistent story being told. That said, for the life of him he couldn't figure out *what* that story was. There were avior and humans and even a couple of gnomes that showed up, but also lots of weather motifs and, well, it was a lot. Maybe it was the story of the tower? That seemed quite plausible.

Honestly, these stairs must have been artificially lengthened. Why would you *do* that? The outside was legitimately shorter, why couldn't they have put the stairs out there?

"C'mon, Kyni. Pleaseeee?" Yathal asked his dog suddenly, panting between each word.

Edwin didn't catch what or how Kynigos replied, but Yathal took on a pleading expression. "Awww. But *whyyyy*. This is *so much* and Mister Lefi says any Skill can be good!"

Kyni gave a short bark in response, making Yathal redouble his puppy-dog look and made Lefi cut off a chuckle. One more quick bark and Yathal hung his head and despondently continued to climb the stairs, breathing hard the entire way.

"What was that about?" Edwin asked Lefi. "I don't speak dog, but you apparently do?"

"Polyglot helps," Lefi gave as a bit of unhelpful clarification, "but Yathal got a Stair-Climbing Skill and wanted Kynigos to let him take it."

Edwin chuckled a bit at that as he continued to secretly float up behind the golden-haired Adventurer. Unlike most animal companion bonds, where the human was the one in charge, *Kynigos* was the one who was able to shape Yathal's Skills.

Looking up wasn't informative as to how much longer it would take unless they were *genuinely* only just barely starting to climb the tower and that wasn't just an optical illusion, but he really, really hoped it was the latter. It wasn't *hard* for him thanks to Flight, but it was tedious.

The faint music grew louder and clearer as they continued to climb, until they eventually reached the top. The stairway just . . . stopped suddenly, letting out into a too-large room at the top of the tower. There were, of course, no handrails around the massive hole in the floor, and Edwin very carefully stepped away from the biggest safety hazard he'd ever seen in a building before looking around.

Wind blew through the room at a steady rate, coming in through massive windows in every direction that *definitely* weren't visible from the outside. The floor consisted of massive stone blocks inset with blue sigils and circles faintly glowing and absolutely *brilliant* to his arcanoception. It felt like swirling winds and brewing storms, but in . . . reverse? Whatever, he could examine it more later on.

There wasn't a whole lot of traditional furniture in the room save for at one end of the chamber, where a few chairs and a couch rested upon a thick rug next to one of the windows. Given the sole occupant of the room was sitting in that window playing the flute, it wasn't hard for Edwin to pick out who Rillah was, though she was sitting with her back to them.

Oh, huh, I know her, Edwin realized as they approached the Adventurer, one eye on her Identify result.

Seasonal Dancer of Whimsy
I passed her on the road. Really good flute player.

While most of her clothing seemed sensible for an Adventurer and the slightly chilly fall breeze passing through the room, her mostly bare back was the primary thing that Edwin could see from his angle, though the top half of it was covered by brown hair. Was she . . . not wearing a shirt? How the heck was she not freezing? There must have been some kind of Skill at play.

"If it isn't the snowbird! I would have thought you might have melted away staying here all this time," Lefi called out with a hint of a smile Edwin wasn't familiar with. Rillah immediately straightened and spun, showing she *was* in fact wearing a turquoise and gold . . . not exactly a shirt, considering it only covered from her collarbones to her midriff, but garment.

Her face brightened, and Edwin caught a glimpse of two different eye colors—one a deep brown and the other a brilliant green while she jumped up from her seat.

"Lefi!" Rillah's voice was melodic and soothing—Edwin clamped down on his mental state, warding off mental Skills—and she brushed a lock of hair away from her eye as she bounded over to them. She wrapped the Adventurer in a hug, and Edwin had to quash an irrational, possibly Skill-caused, pang of jealousy.

After a moment, they separated. "It's so good to see you; I've been cooped up in this little city for *months*, can you believe it?"

"I know, little snowbird. That's why I'm here."

"Have you come to sweep me away to the far corners of the wind?" Her face was one of picture-perfect innocence and curiosity, then broke into a grin. "I'm glad you're here."

She finally turned to the others in their little group, and she bent over to greet Yathal. The boy was doing his customary hide-in-Kyni's-fur routine, but he hesitantly looked up to greet the woman's gentle smile. "And *you* must be Yathal. I've heard so much about you! I'm sure we'll be great friends."

"Really?" Yathal said, barely above a whisper.

"Of course! Unless you don't want to be my friend?" she asked with an exaggerated pout. "Then I'd be sad."

Yathal whispered something into Kyni's ear, who nudged the boy. Seemingly remembering something, the little kid clasped his hands together and bowed deeply. "I would be quite honored if you would accept me in your presence."

"Oh . . . there's no need for that, little buddy! We're *Adventurers*! Do you know what that means?"

Yathal shook his head, so she leaned in conspiratorially and faked a whisper to the boy. "It means we don't have to be proper all the time."

". . . How? Don't you get in trouble?" There was a note of hope or awe in his voice.

"Nope! What are they going to do? Send us to our room? Nuh-uh! We can go wherever and do whatever we want!"

"But Ma always said that being rude to people would mean they wouldn't wanna be your friend."

"Pshhh. Look at me! They've been keeping me here for *months* because I have something none of *them* have. When you're an Adventurer and someone needs you for something, they *really* need you," she said with a twinkle in her eye. "They've needed me so much these past months that they gave me this whole huge tower all to myself! Some of them can't even stand to look me in the eye and they still need to put up with me."

"Whoaaa . . ." Yathal turned starstruck as he looked around the building they were in. "They kicked out the governor for you?"

Rillah bit back a laugh. "No, not quite. The governor's place is *really* nice. It's supermagical, and you know what? He's got a bunch of Adventurers working for him himself."

Yathal's wide-eyed gaze returned to the woman. "Really? I thought nobody wanted Adventurers around."

"That's just what governors like to say so they can get them all to themselves," she said with a wink.

"What do they want them for?"

"Oh . . . all sorts of things. Governor Kos'vilista has a couple of mages working for him, as well as some for . . . other stuff."

"What kind of other stuff? I'm not a mage." The boy pouted a bit, but even Edwin could tell his heart wasn't in it.

"Hmm . . . I'll tell you"—she bopped his nose in emphasis—"when you're older. But some of his guards are Adventurers, you know?"

"Really? But . . ."

Edwin wilted a bit as the two of them carried on for quite a while. He could see what Lefi meant—Rillah had a way with words that put the normally shy boy at ease instantly, bringing him to say more over the course of an hour than Edwin had heard over the entire month and a half trip.

At some point, Edwin and Lefi seated themselves on some of the available chairs. Rillah, for her part, eventually sat cross-legged in front of the entranced boy. Eventually, though, Lefi stood up and gave a good stretch. "It's been wonderful seeing you, snowbird, but I think we need to get going. Come on, Yathal. We need to find a good inn nearby."

"Oh! There's no need for that; you guys can stay here. There's at least three more bedrooms, and I'd love to get the chance to talk to the boy, sorry, the *man* of the hour again." She beamed at Yathal.

Lefi didn't argue—he wouldn't, considering he had been expecting it from what Edwin recalled—and agreed with a quick nod. "Where do we go?"

"Stairs." Rillah lazily indicated them, but a grin crossed her face and revealed she knew *exactly* what it meant. "Talk to Pierash; tell her you'll be here for a while. She'll *love* that."

Lefi chuckled. "Pierash being the Mundanity Assistant? Seems she'd be thrilled to hear that. I could practically feel the dismay radiating from her that Kyni might get dog hair on the floor."

A wry look crossed Rillah's face. "She's the one, yeah."

"Well, excellent. I shall see you in the morning, then?" Lefi waved to Rillah as he started to descend, Kyni gently pulling Yathal along. The kid was the classic combination of "adamant that he was totally fine" and also "nearly falling asleep on Kyni's back." Edwin hoped he wouldn't fall off his ride on the very long climb down.

Edwin, for his part, was glad to escape the social situation that was sitting awkwardly off to the side for several hours, and he tried to slink off following his companions, only to be cut off by Rillah's voice.

"I don't think we've been properly acquainted," she spoke up. "You're Edwin, right? I've heard about you."

"You have?" he asked, confused. "I don't think Lefi sent even a single letter since we ran into each other. How? Also, yes. Hi." He shook his head and extended his hand in greeting. She looked at the motion in curiosity, and Edwin quickly withdrew it. Shaking hands wasn't a thing here, not really.

"Sorry," he muttered.

She just smiled. "It's all right."

Edwin was of two minds about Rillah's friendliness. On the one hand, she was clearly like Lefi: she liked everyone, so he wasn't special. On the other, he did like her more than the clearly-compensating-for-something Adventurer he'd been traveling with, and the attention wasn't *bad*.

Inion would be giving him *such* a hard time next time he saw her.

He realized he'd been sitting in silence for a bit longer than was polite. "Anyway, hi. I'm Edwin." He inclined his head in greeting as she took a seat next to him. She replied with a dazzling grin, which, given his painfully bungled introduction, only confirmed Edwin's suspicions she was just generally friendly.

"Pleasure to meet you, Edwin. I'm Rillah."

"Yeah, I . . . anyway, what did you want to talk about?"

Smooth, Edwin, real smooth.

She innocently shrugged. "Well, I like seeing interesting things, and there haven't been a whole lot of those around lately. You're quite the sight for sore eyes, really." She capped off her statement with a bit of a sparkle in her eye, but Edwin had gotten mildly distracted in the meantime.

Oh, so I'm better than complete boredom, he mused.

Shut up, me. It was obviously meant as a compliment, another part of him retorted.

"Me? Interesting? I mean . . . I don't . . . other than . . . and . . . yeah, I guess." He sighed without any way to really help the conversation avoid him—after all, so long as Rillah didn't know much about him, she was unlikely to dislike him.

"It's okay." She put her hand on Edwin's arm, and he felt a powerful Skill originate from the touch. Instinctively, he jerked his arm back. "I'm sorry!"

She immediately apologized. "I didn't realize that you'd react so negatively. It's not often that Soothing Touch provokes that kind of response."

"It's all right." Edwin mumbled an apology in turn. "I . . . overreacted, sorry. It was a flinch. What . . . what does it do?"

"It's just meant to help you find the contact soothing, help take off a few nerves."

"Can . . ." he started.

Can you turn it off? The question sat unbidden in the forefront of his mind, but Edwin brushed it off slightly. He . . . he could get through this. If nothing else, it was Adaptive Defense training. He didn't think Lefi would leave him alone with someone untrustworthy, so he could probably let his guard down a *bit*, right?

"Can I what?" she prodded slightly.

"Nothing, nothing." He waved off her concerns. "It's nothing important. Can . . . you do that again, I suppose?" he tried asking with a small smile.

"Of course." Rillah returned an even larger smile and placed her hand back on his forearm. He could see the Skill, a sort of dark silver snaking its way through his arm. Once it reached his torso, he relaxed against the chair, resting his head on the back cushion.

"That . . . that feels nice," he remarked, happy to get a smile in response. Then he shook his head, regaining his cognitive functions. "What were we talking about?"

She giggled lightly. "That doesn't really matter all that much, does it? We were talking about you, but if that's not to your liking, we can talk about anything else. You're just so *fascinating*."

Edwin vaguely felt like squirming under the compliment, but managed to quash the impulse in part thanks to Soothing Touch's influence. He could focus, he could be good.

"I guess?"

"Of course you are, Edwin. But how are you enjoying Sheraith?"

"Oh, I don't know. I haven't really been here all that long. Getting out from the wind of the plains was nice though."

"You're welcome."

"Oh? I didn't realize you were responsible for the weather," he jested, but frowned when he saw Rillah's face.

"Wait, what? Are you?" Edwin frowned. "Who *are* you anyway?"

"I told you, silly," she said. "I'm Rillah. We can swap stories about ourselves later if you'd like."

"Maybe," Edwin noncommittally acquiesced. "So . . . weather? I mean, yeah. It's been nice, though still a bit chilly? It's rained a few times lately; that's an experience I haven't had for a while."

"Spent too long inland?"

Edwin nodded. "Yeah, pretty much. I lived for a *year* in the Verdant, you know? Never saw even a drop of rain. *That* was a really weird experience, and then I come out here and it's raining every other day. Feels more familiar, all told."

"You're not from inland, then?"

Edwin shook his head. "Nah. I'm from . . . much farther away."

"Hmm . . ." She narrowed her eyes at him, playfully adding, "I'll learn about you eventually."

Edwin softly chuckled. "Eh, I'm not that interesting. So . . . you do something with the winds? Are you a mage?" He suspected as much; she felt like warm, vigorous winds to his arcanoception.

She nodded. "Yep! I've got a *way* with the winds, so when their old weather mage finally kicked it, they snagged me to help out. They get pretty bad storms, so I'm here to help keep that from happening."

Edwin looked at her with newfound respect. "How powerful do you have to be for *that?*" he asked.

"Oh, most of it isn't *me*. You saw all these?"

Rillah pointed to the inscriptions that filled the majority of the room. "All I need to do is magic it up every day and it does the rest, unless there's something *really* bad that comes around, but that's not so common this time of year. That means it's just a bit of mana, not even enough to tire me out."

"But you're stuck here in the meantime?"

"But I'm stuck here in the meantime." She sighed.

"For how long?" he asked.

"Blast it if I know. They're supposed to be getting some replacement from the capital or whatever eventually, but they've been saying that for months now. If they don't get something new soon, though . . . yeah. They won't be happy." She let out a soft peal of laughter.

"It's as cushy as a *cloud* here, you know? The position gets an absolute fortune for almost no work, not that I see most of that. Because I'm an *Adventurer*, they say that it would just be wasting good coin and it goes right into the pockets of the local politicians." She shrugged. "That's just how it goes, though. And I'm not a Hunter so I don't mind too much. You really can't, not if you want to keep your mind."

She looked at the ceiling. "It *is* a nice place, though. Never lived in a proper tower before, so it was quite the experience for the first couple of weeks. But now? Ugh, I *so* wish I was back on the road. Did I mention how boring it is here?" she asked Edwin, turning to face him more fully. "There's not even enough room here for a proper Dance! And people get mad if I go flying in the streets. Not that it *stops* me, you know, but . . . Oh, I'm sorry. I was rambling."

"Mm." Edwin didn't know quite what to say.

"Hmm. You've had enough of this, I think." Rillah withdrew her hand from Edwin's arm, and while the effect wasn't *instantaneous*, the sensation still felt like being emotionally plunged into a pool of cold water.

He gasped. "Whoa, that was a sudden change." He shook his head. "I hate mental influence Skills."

She hummed slightly in agreement. "Well, you at least kept yourself dignified. That's more than most can boast. Do you have practice?"

"Unfortunately, I've had to directly fight some seriously strong compulsions twice now, and I like to think I'm getting pretty good at it, you know? Apparently relaxation is harder to fight though."

She studied Edwin with a keen green eye. "There's a story there, isn't there? I'll get it from you eventually. You practically *smell* like good stories."

"Uhhh . . ." Edwin wasn't sure how to respond to that.

"It's a Skill! Honest," she tried to reassure him.

Some awkward moments of silence passed while Edwin tried to process the new information.

"So you're a wind mage?" he eventually guessed just to break the silence, based off the feel of her mana, the formations in the room itself, and her supposed job.

"You first."

"Me?"

"Well, it's not often I meet another mage," she explained, "and it's always neat to compare notes. What's your specialty? I'll show you mine if you show me yours." Killah winked.

Edwin returned a smile. Ah, so that was what she found interesting about him. His magic. And here he marginally had hoped it was his personality. But of course it wasn't, why would it be?

Shut up, me. Don't be ridiculous. She met me less than three hours ago. Which is probably about the maximum time that anyone could like my personality for.

Shut up, me.

"I mean . . . I don't know if I'm that interesting or even *have* a specialty. I've got like three Skills that use magic, two of them are evolutions? I started off with Basic Mana Sense, used that to get the Mage Path, got Basic Mana Manipulation with *that*, evolved it into Mana Infusion, then combined Mana Infusion with Packing to get Flight." He shrugged. "So yeah."

"Didn't you get any evolved magical Skills? Unless you're Tier 1?"

"Let's say you go first?" he countered. "I mean, it's not that I don't trust you, it's just . . ."

"You only just met me," she finished. "And I'm this strange and beautiful figure with natural magic and you think I might be a fey or something."

"Funny you say that . . ."

"I'm joking," she said as she brushed her hair to the side. "The System calls it Isochronal Magic, and that means what I'm good at changes with the seasons. This time of year I'm one of the stronger wind mages on the continent—not that there's much competition"—her voice lowered into a grumble—"and is why I'm stuck here."

"What about other times of the year?" he asked.

"Uh-uh-uh! You need to tell me about *your* magic first. Also, it's seasonal. You could probably guess it."

She really liked winking, didn't she? Edwin gave in. "Okay, I have . . . five Tier 2 magical Skills. One is Mana Infusion, lets me make Skills and materials magical." Her eyes widened at that but she didn't say anything. "Then Ritual Intuition, which lets me get a sense for what different kinds of mana are; Overcharge, which Lefi could tell you *all* about, and lets me Mana Infuse myself and my Attributes; Improbable Arsenal, which is a magical Efficient Space; and Basic Thermokinesis, which lets me heat up stuff."

"Well, I wasn't expecting *that*. Quite the impressive collection, I have to say. What about Flight?"

"Haven't evolved that one yet, actually. Only got it a little while ago."

"Aw, a liddle Tier 1 are we?"

"Hey!" he protested. "Lefi is Tier 1 too."

She smirked. "Well, I suppose he is. But you're both children to me. Clearly *I* am the most mature one in this building."

"Really? What about . . . I forgot her name. The Assistant."

"Pierash? Well, *maybe*. If you count being boring and uptight as being mature."

"Wait, that wasn't what you were doing?"

She rolled her eyes and swatted Edwin's arm in response. "Oh, shush. You've known me for less than three hours, you should *not* be so . . ."

"Quick-witted?" Edwin supplied.

"Precocious," she settled on, then frowned. "Wait, no. That doesn't translate well with Polyglot." She continued, "It's a bit strange seeing the guy who raised me look younger than I am, but that's how it is sometimes."

"Wait, Lefi? He's older than you?" At long last, confirmation that Lefi was in fact older than his abnormally young appearance.

She said, "Don't really know how old he is. Depending on when you ask, he's either older than the Adventurer program itself, was one of its first participants, or might 'just' be about twenty years older than you or I. But he's looked the exact same for the last fifteen years, and *acted* the same way too." Rillah shook her head. "He hasn't changed a bit."

"So then, you've known Lefi for fifteen years?"

"Ever since I became an Adventurer. Well, he helped me become one."

"So that means you were what, Yathal's age when you met him?"

She thought for a moment. "That seems about right."

"How'd you become an Adventurer so young?" he asked, but immediately realized he had made a mistake when he saw Rillah's reaction.

"Hmm . . . let's wait until we know each other better for that, 'kay?"

Edwin shrank back. "Sorry. I didn't mean to pry."

"Hey! Hey. It's okay," she tried to reassure him, not wanting to hurt his feelings. "Look, how about . . . you can ask me any question you want and I'll try to answer, okay?"

That didn't *help* him when it came to feeling bad, but whatever. He sat in silence, thinking for a short while before finally deciding.

"Can you teach me magic stuff?" Edwin settled on.

"Why do you think I was trying to talk to you?" She winked yet again. "But you gotta help me in turn, deal?"

Edwin thought a moment. "Sounds good to me, I guess."

"But that can be another time! Tell me, how was your trip? Lefi always exaggerates *so* much, did anything interesting happen on the road to you?"

"Well, there was this spider . . ."

By the time the two of them finished talking, it was late. It was quite possibly the most positive human interaction that Edwin had had in literal years, and he was *exhausted.* The human interaction had started shifting from enjoyable to just draining at some point, but Rillah either was another *extrovert* or had some kind of Skill that gave her social stamina, as she seemed just as cheerful and bright as she had been to begin with.

Finally, she yawned and stretched, giving Edwin a slightly sleepy grin. "Well, *that* was nice, but I think it's about time for bed, yeah?"

He nodded in reply; he was still marginally recovering from not sleeping the night before, but he was essentially fine. "Are the rooms all the way at the bottom?"

She nodded and rolled her eyes. "The tower's *really* old, but pretty much all its masters could fly. They liked to show off their superiority by making everyone climb endless stairs if they wanted to get to any of the magic stuff, whereas living is all done at the bottom.

"Also, I'm pretty sure the top's been knocked over a time or two, so yeah! Sleeping's at the bottom."

"I guess that makes sense. Still, it's a *lot* of stairs to have to go all the way back down."

"Or . . . you could take the fast way!" she called out and fell backward into the stairwell.

Edwin's stomach lurched, but before he even really thought through his actions, he had sprung up and jumped into the void.

Vertigo set in *immediately*, but he wrestled the impulse to the side as he activated Flight and . . .

Oh. Right.

Of course Rillah could fly too. She was a *wind mage*, more or less, and had even said that she could during their conversation.

However, he had expected her flight to be strictly magical, like his was. Maybe a mantle of winds or whatever that wrapped her and allowed her to float effortlessly. He was *not* expecting to watch a pair of massive wings spring from her back—so *that* was why she left it bare, that made sense—filling up most of the airspace with burnt orange, yellow, and red feathers.

Edwin managed to tether himself to the side before he could slam into Rillah, but she slowed down as well, rising up past him and making her wings outright pass through him.

"Aww! So noble, trying to save me from my own jump?"

"I wasn't . . ." he trailed off. "Shut up," he muttered, much to the laughter of Rillah as they floated down a too-tall tower.

And so, Edwin found himself on a proper bed for the first time in nearly two months, studying the ceiling. For all that it had been an exceptionally long and exhausting—in every sense—day, he still felt it was overall a success.

He'd found someone he could stand and who could stand him, not that it was too great of an accomplishment for someone who clearly both just "liked everyone" and had likely been asked by Lefi to help Edwin out of his "shell," just like with Yathal.

He was perfectly in control of his own shell, thank you very much. He didn't need to be pulled out like some scared little kid.

Another part of him said he shouldn't complain about so much personal attention from a pretty girl, but the year and a half he'd lived alone with Inion put *that* part of his brain firmly under his control.

In any case . . .

Edwin sighed. It had been a nice day. He would stick with that. Tomorrow, he'd visit Inion and see if there was any good way to try and smuggle her into the city—maybe she could hide inside a water barrel or something—and maybe start learning a bit about magic from Rillah. Maybe he would stick around for a bit longer, he thought. It . . . wouldn't be awful, at least.

He could enjoy this.

CHAPTER 3

Fight or Flight

"How was the river?" Edwin asked, more out of politeness than anything. He already knew basically what she'd say, after all, and . . .

"Oh, it was really cool! Nobody was in it, though the fish were really fun! There's this *great* waterfall a little ways back there, we should go and visit it! I'm sure you'd love it . . ."

There it was. Edwin nodded idly in agreement as he and Inion slipped through the streets of Sheraith, returning to the tower that was their current residence.

"You know, you really should have just come with us when we entered," Edwin pointed out. "You could have just hidden in a barrel of water inside the carriage."

"Maybe," she cheerfully agreed.

He gave her a side-eye glance. "You're impossible."

"Only sometimes! Besides, this way worked out just fine, you know?"

"I mean, it *did*, but we had no way of *knowing* that. Lefi said that most cities aren't built right next to rivers for that very reason—it's hard to keep some aquatic monster from just slipping into civilization, and those few that do usually have warding like you wouldn't *believe* turned toward that. I'm not actually sure why they *don't*, actually. I'll have to ask Rillah when we get back; she's pretty connected to the magical circles of the city."

"Ah, does that really matter?" Inion said dismissively. "I made it in, and what else could you learn?"

"See, there's *always* something to learn, and you never know if it's worthwhile until after you learn it. So learning everything you possibly can is never a waste of time. Who knows, maybe this is some really pivotal piece of information that will totally define my stay here.

"Maybe some massive river monster will attack and everyone wonders how it could have possibly gotten in, but only I'll know the secret and I feel guilty that I didn't tell anyone because I could have prevented the tragedy but I still somehow ended up really important in the defeat of the monster despite the city guard being constantly ready for that sort of thing and the local Enforcer likely able to come at a moment's notice.

"Actually, should I try to meet the local Enforcer, do you think? Tara was great but I don't know if that will hold true for other Enforcers. But at the same time they're probably really powerful and probably will become relevant at some point.

"I definitely already jinxed my stay by thinking that six smoke grenades would be plenty, I should make more, shouldn't I? Hmm. I need to see about processing some more lybird feathers, but I really need to also make some better weapons so Lefi might see how potent my creations can really be. But *then*—"

"Is this what it's like to live in your brain?" Inion asked.

"I mean . . . probably?" Edwin hazarded, mentally panicking about what he could have said to provoke that kind of reaction from her. Did he say something wrong? He mentally tried to recall what he had said; was it bad?

"It's interesting is all."

Yep, he had definitely said something bad. It couldn't have been about his training, could it? Inion talked about that sometimes herself. Was it about meeting the local Enforcer? Or was it just that he was talking too long? It was probably just talking too long, wasn't it? Dang it, he thought he'd dealt with that particular problem, but apparently not . . . and why was he babbling so much in his own mind again? He was better than this most of the time.

Okay, Edwin. Focus. Why can't you think about something for more than two seconds in a row all of a sudden? Well, actually it's bound to be more than two seconds. I had some pretty impressive coherent thoughts in there.

Gah!

"—Talking but are thinking about things now?"

"Um, maybe?"

She shook her head. "What am I going to do with you?"

"You've done *lots*," he retorted. "But I presume whatever is next will be painful."

"Nah." She waved him off. "I'm going to have you introduce me to this Rillah."

"I thought you said this *wouldn't* be painful." Edwin playfully groaned as he ducked around a young boy—a Junior Apprentice Carpenter—and double-checked to make sure the construct he'd made with Sapper's Apparatus securing his purse was still in place (it was).

"Hey! It's good for you. Humans are *social* creatures."

"Yeah, sure. We also drink water but nobody seems surprised that we can drown."

"Ooh, fey! Never met any of your kind before, but I always heard *stories* from Dad."

"Well, I'll try not to disappoint. Was he of the Old Ways?"

"Nah, he was just from the forest, but he wasn't very reverent. Mainly complained about you being . . ."

Edwin held back a sigh. Inion was getting along great with someone else, and he got to watch Rillah getting along fantastically with someone else as well. He never held any delusions about . . .

Shut it, me.

He seemed to be dipping into his self-destructive social side quite a bit lately, and he couldn't help but wonder why. Was it just the increased exposure to other people, perhaps? Or was it that his brain shoved memories in his face and reminded him of all the reasons nobody could like him?

Edwin knew that his worries had to be fabricated at least on some level, but . . . Which ones, and by how much? Overassuming his familiarity and relationship with someone was something he wanted to avoid *at all costs*, and he paid for that decision a lot, in all honesty.

Someone more open and forthright would definitely have more friends than him.

But he also found meeting and trying to befriend people *exhausting*, and for every friend he might find by being superearnest and up-front, there might be a hundred who really disliked him for it. And he just didn't have the energy to try that many times. He'd sooner approach each person with caution and avoid embarrassing himself.

It did mean that he would definitely be outshone by his more outgoing and personable companions, though. Especially if he was going to stick around for a while with Lefi and/or Rillah; they were very energetic personas, and . . . yeah.

Not getting into that.

Well, at least Inion and Rillah seemed to be getting along well. What was Lefi up to? he wondered.

Edwin's stick scarcely managed to block the punch, sweeping the hand off to the side with a solid *crunch*. Under normal circumstances, Edwin would be worried about the sound. But when fighting Lefi, not only did Edwin *have* to go all out, he couldn't even hurt the guy if he tried.

Genuinely. Back when they were first starting off, Lefi had gotten him to whack him in the face as hard as Edwin could muster. Lefi barely even noticed it. He must have had a triple-digit Health Attribute, as well as possibly Constitution, an Attribute that he claimed flatly reduced damage and harm taken from all sources.

All that to say, if there was a *crack* when they were fighting, it was more likely that Edwin's stick was in need of repair than any part of Lefi. Crunches obeyed the same rule, and so Edwin managed to fight past the sympathetic wince of pain and tried to follow up the sudden opening it provided.

Unsurprisingly, it didn't work. Lefi's own stick came around and struck Edwin's with a clatter. To keep himself from dropping his weapon, Edwin grabbed onto the end with his second hand, reinforcing his grip.

As soon as it was safe to do so, Edwin released his auxiliary grip and snaked it into his belt pouch, withdrawing a small sphere of "potion."

Which potion? Didn't really matter, they were all filled with water at the moment. All that mattered was that if he could hit Lefi with it, Edwin won.

Another feinting probe toward Lefi's face with his stick got the weapon smacked out of his hand for its trouble. That was fine, though. It just meant his right hand was available for throwing his potion as hard as he was really capable of.

The vial sailed through the air directly on target, but Edwin didn't let himself hope, having been in almost that exact same situation previously . . . and there it was. Lefi's own stick collided with the crystal ball and, instead of breaking the fragile object, sent it flying off to the side. As soon as it struck the ground it shattered into blue light.

Okay, so one of Lefi's Skills let him reinforce objects he hit, maybe? It *would* be useful if he trained a lot of people, come to think of it. Edwin didn't have time to think about it too much, though. He grabbed his next prepared weapon and threw *it*, dismissing its apparatite container as he did so and allowing the contained water to spread out into a sizable splash. No way to deflect *that*, now was there?

. . . And Lefi just dodged it.

Edwin should have seen that coming, but it was still amazing to think that the guy could dodge a splatter of water *and* two marbles at the same time.

Hmm.

Edwin pulled out his latest iteration of his marble slick. Hundreds of apparatite spheres, many of them with multiple nested layers, others with caltrops either metal or apparatite in case they were shattered all packed tightly into an expanded and very fragile apparatite box.

He threw the package—a first for their fights; normally they fought on much less even ground than the stone-floored courtyard they were currently on—and it shattered, scattering the marbles in every direction.

Lefi grinned. "Not a bad move there, Edwin! But not good enough!" His feet stepped effortlessly through the crowds of marbles, scarcely even seeming to notice their presence.

Edwin had retreated a short way, using Flight to avoid the hazardous terrain, but the speed at which Lefi was charging at him was still more than he could outpace. He tried to rise farther into the air, but he wasn't fast enough to prevent the Adventurer from grabbing his ankle and slamming him bodily into the ground.

The Combative Mentor—Lefi had tweaked his Class name again for some reason—fell back into a relaxed stance. "You, my friend, need a lesson."

Edwin sighed as he rose to his feet once more. "Okay, Lefi, what is it this time?"

"It's probably best that I provide a demonstration."

He held back a wince. "Demonstrations" were always painful from his experience, so he wasn't likely to enjoy this. "All right, hit me."

Lefi took the invitation for what it was and brought his stick whipping around, making Edwin flinch. The Adventurer didn't actually strike his face, much to his relief, but held the tip of the wooden rod inches away from Edwin's nose.

"When you find yourself fighting someone, what is the most important thing to keep in mind?" Lefi asked.

"Um. Is it how to win?" Edwin tried. "Or are you talking about something more specific?"

"Wrong!" Lefi rapped the top of Edwin's head in admonition. "Try again."

Edwin rubbed his skull. "Fine. Is it what your opponent is going to do next?"

"Closer, but no!" Lefi rapped once again, but Adaptive Defense was already doing its job fighting against both blunt trauma and pain.

"Okay, then I don't know. Maybe what *you* should be doing next?"

"Wrong!"

"Look, I'm clearly not going to be getting it. What are you looking for?"

"The first thing you need to remember in *every* fight is 'how do I survive?'"

"Well, I mean obviously, I could have told you that," Edwin flatly replied.

"Oh?" Lefi was holding back a chuckle. "Then why didn't you?"

"I don't know, it was too obvious?"

"Hmm. I do not believe so! I see in you the same problem I've seen countless times before. You cannot win every fight. Many times, it's all but impossible. Yet you approach every spar with me the exact same way, trying to find a way to land a blow on me instead of avoiding them *from* me."

"Wait, I was supposed to just . . . run away? That's not how spars are supposed to work. It's a way that I can improve how I fight while being at minimal risk."

"They're training. Remember what I said? Fight me like you would if I were trying to kill you."

"Yeah, but . . ." Edwin trailed off. "I got nothing. So what, I guess?"

"Break the habit." Lefi punctuated the point with another rap. "You're at your best when you know exactly what you're facing and when doing so on your terms. You have powerful friends; *use us*. The better leveling from danger is *not* worth your life."

Edwin sighed and asked again, "So what, then? I just run away?"

"Yes. Run hard, run fast. You have Longstrider, Stamina, Flight, and you're a human. Throw one of your smoke bombs down and run."

"I've done that before!" Edwin protested. "And it turned out to be against a *turkey*."

A grin flitted across Lefi's face. "Lybird, not a chicken. But would you rather run away from a fight you could have won, or stuck around if it *was* so dangerous? There is a time and place to stand and fight, but it's not your first resort. Only do it if you can't run; don't see a giant spider and think how you'll take it. Get *out* of there, get information, and then and only then do you try to win. Get friends, make potions. Do what you have to; you don't just charge in and improvise.

"You're pretty good at improvisation, I'll give you that. I've seen you pull out some frankly ludicrous wins, but those aren't a strategy. They're luck. But you? You see something and you can't not do it. If it's a potion, a fight, or even just a question about Skills. You need to know the answer, you need to figure out the solution. You can never *not* get an answer, and that will kill you one day if you don't control it."

"But what? Am I supposed to just not pursue the answer to questions?"

"Yes."

"So I see a potential potion and I don't make it? I learn about a Skill and *don't* try to figure out its limits?"

"Yes."

"That's not living! How do you people manage just going through life so *incurious*? Don't you feel the need to know, the need to learn more and more?"

"Do you?"

"Of course! Asking questions and learning is fundamentally what it is to be human. You can't just *not* know something, or at least not *try* to learn it."

"Yet you're able to control yourself with your experiments, are you not? You perform the same measurement multiple times, check things you already should know intuitively, all the time."

"I *try*. I have to try," Edwin admitted. "You have *no* idea how hard it is for me to make sure I keep going with proper experimental procedure, and even then I don't make it all the time. There's just so much cool stuff, I want to test it all, use it all!"

"And you can. You likely *will*, if you don't kill yourself chasing some battle you didn't need to be in."

"Hold on," Edwin recalled. "Weren't you talking about how I needed to learn how to win fights back when you and Inion were scheming about how best to tor— train me? Like how I couldn't just rely on people to do the job for me?"

"That hasn't changed, not truly. The primary difference is what you are prepared for."

"Oh, so I'm not ready to actually fight people then?" he accused.

"You are. You possess far more combat training than the average person, yet it is insignificant in the face of a true warrior. But training you to defeat *them* is not my intention—preparation is where you shine, is it not? I've seen you master a Skill with just a few days of preparation and the right herbs by which you could create a potion. You are an alchemist, as you are so fond of saying. Alchemists are not warriors, and neither are you."

"Yeah, I know. That's why you have me using these fake-potion things, so we pretend that I have the perfect counter for whatever it is that I'm fighting. Sure, I might need to run in an initial fight, but I'll need to come back at *some* point unless I rely on other people entirely. Which you said I shouldn't do."

"You should not. And yet you still face me head-on, do you not?"

"I mean, sure. But I also don't want to use up all my smoke bombs in training. I'll make a few more at some point but Refining that much material is still a pain." A thought struck Edwin. "Hmm. I wonder if I can automate the process somehow? Would . . . no, it requires manual input. But maybe . . . no. Anyway, sorry. Where were we?"

"You must first learn how it is that you can survive! I shall alter your training from fighting to survival. The latter is more important for you."

"But I got a lot of that from Inion," he pointed out. "You said that alone wouldn't be sufficient."

"Survival is about more than not being hit, my friend. It is about hitting back as well, with everything you have at your disposal. The most important thing is where your instincts lie. And right now, they do not lie with survival."

"Hey, I want to survive," Edwin complained. "It's literally my primary goal."

Lefi held up a hand and counted off fingers. "The Catabolic Alchemist and his minions."

"The *only* reason I stuck around and fought Niall and his goons was because of *your* Skill influencing my brain, and you know it."

"Charging at an aggressive wild beast, shoving your hand down its throat, then setting your hand *on fire* to defeat it."

Edwin frowned. "How did you know about *that?* Have you been talking to Inion again?"

"Turning your own kiln into a bomb and hoping that a just-obtained Health Attribute would be sufficient to help you survive."

"In my defense, the alternative was *certain* death. That assassin was serious business, and the explosion was also meant to call Inion back from her explorations."

"Wholly disregarding the threat that another presented to you because you did not feel as though you were in any particular danger."

"Okay, two things with that. One, my instincts are usually pretty good. Two, yes that was a mistake and I can do better than that. I was overconfident, slipped up, and paid the price."

"Charging at a Titan Spider mostly unarmed and unarmored."

"Okay, but I did learn my lesson from that one and I won anyway."

"Yet here you are, and have you yet run away from a single fight?"

"I mean, at least one if you count the lybird. Two, if you count me fighting the dwarves, back when they were keeping me prisoner and my entire goal was to get away from them."

"We can count the lybird. What other accomplishments in this regard?"

"So we're just ignoring the dwarves?"

"You willfully attacked them to accomplish a goal; you did not retreat from a fight you could possibly avoid. I should arguably have included them as a point of *failure* for you."

"Okay, sure. I see your point," Edwin acquiesced. "I'll do it."

"Oh?" Lefi was clearly skeptical. "Just like that?"

"Just like that." Edwin sighed. "Obviously I'll probably fail a *lot*, but it'll be my goal. You're the combat expert here, and I know that I should definitely try to listen to you. I mean, it's not what I want to do, but if you think it's a good idea . . . Run from any fight I'm not prepared for if I have any chance, because I can't protect myself. I mean, now that I know you want me to literally run away from training, I will *happily* oblige."

Lefi assessed Edwin with a skeptical eye, then gave a curt nod. "Excellent. Now, back to our sparring. Begin in three, two, one . . . go!"

As Lefi lunged for the attack, Edwin activated Longstrider. In the blink of an eye, Lefi's stick passed through where Edwin had been mere moments before, but Edwin was already ten feet away and running.

"Strike!" Lefi called out, as his stick snapped into position on Edwin's torso, sending him sprawling.

Edwin got to his feet, wincing slightly. As it turned out, running wasn't as easy as Lefi liked to make it sound. The guy was *wickedly* fast and incredibly accurate with all his weapons. Right now, Lefi was trying to teach Edwin the proper ways to disengage, and while he appreciated the lesson in *theory*, he wasn't sure he was actually learning anything other than the fact Lefi was somehow able to strike him from behind *while in front of him.*

"Stand!"

After a few tests to make sure that Edwin knew how to run away properly—he did—Lefi had pivoted their lessons to making sure that

Edwin was ready to either fight or run at a moment's notice. Threat assessment, he called it.

In practice, it meant that now Edwin was getting a few moments of reprieve between half of his times being beaten into the ground. Because of course Lefi wasn't going to just let Edwin *run away*, no. He now needed to learn a fighting withdraw against even Lefi.

Block, block, step back . . .

"Strike!" The stick connected with Edwin's wrist that time, making him drop his own weapon. He grimaced, but retrieved the rod and took his stance once more.

"Run!"

Step back, step back. Use Flight to pull, drop marble, block, and—

"Strike!"

Gah, the wrist *again*. Without saying a word, Lefi returned to his starting position, and Edwin followed.

"Stand!"

Block, block . . . instead of stepping back, Edwin tried blocking again this time.

"Strike!"

His wrist was *really* starting to hurt and would probably need a potion by the time they were done. What the heck was he doing that constantly provoked the attack?

"What am I doing wrong?" he asked.

"Hmm? You'll get it!"

"Couldn't you just tell me, so I can figure it out sooner?"

"Run!"

Step back, use Flight to suddenly veer off to the side . . .

"Strike!"

Okay, what did Lefi have against his wrist?

"Strike!" That one *hurt*, clipping the side of his head and directly hitting his ear.

"Gah!" Edwin felt a bubble of frustration envelop him. He fought it, trying to force it down, force it into line, but it pushed back even harder. He threw down his stick in frustration, sending it clattering across the stone as he cradled his ear. Was it bleeding? "I'm done!"

Lefi lowered his stance. "What do you mean? You're performing remarkably."

Edwin tried desperately to wrestle his emotions back in line, to no avail. "I'm not improving! All that's happening is you're having me try again and again to hit you and I keep failing time and time again. I have better things to do with my time, you know. I'm not *getting* anything from this training now that you've told me to just run away, or when you tell me to stand and fight! You're not teaching me anything, and I'm not getting any better on my own!"

"Nonsense! While it may take a while, your Skills will surely prevail shortly! It will just be a bit longer, then you will become a master!"

"Oh, shut up!" he snapped, his emotional restraints disappearing. "I don't have a combat Skill, Lefi! Other than Throwing Weapons, which doesn't apply at *all* here. I want to learn how to use my Skills to fight, not the other way around. The only way I'm going to get better is if you *teach* me to get better, you can't just let the System do all the work for you again! Honestly, do you ever do anything for *yourself*, or do you just coast on your hundreds of Skills?"

Lefi seemed struck speechless by Edwin's sudden outburst. Before the Adventurer could formulate a response, Edwin's brain caught up with his mouth and was instantly mortified.

"Gah! No! I didn't . . ." He could practically feel all the goodwill he'd built up with Lefi fading away in a single calamitous moment, where his emotions finally managed to break free in the very worst way. He wanted to collapse into a ball, but instead he pulled on every Skill he could manage to just *flee*.

Next thing Edwin could properly remember, he was in his room, curled up on his bed with his head between his hands. His emotions were in shambles, his control over all of them breaking and refusing to behave as he tried to shove them back in their boxes. Regret and sorrow mixed with anger, primarily aimed at himself. If only he'd been able to keep a better control over his anger, this could have all been avoided. Why did his control slip right then, when the Adventurer was trying to help him?

This was why he didn't have any friends, wasn't it? He could keep his emotions in check almost all the time, but on the rare occasion that they did slip out . . . who would want to be around him? He certainly wouldn't. Not when he so habitually lashed out at people around him *helping* him. He was intolerable at the best of times, and it only got worse from there.

There was a knock at the door.

"Go 'way!" he yelled, lifting his head from his pillow just barely enough to speak.

"Edwin?" He expected Inion's voice but was surprised to hear Rillah's.

"Oh, uh! Sorry!" he hastily clarified, embarrassed at the thought she might see him in such a state, the surprise sufficient for him to get his emotions to mutely hop back in their boxes. "I thought you were, oh never mind." A quick glance around his room didn't reveal anything he wasn't supposed to be showing. "You can come in, I suppose."

He sat up on his bed while the girl joined him, hopping cross-legged onto his mattress. Despite being made of . . . he didn't actually know what beds were made of on Joriah, come to think of it. At least not these. But in any case, they were just as, if not *more*, comfortable than his was before he was ripped away from Earth and nope! He was trying to stay presentable, and he wasn't allowing his emotions to run rampant *again* today.

"Lefi is such a pain, isn't he?" she started.

. . . Of all the opening lines Edwin had expected, that was *not* one of them. Didn't they get along great or whatever?

"Um, I don't think that I'm a very good person to comment on that. I find most people to be pretty annoying to be around, just because . . ."

"Oh, even me? Am I really so bad?" she asked with false offense, leaving Edwin marginally stumbling over his words.

"I mean, no, but also yes? Wait, no. Um, so you see . . ." He struggled to formulate his words.

He didn't dislike being around her, sure, but that didn't mean he was *comfortable* around her either. Rillah was a new person he wanted to make a good impression on. Emotional vulnerability *was* useful in that regard, yes—so long as he didn't go so far as to evoke pity—so this wasn't an inherent loss of a conversation. But how did you explain to someone that no, you *did* find their presence a drag while still marginally enjoying being around them?

"I *do* like being around you," he eventually settled on a small, hesitant lie, "but also, I just don't know."

"It's okay." She smiled. "You just met me, it's understandable."

"Sure," he settled on.

"Lefi is just a pain at times though, you know?" she continued. "I've known the guy for most of my life, and while I love him to pieces, we don't travel together for a reason. Part of that is of course that I want to go wherever the wind takes me whereas he prefers his 'Quests!'" She said the last word in a surprisingly accurate rendition of Lefi's voice.

"But other parts of it are just that he doesn't truly understand and empathize with the difficulties that most people have. For him, he *always* uses the System. For everything. People make jokes about Adventurers, and half the time even their most ridiculous speculation is less than what he has.

"He once told me he has *three* different Skills dedicated to baking bread specifically. Three! Why he has them, or how he got them—well, I actually *do* know that," she said with a sly grin. "But that's not my secret to tell. But he's never needed a teacher because he knows the System will help him out. By that same aspect, he knows what helps *him* and just can't understand that not everyone has a hundred Skills whispering secrets of success to them. All he knows is how to help the Skills level.

"He's very good at that, though. He's *really* good at that. Ask him about any Skill you have and he'll know exactly how to level it, and his Skills will help you level it even faster. But he's trying to make you a fighter, and that's just not who you are, is it?"

Edwin started slightly as the conversation shifted back to him and he had to reengage his ability to speak. "No. I . . . don't think so. When I first—well, when I first arrived in Liras, I thought that I might be able to be this supercool action hero, the kind you see in stories, you know? I was actually really good at it, too, or so I thought.

"I took stupid risks but they paid off. I fought my way out of captivity and managed to subdue a small bandit group. I killed a house-size bear, burned a panther to death by my own hand. And I really liked it!

"But I also burned that panther to death *with my own hand* shoved *down its throat* as *fuel,* had to cauterize an arrow wound in my shoulder, was nearly crushed by rocks, dropped myself through rotten floorboards, and more. It's just not what I enjoy.

"Well, no. I *do* like it. Fighting brings a kind of clarity, and with my toolbox, it's like every fight I enter will be some kind of puzzle. I *do* enjoy that, but not the danger. No, that's not quite right, either. I dislike the stakes, I guess? No. That's not right."

"Do you not appreciate the wounds you take?"

"Eh?" Edwin raised and lowered his hands in a display of uncertainty, mindful of the scars they'd accumulated so recently. "I mean I don't *like* getting hurt, and I think if you do it's probably a problem, but that's not the issue. I think . . . I don't like the margin of error."

"Oh? Could you elaborate?" Rillah had produced two clay mugs filled with something vaguely tealike from *somewhere* and offered one to Edwin.

"Margin of error? That's basically how close you have to be to perfection before it's a success."

"Oh? Interesting. But that's not what I'm asking about. What do you mean you don't like the margin of error for fighting?"

"Well . . ." Edwin struggled to formulate his thoughts properly. Why couldn't this have been one of the internal debates he'd had with himself preparing his every point and counterpoint for the event where somebody asked him why he thought that bringing dinosaurs to life was a good idea?

"Okay, it's kind of like this. I'm an alchemist, a *scientist*. Messing things up is almost literally my job description. I'm supposed to do something wrong in every possible way, so I can figure out the exact parameters for what is *right*. But with a fight, if I mess up even once, I don't get a second try. It's experiment over, no more testing. And that just doesn't appeal to me, I don't think.

"It's a *rush*, don't get me wrong. But the stakes are too high, the room for error too small. There's no time to make sure all my work is right, I just have to make a call and live with it. Some people would find that thrilling and I suppose I kind of do too. But it's also *so exhausting*, I just can't live with it. There's better ways to get that rush. I know it's damaging to my mind, and . . ."

My mind is screwed up enough already.

"So then, what's the problem? Most people never fight once, you know."

"It's Lefi, I suppose? He wants me to be good at fighting but he's also trying to teach me how to avoid fights, and he just sort of assumes that everyone will think like him and that *of course* it's superimportant for me to learn how to fight!

"He's not wrong, I think. I *do* want to be able to protect myself, and take care of myself without relying purely on the goodwill of others. Heck, before all this, I probably would have agreed with him, too, that I needed to be good at and would benefit from fighting and learning to fight. But after two months of being beaten into the dirt time and time again? I like to think I'm resilient, but it's a bit much. Not to mention it doesn't actually feel like I'm improving. He says I am, but what does that really compare to? I'm no closer to measuring up to him than I was a month and a half ago."

"He does tend to do that, doesn't he? He just doesn't understand that without a Skill to guide you, no amount of throwing you around will actually make you better at fighting, not truly."

"Yeah, that sounds about right."

"So"—Rillah pivoted to another topic—"why do you feel so strongly that you *need* to control your life? It's not that often I come across such a similar desire to my own."

"Well, I . . . actually, why am I telling you all this? I'm sure that I'm just tremendously boring, I'm so sorry. I didn't want to drag you into all my emotional insecurities."

Come on, poke and prod just a bit, a tiny corner of him rooted. *Please, show more than cursory interest in me. If you actually care about me, and aren't just trying to cheer me up, surely . . .*

"Are you sure?" she asked. Not an outright prod, but it was prod-adjacent. He'd let it slide.

"Yeah, I mean . . . yeah. I don't want to spiral down in that direction, which talking about that sort of thing would probably do," he admitted. Still room for a prod, now it was back to her . . .

"Well," she settled on, "okay. But you'll tell me sometime!"

Edwin shrugged. He could commit to the vague future-that-is-never about that suite of emotional vulnerability, no problem. It would be easy enough to deflect and never actually have to dig into his core any time soon.

A thought seemed to cross her mind. "I know just the thing that you'll *really* like."

"Oh?" Edwin asked, interest piqued. "And what might that be?"

There was a sudden gust in the room as Rillah's autumnal wings twisted into existence, the skin of her back flowing like water and flickering like an illusion into creating the wings.

"Let's go flying!"

"Did I mention I don't like heights?" Edwin hazarded, cautiously peering over the edge of the tower's roof, fighting back a bit of vertigo.

"You don't? How on Joriah did you ever get the Flight Skill then?"

"Brute force and scientific understanding," he absently replied. "Though saying I dislike *falling* might be more accurate."

"You can fly!" Rillah encouraged, hovering in front of him. She didn't actually need to flap her wings to float, apparently, and they were mainly used to help her maneuverability or so she claimed. "You'll have *no* problem catching yourself. I know, it's pretty intimidating the first few times, but I'm sure you'll manage it!"

"I can only extend two meters from my anchor point, though," he protested. "Any farther than that and I'll actually just fall."

"You'll be fine! Come on, you can attach to me."

". . . Are you sure?"

"Yes, yes. Don't worry, my wings are *really* strong. You explained how your Skill works, and it's at least worth a try." She held out a hand and assumed a pleading expression. "Do it for me?" she asked.

Well, when she put it like *that* . . .

Edwin took a deep breath and steeled himself. Rillah was asking him to put his life into her hands, so to speak. He'd just met her yesterday. She was still almost a complete stranger . . . Could he trust her? What would he get out of it? Maybe a bit of fun? And what did he risk? Almost everything.

"Please?" she asked, wiggling her fingers in a clear invitation to grab on.

It would always be risky, wouldn't it? He'd forever have reasons to not jump off the roof, and it would be good for his Skills.

Yes! It would be good for his Flight Skill. The sooner he could evolve that, the sooner he could take Stamina Manipulation and explore his abilities all the more.

It was still a risk, though.

It will always be a risk.

Edwin took her hand.

CHAPTER 4

Sights to See

Flight was absolutely amazing.

Sure, he'd experienced glimmers of what it was truly like to fly from time to time, but Edwin was always so limited in what he could do. Most of the time, the Skill was relegated to just enhancing his existing mobility capabilities and slowly drifting through the air like what Inion tended to do.

But this? This was *so much better*.

Rillah zipped through the air on her leaf-covered wings, pulling Edwin along as she did so. He could probably gain some control over his trajectory if he let go of her hand, but if he did, all he would really be able to do was to move relative to Rillah, and even that was bound to be limited. Even *with* a tight grip on her hand, he needed to put most of his mana into Flight's tether strength, something he previously didn't even know was an *option*.

Rillah was really, *really* good at flying, too. Dipping into Skillful Assessment, Edwin watched the veritable symphony of Skills working in concert . . . he saw the Skill-based skeleton of her wings connecting at her shoulders, providing a massive framework for her flight to base itself off. The rest was filled in presumably by magic, but that magic was interwoven with a wholly separate set of Skills that allowed her every twitch to help her turn, her every flap making her go faster. True to her word, her flight was powerful enough that he was barely an additional strain, and he couldn't help but wonder what sort of Skill was involved and how he could get that sort of thing himself.

If he were to guess based on what he was seeing, she had gotten her Wings as a Skill evolution at some point, and then picked up a new basic Skill built around its functionality. He could ask later. For now, he was going to enjoy this.

They had started off with a dramatic swoop toward the ground, and Edwin had almost flinched at the speed they were hurtling toward the stone building at the base of the tower. He nearly broke off . . . but he was trying to trust, so he held fast.

It was well rewarded, as she pulled up into a *wickedly* fast flight forward, darting to and past the wall surrounding the tower's property. He had squeezed her hand tightly in concern, but she had just laughed and brought them just barely over the wall—closer than .22 meters, that was for certain—and . . . that was already higher resolution than he could normally get from Numeracy. He was getting some serious levels, it would seem.

The part of him responsible for keeping an eye on Numeracy informed him that they were going some fifty meters per second, and the rest of Edwin unanimously declared that he should pay more attention to the experience.

He came back to himself fully to see Rillah not looking where she was flying—but still effortlessly dodging every obstacle, of course—but instead looking at *him*. She gave his hand a quick squeeze; what was she . . . oh, of course.

"You've got this!" she promised, and Edwin hesitated . . . then let go of her hand.

He doubled down instead on his tether and let her pull him along like he was at the end of a fairly stretchy rope as they dove into the city streets themselves. The crowds of people below them parted as Rillah dove through them. When one of her wings did occasionally run into something—either an object or a person—they just passed straight through without so much as a hint of a collision. That she didn't have to worry about decapitating people was certainly a relief, but it just as much pushed her to go and take *even more* risks. At least Edwin was able to navigate into the space in the crowds left by her passage to avoid hitting anything.

Rillah pulled into a tight spiral, circling around one of the rare columns out in public, carrying Edwin into a whirlwind spin as she recovered some height. Another flap of her wings and she'd risen farther above the city, and then she pulled them back into a dive, swooping down to the streets and rising back up.

She jetted around buildings, spinning around and narrowly dodging people as she swept close to the ground. Edwin decided to play it a bit safe this time and flew so he was above and mostly in sync with her, but she was at the point where her wings were brushing the ground.

"I thought you said people got annoyed at you when you did this!" he called out.

"Yeah, well, they're all a bunch of hypocrites! You think they don't do this? Only if they can't! I think I also said that I just *don't care*! Take that, Vsarin! You and your stupid furry snakes!"

"Who and their what?"

"Don't worry about it!"

With a quick flap of her wings, Rillah took off from the ground, leaving the puny humans and the resulting chaos of her flight through their midst behind, and jetted into the sky, where flocks of avior were similarly undergoing their normal routine.

The air was thick with Skills, though primarily concentrated within the bodies of their airborne companions; very few had active Flight Skills, and so far as Edwin could tell, all external Skills *were* active.

Rillah swooped through one of the few places where Edwin could see a Skill active in the air, and she immediately jetted up, the Updraft Skill effect pushing her into the sky and pulling Edwin along for the ride. The Veteran Overseer responsible for the Skill screeched something that was snatched away by the wind as they pushed past him and continued on, farther and farther into the sky.

The wind this far up almost froze Edwin to the bone at first, but he felt Adaptive Defense kick in and swiftly reduce it to "chilly but manageable." From this far above, the sight looked spectacular. This bird's-eye view was something that he never thought he'd see and was far better than the measly view he had gotten even on airplanes back on Earth. Here, he had a completely unobstructed view of everything in all directions.

Far below him, the gray and brown of the city stood in sharp contrast to the greens and wheat-golden patchwork of land that surrounded it in all directions. The roads were oddly gray straight lines cutting straight through the landscape, clusters of farmhouses making villages tiny brown dots scattered some distance away from the city, and distant forest making a patchy, dark green carpet. Even the river was a brilliant sapphire far below them, winding to and fro as it meandered downstream. Upstream, Edwin thought he could see the waterfall Inion had mentioned as the terrain stepped up as it headed toward the massive mountains that dominated so much of the surroundings.

From up here, though, Edwin could see they were nearly at the tail end of the Highpeak Mountains, and that far off in the distance an ocean glittered. A tiny wisp cloud drifted by beneath them, and the azure sky offered an infinite backdrop behind them.

"Wow," Edwin couldn't help but remark, and Rillah grinned.

"Quite the sight, isn't it?"

"Yeah. It's . . . I've seen some views in the past, but this is something else."

"Flying is great, isn't it?" she asked, and Edwin nodded mutely. "But it's nothing compared to seeing everything down there up close. What might be a tiny dot of color from up here could be the most interesting place that's ever existed. A patch of forest might have some rare and beautiful flower, a person you meet on the road may have truly fascinating stories. Seeing things from this far up, you can see everything . . . but also nothing. It's like being in the tower. To see anything *worthwhile*, you gotta get close, you gotta go and interact with stuff."

"Is this why you travel?"

She chuckled. "No, I loved to travel long before I ever could fly. This is perhaps the greatest perspective, but like anything, it can only be interesting for so long."

"You find this *boring*?" Edwin asked incredulously.

"No, not *boring*. The awe goes away eventually, but the sights are always just as amazing. Being up here during the sunset casts it all in truly wonderful colors, or right after a rainstorm you might be able to see a rainbow that's actually a full circle. Sights from up here really make everything seem so small, and . . . it almost makes sense why avior look down on the poor earthbound humans so much."

Edwin nodded, drifting slightly farther away from Rillah to better enjoy the view. He could understand why he might eventually get bored, but the novelty still had very much *not* worn off yet, and he would appreciate that while he could.

"You ready?" Rillah's question broke him out of his thoughts. Ready for what?

"Let's go!" She made a sudden turn, jetting off to the side with almost no warning . . . well fine, he had a warning, but it wasn't *sufficient*.

The sudden movement caught Edwin completely by surprise, and before he could adjust to double down on the strength of his tether, it was already too late, and she had gone past his limit.

His stomach dropped as Flight's tether snapped, torn like a cobweb in the blink of an eye. All at once, the security the Skill provided dropped away, and Edwin suddenly found himself very, very far off the ground and falling very, very fast.

"Rillah!" he yelled out, eyes wide as he tumbled through the sky. "Help me!"

Flight.

Flight!

Flight!

FLIGHT!

"Aaaahhhhhh helpmeeeeee!" Edwin frantically tried to reengage Flight, but without Rillah as an anchor point, his Skill had nothing to latch onto. That, or he was just too panicked. His heart dropped into his stomach as he tumbled through the air chaotically.

Everything seemed to darken around him as his brain tried to reboot, but he *refused* to pass out.

His thoughts.

His thoughts were sluggish.

His awareness shrank into a pinpoint of light. Wh-what should he do?

What *could* he do?

Um, there was . . .

It felt like he had been falling for *hours*, surely the ground was coming soon?

He needed to . . . he needed to what?

Come on, think . . .

AAAAAAAAAHHHHHHHHHHHH

Think *productively!*

He blinked his Status open to try and see what might help him, but . . . what? He had something that would help him survive impacts, what was . . .

Overcharge!

The world sharpened and slowed around him, putting away his worries that he might pass out from the experience. The ground was still quite a ways away, and the wind rustled through his hair and past his ears, drowning out all other sounds. He didn't think he was screaming, was he screaming?

He should be safe, probably. He had Overcharge up, and that could help him survive splatting into the ground at terminal velocity, right? Edwin suddenly realized that they'd only ever tested his defenses against Skill-enhanced impacts and injuries. Granted, that was the majority of what he cared about, but it meant he didn't know how a high-speed impact might stack up against his defenses.

Once he got close enough to the ground, he could activate Flight and hopefully use that to dampen his impact like he was running into a giant pillow. The closer he got to the ground, the more force he could exert and it would hopefully be enough to soften his impact?

Assume a spherical physicist is falling at terminal velocity and is about to collide into a two-meter spring . . .

A pair of arms wrapped around him, as Rillah pulled him into an embrace to catch him. His muscles weren't very responsive, but he was at least able to wrap his arms around her in turn, holding on for dear life with all the strength—wait, no. Overcharge. Bad idea—about a quarter of the strength he could muster.

He didn't jerk to a stop. No, more likely she had flown up behind him and matched his speed, now was slowly pulling them back to a more sedate pace. The ground seemed to be approaching awfully fast, though. How were they going to—

Whomp!

A massive gust of wind struck the ground beneath them as a pair of powerful wings blasted a cushion of air for them to land on. Then they were back on the ground, and Edwin breathed a sigh of relief as they returned to the tower's lawn.

Rillah was saying something, what . . . oh, he was still desperately clinging to her, wasn't he? She didn't have her wings out anymore, but he was still really tightly hugging her. And making some embarrassing noises, he was certain.

Edwin released his death grip and collapsed onto the ground, panting wildly. He wasn't sure if it was psychosomatic or his body had just flatly adjusted to the Skill's presence, but Breathing didn't seem to stop him from getting winded in high-stress situations.

His mind raced a thousand kilometers a second, desperately trying to put itself back together from that . . . harrowing experience. Suspecting that he could survive a fall at terminal velocity was one thing, but actually experimenting with that was not something he was *ever* eager to test. Though he probably should, shouldn't he?

Overcharge wore off suddenly, and that added a whole new layer of complication and pain to things. Exposure to the extraconcentrated version of the Skill he'd been experimenting with when it was constrained to his arm had numbed the pain of the normal variety somewhat. He also knew that with a bit of rest he would even be up for some light magical exertion. But it still hurt worse than a failed exam, and until he *did* get a few minutes, he'd be in a lot of pain.

Putting all that aside, though . . . Only including the effects the extended period of free fall did on his psyche, it would be at least a few minutes before he was coherent enough to do anything but babble about . . . something—he didn't know what but hoped it wasn't too bad—and shakily walk around. His Flight Skill categorically refused to activate, though he suspected that was related to his general lack of coordination.

Rillah seemed . . . not exactly concerned, but she didn't brush him off either. Did she say something about having seen this before? Probably not, but his brain was telling him all sorts of things that were probably inaccurate.

She laughed about something—probably at him—and brushed his arm with her fingers, instantly bringing him back to reality.

The human contact was nice, sure, but what was definitely more useful was the massive amount of Calming Touch she included in the caress. A few minutes later, Edwin was stable even without the Skill acting as a crutch, and he glanced at his notifications.

Level Up!
Skill Points 885→895 (Average level: 48)
Flight Level 44→50
Numeracy Level 42→44
Overcharge Level 26→27
Skillful Assessment Level 41→42

"Thanks," he actually remembered to say. "I don't know how long I would have been like that otherwise."

"Happy to help," Rillah said. "It *was* my fault after all."

"It's *not* your fault. Besides, you couldn't have really known how badly I'd react."

"No," she admitted, "but I still was insensitive and careless, and for that I am sorry."

It was so nice, finding a person who cared about his feelings. It was . . . novel. Edwin wasn't sure it really *helped* his social anxiety, though, because now he just was extraworried about not chasing her off.

He *knew* that was being unreasonable, though. He should just "be himself," apparently. Never mind that unfiltered Edwin was unbearable to even *himself*, how could anyone like that? He knew that people didn't truly want people to be their natural, annoying selves. That just meant that . . . honestly, he didn't know what. Hopefully he'd figure it out.

"So, you going to say anything about *why* you reacted so badly?"

"Oh, right. I suppose I can." Edwin had been sitting in silence for an awkward amount of time again, hadn't he? Gah, social stuff was so hard . . . and he was doing it again.

"I'm not sure I can *really* explain it adequately, because it is a fear of mine and those are always irrational. But I suppose if I were to point to some time where it *really* started up was probably the last time I fell from the sky."

"The *last* time? How in Xares's name did you fall from the sky *before*? I thought you hadn't free-flown before?"

"I haven't. This was before I got the Flight Skill anyway."

Rillah raised a very skeptical eyebrow, green eye practically radiating disbelief. "And how exactly did you fall from the sky? Wait—don't tell me. Are you from Vis'Daric?"

"Um, no actually. Have you been there?"

She shook her head. "One day; haven't made it to a Docking City in time before."

"Oh, cool, we can go togetherrrrr . . . if you want to, of course." Edwin's brain went into panicked recovery mode. "I don't want to assume that you'd want to travel with me anywhere, you know? I mean, I kind of *hope* that you'd want to go with me to places, but not in a weird way! I just enjoy . . . actually, I'm going to stop talking now."

She laughed. "Edwin. It's *all right*. If you want to go that way, and think you'll make it, *absolutely* let me know. Visiting the Brass Sun is a longtime goal of mine."

"Brass Sun?"

"Uh-uh! No changing the topic. If you've never been there, how did you fall out of the sky? Did you make some avior mad?"

"Oh, right. Vis'Daric." Edwin refocused, then finished processing her statement. "Um, I don't think so. I don't actually know *how* I got there, if I'm being honest. I don't have any memories of the arrival, I just remember . . ."

He suppressed a shudder as he recalled his first moments on Joriah, plummeting to his doom and passing out.

"A lot of falling. But yeah, that was terrifying. Didn't have any Skills that would help me, tumbling through the air . . . it was pretty terrifying. I think I actually blacked out."

"You didn't have *any* applicable Skills? What the *gashith* did you do?"

"I survived."

"No, really? Never would have guessed. So you don't have the Eleven Lives Skill?"

"Wait." Edwin's mind was racing. "Is that a thing?"

She let out a snort. "Ha. No. Well, it might be. Who even knows?"

They sat in silence for a moment.

"Lefi would," they said in unison, then broke into laughter.

Once they'd composed themselves, they spent an amicable moment of silence simply recovering and formulating their next thoughts.

"Hmm," Edwin noted. "I'm hungry. You want something? I think I saw a bakery while we were flying around earlier."

Rillah nodded. "Sure! Free food is great."

"Great. I'll be right back."

"Here you go." Edwin tossed Rillah a small apparatite box, a pastry visible albeit steam obscured inside. She snagged it from the air before it could slip past her fingers and fall to the bottom of the tower. Edwin dismissed the Sapper's Apparatus construct, and she eagerly bit into it.

"Ooh, thanks. Oh wow, that's good. Where'd you get it, and how much was it? I need to stop by there sometime."

"Oh? I would have thought . . . no, actually you wouldn't know every bakery in the city would you? Anyway, it was just down the street and . . ." Edwin gave quick directions as he joined her on the tower's roof, gratefully releasing his mana tether. Rillah nodded. "And it was pretty cheap, just a couple ager for everything in total."

She choked on her food, coughing and spluttering to the point Edwin wasn't sure if he should do something.

"Right. Give me your pouch. You clearly can't be trusted with anything beyond a few ves."

"What? Why? I'm perfectly capable of managing my own money, thank you very much."

"Not if you're spending more than an ager on two things from a bakery!"

"Well, I did get some other stuff . . ." he protested.

"Nuh-uh. Doesn't matter. If you didn't buy nearly the entire shop, nothing you got should have been valued in more than a couple ves."

"What are you talking about?" he protested.

"Edwin"—she clapped her hands on her leg—"you just spent about a week's worth of wages for a laborer on *two pastries*, and you thought that was a *good* deal. Carrying around all that money with that disconnect is probably alerting everyone with Value Assessment in the *city* they can charge you at least twelve times what they normally would.

"Now, *give me your pouch.*"

"I met you *yesterday*. I'll buy you a pastry—and put my life in your hands—but I'm not about to just hand you all my money! Doubly so after you just *dropped* me. I'll . . . lock it up or something."

"Hey! I said I was sorry. Anyway, *no!* Coin-Scent is *the* most common thief Adventurer Skill, it'll lead them right there."

"You live in a *tower*! How is that not safe? Don't you have a vault or whatever?"

"Gimme!"

"No!"

In the end, they concealed his coins in at least a hundred layers of apparatite and locked it in the vaultlike safe alongside *Rillah*'s money—a revelation that Edwin felt extremely vindicated to discover. He did keep a single half grai in his boot as insurance, but bleh. Otherwise, he only had half an ager and thirty ves in his belt pouch.

Honestly, why did everyone treat him as a child? He was responsible . . . He *could* be responsible!

"Hey, hey. It's all right." Edwin was trying to pacify Inion. "It was an accident, there's no reason to go so . . . apoplectic."

"She dropped you!" Was it his imagination, or was the lighting on her face starting to shift? He did *not* want to deal with a furious fey.

"Look, it was kind of my fault, too, okay? I probably could have prevented the whole thing if I was more careful."

"You trusted her and then she *literally* dropped you! I *will* hurt her." *That's hardly new— Shut up, me.*

"Look, you guys got along great before! Just think about that? Like, yes, she dropped me. But then she caught me! She even apologized of her own volition! Look, it's totally fine. Completely and totally fine. I promise."

Edwin gave a big smile to try and persuade Inion but was met with a flat glare, only slightly spoiled by a lock of her hair slowly drifting in front of her eyes.

". . . Fine," she conceded. "But I'm keeping Identify close with her."

Edwin took a deep breath. He could do this, no matter how painful it was. He'd faced down giant bears and spiders, this was nowhere *close* to the scariest thing he did on a regular basis anymore.

"Hey, sorry for storming out on you earlier," he said, turning to Lefi.

Lefi looked at him in surprise. "Oh? Ah, but you needn't worry about such things! Frustration is understandable."

"Yeah, but I lost control of my emotions and I *really* shouldn't have snapped at you. I just was frustrated, because it felt like I wasn't improving at all. Oh, I, uh . . . also brought you this."

He pulled out an apology flask of ale from his belt. It was apparently about the size of a barrel on the inside, and he'd traded two whole healing potions for it; he was probably being ripped off again, but what else was new?

"It is perfectly all right, my friend!" Lefi said. "All would be forgiven even without the gift! Do you wish to have some yourself?"

"Ah, thanks, but I don't drink," Edwin declined.

"Your loss! Ah, Rillah shall be so envious! She does love this."

Edwin raised an eyebrow at that as the Adventurer took a quick drink. "Ah! Absolutely wonderful."

"Glad you like it," he said. "It was the only thing I could think of."

"You thought marvelously! I hope you were not overcharged too severely!"

Edwin sighed. "How did you hear about that *already*? But yeah, I might be absolutely awful at this people stuff, but I still like to *try*."

Lefi laughed, then broached the question Edwin had been waiting for. "Do you wish to continue your training?"

"Do you think it'll actually help?" Edwin asked. "Like genuinely, actually help. Because I can certainly try, but I would like a bit more feedback on what I'm doing wrong."

Lefi smiled. "I can certainly try myself."

A few ager—not spent by him, but by Rillah, who knew the city best—had gotten Edwin a pauldron made to his specifications almost impressively well. The metal cuff fit snugly around his shoulder, and the line of pinholes were perfectly aligned with where he'd found them to be most effective—that had been a very long, very painful day of testing. At least he'd come out of it with a good idea as to how to maximize his one-arm Overcharge. But best of all, it articulated perfectly with his joint, barely impeding his range of motion. It still *slightly* harmed how much he could stretch, of course, but that just came with the territory of level 74 Flexibility. Random pieces of loose clothing impeded his mobility.

For some reason, his more generic tunics, let alone his pants, didn't seem to anticipate his ability to put his knees behind his head for extended periods of time. Honestly, though, they should. Sure, Attributes may not have been *that* common, but apparently it was common enough for artisans to get the Dexterity Attribute, so shouldn't they be able to make clothing that accommodated for that?

The answer to that was no, because Dexterity didn't actually improve your flexibility or range of motion, just let you have greater control over your body, and it was generally focused on the fingers for the people who used it anyway.

He should probably try and get the Artisan Path, though. Dexterity sounded like a good attribute for him to have, and it would at least help him with his current task. As it stood, it took an impressive amount of focus to keep his fingers from trembling and ruining all his progress.

Alchemical Dismantling helped *somewhat*, but not overmuch. It made the entire procedure possible, but a certain amount of finesse still was required to cut the quill out of a feather—or more accurately, the feathery parts away from the stem.

He'd found in his Refining that the quill of the lybird's peacocklike feather wasn't helpful in his refinement of obscuring illusion dust. It seemed to have more to do with . . . fear and darkness. If he were to guess, it served as some sort of control function, helping the rest of the glorified turkey's magic to be aimed properly.

Whatever the case, all Edwin needed were the iridescent vanes, glittering black and green. How you could have black iridescence he wasn't entirely sure, but it looked *really* cool. His initial experiments had shown that the final result was just as potent, produced comparable amounts of dust, and most importantly was *way* easier to Refine. The only hitch was that he had to cut *right* at the base of the barbs. He'd found out the hard way that just trying to shave off a bit of the feather didn't work for some reason. It was either the entire blade of the feather or nothing.

The minced feathers probably still had *some* use, sure, but they were far less effective for his goals at the moment, and he couldn't get distracted trying to find out everything about them.

Just by omitting the shaft—whatever it was called—he could cut his time almost in half, and given how much harder the process got, the longer he took was huge. Sure, the bulk of the time he spent Refining was trying to get his mana into a Refined state, and that was taking less and less time as he got better and better at the process, but after about the first hour spent actually Refining an object, his mana got unruly.

Considering he could practically double his output each additional ten minutes—five minutes, now—that he took Refining things, cutting the time it took to get the first feather properly Refined from half an hour to fifteen minutes was absolutely massive.

Heck, if he wasn't careful he would have to start rationing his use of the feathers in case he found something else that he wanted to use them for in the future. That was a problem for future-Edwin, though.

Right now, it was just him, his knife, and his sample. One last deft swipe with his blade—that Knives Skill was starting to look rather tempting—and the feather was done, the dismantled parts going in their respective jars.

Two thousand lybird feathers in the jar, two thousand lybird feathers. Take one out, slice it up, one thousand nine hundred and ninety-nine feathers in the jar. . .

Edwin had asked for and been assigned a small stone workshop in the tower to perform his latest experiments in, as he didn't want to accidentally burn down his carriage with his current project.

Simply put, he was seriously overdue for plain, no-frills explosives. He'd made flash-bangs, smoke bombs, fire cocktails, and more. But he hadn't made a single concussive bomb since either the dwarves or blowing up his kiln, depending on what he decided to count.

And that was just far, far too long. He highly doubted that many people would have shock wave resistance via Skills, and while Health would help put a damper on the sorts of internal damage that could be caused . . . nobody would be very well-off from having a bomb detonate right in front of their face. He could probably even manage that with Throwing Weapons and Firestarting, which was a truly terrifying prospect.

Sure, there were lots of problems with the idea, and lots of danger to be had.

But when it came to making things blow up . . . Edwin surveyed his tools and materials eagerly.

He could put aside his concerns.

It was time to make things go *boom*.

C H A P T E R 5

Booming Business

Explosions were very cool. That was just a fact of life. Paradoxically, they were both very hard to make work and also hard to *prevent*. As Edwin knew from experience, dust explosions could happen at any time when one was working with something flammable. But he was finding out getting explosions to happen consistently was much harder than he had anticipated. Even Bomb Throwing didn't always cooperate, though he could at least reliably turn it *off*.

Really, it was just a matter of control. Explosions were in some ways the maximum demonstration of chaos, and it was phenomenally tricky to make chaos do exactly what you wanted it to. It wasn't even because chaos was some sort of metaphysical force whose bounds transcended mathematics.

No, it was much more sinister than that.

It was *statistics*.

Simply put, there were very few ways that an undetonated bomb could be put together. Molecules needed to be in the right positions, the detonator needed to be aligned properly, so on and so forth. But a bomb *after* it had blown up? Well, that had nigh-infinite ways it could exist. That was the secret of entropy, after all. It wasn't inevitable, it wasn't some cosmic law that entropy *had* to increase. It was just overwhelmingly statistically likely because an object could be put together way more ways *incorrectly* than the handful of *correct* states it could exist in instead.

. . . where was he? Oh yes, explosions.

Explosions were hard to predict because fundamentally what you needed to make an explosion was a very, very fast and powerful reaction. To get that, you needed a substance that could, within just a few seconds, react in such a way that also released a *lot* of energy. Of course, the problem was that simply having a substance with that much potential energy meant the substance had a *lot* of energy it was trying to get rid of. So you needed a substance that both had a lot of potential energy bound up in it—was reactive—and wouldn't release that energy on a whim—wasn't volatile. And finding a substance that was reactive but not volatile was very, *very* hard.

Edwin couldn't even properly cheat with his magic, simply because there was no single "explosion" reaction, not *truly*. Explosions were just the by-product of some mass in a small volume suddenly trying to occupy a much *bigger* volume. If left unconstrained, that would just result in a movie-style fireball. Cool, but without much force. However, if in a container where that pressure could *build*, and then release all at once . . .

His steam bomb from his time with the dwarves was a perfect example. It was just flash-boiled water trying to expand into steam and not being able to. He knew from experience that the sudden cloud of superheated steam could definitely be dangerous, but at the same time it wasn't *that* bad. Certainly not enough to seriously harm the sorts of creatures he was regularly facing. It was only when he'd encased it in mortar and gave the steam a casing to build up pressure in and shrapnel that it could propel outward that it became formidable.

Of course, some explosives didn't need any kind of container to undergo a genuine explosion. C4 came to mind, among other high explosives. In those cases, the air itself filled the role of a sort of container, with the explosive trying to spread out faster than the speed of sound—that was, the speed of air—and creating a shock wave.

Of course, most detonations *weren't* the result of high explosives, and so he'd probably need a container of some form. Fireballs were all good in Hollywood, after all, when they didn't need actual danger and really *preferred* spectacle. But as a defensive tool? Well, there were three main possible ways to be injured by an explosion. Well, not counting incidental injuries like smoke inhalation or collapsing structures, anyway.

The first was the shock wave itself. If it was powerful enough, it could do some serious internal damage as it passed through squishy tissues and organs, bursting air vessels in the lungs and so on. Edwin was somewhat skeptical of its use against someone with Health, but at the same time it would probably be a *great* way to stress the Attribute, leaving them more vulnerable to other attacks.

The second was in some ways even more limited, and that was the direct heat of the explosion. Depending on what the explosive was, it could be seriously devastating, but for his purposes he doubted setting things on fire would be all *that* helpful. Overall, he figured it was a minor contributor in comparison to the other two, but it bore mentioning.

The final and most functional method was kinetic projectiles. The idea was simple: put something strong but either brittle or small in the way of the explosion, and let the rapidly onrushing gases blow it away. As the saying went, it's not *that* the wind is blowing, it's *what* the wind is blowing. Yes, that was technically about hurricanes, but it applied just fine to shrapnel as well. That was how grenades and guns alike worked, after all. Using an explosion to put a lot of kinetic energy into a metal projectile very quickly. And assuming he could get Bomb Throwing up to an appreciable level, the System would only make things stronger.

So, on his task list . . . make a gun. He could do that. Grenades could come later, but he was hopeful to get a baseline idea of the strength of his explosives before he started bringing Skills into the mix. Grenades would *definitely* be affected by the Skill, whereas guns . . . probably not.

While perhaps the obvious candidate for making a gun was, well, black powder, Edwin didn't know where he could get the stuff for it. Neither Lefi nor Rillah knew where he could get saltpeter, and while thanks to Memory he knew he could synthesize it from guano, neither of his companions knew where he could find bat caves, either. Without that, the only accessible way to make saltpeter would take him at least a year of *very* disgusting work, which he just didn't have time for now. He also didn't have the inclination to work with massive amounts of sewage, either.

He'd prodded his companions a bit as to the absence of the substance, considering he was pretty sure it had been in wide use for centuries if not millennia back on Earth. Apparently, it had just . . . never been needed.

According to the few mentions he'd found about it in the tower's library, they knew of its *existence*, at least societally, but other than as a mild curiosity nobody really needed it. Thinking about some of its uses, he could almost understand. There were Skills for both meat preservation and fertilization, and alchemists cared more about magical substances over their more mundane chemical counterparts, thanks to the higher-level yields the former gave. Why would anyone bother performing the disgusting procedures that had been needed back on Earth to make it?

In all honesty, though, it might well be just as easy for him to make *nitroglycerin* than it would be for normal black powder, and certainly more worthwhile. If he got his hands on sulfur he could *probably* make sulfuric acid, and once he had that, if he *did* get his hands on saltpeter somehow, he could make nitric acid. Mix those together with some glycerin, and well . . . boom.

All of that was still a ways off, though. Edwin wasn't stable enough—nor desperate enough—to start the yearlong process of making saltpeter that was mixing manure with sawdust and letting it decompose for a year while keeping it wet with urine the entire time. Besides, he was an alchemist; he could come up with something better than that.

He *hoped* he could come up with something better than that. He had serious questions for whoever discovered *that* particular method of saltpeter synthesis. Like, come on. The sheer amount of *human waste* that it involved was flatly disgusting.

Fortunately, while he might have been lacking in archaic yet common-on-Earth chemicals, he had elemental magnesium and phosphorus in abundance. It was . . . really kind of absurd. But was he complaining?

Okay, maybe he was, a bit.

"Step . . . up!"

True to his word, Lefi had actually gotten *significantly* better at teaching recently. It was really startling, but Edwin supposed that was just what happened with Skills when someone was "Exceptional." A massive experience boost definitely would explain why he'd managed to improve, but there *had* to be more to it. Some Skill that boosted the efficacy of other Skills? He didn't have any evidence for the idea, as there weren't any obvious candidates in the chaotic maelstrom that was Lefi's Skills, but it would explain why Lefi was seemingly good at *everything* and could become a veritable master overnight.

While drills might have been boring, Edwin was immensely glad that his latest training sessions left *just* his Stamina exhausted, and not his Health as well. Plus, he was actually *learning*. Lefi had a lot of experience using his Skills, and when not just trying to get Edwin to figure it all out on his own, things went way faster.

"Step . . . up!"

Longstrider flashed, and Edwin jumped forward almost seven meters. Using the Skill properly in combat was *significantly* harder than Edwin had first thought it would be, because you still *traveled* through the intervening space. To the outside observer, it looked like he was gliding across the ground, and to someone in the know, it was really easy to intercept the movement unless you took really short steps. Doing that was *fine*, but if that was to be your primary use of the Skill, there were better choices out there.

It was, apparently, why the Skill was a relatively low priority for combatants, who generally preferred Footwork (in the case of guards and mercenaries) or Marching (for soldiers). Lefi apparently disagreed, though. He said that the people who could only travel in a straight line were wasting their potential, and Longstrider was one of the single most important Skills when fighting.

Even Edwin knew that positioning was everything in a melee fight. But apparently the weaknesses of Longstrider were just too great most of the time. You couldn't change directions in the middle of a Longstride any more than you could turn after committing to a normal step. Unless, of course, you had a shortcut.

"Step . . . up!"

Lefi, of course, had a Skill that just let him change direction midstride, ducking around obstacles at an absolutely insane pace, that was wholly separate from his Walking chain. Heel-Face Turn or something like that.

Edwin couldn't do that. Not really.

But he *could* use Flight.

Longstrider and Flight just weren't compatible. Longstrider only worked while his feet were firmly planted on the ground, and while he could have Flight *active*, he couldn't use it. Or at least, that was what he had thought for a while.

Lefi had pointed out that at the very least Edwin could use Flight to cancel Longstrider midstep, which had its own set of uses. The experience was disorienting, because momentum with Longstrider was . . . wonky. From Edwin's perspective, he was going the same speed either flying or using Longstrider, but switching between them always included a lurch.

"Step . . . up!"

Right now, he was practicing switching between them at a moment's notice, and little by little, he *was* improving. He'd even been offered a Skill for it, but it was too niche to really be worth taking and disrupting his current plans.

It was just a matter of practice, and with a good teacher . . . Well, anything was possible.

Edwin carefully broke off a piece of phosphorus from his supply. He had plenty for the foreseeable future, which was nice, but he made sure to keep it all underwater just to be on the safe side.

"It's really nerve-racking working with this stuff, so you know."

"Does it really present any danger?" Lefi asked.

"Honestly? I'm not sure, and I don't want to find out. White phosphorus's flames are hot enough to boil iron, so if pretty much any gets on my gloves, they're being thrown in the corner."

Edwin wasn't stupid, he was using Fey's Caress under the gloves keyed off a steel bracelet he'd picked up some time back, and having hands magically transmuted into metal *should* be sufficient protection. But he wanted to make sure Lefi knew that it wasn't to be trifled with.

"Anyone without the right Skills got this on them? They're in for a very bad time at *best*. If they somehow got any *inside* of them, well . . . I'm not sure if even *you'd* survive. Basically, this stuff is very bad news and you need to be careful around it at all times."

"Understandable." Lefi didn't seem overly concerned about the substance, but Edwin didn't really expect him to. The important thing was just that he knew how to behave in the lab. Obeying proper lab safety was, after all, one of Edwin's main conditions for the Adventurer to get some alchemy lessons. It was only fair, after all, given how much help he had been providing with *Edwin's* Skills.

"But this will be something of a good, if volatile explosive. It ignites on contact with warm air, which I know I said before but it's worth repeating, but that also means all we need to do to *get* it to explode is to just expose it to air. Now, it's not instantaneous, but that's not too much of a problem for me at least."

"Your Firestarting?" Lefi asked, and Edwin nodded. The Adventurer shook his head and chuckled. "I still don't understand how you managed to transform a passive Skill into an active one."

"Neither do I," Edwin admitted. "Though Firestarting is already half active at least, given it reaches out of the body."

"Is that what you've found is the difference?"

"Well, it's not a perfect definition, but it generally looks to be true. And Firestarting isn't always active; otherwise, a high enough level in the Skill would just spontaneously start fires wherever you went. Anyway, that's getting off track again and don't *you* have a Skill for that?

"So, by grinding this stuff into a powder, it will make it burn hotter and faster, but only if it's not *too* small," he explained, using a mortar and rough pestle to grind the waxy substance into granules, entirely submerged in a basin of distilled water.

"Why is that?"

"Okay, so fire needs air to burn, you know that, right?"

"Yes, you said that this creates fire when exposed to air, I recall."

"Well, I mean more generally . . . anyway, that's not relevant right now. Basically, all fire needs air to burn . . . though that's not entirely true strictly speaking, it just needs some kind of oxidizer." Edwin shook his head. "I'm getting distracted again. Basically, there needs to be all the stuff for your explosive to freely detonate available, and in this case that's exposure to air. So, you want to maximize the surface area of the phosphorus relative to its volume, which if it's all one block obviously isn't happening and if it's *too* small, then air can't get through but . . ."

* * *

Grinding the phosphorus proved to be easy enough, and Edwin found that by pulling on Alchemical Dismantling, he could make the granules a really consistent size with a minimal amount of work. Lefi had a Skill that worked almost identically to Dismantling, *of course*, so he was almost as good as Edwin at it right off the start, and by the end he was even *better*.

Edwin knew he shouldn't be jealous, but it was kind of hard to not be. This was supposed to be *his* thing, but of course Lefi could match him even here. But no, Edwin was being supportive, so he'd see how far he could push the Adventurer—no matter how frustrating it could be to watch the totally-not-a-protagonist outclass him in everything.

It's not like I should have expected anything else . . . oy, shut up, me.

No, he was not going to get all mopey and socially self-destructive anymore. He knew that people wanted to be with him! He was a valuable team member, and wasn't that what he had always wanted? He *loved* being the sort of person who could help out, and explaining things to people was something he truly enjoyed. He was supposed to be happy, darn it, and he would *not* let his emotions get in the way of that.

In any case, processing his excessive amounts of phosphorus, courtesy of his time in Panastalis, proved to be quite easy, but it also presented a bit of a dilemma. How was he going to get the explosives dry without them igniting? Once the water was gone, he could seal it in an apparatite container and hope that whatever minuscule amounts of air were trapped alongside it wouldn't be enough to make it explode.

A few tests confirmed that yes, the granules did indeed ignite if he left them out for an extended period of time to dry, but he eventually managed to get a system down. With a bit of help from Rillah (this was quickly becoming a team effort), Edwin was able to make a cold box at refrigerator-like temperatures, well below what phosphorus needed to ignite, and let the granules dry there. Of course, it took a fair bit of time for the granules *to* dry, definitely longer than was feasible for Rillah to stay there constantly channeling magic into it.

So Edwin cheated a bit. He used Basic Thermokinesis on the container it was stored in but added almost no heat to the system, instead allowing the Skill's inherent insulation to help keep the interior cold.

He was really proud of that workaround, even if it meant that he lost a night of sleep to keep the system properly chilled for long enough.

By working quickly, he was able to load up a lot of apparatite casings, and while there *were some* small fires that broke out inside some of his shells, none of them grew out of hand, and Edwin considered the endeavor as a whole a success.

Initial explosive tests were confusing, because when he tried to use Firestarting on the capsules, nothing happened. Even Infusing the Skill didn't do anything beyond creating a tiny puff of smoke.

Then Edwin realized he was being stupid. Phosphorus didn't have any internal oxidizer. It was that very fact he was relying on to keep the fuel stable, but he had still managed to forget that when actually *trying* to blow it up. Hmm. Some changes to the plan were required.

A bit of testing showed that they worked as Edwin hoped. Bomb Throwing didn't seem to activate, possibly because he wasn't throwing it? Or maybe it didn't count as a bomb? Anyway, if he dispelled the phosphorus's casing and exposed it to free air then applied Firestarting, the end result was a *lovely* fountain of ridiculously hot flames and sparks.

Now, all that was left was to turn it into a gun.

The end result looked a lot like a miniature potato cannon. A grate sat at the end of the barrel right before it opened into the explosives chamber and a specially made apparatite projectile was loaded in. Edwin released the container of phosphorus and ignited it, ducking behind his barrier—a very solid wooden table tipped over on its side. Given the solidity of the construction, it was probably overkill, but . . .

BANG!

Edwin suddenly felt like his shield was *very* inadequate as his prototype exploded. Fortunately, the fact it was made of apparatite meant that instead of sending deadly shrapnel all over the place, blue sparks slowly settled to the floor, but that didn't stop some unexploded phosphorus from raining all over his workshop, igniting and filling the room with smoke. He was once again reminded of just how glad he was to have Fresh Air.

In hindsight, he wasn't sure what he expected of a literal glass cannon.

Three iterations later, he'd figured out how thick he needed to ensure that his gun *didn't* explode, but the scales he was working with definitely weren't enough to be usable in any practical sense.

Was scaling it up probably just going to be a waste of time? Maybe. He'd need to rework most of it once he had better explosives with their own oxidizers, but he'd come this far. Who knew what sort of things he might learn? Certainly not him. That's why it was an experiment!

Edwin cracked his knuckles.

He was going to need a bigger gun. And . . . Edwin looked around at the chaos repeated explosions had wrought in his lab, the white haze hanging in the air.

. . . He should probably do this outside.

Version two of the gun was complete. Its walls were *significantly* thicker, and it had a two-meter barrel and one-meter blasting chamber, had a screw-on cap for allowing more air into the chamber after each shot, used a well-fitted stone for a projectile instead of an apparatite bullet, and had a thousand little improvements over its little brother.

And now, in a small meadow close enough to Sheraith that it was feasible to fly a really heavy apparatite object to, but far enough away that the sound was unlikely to reach the city, he was ready to test it.

Edwin dismissed the phosphorus's casing, releasing almost a full kilo of powder into the combustion chamber, and quickly joined the others as he dashed behind his blast barrier, a few stones ripped from the earth and arranged into a low wall. He anxiously peered over the rocks and focused on the phosphorus. Hopefully this was close enough . . .

Firestarting.

BOOM!

The noise shattered the natural soundscapes of their surroundings, sending flocks of birds cascading into the sky, shaking the clearing and knocking more than a few leaves from the nearby trees to the ground. White smoke drifted up from where the gun had landed, but the clearing primarily smelled like freshly cut wood and upturned dirt, which . . .

"That was awesome!" Yathal expressed his glee, a sentiment clearly shared by Kyni.

Inion looked similarly impressed, though she didn't say anything.

Lefi was clearly taken aback. "That was without a single Skill?"

Rillah gave Edwin an encouraging pat on his back as he nodded to Lefi. "I've never seen *anything* like that, and you say you can make even cooler stuff than that?"

Edwin nodded absently as he looked on with absolute glee at the (intentional) devastation his creation had wrought. Even without Bomb Throwing activating at all, the stone had utterly demolished the tree it had been aimed at, leaving only a splintered trunk and a significant amount of shattered wood behind. He'd need to get Lefi in to test its efficacy against Skilled opponents, but it would be *amazing* at imparting a lot of kinetic energy very, very quickly.

His enthusiasm was dampened slightly when he looked at the barrel. It had been thrown across the clearing, and several parts had broken into blue motes of energy, including part of the barrel. Edwin sighed. That would take *forever* to fix, to say nothing of figuring out what he would need to do to prevent that level of recoil from happening again. At least it hadn't exploded this time.

Two test firings later—about one week after his first test, thanks to the absolutely insane amount of apparatite he'd needed to conjure—Edwin had figured out that if he didn't want the recoil on the gun to send it flying, he'd need to make the apparatite body so big and bulky that even *he* couldn't lift it easily. At first, he'd tried using supports that would lock the barrel in place, bracing it against a nearby tree and digging into the soil, but apparatite just wasn't strong enough, apparently. The next model would need to include handholds, because he was *not* reconjuring the exterior and had forgotten them until it was too late. At least he'd been able to make it on-site.

Yes, it was functionally immobile, unless someone wanted to personally pick it up, and stuck in a random clearing miles from the nearest city. Yes, it required him to repair a bunch of the parts every time he fired it. Yes, it used an absolutely absurd amount of phosphorus per shot fired. But those problems could be fixed.

He could make it out of metal and figure out a better recoil-absorbing method (wheels, perhaps?; or maybe when he used metal, the bracers would be strong enough), and he could experiment with better propellants (particularly ones with their own oxidizers) and projectiles. A lot of this would probably be invalidated once he started messing around with magical explosives, anyway, but he was glad he'd done it for the lessons learned. It would be a long-term project for certain, simply because of the scale of everything he needed.

But he *would* make it work.

Because despite all of its issues, a simple fact remained:

He had a *cannon*. All other arguments were invalid.

Previously, Edwin's efforts to learn about magic had been stymied by insufficient information. He was mostly limited to just himself and his own experiments. Inion had never been very useful, either, because she said she didn't know how to teach the basics. When he'd pushed for some instruction, anyway, he'd just been left confused.

Considering he wanted to start to dive into magical explosives, Edwin figured he should probably make sure he had a slightly better grasp on *both* halves of that statement before rushing forward recklessly. Fortunately for him, he finally had another mage to talk to!

"Mana is all around and inside everyone, just like blood or breath," Rillah explained, sitting cross-legged. "But most people can't touch it, any more than most people can control their heartbeat. When you woke up your mage talent by getting the Attribute, you started being able to touch it."

"I mean, I'm still pretty sure I wasn't magical before then."

"Of course you were. That's how you got Basic Mana Sense. Anyway, you said your mana started at one, right?"

Edwin nodded.

"Yeah. It was just really weak. But once you could touch it, that's when your Skills started including it in their effects? That's the difference between a mage and someone who just managed to get a magical Skill."

"I might have misheard you, or Polyglot might be acting up." Edwin frowned. "But you said that the way you know someone is a mage is because their Skills include it, and then promptly said that someone with a magical Skill isn't always a mage."

"Basic Skill," she clarified. "Someone who's a mage has magical Tier 1 Skills."

"Okay, but sure. Shelving that for the moment. So how *does* a mage use their magic for anything, then?"

"It's a bit like using a Skill," she explained. "But without the System, it's all much harder. For me, I imagine my magic as a storm that changes with the seasons. It'll be a hurricane, blizzard, rainstorm, or drought."

"Droughts aren't a type of storm, though?"

"Yes, but shush. I'm making a point. The more I call on my magic, the weaker the storm gets and it takes quite a bit of time to recover. I know another mage who views their mana as a reflecting pool where powerful reflections can disrupt the surface, another who visualizes it as a stream and they can only use so much at a time but with no real exhaustion, and a third who pictures their workings as plants they grow, and the larger the growth, the more powerful their magic."

"What do they all have in common?" she prompted.

"They all have *some* kind of limit," he said, catching on. "It doesn't really matter what, just that it exists. You can call on lots of power, but not consistently. The mirror guy can only use so much power before things go haywire, and the stream . . . a similar thing, but just visualized in a different way? Then the plant guy is the opposite. The longer he spends on it, the stronger it is, but without other restrictions?"

"Nice! Yes, magic isn't unlimited. Incomprehensibly vast, but limited all the same."

"So what does that mean for me?"

"Well, the first step of using magic is calling on it. To do that, you need to know what you're calling on. Close your eyes and think for a while about what your magic looks like to you, and what that means."

Edwin nodded and closed his eyes, poking at his mana pool with all his senses.

"There's definitely two conflicting feelings . . . is that bad?" Edwin thought for a moment, trying to visualize the energy. "One part of me feels like it's a fire or sun that's radiating power, but I also feel like a pool of water that can empty out."

"It's not ideal but also not uncommon. In fact, most people have conflicting ideas about their mana at first, and overcoming that is the biggest step to actually controlling your magic. Molding your ideas into a clear, singular picture of what your mana is like will be a tremendous help in your casting, as it will naturally tend toward directly enacting your image into the world. Like how I can use weather magic so easily. But you definitely need to be able to call all of your magic at once, so it should all fit together neatly."

Edwin frowned, and she continued, "Look at mine. Because of my magic, it took me a long time to bring it all into a single concept. I had to figure out how to incorporate the unpredictability of the seasons—the overwhelming chill of a blizzard, the untamability of wind, the life-giving rains of spring, and the heat of summer—all into one. Of course, now it's obvious how they should fit together, a single eternal storm whose form changes with the seasons, but it took me a really long time to put it together."

Edwin nodded as he closed his eyes to visualize his mana pool. It was definitely a *pool*, and he could still feel the miniature sun nestled between his collarbones that was the source of his magic. The sun could burn away, the pool could empty out. Hmm. Light, heat, and water . . .

His mind flashed through possibilities. Lava? No, definitely not right. Molten steel? Eh, similar problem. Maybe nitroglycerin? No, that still didn't feel right.

What about a volcano? If the sort of magic he could use was tied to how he visualized his mana, volcanoes were pretty hard to beat for sheer power and versatility.

Ooh! No, what about a hydroelectric dam? Incorporating electricity directly into it and really go wild. Hmm. No, no. It didn't fit. Also . . .

"How complex can this be?" he asked.

"The important thing is that you can visualize it properly. The better you can visualize it, the easier it will be to use magic."

"So simpler is better?"

"Generally, yes. If you need to spin some elaborate yarn as to how all your magic fits together, it will be exceptionally difficult to use for anything but the most basic of powers. I heard of one mage whose magic apparently took the form of the entire Brass Sun, and all its inhabitants and magic within. It's probably just a story, but it was said that although he had an impressive array of capabilities once he was actually able to use it, but it took him outright hours to properly visualize his magic *to* use it."

"Oh, so I need to be able to picture it whenever I use my mana?"

"Unless you directly use a Skill, yes."

Okay, so the hydroelectric dam and volcanoes were definitely out.

He needed a practical way to visualize his ability to trickle out mana like drops of water, but also adequately reflected the power crackling within it and was positively radiant. Some kind of radioactive liquid, maybe? His mind raced, Visualization helping him imagine a hundred different possibilities. What else would . . .

Oh.

Oh, of course.

A triumphant grin crept across Edwin's face.

Congratulations! For firing a cannon, you have unlocked the Artillerist Path!

Congratulations! For creating a prototype weapon of war, you have unlocked the Sapper Path!

Congratulations! For successfully creating a Visualization for your personal mana, you have unlocked the Schooled Mage Path!

Level Up!

Skill Points 895→939 (Average level: 49)

Adaptive Defense Level 32→33

Alchemical Analysis Level 34→35

Alchemical Dismantling Level 42→45

Alchemy Level 91→92

Basic Thermokinesis Level 28→31

Bomb Throwing Level 51→52

Fey's Caress Level 38→40

Flight Level 50→53

Fresh Air Level 34→38

Improbable Arsenal Level 33→34

Longstrider Level 35→40

Numeracy Level 44→47

Outsider's Almanac Level 134→135

Polyglot Level 68→69

Prototyping Level 34→36
Ritual Intuition Level 30→34
Sapper's Apparatus Level 54→57
Skillful Assessment Level 42→45
Watchful Rest Level 31→34

CHAPTER 6

Mind-blowing Revelations

"Got it." Edwin opened his eyes.

"Wait, really?" Rillah seemed genuinely taken aback. "That was so fast! How did you— What did you settle on?"

"I mean, I *do* literally have a Skill for Visualization. Anyway, it was . . ."—Edwin decided to be dramatic—"a potion."

"A potion?"

"Yeah," he explained. "Like one of the bottles I have in my workshop for illumination. You said it should be simple and easy to visualize, but potent. Well, I work with that sort of thing all the time, and I can pretty readily imagine a bottle of liquid sunlight, or liquid fire. It's, you know, a potion. There's a bottle of it and I can pour it out and use it in stuff. It glows and has really fast effects, but it's also a liquid and that tracks with what I've been imagining mana as so far."

She remained skeptical. "It sounds like you have a very small amount of mana to call on with that image. Are you sure that's a good idea?"

Edwin shrugged. "I've literally never run out of mana. I suppose more potion is being made all the time or something." He thought for a moment. "Yeah, I can actually imagine it perfectly, a bunch of alembics and pipes and stuff all hooked together constantly adding to the batch. But it works so well! It's basically just glowing water, so I should be able to call it up pretty quickly, but it also has lots of variety!"

She shook her head. "Leave it to you to make your analogy for magic *include* magic."

Edwin looked at her helplessly. "Well, anyway. What's next?"

"Well, I wasn't expecting you to be done with that *today*, let alone before we landed."

Edwin grinned, glad that, thanks to all the practice he and Rillah had done, he could use Flight with basically no more trouble than just standing around.

"But since you *did*, now you just need to keep that image in mind. You got it? Okay, so then in my case I imagine standing in the middle of the storm, and I make the mana *pulse*, I guess. Don't know what else to call it. Then I . . . you know what, I'll just show you."

The two of them stood in Edwin's firing range meadow. All the reasons they had used it before—a convenient, yet remote distance from Sheraith, a lack of anything fragile—worked just as well for demonstrating magic as explosives, after all. Plus, they were already halfway there on their flight.

He could definitely feel Rillah's mana surging from her and around them, a fierce and dry wind whipping from within her core. As the weeks had passed, it had begun taking on a colder and colder tone to it, which was apparently connected to her magic shifting toward more ice and snow abilities.

Rillah let out a low hum and the air around them thrummed in much the same tone, harmonizing together. She wordlessly sang a few other notes, jilted and harsh, that seemed to hang in the air, preparing it for something. There wasn't any obvious effect, though—

A brilliant bolt of lightning flashed through the air, momentarily blinding Edwin, just before the heat and shock wave blasted past him. He shook his head to clear it slightly, left otherwise unfazed by the veritable explosion—he was probably getting far too comfortable with stuff blowing up in his face, wasn't he?—and nodded in appreciation.

"And that was *without* a Skill?" he confirmed. "That's pretty potent for something you can do just by humming for a minute."

Rillah beamed at him, green and brown eyes glistening. "Yep! I've been offered the Skill a few times—Lightning Strike—but I've never used it often enough to make it worth a whole Skill. It takes a lot of wind from my storm, but it doesn't really matter."

Edwin nodded. "You said you were Tier 4, right? I bet that's a pain and a half to try and deal with every time you want to add a new Skill."

Rillah nodded. "Be glad you can still add Skills to your set without slowing yourself down too much. I *still* haven't gotten my Flying Skill chain up to the fourth tier and I've had it for three years now. It doesn't help that all the really good Flying Path combinations are sixty points at *least*, and I can't even look up a Record because of the species differences!"

"So what was up with the humming?"

"Ah! Well, a storm can't really be controlled, but a song can be controlled."

Edwin blinked. "I don't see the connection."

"It's . . . well, I've never really tried to explain it. It makes sense to me? I can sing, or use my flute, and that's how I can shape what the storm does. It's kind of like if you have your potion magic, would you directly make a potion?"

"Is that not how magic works?"

"Well, no. Did I not explain that?"

Edwin shook his head.

"Oops! I guess that's what happens when you figure out an image within ten minutes about me first mentioning them, I forget stuff. At least it went well. Probably.

"So, if you want to make a magical effect, you need to control your mana, and I guess you might do your whole potion-brewing thing to make magic? Like, mixing your stuff together or whatever . . . I can't help with that, sorry."

"Well, I'm glad I didn't go for the hydroelectric dam, then," he muttered, and he waved off Rillah when she perked her eyebrows up. "Doesn't matter. Just an overcomplicated visualization."

She nodded in understanding, though still looked somewhat confused.

"So what else do you have?" Edwin asked.

"Haven't we been over this?" she retorted.

"I'll stop asking if you stop looking like you're about to laugh with every admonishment."

She considered that for a moment. "Fair enough. I just have one base Skill for each season. This time of year, it's obviously Autumnal Gust."

A Mana-Infused Skill blossomed around her and the wind picked up dramatically, flattening the grass around them. As she continued, Edwin felt another Skill enter the mix and saw crescents of Skill energy scythe through their surroundings, cutting grass and letting the clippings fly into the air, buffeted by the wind and pulled into a tight spiral around Rillah.

She stood in the middle of the miniature tornado, without so much as a hair out of place. Some of her loose clothing fluttered slightly, but Edwin could see she was actually *cheating*, a Skill manually moving the cloth wholly separate from the localized windstorm. He wasn't sure what to think about that. A cloth-fluttering Skill was what he expected from *Lefi*, sure, but not Rillah. Maybe it was the by-product of a different one?

Then, the wind died down, and the meadow settled back into normalcy.

"No music?" he asked.

"The Skill takes care of most of that for me. Other than providing the mana and unlocking the Skill to begin with, I don't actually need to do anything. Surely you're familiar with the idea?"

Edwin nodded. "So can you not use your other magic when it's not in the right season?"

"Oh, I can. It's just weaker. The equinoxes and solstices are when my magic is purest, but I can always use all my magic at any time."

"Wait, how does that tie into the constant storm? Like ice in a snowstorm or whatever."

"It . . . well, it's more of a symbolic representation, you know? The storm is a common point but it doesn't always fit with my magic."

"Weren't you just telling me how it strictly limited what you could accomplish with magic."

"Yes, but . . . Okay, look. I've had my magic for more than a dozen years; that's a lot of time where I can push the limits of my imagination and magic, and it won't all make sense when I explain it."

"I suppose that's fair," Edwin conceded. "Any chance I could get a demonstration of the other Skills?"

"Ask me again later. Don't you know it's rude to ask a lady her Skills?"

"Oh, so it's fine to ask a guy, then? Does Lefi know all your Skills? Should I ask him?" he shot back with a grin.

Rillah flashed a mischievous grin in response and summoned a gust of wind, blowing him into the air. Edwin caught himself without trouble and dove forward to try and catch her off guard. She was expecting the move, though, or at least reacted fast enough he didn't even come close, but it *did* set off a midair game of tag, which was . . . quite fun.

As he lay in bed that night, his Skill aching like a sore muscle, Edwin reflected that it had been a good while since he'd just enjoyed himself so much.

Edwin held his grenade up to the light, taking one last look before the test. The majority of what he could see through the apparatite, of course, was just the phosphorus. Inside, though, he knew there was a tiny, fragile vial of firevine sap, held in place by a combination of crystal and phosphorus itself. What was empty space in the container around the explosive itself would one day hold tiny bits of shrapnel, including them for this test was just taking a stupid risk. He cared about its potency, not how many iron filings he could pack in around it.

If this worked well, he'd have to see about getting proper casings made up as well. Though apparatite might work just fine for this. It was fragile enough to shatter easily, after all, but not so easy that the grenade should outright fail.

Satisfied with the basic form of the grenade, Edwin set it on his workbench and gave his safety equipment a final check-over. He didn't want to do this outside for many reasons—mainly that he didn't want to set off explosives in the city, and the meadow was too far away for this sort of thing—but he'd strengthened his blast defenses and was doing this in an otherwise empty room, so it *should* be fine.

Test one, mundane phosphorus and firevine oil, he narrated to Almanac. *Held in an apparatite container with separate containers for oil, phosphorus pellets, and expanded air canister. When struck, a primed explosive—see PhosphateGrenadePrototype7—will have the intentionally fragile separators between partitions break and allow the components required for a detonation to intermix and hopefully ignite.*

Edwin removed the protective cap, allowing the oh-so-fragile crystal protrusions to stick up above the explosive's main body. Satisfied, he stepped back to the far side of the room, sheltered behind his blast screen, and threw his detonator pebble.

The tiny rock, smaller than even his fingernail and guided by his Throwing Weapons Skill, flew true, perfectly striking the detonator pins. There was a brief, tiny flash of blue light, then . . .

WHOMP!

Smoke and fire billowed into the room, filling it with the ever-familiar scent of garlic that phosphorus produced for whatever reason.

Hmm, okay. Definitely good, and certainly a viable alternative for his smoke bombs if he didn't mind the smoke being both toxic and spreading fires everywhere. So . . . not really practical for those purposes. But that was fine! It was why he had dedicated smoke bombs anyway. Also, setting things in a wide area on fire wasn't exactly a *bad* tool to have, and so long as there wasn't anything flammable around, he could pretty easily make the phosphorus burn itself out just with some quick applications of Firestarting, anyway . . . which he should definitely do now.

He also knew that his grenade design worked! That was cause for celebration in itself.

It took a little while for the smoke to clear enough for another bomb test, but after some time spent fruitlessly trying to master his newfound—well, newly *defined*—magical powers, Edwin was eager to move on with his experiments.

His next bomb would be Infused, and Edwin was already expecting a much larger explosion as a result. He hypothesized that the mana he stored within the phosphorus would be released in the detonation, bringing a proper fireball into existence.

Test two, Infused phosphorus and firevine oil. Testing methodology a match for PhosphorusExplosivesTest1.

He set his grenade prototype on the counter, took shelter behind his reinforced barricade, triple-checked that all his protective gear was in place, and threw his detonator pebble. Everything was going just as planned . . .

Wait, wait, no. Why was—

BANG!

—Bomb Throwing activating?

A fireball filled the room, the sudden explosion and shock wave magnifying in volume as it bounced around the enclosed space. The world went orange and then white, and it took Edwin way too long to realize it was because his apparatite face mask had just been coated with phosphorus pentoxide. His earplugs had probably saved his hearing, and he dispelled them to see if anyone was— Ah, there it was.

"Are you okay?" Inion asked, her voice echoing through the room. Apparently the explosion had caught her attention, because she had *not* been nearby earlier.

"Yeah, yeah!" he called back, wiping off his mask to reveal the workshop *was* indeed very smoky, but strangely, the workbench was also coated in a thin layer of black dust in the perfect shape of a scorch mark. Where had *that* come from? It was made of *stone* and hadn't been there with the mundane test. Perhaps just as strange was the distinct lack of phosphor fires *anywhere*. "I'm fine!"

He coughed more out of a sense of obligation than anything, but he had no doubt that he had just given Fresh Air quite the workout. He frowned at the soot covering the table. What *was* that stuff, and why was it black? Was it from the firevine? Phosphorus pentoxide—the usual result of burning the element—was *white*. And yes, there was a lot of that everywhere, but what the heck was *this*?

Alchemical Analysis.

>83% Elemental Phosphorus

What the *heck*?

"It just worked way better than I had anticipated!" he called to Inion. "Way, *way* better. I'd stay out there if I were you while I clean this up!"

Hmm. Why did Bomb Throwing trigger for this one but not the previous? Did it have to do with the amount of magic present in the latter? Why was there a black phosphorus scorch mark on his bench, and was it *actually* black phosphorus? Where were the lingering remnants of burning white phosphorus spread throughout the room?

A bit more testing showed that, no, it was not the amount of magic present. In fact, Edwin couldn't figure out *why* sometimes it came into play and other times it didn't. Sometimes, Bomb Throwing activated for the mundane grenades, sometimes it didn't activate for the magical ones with no apparent difference in his experiments.

He grumbled in frustration. What was this stupid thing doing that he couldn't control when the Skill would or wouldn't engage? It made it very hard to determine appropriate blast shields for testing when at any moment a given explosive might suddenly be ten times as powerful. He clearly needed to get a better handle on how to *not* make a Skill activate . . . hmm. Maybe he could just make Bomb Throwing an active Skill instead of a passive one? He'd done it with Firestarting, after all.

It wasn't a *perfect* solution by any means, of course. From a raw Skill-comprehension angle it was far better to understand the limits for a Skill's activation than it was to just brute-force keep it from working, but he *did* need to make sure he wouldn't blow himself up by accident if he started working with nitroglycerin at some point, so it was some-thing to work on if nothing else.

He'd need to move to a room with better ventilation, as well. Fresh Air had made him sloppy with that particular bit of safety, but if noth-ing else, it was a pain waiting for all the smoke to clear every time he tested a bomb.

Seriously, though. What was up with Bomb Throwing?

That said, at least the Infused grenades did reliably produce the fire-ball and black phosphorus soot, just without Bomb Throwing getting involved they were much more manageable sizes. He also hadn't man-aged to *prove* what the black, graphitelike substance that his Fireballs left behind was, but he was pretty sure that it was genuinely black phos-phorus. If it was, that raised a *ton* of questions about the explosion and why there was black phosphorus—which was normally only produced in a lab, under seriously extreme pressures—created in the detonation.

Edwin considered himself lucky that the particular allotrope he was dealing with was stable, if nothing else. His fireball had enough prob-lems, what with leaving clouds of caustic material hanging around. But where the *heck* was the extra energy to create the black phosphorus coming from?

Yes, yes. It was certainly magic. He was dealing with magical phos-phorus, after all. He hadn't seen anything that suggested mana cared about conservation of energy. At the very least, he hadn't noticed any sort of consistency in how much energy some fixed amount of mana was equivalent to.

Heck, he could *fly*, and the energy requirements for that sort of thing were . . . insane, unless using clever aerodynamic tricks to help out, which he wasn't. But also, that was *with* the aid of his Packing Skill. Considering Edwin could lift giant boulders with only a bit of effort these days, that Skill definitely did a *lot* of heavy lifting, pun intended. And if that had been everything, he would have just dismissed it as "just magic."

But that *wasn't* everything. Why did a bigger explosion create a by-product that took some truly insane pressures—something like twelve *gigapascals* if Memory served—to make? Was it connected to the fact that Infused phosphorus was a high explosive, albeit a weak one? It was either by accident or a deliberate—so to speak—part of the process. There was *something* strange here going on, and he *would* figure out what it was no matter what it took.

Edwin was deep in thought when Kynigos dragged him from the lab and out into the daylight before running off. Though he hissed in frustration at not being able to continue his testing, most of his reluctance vanished when he saw Rillah waiting for him. What was she doing?

"Come on, let's go flying!"

"What do you need me for to do that, though?" he protested. "Last I checked, I needed you to fly and not the other way around. I've got stuff in the lab to do! There's something strange going on and I want to investigate."

"I *don't* need you to fly. But you haven't been outside for a week! Your lab will be there when you get back, but it's a great day for flying! Those'll be rare as we keep going."

It was actually true, especially since his training with Lefi, currently at about an hour a day, was predominantly indoors. Edwin definitely felt that he was actually learning stuff . . . not that it made any difference in how his Skill was stacking up against Lefi.

"Don't you have time to spend with Yathal or whatever? You seem to have gotten Kyni on your side, but what about his boy?"

"Nope! Lefi's keeping an eye on them right now."

"Well . . . aren't you in charge of scheduling the weather? Can't you just make nicer days?"

"Oh, please. You *know* it doesn't work like that. Besides, I can really only create seasonal-appropriate weather. I can't make it *warmer* when we're past the equinox."

Edwin sighed, only really putting up a token amount of additional resistance, though from the sounds of it he was still her last choice for someone to spend time with. Still, he wasn't about to *decline* spending time with a pretty girl. Besides, it was kinda fun. Also, it was great Flight training, he'd been getting so many levels in it thanks to their outings.

"Do you have some sort of appearance-based Skill?" he idly mused as they rose above the tower, then promptly realized his mistake. "Uh! Sorry, I didn't mean to ask that. I, um. I don't actually have an excuse. I just didn't think first."

She laughed and floated close enough to ruffle his hair slightly. "Why, Edwin. A lady loves to hear she looks pretty."

"Well, sure. But I just figured . . . you know what, never mind."

"I'll tell you . . . if you tell me what your crystal-making trophy Skill is that Lefi loves so much."

"Wait, Lefi likes Apparatus? He's barely mentioned that to me," he asked.

"Apparatus?"

"Sapper's Apparatus," he explained. "Evolution of Construction with Superior Alchemist. Quite useful, all told."

"Really? Huh! How'd you get that Path?"

"Beat up a band of bandits; their leader was an alchemist."

"Oh, yes! I remember that story. Anyway, to answer your question, it's an evolution of Unweathered Form."

"Unweathered Form?"

She nodded. "It's really important for my magic that I'm not really affected by weather or by the seasons. So I made sure to get a Skill that keeps me from getting too hot or too cold, which is very important for me."

"Because of your wings and your corresponding . . . inability to wear shirts?" Edwin knew he was on thin ice, socially speaking, but he persisted nonetheless. Probably a bad idea, but . . .

Rillah gave him an arch look. "I'll have you know that this is the *height* of fashion in the capital."

Edwin raised a skeptical eye as they drifted through the sky.

"It is!"

"What, how does that . . ." Edwin trailed off in thought. Hmm. From what he'd seen of fashion, avior tended to not wear overmuch, and while humans and the like tended to still wear clothing more reminiscent of medieval garb, he could definitely see Rillah's outfit—heavy garb on the waist and below, very little on the torso—being more common. Though that would only make sense if . . .

"Is the capital farther south from here?"

Rillah paused and looked at him curiously. "Yes, how did you know?"

"Well, basically not everyone will have your Skill to prevent them from getting too cold while wearing that, so it would have to be a lot warmer on average down there," he explained. "So, farther south."

She pursed her lips. "Well-reasoned. Even when I'm just messing with you, you figure stuff out." She ruffled his hair again, and Edwin started feeling a bit self-conscious. He hadn't really washed himself lately, so his hair was likely filthy with smoke and oils and *probably* caustic desiccants from all his experiments. Actually, what did he *look* like? Did he have a patina of smoke covering him? When was the last time he'd washed his clothing?

He'd take a bath when they landed, he told himself. There was a bath off in one corner of the tower, and the water was actually *heated* (and kept clean) by some magical object embedded in the corner.

At least Purify made washing himself relatively easy, and incidental use of the Skill while Refining stuff meant his hands were practically *sparkling*. He'd still need to rinse off first to keep the water from turning into phosphoric acid, though Adaptive Defense was *probably* pretty much completely protecting him from the stuff these days.

"What were we talking about?" Edwin realized. "I got distracted."

"Me," Rillah readily supplied.

Her? But . . . *Oh, right.*

"So Greater Unweathered Form?"

"Similar ability but *much* more potent and with a wider array of uses. It's *great* in the rain. Keeps me completely dry."

"And . . . Idyllic Form?"

"That's what makes me so *pretty*," she teased. "Makes me 'Possess the natural beauty of a fresh snowfall,' I'll have you know. I'm quite happy with the level I got it to."

"Oh, so you've evolved it too? What is it now?"

She gasped in mock offense. "Honestly, so many personal questions? I asked you once already . . . Don't you know it's rude to ask about Skills?"

Edwin frowned. "Oh come on, don't flip on me like that. You were *just* telling me about your Skills. Besides, I thought you were all for not being formal and that sort of thing. Actually, now that I think about it, aren't the *vast* majority of Classes and Skills public knowledge in the Empire? How does that translate to them also being really private?"

"What?"

"Rillah, I *know* you can hear me." Edwin didn't need to speak up even with the onrushing wind from their dive. "You have at least three Skills constantly active concentrated around your ears, and I'm pretty sure it's your Hearing Skill that lights up every time I talk to you."

She continued her pretense of not hearing him, and Edwin sighed before returning his attention to enjoying his Flight through the clouds.

"Step! Up! Up! Left! Dive! Step! Right! Step! Jump!"

Edwin had gotten used to switching between Flight and Longstrider in a single instant, to the point where Lefi had chained multiple commands together. That training exercise lasted for about a week before Edwin could do it in his sleep.

Then, however, Edwin had figured out something new with Longstrider. Namely, its Infused effect. Most, and in theory all, of his mundane Skills had some sort of magical effect when paired with his third-highest-level Skill, even if it wasn't always obvious. His magical Skills on the other hand couldn't be Infused, but that made sense.

"Jump! Step! Up! Right! Right! Back! Left! Down!"

Most of them directly *utilized* Mana Infusion in some way or another, and you couldn't use the same Skill twice simultaneously any more than you could hold two big objects in the same hand or speak two words simultaneously. Okay, that wasn't entirely true. He could use one of his magical Skills while also Infusing something else. He did it *constantly* with Flight, after all. Improbable Arsenal explicitly changed the effect his Infusions had on container-like objects, Flight was literally made by combining Mana Infusion and Packing, and while Edwin was still trying to figure out if Fey's Caress was magical or not he did suspect the shape-shifting Skill used Mana Infusion *somehow* in its base effects.

"Down! Left! Left! Left! Left! Jump! Right!"

But in any case, Mana Infusion was great, *if* he could figure out how to use it correctly. There were three layers of difficulty in Infusing his Skills. First was just figuring out where the Skill *could* be infused and how to shove his mana in. It was like trying to plug in a USB drive where the USB was invisible, the computer was invisible, and the drive had twenty different possible orientations.

"Up! Up! Down! Down! Left!"

The second difficulty was figuring out if anything else needed to be Infused simultaneously. Well, technically not *simultaneously*, just in unison. Some Skills didn't seem to have any effect when Infused on their own. Even Firestarting, Edwin's premiere Infused Skill, still required him to Infuse the air near his fingertips in addition to the Skill itself before it would deign to create sparks. Others, like Seeing, seemed to have the effect of "can combine with another Skill," and he needed to figure out *what* other Skill was needed for there to be any effect. Of course, that tied into and was made all the more difficult by the *third* component of Infusing a Skill.

"Right! Left! Right! Jump! Step!"

Namely, *figuring out* what the Skill did. His Skills didn't come with instruction manuals, and Infused Skills doubly so. He *still* didn't know what Nutrition and Survival did when Infused in a pair—heck, he didn't know what Infused Survival on its *own* did—despite sporadically working on it for nearly two years. Most of the time, it was just luck that Edwin found some new application of an Infused Skill, and his Longstrider discovery definitely qualified.

"Jump! Jump! Jump! Jump! Up! Right! Back!"

It had been the result of an overly tired slipup, amusingly. He had been at the end of a particularly long training session trying to figure out exactly *what* Infused Longstrider did, when his exhaustion—Longstrider could be *really* tiring when he was pushing at its limits for hours on end—had led him to tripping over his own two feet during a particularly quick turn, and his panicked attempt to straighten his legs and catch himself had launched him over ten feet through the air.

He could *jump*. Now, that may have sounded like a really stupid magical application of Longstrider, but for a Skill whose primary limitation was that one foot had to be either firmly planted on the ground at all times, it was impressive. Well, you had to have your feet planted unless you were running, in which case it was a little more flexible. But other than *that*, the Skill had a very clear requirement: firm footing on or near the ground.

When it was Infused, though? All the Skill required was that he had a solid foothold at the point of his jump's *start*.

"Back! Left! Up! Jump!"

Edwin was in pretty good physical shape, all told. He was still scrawny, sure, but he was very physically active and had *several* Skills giving him a pretty much perfectly nutritious diet when he ate—and when he was especially active, he ate regularly. That was to say nothing of Athletics and Flexibility giving him downright *superhuman* levels of fitness. Without Longstrider boosting his jump, he could very easily jump more than a meter in the air.

With the Skill, though?

Well, he could clear almost *eight times* that.

"Jump! Down! Right! Forward! Jump!"

And it was *awesome*.

Edwin certainly never felt bored, as he didn't let his work with alchemy slack, either, and he spent many an hour explaining to Lefi what he was doing and why it worked, along with all sorts of questions the man had about chemistry and science. Considering the amount of progress he had been helping Edwin make in his Longstrider and other Skills, though, it was a well worthwhile trade.

He had tried Refining phosphorus into being more explosive, and it didn't really do much? Not that "explosive" was a property he could really refine, but neither speed of combustion nor temperature impacted the destructive potential of his grenades.

It left him puzzled for quite a while, and it was only when he managed to get an accurate read on a fast-explosive's temperature one time that it finally became clear to him. Explosions were basically the result of a material getting *really* hot *really* fast, either tearing itself apart or heating up the air to increase its volume.

But his Refined phosphorus only burned hot *or* fast, not both, and the properties changed at essentially the same rate, leaving the overall explosion the same size. It was a frustrating conundrum, but Edwin figured he shouldn't complain *too* much. It had been an interesting diversion, but he was pretty sure the only way he could make pure phosphorus be any more explosive via purely alchemical means was by making the entire thing catch on fire at once.

He had hoped that Firestarting might come to his rescue, but it seemed not. He was pretty sure that the only reason he could ignite an entire log simultaneously was because the organic compounds did have *some* amount of oxygen locked away inside of it . . . or something like that, anyway. If he wanted to improve his burn rate of phosphorus, he'd need to make it into a gas and allow every molecule to combust simultaneously.

It was an amusing idea, but how would that even *work*? Phosphorus only sublimated at temperatures around 1000° C, and, well . . .

"Sub . . . limated? Vanished?" Lefi asked, breaking Edwin out of his lecturing mode.

"Sublimated? It's like evaporation, but with solids instead of liquids." The explanation got a confused stare from the Adventurer, and Edwin continued, "So there's three forms of matter, remember me saying that? Well, technically there's like *seventeen* if you want to be comprehensive, but while time crystals are *cool*, literally, they aren't relevant right now. Three states of matter that matter right now. Normally, you have a solid—like ice—that melts, and then boils or evaporates into a gas—like steam. With me so far?"

"Time crystals?"

"Just ignore that. It's this weird state of matter at hypercold temperatures where particle motion has no energy because of how cold it is . . . I read like *one* paper on the stuff years ago, and I haven't even begun to explain the absolute basics of the stuff that *you* would need to understand how it's even theoretically possible. Moving on. So . . . solids, liquids, and gases. You with me?"

"I do believe so."

"Great. Well, sometimes a substance can skip the liquid phase and jump straight to a gas. That's what phosphorus does. Heating it to a thousand degrees Celsius would give diphosphorus, and that's super-reactive like the hellish element it is. But it also wouldn't be practical to really *have*, because it would need to *stay* that temperature, and I think I'd need to be like level ninety in Basic Thermokinesis to make it work. But what *might* work is if I was somehow able to powder normal white phosphorus to the molecular level and then somehow distribute that powder over an area, then *that* would create quite the . . ."

He trailed off in realization, "Fireball."

"Edwin?" Lefi asked.

"Yeah, yeah." He vaguely waved his hand at the Adventurer, springing up from his chair, mind racing.

"I need to get to my lab. I think I figured it out!"

Congratulations! For receiving extensive lessons from ??? Lefi Forolova, you have unlocked the Student of Power Path!

Congratulations! For successfully developing a new application for the Longstrider Skill, you have unlocked the Athlete Path!

Level Up!

Skill Points 939→995 (Average level: 52)

Adaptive Defense Level 33→41

Alchemical Analysis Level 35→37

Alchemical Dismantling Level 45→46

Basic Thermokinesis Level 31→32

Bomb Throwing Level 52→55

Fey's Caress Level 40→41

Flight Level 53→56

Fresh Air Level 38→44

Improbable Arsenal Level 34→36

Longstrider Level 40→46

Mana Infusion Level 88→89

Memory Level 64→65

Numeracy Level 47→48
Polyglot Level 69→70
Prototyping Level 36→39
Refine Level 35→36
Ritual Intuition Level 34→43
Sapper's Apparatus Level 57→59
Skillful Assessment Level 45→48
Watchful Rest Level 34→36

CHAPTER 7

Fire, Water, Sky

"What is it which you have managed to determine?" Lefi asked, confused as he followed behind a very eager Edwin.

"Remember what I was saying about the soot stains on my lab bench?" he prompted the Adventurer, getting a nod. "Yeah. There was nothing in the explosion that should be able to create soot, but I figured out that it was black phosphorus, which is *plenty* stable. Of course, that's not much better for really explaining what's going on, because normally it can only be created with insane amounts of pressure, and besides, it should burn up in the fireball. So I didn't know where it was coming from.

"Well, I was *also* wondering what was up with the fireball itself. Somehow, it became a high explosive, and that means that the entire thing has to ignite simultaneously. Like, every single molecule at the exact same time. Or, I suppose, the magic itself could create a shock wave at the surface of the explosion, but it doesn't feel like that. The magic feels like a fireball, not kinetic energy or . . . sound, I suppose. So one of my senses would be lying to me if that were the case.

"Now, I need to perform a couple of tests, but I think I finally know what's going on. I need to focus for a few minutes, but I'll answer your questions afterward."

Edwin stopped in his storage room to grab some munitions test samples. Well, it was more of a closet than an actual room, but that didn't really matter. For obvious reasons, he kept his materials separate from his actual *experiment* room.

He stepped inside his lab, motioning for Lefi to stay back, and placed the crystal-covered substance on the windowsill—not *quite* a replacement for a fume hood, but thanks to Fresh Air it was sufficient for his new workshop.

Okay, test one. If this failed, then there was clearly something else going on.

Phosphorus was flammable enough that he didn't even need to Infuse Firestarting to make it burst into flames. A simple finger-gun was enough to get him into the proper mindset for selective ignition, and he aimed at the tiny, sealed chunk of explosives before pulling the metaphorical trigger.

BANG!

Edwin nodded to himself as the fireball faded. He should have tried anerobic tests of Infused phosphorus, but he hadn't really thought of it as an actual *test*. Just a stupid mistake he'd made early on in his experiments with the mundane variety. But the broken apparatite, and accompanying fireball, confirmed that he didn't have to be *too* worried about adequate oxidation in his actual weapons, at least. Well . . . depending on if he was right about how this worked, it might only affect his grenades, but that was fine.

There seemed to be a slightly larger "soot stain" than usual, but that might have just been his imagination. He still needed another test before making any further conclusions. After all, once the apparatite container had burst, the phosphorus was able to combust as usual. What would have happened if it hadn't broken free or was unable to combust?

For his next experiment, Edwin summoned an apparatite container around the casing, Infusing it with Improbable Arsenal as he did so. He'd found that if he used the two Skills *simultaneously*, instead of creating an object with Apparatus and then expanding it, he could get a larger expansion ratio, and he'd need as much volume inside as possible. Inside the testing box, he dismissed the Infused phosphorus's casing, allowing the yellowish pellets to spill out into the larger space. That accomplished, he put the box on the windowsill—it *shouldn't* explode, but Edwin was rather attached to his fingers and would rather not lose any—and ignited it.

Inside, the phosphorus sparked, glowing slightly as it erupted into a ball of black dust that filled the expanded space in complete silence—thanks to the near vacuum inside—before settling into a layer on the bottom.

"Yes!" Edwin cheered.

"I'm afraid I do not comprehend that which you just managed to confirm?"

"So"—Edwin slowed down—"so far as I can tell, when I try to ignite Infused phosphorus—I need to come up with a better name for that—the magic *tries* to burn the phosphorus, but it isn't able to. So instead, it manages to convince white phosphorus to transmute into black phosphorus. Because black phosphorus is more stable, the transmutation gives off energy, which blows the block apart. Then I *suppose* the excess heat manages to ignite some of the black phosphorus and then that burns more and more until most of the black phosphorus is gone.

"That's why, when it was in a vacuum, it just poofed into a cloud of black dust. With no air, it didn't have anything to burn for fuel and so it all fell apart into molecular dust; don't inhale that, by the way. It *might* be stable inside of you, but I really wouldn't take the chance."

"I presume that made sense to you, but is there some benefit to this? Not that there needs to be! Such a discovery is marvelous unto itself, is it not?"

"Well, you're right on one part. Knowledge is always better than ignorance, but in this case . . ." Edwin said, a twinkle in his eye, "it means I can do *this*."

They'd reached the chest of phosphorus, and so Edwin resheathed his hand in steel, drew his apparatite knife, and sliced off a chunk of phosphorus from inside its watery basin. It started smoking almost immediately, of course, but that didn't matter this time, nor that it was slightly wet. Instead, he tossed the element into the room, arcing toward the window as he took aim with his Skill.

Firestarting.
BANG!

It exploded midarc, and Edwin's face stretched into a wide grin. He could circumvent *so much* preparation like this. And! For the first time, he knew what his magic did, physically.

Spell unlocked, he thought in triumph, *fireball.*

". . . And then, Kyni ran at the guy and took a big bite right outta his club like he was playing! It was so cool. So then this guy just looks at his stick an' tries to hit Kyni, but he isn't about to let somethin' like that stop him! So he grew and just swallowed the whole thing! He kept on shoutin' about how Kyni was such a big dog and how he could never stand against such a big and strong dog and then he ran off after just a little bark! It was so supercool!"

"Oh?" Rillah prompted as she brushed out Yathal's hair. Kyni's coat had been already finished and the dog's fur gleamed in the dim light. "Are you picking up Sherrish, then?"

"Well . . . not *really*," the boy admitted. "But it was obvious what he was saying!"

Yathal didn't have Polyglot, which really hindered his ability to interact with pretty much anyone without the Skill. Fortunately, it was a relatively common Skill for everyone from guards to merchants— anyone who was likely to interact with nonlocals, basically—but it was also all but required for any half-decent Adventurer according to both Lefi and Rillah.

Its evolution Path was at least straightforward enough—just evolve Language with Linguist, both of which strongly preferred the other. Unfortunately for Yathal, the most common method of unlocking the Linguist Path was by learning a new language, and the kid was definitely still a ways away from that goal.

"Are we not concerned about the fact somebody tried to mug Yathal, then? When did they even leave the tower?" Edwin asked Lefi, who just shrugged.

The six—five if you didn't count Kynigos—of them were all sitting in one of the tower's lounges, eating a rare meal together. It was never really *planned*, it just tended to happen, but Yathal had really wanted to tell them all about what his day had been like and so had insisted they all meet.

"Yathal would never come to harm, not with Kynigos watching over him, and it's better that he has the opportunity to get used to being in unfamiliar places. Besides, between the two of them, it's Kynigos who must learn to be responsible, and it's important to teach him the sort of trouble Yathal can get into with cities."

"Fair enough, but like . . . shouldn't we keep a bit of a better eye on them or whatever?"

"Life is harsh."

"Sure, but just throwing someone into a river isn't a good way to teach them how to swim."

That got a skeptical look from Lefi, and Edwin realized his mistake. He buried his head in his hands. "Please tell me you'd at least fish them out if it looks like they'd drown."

"Oh, but of course!"

"I mean, sure. I've been spending a fair amount of time with Rillah. Among other things, she's *nice*," Edwin pointedly teased his friend. "And she is *definitely* better at teaching me magic than you are." He splashed Inion with a bit of water.

One unexpected benefit of Adaptive Defense was that he could stay in the bath for a basically indefinite period of time without getting wrinkly, and he'd never overheat from the water either. So he tended to stay in it for several hours at a time.

Inion had figured out his habit and started joining him after the third time, and what had once been Edwin's last "alone with his thoughts" time—after he'd started doing alchemy with Lefi around much of the time—had become "spend time with Inion." It was kind of hard to complain about getting the chance to bathe with her for obvious reasons—he had long since been inured to having no privacy from the fey, this wasn't really different—but he *was* starting to get a bit people-worn.

"Hmm," Inion said as she floated by him, "how many people do you like being around?"

"I mean, I don't *know* that many people on Joriah," he reminded her. "So it's not really a fair comparison."

"Yes, but she's definitely spending a lot of time with you. You should be a bit more careful with that."

"Yeah, she's teaching me *magic* and is tons of help leveling Flight. Oh, what? Another girl wants to spend time with me and you're suddenly suspicious of her? Are you sure you aren't just jealous?"

She rolled her eyes. "Edwin. I'm older than this entire *w— Empire.* Me getting jealous of you spending time with a girl is utterly *absurd.* What would I even be jealous *of?* That we don't spend as much time together as we did before?"

"Yes?"

"Please. You know I don't care about that."

Edwin wrenched his brain away from the interpretation that she *didn't* care about spending time with him and tried to spin it more positively. She was clearly . . . just happy that he was being social, clearly. Did she care about that? Wait, yes. She did.

"So then what *is* your problem? Is this still about her dropping me?"

"You were in serious danger! She clearly doesn't care about your well-being, and you don't know how much you can trust her but you're still telling her all about your Skills."

Edwin rolled his eyes. "It was one time! And she apologized anyway. I can take care of myself, you know. I could have just Overcharged and been fine. I actually *tested* that. I dropped a rock onto my head while I had the Skill active and it broke on *me*, not the other way around."

She raised a very skeptical eyebrow.

"It was safe! I worked my way up. I didn't just drop a boulder on my head to see if I'd be all right. Come on, you know me."

"Yes, because you would *never* perform an 'experiment' that might seriously harm you if it went wrong."

"Again, that was *one time!*"

Inion leveled a stare at him, and Edwin withered under her gaze.

"Okay, it was *technically* twice.

"Look, I don't know, okay, *fine.* I suppose you *could* count those as separate instances, so *maybe* it was three times.

"Okay, that time just flat out doesn't count. I was in *no* danger the entire process.

"Stop looking at me like that!"

* * *

"So, yeah, Inion doesn't like you."

"Doesn't surprise me, she does strike me as very possessive."

"She's not . . . okay, maybe she is, a bit. I just wish I knew how to help!"

"You know I'd never take advantage of you, right?"

"I mean, *I* know that—"

Probably. How would I be able to tell?

"It's just a matter of convincing *her*, and I don't know how to do that."

"If I think of something, I'll let you know. *Anything* to help you out," Rillah said mischievously.

"Oh, really? In that case, what about telling me about every one of your Skills?" Edwin joked. He tried to not bring it up *too* much, but his mind never really was able to go anywhere else, and he'd need to think of what he'd bring up next after she refused.

"Sure!"

"Wait, actually?" Edwin asked, discarding his musings. "Are you sure? Not that I *don't* want to know what Skills you have going on, especially with your ears. Only one of them seems to be Hearing; what are the others? But anyway, what happened to that being private, or it not being proper?"

"Oh, are you complaining?"

"No! No. I love learning about you. Wait, no, that's not right."

"Oh, you *don't* like learning about me?" she shot back, and Edwin panicked. This was exactly the sort of thing that drove people away from him, just sticking his foot in his mouth.

"No, no. It's not learning about *you*, it's learning about your magic. Wait, that's worse."

I said stop *sticking your foot in your mouth.*

"I like learning about *everything* and . . . I'm . . . just going to stop there." He sighed.

At least she didn't seem too offended and just laughed off his blunder. Edwin couldn't help but wonder how much damage he'd done to her mental image of him, though.

"I'm just messing with you, don't worry. But for working with me? It was never going to take long, Edwin. Especially not with you working so much with Lefi. Yes, it matters that you keep your guard up with people. But we're Adventurers, for better and worse. We need to constantly keep an eye out for people who will try and take advantage of our lack of support. That means keeping things close to the chest, yes. There are those who hate Adventurers and will look to hunt them down, others will just refuse to pay you for jobs you perform."

She shrugged. "But the other side of that is that it's more important for us to *make* those support networks. Because there's so few people that we can really trust. Imagine what would have happened to Yathal and Kynigos if Lefi hadn't gotten them and brought them here. It's important to weather the storms in groups, and those groups need to be honest with one another."

"Yeah, but . . . why me? Is this just because of Inion?"

She gave him a smile and a bit of a laugh. "No, it's not *just* because of Inion. Most of it is because you're honest."

Edwin started. "What? Do you have any idea how many secrets—"

She chuckled slightly. "I'm not talking about your secrets, whatever those are. We all have those. You're just very straightforward. When you say something, you mean exactly that. No hidden agendas, nothing."

"I think you might just be spending too much time with politicians."

"No more than I can help," she said. "The nobles still insist on weekly meetings with me, but it's *always the same*. Oh, due to unexpected delays my replacement is not coming quite yet, but any day now I should expect them, whoever it is, to begin the trip. But I better not get the idea that I'm actually doing something they couldn't do *without* me, I'm not *valuable* to them or anything."

"Any time with a politician is too much time with them."

"I won't disagree with you there."

"So why *don't* you just leave? I mean, I could get it if they were paying you a good amount or whatever, or if you had someone in the city you liked seeing, but why don't you just"—he waved his hand in the air—"fly off?"

"Well, you keep things interesting for one. Between your lab stuff and Yathal's antics? There's never a boring moment with you around. But as it's coming to winter, well . . . I usually settle down for a while, and the tower certainly is a nice place for that. Much nicer than most places I winter, anyway. I lost my autumn, which is always sad because it's the *best* time for flying, but no point dwelling on it."

"Sure, but why did you stay this long?"

"Well, because they needed my help. Come on, Edwin. I know you understand that."

"I mean . . . sure. I wouldn't say I'm *obligated* to help random people; that gets into a whole *mess* of Ethics. Like an inherent obligation of action just isn't a thing that can or really *should* even exist."

"Edwin."

"Yes?"

"Stay focused."

"Right. Basically, positive obligations are a *huge* moral mess, and—"

"Edwin . . ."

"Sorry, sorry. What were we talking about?"

She sighed. "Would you help people that needed you, even if you didn't know them?"

"I mean . . . probably, I guess," he conceded. "But, like, if they asked me . . . yeah. But I do have limits."

"So do I," she agreed. "I won't stay here forever, but I also don't want Enforcer Finnas to hunt me down."

"Okay, that answers my question somewhat, but what *is* up with that? I haven't gotten the impression many people actually *want* you here, but you also can't leave?"

"Oh, that's simple," she said as they drifted through the sky. "They've done such a great job persuading everyone that they don't need me, they've convinced themselves too."

"I don't follow," Edwin admitted. "So they think they don't want you, but also won't let you leave?"

"The city enchantments *need* to stay active, and they require a steady source of wind magic to protect everything, but the nobles couldn't bear to admit to their subjects that they need to rely on an *Adventurer*, so they spin everything in a way that makes me look absolutely useless, or like I'm threatening or sleeping my way into the position. I'm somewhat flattered by the former, but the latter is just *ridiculous*."

"Oh, why's that?"

"Because they don't have *nearly* enough towers if that's what it took to get into one," she replied with a grin.

Edwin chuckled. "I'll take your word for it. But that does seem to be the case, yeah. I've heard several things that sound like insults about you when I'm out and about. Whatever slander campaign they ran against you is rather impressive, I have to admit."

"Oh, believe me. I've heard it all myself. But it's all because of how important it is to them that they retain the appearance of complete competency, and the idea that anyone could do anything without their support doesn't work with that.

"In other places, the local Enforcer might stand as a counterpoint to the governor, and they can play out their little power struggles on that axis. Here, though? Enforcer Finnas is in the middle of it all and it doesn't look good for his power if he can't do everything."

"So what? You just *let* them mock you?"

"You can't be a successful Adventurer if you put too much into caring what people will think about you. Look at Lefi."

"People are overrated," Edwin grumbled slightly, and Rillah laughed.

"They can be. And it's good to see you're already in the right mindset. But that brings me around to my original point. I'm helping you because you're helping me."

"Helping you? I'm not doing *anything*," he protested. "And I have to keep shoving my guilt down because there's nothing I *can* do. It's only because of you that we're able to stay here, and it's not like I'm providing anything useful. Heck, I can't even help out by making food every once in a while because my stupid cooking Skill is addictive!"

"Edwin," she gently admonished, "do you blame Yathal for not being as strong as us?"

"Oh, so I'm a kid now?" Edwin snapped, then winced. "Sorry. That was uncalled for."

She gently stroked the side of his head. "You're not a kid, you're just new to this is all."

"What do you know of my past?" Edwin guardedly asked.

I swear, if another *person knows about me being an Outsider. . . I don't know.*

"Not much," she said. "Lefi will only tell me that you're from very far away, but that anything more isn't his secret to tell."

"And you haven't been bugging me about that?" Edwin was surprised. "You who wants to know everything?"

She waved her finger in admonishment—they used the little finger in Joriah, but it was still unmistakably the same motion. "You're the one who wants to *know* everything. I want to *experience* it."

"You want to experience *everything*?" Edwin teased.

"Oh, of course not *everything*, no more than you want to learn every little nuance to that one process you were telling me about? The nitrac-thing? Oh you know, the preserver-explosive thing."

Edwin wrinkled his nose. "Point taken."

"You don't need to be useful *now* to be very clearly useful in the future or in many other situations. I've seen what you make, and you're clearly shaping up to be a promising alchemist. If you're ever able to make even half the stuff that comes out of Panastalis, yeah, I want to get on your good side now. Can you at least believe that?" She shot him a smile as they fell into a dive.

"Yeah, yeah. So what I'm hearing is, I'm not *actually* helpful right now for anything but entertainment; you just think I might be eventually."

Edwin tried to believe that she meant it, but his brain . . . wasn't convinced. He was useless! That they were willing to patronize him didn't make it *better*; why couldn't they just tell him the truth? Or worse, were they expecting him to be able to make arycal and midnight dust and all the other stuff alchemists could make? What would Rillah say if she found out he was totally incapable of making *any* of that stuff?

"Edwin, no," she gently said, coming to a stop and turning around to look at him, hovering in the air far above the tower.

He sighed. "Look, I'm sorry. I shouldn't have gotten after you. Can we end the flight for today? I don't want you to have to deal with me anymore today."

"Oh? You don't want to hear anything more about my Skills? Not even my ears? I promise, you'll find some of them *fun*!" Her voice picked up a slightly melodic tone as she talked.

"No, not today. I mean, I could, I just— Can we talk about them at some later time? I just . . . I'm not feeling it right now."

Rillah reached out to grab his hand, and while Edwin initially felt like refusing it, sense won out over spite and he hesitantly reached out to take it. Her hand was so very nice and soft . . .

Edwin fought back a bit of a sigh. Human physical contact may not have been quite the same as emotional closeness, but it was a nice enough substitute. He still couldn't look her in the eyes, and he shoved back a sudden surge of longing.

"Of course we can. One last dive?"

A wan smile crossed Edwin's face. "Sure. One last dive."

"Oh, hey," Edwin noted as they landed.

"What's up?" Rillah asked. "Feeling better?"

"I mean, I guess a bit? Anyway, Flight leveled again."

"Oh, nice! It's been a few days, hasn't it? What's it at now?"

"Yeah," he agreed. "Fifty-nine. One more until I start looking at evolving it."

"That's great!" She made a quick twisting motion with her out-splayed fingers in a "congratulations." "You've been growing so fast!"

He shrugged. "Guess you can thank Lefi and Inion for that." Edwin's eyes widened. "Oh, and you. Definitely you, and getting me to go flying so often," he hastily added.

Rillah gave him a warm smile. "It's my pleasure."

"Gah!" Edwin threw the rock he was holding on the ground in frustration. He was useless even in his *magic practice*. Sure, he could make slightly different types of mana by focusing on different kinds of potions, but when he tried to mix them to create anything slightly more complicated, or even just to practice, they just absolutely refused to cooperate.

Inion looked up, curious, and put aside what she was working on—some braided flowers from the tower's garden, still flourishing even in late fall. "What's wrong?"

"This magic! It's just . . ." He sighed, frustration gone. "Just a momentary bit of frustration. I thought for *sure* I had it that time, but the drops separated just before they finished mixing. Why, well, I mean I *expected* it to be hard."

"So what's the trouble?"

He shook his head. "Nothing, really. Rillah just makes it look so easy. And I know that's because of practice and lots of Skills, especially given I kneecapped myself way back when. I'm just so far behind everyone else it's ridiculous. Oh, look at me! I can start a fire with the snap of my fingers, I can mix a healing potion. Then you have Lefi, who okay, I'll admit that he's not a good point of comparison. But then you have *Kyni*, who can at the very least heal Yathal with no difficulties and straight up outrun the wind when he's really trying."

"Edwin, you've been on Joriah for less than *two years*."

"Yeah, I know! But look at my company! I've barely so much as ruffled Lefi's cloak when we spar, Rillah outclasses me in *everything*, and I can't even get this to work despite having two Skills practically dedicated to it! And don't even get me started on *you*.

"It doesn't *matter* that I'm getting better because I'm not getting better fast enough. What matters is that I *am* behind, and I'm just not catching up fast enough! Sure, Flight will probably hit level sixty in the next few weeks, and I suppose I really need to start thinking about what I'll do for that . . . But that still only puts me at Tier *2*. Then everyone keeps patronizing me over it! And that's without even talking about all the non-Skill ways that they're better than me. Rillah's actually able to put up with me, even when I get annoyed!"

Inion glared at him.

"What?"

"You're an idiot, you know that?"

". . . Why?" Edwin's mind raced with everything he might have just said. What had he done wrong? He needed to . . .

"Lefi is the Empire's strongest Adventurer and has been improving his Skills for nearly a century." She counted off her fingers. "*That girl* is your age, yes, but has had Skills for her entire life and has been a potent mage for most of that time. She's spent more time getting a single Skill to Tier 4 than you've spent *on Joriah*. And then *I've* had Skills longer than this entire Empire has existed, and while I was asleep for most of that I still had *centuries* to grow my Skills and really master them. You'd be an utter *freak* if you somehow were able to already be as strong as any of us."

"How do you know all that stuff?"

"I *talk* to people, Edwin."

"I do that too!" he protested. "Though . . . yeah, not about that, I suppose."

He huffed out a breath in frustration. "So basically, I should focus more on my true peers? I'm doing better than toddlers? What?"

"Yes. Though you could well pass into Tier 3 at any point if you so choose and you know it."

"Sure, but then I'd be dealing with a bunch of really weak Paths, which doesn't *really* help. And I'm not being compared to toddlers!"

"Even most laborers and such might have but a single sixty-point Path, you know that, ya? If you wanted, you could surpass them all at will. Really, you already have. Whatever your Flight Skill becomes will be impressive enough.

"You had education back on Earth, did you not?" she continued.

Edwin nodded. "Yep. Ages five through . . . well, you could go until you were like thirty, but most just went until eighteen."

"Here, you started your schooling two years ago, and now you're upset that you've *only* gotten twelve years' worth of Skill growth since then."

"Yeah, but . . ."

"Both of them are known across the Empire as being exceptionally powerful. Lefi in particular, but do you really think there wasn't a single other wind mage Sheraith could have called upon instead of her?"

"That doesn't really *matter*, though, does it?" Edwin snatched his identification tokens from his necklace and dangled them in front of Inion's face. "I've got *these* telling people what to expect of me. If I find myself in front of some really important governor, or a guildmaster, or an Enforcer, or some kind of bandit, they aren't going to care that I've only been working on this for two years! They're going to care that *I'm weak*, that my Skills are subpar and I just don't have the power to back up *anything I want to do*."

"For now. What about two years from now? Five? Ten? Edwin, you've got your whole life ahead of you; you *will* catch up. And you don't even need *to* catch up! Edwin. Edwin, look at me. It's *okay*. It doesn't even matter that you may be lacking in some common areas, because the places you *are* special, you're so far ahead of everyone else that what Skills you have for it doesn't even matter. For the people who matter, you're special enough."

That . . . was true. And entirely fair. Though way too cheesy to be sincere. Still, it was enough for Edwin's brain to calm down enough that he could shove his panic into the box where it belonged.

"And Rillah was just talking to me about this, too. I need better benchmarks, don't I?" He sighed. "Not that I really *have* any available."

He sat in silence for a moment before steeling himself. "Any idea what I should do about that with my magic?"

"You said you picture it as a potion, yes?"

"Yeah. What's yours, like a stream or something?"

She nodded, floating over to him. "Close enough. Summon a bit for me?"

Edwin obliged, mentally tipping over the potion bottle and letting some of the radiant liquid run down his arm and pool in his hand. The Visualization Skill was already showing its worth—he would have never been able to hold that much mana before he knew to imagine it as a potion. Now, the difficulty wasn't in keeping the mana together as it was to keep it against his hand, a *significantly* easier task.

Inion nodded, and he felt her mana, so reminiscent of a shaded spring, burble up from her palm and gather in her hand the same way Edwin's had.

"When you use your mana, you must determine how it is that you shape it. For me, water is an extension of my body, so I can control the water itself. You have a much harder job; how is it that you see yourself directing your mana?"

"Well, I'm trying to get it to mix properly."

"What is your goal?"

"I don't really have one. I'm just trying to feed two slightly different types of mana together and mix them *somehow*, just to get a bit of practice. But they're always staying either distinct or just canceling each other out. I'm starting to wonder if going with potions was a bad idea. Rillah uses sounds and music, and she does all this harmonizing stuff where two notes can have their individual effects but combine to make a third . . . how *does* that work, anyway? Can you cripple your magic by choosing a bad visual?"

"The mana doesn't *change* with your visualization," Inion explained. "Not by itself. Your mana is no different than it was before, not really. It behaves a bit different, and that's it. But! With a clear picture in mind you can make different applications *way* easier than normal. As you get better with the picture, the easier it'll be to get it to work the way you want."

"Oh, so they're . . . more like models, then?"

"Mah-dels? You say that word and I hear at *least* three different terms."

"Um . . . so in physics, there are things that don't conform to normal experiences. Electrons and photons—don't worry about it—are the major ones. There's different models you can work with that focus on different properties of the things, and depending on what model you use, different calculations might be easier."

"I have no idea what you just said."

"Could you look at someone's mana and tell what their visualization is?"

"Not to any *detail*, nah. Though that only applies if they aren't using it at all, but if they are you can infer quite a bit."

"Okay, great. So yeah. It's not that the *mana* itself changes, but the way you approach it can make certain tasks easier or harder."

Inion raised an eyebrow.

"Yes, I know that's exactly what you said, but now I understand it. So how does that help?"

"Well, you'll get better with practice."

"Yes, I *know* that, but I can't even get *started*. Hard to practice when you fail all the time." His lips quirked up slightly. "Just look at my training times with Lefi."

"You said he was doing better, didn't you?"

"Well, okay, he is, but . . . never mind. It was a bad joke. How am I supposed to practice it, though?"

"You spend at *least* an hour in your workshop each day doing potion work, don't you?"

"Yes? What does . . . oh!"

"Use Mana Infusion at first to get used to it, I'd say. *Then* try to freehand it."

Edwin jumped up. "Inion, I could kiss you! That's perfect!"

"Oh? Do you want to?"

Edwin's face must have gone through some very complex and very amusing emotions, because Inion just laughed at him while he went red from embarrassment and tried to hide his face.

Level Up!

Skill Points 995→1020 (Average level: 53)

Adaptive Defense Level 41→42

Alchemical Analysis Level 37→40

Alchemy Level 92→93

Arcadian Elixir Level 32→35

Bomb Throwing Level 55→56

Fey's Caress Level 41→43

Flight Level 56→59

Fresh Air Level 44→45

Improbable Arsenal Level 36→39

Longstrider Level 46→48

Mana Infusion Level 89→90

Prototyping Level 39→40

Ritual Intuition Level 43→46

Sapper's Apparatus Level 59→60

Skillful Assessment Level 48→49

Watchful Rest Level 36→37

Name

Edwin Maxlin

Age

2

Race

Extraplanar Human

Class

Alchemist-Errant

Attributes

Health 25

Impact 7

Mana 33

Perception 19

Stamina 30

Skills

Alchemical

Alchemy 93, Alchemical Analysis 40, Refining 36, Alchemical
Dismantling 46, Sapper's Apparatus 60

(Purify: 75)

Magical

Basic Thermokinesis 32, Fey's Caress 43, Ritual Intuition 43,
Mana Infusion 88

Flight 59, (Basic Mana Sense: 82), (Basic Mana Manipulation: 9)

Physical

Overcharge 27, Longstrider 48, Fresh Air 44

(Athletics: 81), (Breathing: 76), (Flexibility: 74), (Nutrition:
73), (Packing: 92), (Seeing: 72), (Sleeping: 73), (Survival: 76),
(Walking: 74)

Mental

Numeracy 48, Prototyping 40, Anatomy 43, Polyglot 70, Memory
65

(Language: 36), (Mathematics: 74), (Research: 50), (Visualization:
80)

Combat

Bomb Throwing 56, Adaptive Defense 42

(Throwing Weapons: 48)

Utility

Outsider's Almanac 134, Watchful Rest 31, Skillful Assessment
41, Arcadian Elixir 32, Improbable Arsenal 33

(Firestarting: 94), (Improvisation: 14), (Status: 22), (Identify: 80),
(First Aid: 82), (Harvesting: 76), (Construction: 77)

Paths

Skill Points: 1,020

Combat

Assassin 0/60, Bomber 0/60, Giant Slayer 0/60, Heedless Hunter
0/60, Hunter 0/30, Killer 0/30, Titan Slayer 0/90, Warrior 0/60,

Way of the Empty Hand 0/60, Trapper 0/60, Artillerist 0/60, Sapper 0/60

Alchemy

Alchemical Medic 0/60, Demolitionist 0/60, Makeshift Alchemist 0/60, Potioneer 0/60, Practical Alchemist 0/60, Mystic Alchemist 0/90

Science

Chemist 0/60, Experimenter 0/60, Researcher 0/60, Purifier 0/30, Scientific Revolutionary 0/90, Scientist 0/60, Engineer 0/60, Physicist 0/60, Mathematician 0/60, Material Scientist 0/60

Magic

Aerialist 0/60, Fey Friend 0/60, Feybound 0/60, Feycaller 0/60, Mage 0/60, Magical Gardener 0/60, Micro-Biomancer 0/90, Primal Constructor 0/90, Primal Ritualist 0/90, Realm Traveler 0/120, Skilled Arcanist 0/60, Fey Supplicant 0/60, Feykind 0/90, Attuner 0/30

Mental

Dedicated Student 0/60, Lecturer 0/30, Scholar 0/60, Unbowed 0/90, Canny 0/60, Steady Mind 0/60, Mentalist 0/60

System

Almanac Administrator 0/60, Forerunner 0/60, Outsider's Almanac Specialist 0/90, Pioneer 0/60, Skill Researcher 0/60, System Scholar 0/60

Trophy

Blackstone Conqueror 0/60, Deepwoods Panther-Hunter 0/60, Stonehide Vanquisher 0/60

Career

Brickmaker 0/30, Butcher 0/30, Diver 0/30, Gardener 0/30, Lumberjack 0/60, Merchant 0/30, Potter 0/30, Scribe 0/30, Woodsman 0/30

Physical

Ascetic 0/60, Daredevil 0/60, Physical Alchemist 0/90, Survivor 0/60, Physical Laborer 0/30, Athlete 0/60

Traveling

Escapee 0/30, Exile 0/30, Traveler 0/30, World Traveler 0/60

Medical

Field Medic 0/60, Medic 0/30, Steadfast Medic 0/60, Medical Lecturer 0/60

Misc

Arsonist 0/60, Autopyromaniac 0/60, Burglar 0/60, Child 0/12, Expert 0/60, Imperial Ally 0/60, Novice 0/12, Pyromaniac 0/30, Razer of the Ruined Tower 0/60, Rebel 0/30, Slave 0/12, Trainee 0/60, Traitor 0/60, Brushed by Power 0/60, Lirasian Citizen 0/30, Royal Advisor 0/60, Favored by Power 0/90, Insomniac 0/30, Sleepless Disciple 0/60, Student of Power 0/60

Completed Paths

CharLimitCanttalkmuchNocluewhathappenedDidmybesttohelpyouli, Mage, Skilled Arcanist, Physical Alchemist, Bomber, Linguist, Beginner, Warrior, Path Less Traveled, Athlete, Scout, Unkillable, Superior Alchemist, Adventurer, Explorer, Outsider, Skill Researcher, Wanderer, Alchemical Warrior, Novice Pyromancer, Novice Ritualist, Alchemist, Physicist, Engineer, Physical Arcanist, Biologist, Practical Alchemist, Fey Scion, Feytouched

CHAPTER 8

Evolving Awareness

Edwin felt like an idiot at times. After so much time trying to figure out how he could replicate alchemical reactions inside of rocks and pebbles to no avail, it was really embarrassing to have to be reminded that he had the *perfect* setup for mimicking alchemical reactions already.

Namely, him *actually performing* alchemical reactions.

It would be fairly straightforward, too. He was working with metaphorical training wheels, after all. The goal would be the ability to mix up spell "potions" on the fly, whenever, wherever, and with whatever he wanted, but one step at a time.

So here he was, back at square one, going through the motions of making something actually useful as he trained his magic to cooperate.

He would have preferred to make health potions, of course. He could make those practically in his sleep these days—given Watchful Rest, possibly literally—but he couldn't introduce his personal mana into the equation without messing everything up.

Failing *that*, he wanted to at least do *something* productive, but he really didn't *have* any nonmagical reactions that utilized liquids at the moment. If he had nitric acid, then things would be *very* different, but he *didn't* have nitric acid and the steps to *get* it were so obscenely complicated it was a wonder that he could even call it up with Memory, to say nothing of the people who figured it out in the first place. It was the cornerstone of modern chemistry for a reason. Chemistry, because of how much stuff fixed nitrogen was involved in, and *modern* because of all the *stuff* needed to make it work on a commercial scale.

He broke himself out of a slight daydream where he had been imagining himself with magic that could break down atomic bonds and bypass all the complications required in "fixing" nitrogen, that was, pulling the *most common gas* out of the atmosphere and just shoving it into a beaker of water. Instead, he pulled his attention back to *water*.

It was in theory the most trivial experiment possible. Mixing water with water, what could the outcome possibly be? Still, for all its simplicity, it *did* have its advantages. Mainly, that there was no way it could go wrong in some dangerous way. Almost as valuable was the fact that water and water were perfectly miscible. He should have no problems with the normal oil-and-water issues his types of mana had with itself. Or if he did, then that would be interesting as well.

Win-win, really.

Edwin forced himself to imagine his Mana Infusion as pouring out a bottle of mana potion, but unlike most of the time he used the Skill, he didn't let go at the end, instead maintaining a small measure of contact with his mana as it settled into the water. It was a bit of an odd sensation, but not one that was particularly unpleasant.

With his other hand, he repeated the process. For his first experiment, he wasn't changing anything about either of the Infusions, it was purely a test to see how they behaved when combined.

Experiment one. Unaltered mana Infused into waters A and B. B added into A slowly while stirring. As predicted, A and B mixed with no incident or notable interrupts.

Experiment two . . .

Edwin kicked his feet through the air near the tower, mildly miming the motion of swimming on his back as he lazily chatted with Rillah. He just felt . . . so at ease around her, even when she wasn't using Calming Touch. It was very nice.

"Okay . . . so is it an appearance Skill, then?" he guessed. "Like I can see some of the resemblance to what I think is Idyllic Form. What, do you just really hate the way your ears look or something? Is it some kind of Skill that lets you reshape your body a bit?"

The Adventurer looked at him like he was an idiot.

"Actually?" Edwin sat up in surprise. "I was *not* expecting that. Um, don't tell me." He cupped his hands in front of his mouth in thought. "Seasonal Appearance?"

"Close guess! Mercurial Form."

"Wait . . ." He again thought for a moment. "So then that Skill line goes"—he counted them off on his fingers—"Unweathered Form, Greater Unweathered Form, Idyllic Appearance, and then back to Mercurial *Form*?"

She scratched her head. "I don't see what you're going on about."

"Well, most of them are something-Form, but number three is Idyllic Appearance."

The girl raised an eyebrow. "Is there something different? Oh! They Polyglot differently for you?"

"Oh, yeah. I guess so. Anyway, shape-shifting?"

She looked to the sky, muttering something unintelligible.

"What?" he asked. "It's a cool Skill. And I'm kind of curious as to whether your DNA would change, or if you could do something with your blood type to make you an *actual* universal donor. Also, can you make yourself grow an extra finger or something?"

". . . What? Why?"

Was that suspicion in her voice? Eh.

He shrugged. "Just to see if you can. Is your skeletal structure mutable? Can you look like different people? How much can you actually change?"

"Oh. That's . . . better." She waved off Edwin's implied question as to what she meant by that. "I don't think I can do much other than some cosmetic changes. Well, maybe. But it's rather limited, and not one I've played with that much. Mainly, I just use it on my hair and ears to avoid getting *too* much attention."

"Wait, hair? Why? Also, if you're trying to avoid attention, why not use it on your eyes?"

She glared at him, and he raised his hands in defense and apology. "Sorry. Touchy subject, I see."

"Well, those *are* the color of my eyes for one, and for another, they won't change color with the Skill. Last, I like them that way. As for my hair, *it* changes color with the seasons too."

I'm surrounded by anime protagonists, he thought, mentally sighing. "Too? Wait, so then that means your eyes change color?"

"How . . . how do you make every question I'm so sick of sound so reasonable?"

"Uhhhhh . . ." Edwin had *no* clue how to respond to that one. Should he apologize? Make a joke? Sympathize?

"My eyes change with my magic, yes. Surely you've noticed them lightening?"

"You think I notice stuff like that? You have one green eye and one brown eye, that's about all I can *ever* remember."

"Yes, well, that's just in the fall and spring. Blue and amber in the summer and winter."

He nodded. "Very cool, I see why you like them. What about your hair then?"

"Brown in the spring and fall, red in the summer, blond or almost white in the winter."

"And you went with brown year-round?"

"I like it. It's less eye-catching."

"Ah, yes. Less eye-catching. That's *exactly* how I would describe you."

She half-heartedly swatted at him. "Jerk."

Edwin chuckled. "We got *way* off topic. So . . . your ears? What do you need to change about them? Don't tell me *they* change with the seasons as well."

She hesitated, clearly deliberating what she wanted to say.

"I can promise that no matter what it is, I won't laugh or make fun of you about it," he reassured her, then paused in thought. "Unless it's *really* funny, in which case I might be unable to control a small laugh when I first see them, and I *might* tease you about it if you seem amenable to the idea later on."

Rillah glared at him.

He dramatically lifted his arms. "What? Didn't you say you liked my honesty?"

"*That's* true." She sighed and rolled her eyes. *Agh. Was that a joke or was that actual exasperation? Um, shoot. Ah, damage control, damage control . . .*

"I can lie if you want!" he blurted out.

She glared at him again.

"Or not!" He made vaguely helpless motions with his hands. "I don't know! Look, if you just keep scowling at me, I'm going to have no clue what you mean."

She shook her head, as if to get rid of her irritation, then said, "You're fine, Edwin."

"Are you sure, because . . ." He trailed off, but his mind filled in the blanks, *Because that's exactly what I would say to someone I was exasperated with and just waiting for a chance to get rid of but didn't want them to feel bad about it. And I don't want to chase off* another *person who I actually like spending time with. I don't have enough to begin with!*

"I'm sure," she tried to reassure him, and explained, "It's just been a while is all."

Edwin was about to ask about what she meant, when he saw the Skill working. Her ears quickly shifted from normal to *distinctly* pointed. *Pointy ears, pretty girl . . .*

His eyes got *very* wide. "Are you an elf?"

"What? No!" she shushed him.

Sorry, he mouthed, eyes wide.

Rillah said, "It's all right. I should have warned you to stay quiet. You've never met an elf, I take it?" Edwin shook his head. "That's what I thought. You'd never think I was one if you had. I don't have horns *at all*, though admittedly that *is* within Mercurial Form's power."

"Oh? Well, does that mean you're . . . what, half elf, then? That's still *so cool!*"

Rillah raised an eyebrow. "Not what I was expecting."

"Rillah, I don't know how to break this to you."

She tilted her head in an indication to continue.

"I'm from *very* far away. I get that I 'react unusually' a lot. If you're expecting me to be anything *close* to normal, then hi, I'm Edwin and we *clearly* have never met."

She laughed, and Edwin immediately felt better. *Hmm. Was that a Skill? Joyful Laughter?* He shook his head slightly to try and focus it.

"I just thought you knew."

"Well, I just . . . didn't, I guess." Dang it, he'd really screwed up this time, hadn't he? He was usually better at . . . well, not being asked questions about people he knew.

"Huh. I could have sworn I told you at some point, or at least mentioned it while you were around."

"Okay, clarifying question though: Was I involved in an experiment, planning an experiment, or had literally anything other than just directly talking to you going on when you said this?"

"Edwin, is there *ever* a time when one of those don't apply?"

"I mean . . . you could definitely grab my attention whenever you wanted," he joked, and then he had to fight back a wince. It sounded . . . much better in his head.

"Hmm." She assessed him. "We'll see."

"So what's that like?"

"What's it like being a human?"

Edwin paused. "Point taken. But like . . . what sorts of reactions do you get?"

"Edwin, I keep my ears permanently disguised as human, what do you think?"

He wasn't able to hold the wince in that time. "Right."

Then he thought about it a bit more. "Wait, but why? I feel like I've seen at least six different species living in the Empire essentially in harmony. Avior, humans, gnomes, halflings, dwarves, and . . . okay, maybe just five, unless there's another that looks really similar to one of those guys. But still! Why elves, or not even *full* elves?"

"Where have you *been*?"

"Highpeaks, traveling, Vinstead, the middle of the woods, Panastalis, and here."

"Ah, never seen Kinea?"

"Can't say I've heard of it, no."

"That'd do it. Also, just try visiting the mainland. Not as many humans, way more strange looks. It's even worse if you're not *actually* human. But beyond that, there's lots of bad blood between Kinea and Quoena."

"Oh, hey, I know that one . . . that's the elven city, right? But why would . . . oh, who am I kidding. People are awful. And that holds in the rest of the Empire, then? Sheesh. So . . . Dad?" he guessed. "I presume if it were your mom, you'd be living in the elf place, or if you *were* an outcast from there you wouldn't be a normal Adventurer. What *is* the normal procedure for people from another nation visiting the Empire, actually?"

"You're clever, you know that?"

"That's what people tell me," Edwin awkwardly deflected. "Feels like I'm wrong more than I'm right, though."

"Nonsense. But yeah, Mum was the one to have the scandal, and here I am. She spent too much time in the Verdant, I suppose."

"So . . . where are you from, then? Not Kinea?"

"Rhothos."

Edwin frowned. "Is *everyone* from Rhothos? I know Yathal's from there, and I'm pretty sure Lefi is as well. At least, that's where his Registrar is. Then you're from there too?"

"Nah, Lefi's not from Rhothos. Don't know where he *is* from, but he just likes Vinstead. The province *is* quite well-populated and is friendly to Adventurers, though."

"I never got that sense while I was there."

"Most other places are worse."

"I'll take your word for it. You *are* the well-traveled one, even if—"

"Even if *you* have the World Traveler Path; yes, I know. Rub it in a bit more, why don't you?"

"Oh, only if you insist," he teased. "In fact—"

Edwin didn't finish his sentence, distracted as he was by something else. A grin crept across his face. "I hit it!"

"What?"

"Flight! I just got the notification, it hit level 60!" He fist-pumped the air. "I was hoping I might finally get it today. I need to figure out what I'm doing with it now."

"Well, what do you have for Paths?"

"Just a second. Hmm. There's no way to show someone else your System stuff, is there?"

Rillah shook her head.

"Ah, pity. Well, this will take a minute, then . . ."

Combat
Assassin 0/60, Bomber 0/60, Giant Slayer 0/60, Heedless Hunter 0/60, Hunter 0/30, Killer 0/30, Titan Slayer 0/90, Warrior 0/60, Way of the Empty Hand 0/60, Trapper 0/60, Artillerist 0/60, Sapper 0/60

Alchemy
Alchemical Medic 0/60, Demolitionist 0/60, Makeshift Alchemist 0/60, Potioneer 0/60, Practical Alchemist 0/60, Mystic Alchemist 0/90

Science
Chemist 0/60, Experimenter 0/60, Researcher 0/60, Purifier 0/30, Scientific Revolutionary 0/90, Scientist 0/60, Engineer 0/60, Physicist 0/60, Mathematician 0/60, Material Scientist 0/60

Magic
Aerialist 0/60, Fey Friend 0/60, Feybound 0/60, Feycaller 0/60, Mage 0/60, Magical Gardener 0/60, Micro-Biomancer 0/90, Primal Constructor 0/90, Primal Ritualist 0/90, Realm Traveler 0/120, Skilled Arcanist 0/60, Fey Supplicant 0/60, Feykind 0/90, Attuner 0/30

Mental
Dedicated Student 0/60, Lecturer 0/30, Scholar 0/60, Unbowed 0/90, Canny 0/60, Steady Mind 0/60, Mentalist 0/60

System
Almanac Administrator 0/60, Forerunner 0/60, Outsider's Almanac Specialist 0/90, Pioneer 0/60, Skill Researcher 0/60, System Scholar 0/60

Trophy
Blackstone Conqueror 0/60, Deepwoods Panther-Hunter 0/60, Stonehide Vanquisher 0/60, Titan Spider-Slayer 0/60

Career
Brickmaker 0/30, Butcher 0/30, Diver 0/30, Gardener 0/30, Lumberjack 0/60, Merchant 0/30, Potter 0/30, Scribe 0/30, Woodsman 0/30

Physical
Ascetic 0/60, Daredevil 0/60, Physical Alchemist 0/90, Survivor 0/60, Physical Laborer 0/30, Athlete 0/60

Traveling
Escapee 0/30, Exile 0/30, Traveler 0/30, World Traveler 0/60
Medical
Field Medic 0/60, Medic 0/30, Steadfast Medic 0/60, Medical
Lecturer 0/60
Misc
Arsonist 0/60, Autopyromaniac 0/60, Burglar 0/60, Child
0/12, Expert 0/60, Imperial Ally 0/60, Novice 0/12,
Pyromaniac 0/30, Razer of the Ruined Tower 0/60, Rebel 0/30,
Slave 0/12, Trainee 0/60, Traitor 0/60, Brushed by Power 0/60,
Lirasian Citizen 0/30, Royal Advisor 0/60, Favored by Power
0/90, Insomniac 0/30, Sleepless Disciple 0/60, Student of
Power 0/60

"What do you think?"

"Well, your Flight Skill is different from my own, so I can't say for certain. But what do you want from it?"

That was a good question. "I'm not sure I really can answer that. I *could* use another combat Skill, *maybe*. But I also don't really think I want to be locked into something that would only help when I'm flying, and I definitely don't want to lose out on something really cool and interesting when if I actually needed a combat Skill, I could just *get* one. What sorts of things would even *be* available?"

"Lefi would know . . . hey, Lefi!" Rillah yelled, getting the golden-haired man's attention. He was relatively close, tossing a ball back and forth with Yathal at the base of the tower. Kynigos was between the two of them and trying to intercept their thrown ball, jumping all over the place trying to catch the ever-stranger throws Lefi could pull off.

"Yes?" he called back, absently catching and returning the ball to Yathal, narrowly threading it just below Kyni's snapping mouth and sending it corkscrewing through the air.

"Edwin's evolving a Skill, we need your advice!"

"Marvelous! I shall be right there!"

"You know, Edwin is better off with *my* advice," Inion interjected, glowering at Rillah as she floated up to meet them as they descended.

"Oh, why's that? Because you know how to float five feet off the ground without wings?" the Dancer shot back.

"No, because I'm far older than all of you combined and have far more experience with magical Skills than you do. Also yes, because I know more about Edwin's Flight than you do. You clearly don't know how to make it work."

"Oh, is *that* right? Well, remind me—"

"Look, look." Edwin stepped in. "I want all of your guys' opinions, all right? Rillah's been helping me get tons of experience; Inion, you know *stuff* about Skills from way back when; and Lefi probably has more Skill evolution experience than both of you put together. Just let everyone talk, please?"

They seemed unconvinced. "Look, I'm not going to be able to give this the proper amount of thought if you're arguing the whole time. Can you at least shelve it for a *little* while?"

Both glared at the other, but Rillah was the first to break the silence. "I have no problem with her unless she makes one."

Inion opened her mouth to reply but was cut off by Lefi finally joining the little discussion with all the subtlety of a bull. "Marvelous! So what Skill do you seek to evolve, Edwin, what level is it, and what Paths do you have at present?"

"Oh, he's trying to evolve Flight. Level sixty, and he's got—"

"Inion, I can speak for myself."

Edwin quickly summarized the situation for Lefi, who stroked his chin in thought. "Most interesting! What do you desire?"

"I don't really know, honestly. Not without knowing my options. I want something good and strong that'll maybe help alleviate some of Flight's weaknesses."

"Don't evolve it then! Continue to level it until it is at a capacity that you are comfortable with!"

Edwin shrugged. "I mean . . . I could? But like . . . Longstrider is already a better vertical and horizontal movement Skill for most situations, and Flight is only really helpful if I have help"—he nodded at Rillah—"or I'm just trying to float around in general. I guess I just don't know what it *could* become."

"Your Trophy Paths might give you wings of some form," Rillah added. "That might help with your free-flight issues. Or perhaps some sort of glider-web, if you take that spider Path. I don't know what a bear might give you."

"Hmm, maybe," he said. "I did defeat the bear by tricking it into falling off a cliff; is that likely to influence anything?"

Rillah and Lefi shook their heads. Inion just looked lost in thought, and Edwin wasn't sure if she'd heard him.

"Okay, good to know. Though I don't know if that spider spun webs. Would it be better if I doubled down on its combat potential?"

"Feykind would likely grant wings," Inion opined. "Quite good ones even. Most fey are good at flying; that would help you fly with more precision."

"That *would* be useful," he conceded. "But then I'd need to raise Flight to level ninety to go neutral with the Skill, and I'm not sure if I want to wait that long. Even just the last level took *far* too much time and I kind of want to get Basic Stamina Manipulation, you know?"

"Why bother? Take more time! What rush are you in?"

"Well, I kind of just want to make myself more useful? I don't feel like I can really do that much, and evolving my Skills will definitely give me a larger toolbox."

"Nonsense! You are tremendously useful!"

"I'm objectively *not*," he countered. "But what do you think might happen if I took an Alchemy Path with it?"

That seemed to stump everyone, but *Kynigos*, of all . . . people (When did they get here? Was it safe to be discussing this sort of thing around a kid?), barked up and Yathal looked thoughtful. "Alcimmy is the thing you can do wit the smoke and bombs and healing stuff right? Well, Kyni thinks you might be able to fly with your explosions or something, or maybe you could make other people fly!"

"Marvelous idea, Kynigos!" Lefi praised. "That is most likely!"

The brown-and-white dog gave a gleeful bark, and Edwin nodded in thought.

"It's not the *worst* idea. Can't say I'd want to be rocket-powered, though it might be able to give me some extra combat options. Some sort of flight potion, though . . . Potioneer or Mystic Alchemist, maybe? Mystic is also ninety points, but it could be useful."

"What about the Agile Acrobat Path? That would likely greatly enhance your nimbility when airborne!"

"Okay, I mean . . . maybe. But I feel like I'd probably already have a Path that could do that sort of thing, and also could we please keep this constrained to the Paths I currently have right now? If you think of something superamazing that I don't have but you know how to get *easily*, then maybe. But this will be hard enough just looking at what I have right *now*."

It took them quite a while to continue discussing his options, during which time Yathal had gotten bored and walked off, followed by Kynigos of course to keep an eye on his boy. But in that time, they'd gotten some amount of speculation in for each of Edwin's Paths and eliminated the obviously worst option. Now, Edwin was mulling over his list of speculated Skill possibilities.

Because Flight was, at the moment, his only unevolved Skill; no matter what Path he took, it was guaranteed to evolve Flight specifically. Unless, of course, it unlocked an Attribute, but he wasn't counting that. But that meant he could be very specific with the Path he completed, and accordingly get an evolution he might not normally be able to obtain.

Assassin/Hunter/Burglar: Silent Flight/Aerial Ambush—airborne Stealth Skill

Bomber/Demolitionist: Carpet Bombing?—bonus to using bombs while in midair

Giant Slayer/Titan Slayer/Killer/Warrior: Some combat boost while midair

Heedless Hunter/Way of the Empty Hand: Kamikaze—flying charge attack

Trapper: Make motion-based traps?

Artillerist: Some kind of artillery-based telekinesis?

Potioneer/Practical Alchemist/Mystic Alchemist/Chemist?: Flying Potion—grant ability to fly

Makeshift Alchemist: Make potions on the fly

Sapper/Engineer/Physicist: Aeronautics—make flying contraptions

Experimenter/Researcher/Scientific Revolutionary/Scientist/Scholar/Mathematician: Some kind of measuring Skill

Material Scientist/Physical Alchemist: Floatstone—make flying materials

Aerialist/Mage: Improved Flight/Flying—more of the same, just with a reset level and better return

Fey Friend/Feybound/Feycaller/Feykind/Fey Supplicant: Fairy Wings—manifested wings for unknown benefits

Skilled Arcanist: Improved Flight like Mage or an integration into other Skill, possibly using Overcharge or Mana Infusion

Magical Gardener: Flying Garden?—helps growing flying plants

Primal Constructor: Possible ability to *build* magical wings

Primal Ritualist: Shift to a more wind-based form of flight

Attuner: Flight Magic specialist—benefits when using flight-type magic

Pioneer: Vanguard—some kind of exploration-based Flight Skill

Skill Researcher/System Scholar: Something meta. An elevated view, perhaps?

Diver: Diving—flight, but underwater, probably without a tether

Physical Laborer: Normally might be something like Packing, but because I already have that . . . who knows.

Ascetic: Untether—reduced need to touch the ground

Daredevil: Crash Resistance/Stunt Flying—something to either help survivability or mobility

Survivor: Crash Landing—something to help survivability

Athlete: Flying—improved mobility while flying

Escapee/Exile: Free Flight—increased ability to fly free of restraints. Alternatively: Increased tether length? Possible, but unlikely and if so possibly *only* would increase range instead of unilateral improvement.

Traveler/World Traveler: Overland Flight—bonuses to endurance

Arsonist/Pyromaniac/Autopyromaniac: Firefly—leave burning trails when flying or light on fire when flying

**Insomniac/Sleepless Disciple: Night Owl—fly while sleeping
Student of Power/Brushed by Power: Ascent—Generally
improved/more powerful flight**

They just had no clue what a few of them might do, such as Purifier, Royal Advisor, his Trophy Paths and most of his Mental and Medical Paths. To make things *slightly* easier on himself, Edwin had decided to just eliminate them from consideration. This would be hard enough already without bringing complete unknowns into the mix that stood a decent chance of *radically* changing how Flight worked, possibly not building on it in the slightest, a fate Edwin generally wanted to avoid.

For a similar reason, Edwin was leaning toward eliminating Makeshift Alchemy. Lefi refused to explain whether or not Skill evolutions *actually* worked in the way he'd suggested, but they didn't have anything better and the pun apparently transcended Polyglot. Edwin was *almost* tempted to take it just to see, but that also seemed like a really bad idea because he *liked* being able to fly, and he *did* want his next Skill to still involve it.

Artillerist was interesting if it really went the route of telekinesis, because that was a stupidly strong ability. Unfortunately, it was far from assured and, if anything, was rather *unlikely*. He also couldn't say he needed *further* Skills involving his explosives at the moment, which was the other way that particular Path might take it. He could eliminate Bomber as well, then.

He likewise didn't really need another information-based Skill. Knowledge was power and all that, but Edwin was *really* skeptical that he would get anything more interesting than perhaps a more accurate altimeter than Numeracy could currently provide. That eliminated a half-dozen options at once, too.

Escapee or Exile . . . well, they'd likely remove his Slave Path from his Status once they were completed, and he'd be *quite* happy to be rid of that particular one from his Status, but he wasn't sure how useful the actual *evolution* would be. Sure, if he could just make restraints or hindrances less, well, hindering, that would be useful but also *incredibly* niche. It might also improve his Flight speed or tether length, which was tempting . . . Hmm. Eh, as a thirty-point Path, Escapee likely wouldn't have that grand of an effect, and he'd definitely prefer Mage over Exile for a general Flight boost.

He also took off the Fey Paths. While useful, he didn't think they were quite appropriate, and he *was* still hesitant to turn himself *too* much into a feylike being. He liked being human, after all, and Inion could be a bit pushy with that kind of choice and he wanted to push back.

Okay . . . Speed round.

He didn't need to be better at swimming, was perfectly fine walking at times and would use it as his primary method of long-distance transport. He wanted to be able to fly *without* being a fire hazard, didn't really care if he was floating while asleep (and could probably do it eventually with Watchful Rest anyway), and didn't have any flying plants to grow. He didn't have enough flight-type magic Skills to make Attuner worthwhile, didn't need to be able to build magical wings, Trapper was too limiting, he really *didn't* want to use his Flight Skill to get *close* to people, and on further thought didn't want to risk his "of Power" Paths on a useless or redundant effect.

That made it . . . better.

He also got rid of the Warrior-related Paths, as he had a suspicion they might involve more melee combat. That brought it down to *functionally* ten options, even if he still had almost twice as many individual Paths to choose from—Assassin, Hunter, Burglar, Potioneer, Practical Alchemist, Mystic Alchemist, Physical Alchemist, Chemist, Sapper, Engineer, Physicist, Material Scientist, Aerialist, Mage, Skilled Arcanist, Primal Ritualist, Primal Constructor, Daredevil, Survivor, and Athlete.

Within each of the "categories," so to speak, Edwin quickly picked out whichever Path he liked most, based largely on which he felt was *most* likely to give the effect he might want. Once he'd pared that down, he chatted a bit more, first with Inion who had stuck around for the entire time.

Then, he found Rillah and Lefi, who were back outside tossing a ball around with Yathal and Kyni. He managed to get some time in talking with them about the benefits and drawbacks of each possible Skill effect, until he felt there wasn't anything more *to* be gained, and it was very late.

He ventured back inside. He couldn't find Inion, but that was fine, he'd track her down later. He still had . . . major decisions to make.

Assassin: Silent Flight/Aerial Ambush
Speculation: Stealth-type Skill, possibly with some kind of combat bent to it.
Pros: Provides an invaluable Skill effect in stealth, which is *immensely* useful for a largely noncombatant. Even a combatant would likely benefit somewhat, though the exact amounts are unknown.
Cons: Unlikely to actually help with *flight* capabilities, meaning current limits on flying are likely to stay. If there are any combat benefits, they would likely be predicated on being hidden.

Mystic Alchemist: Flying Potion
Speculation: Grant the ability to fly to another person.
Pros: Many situations in which having a different type of mobility would be very useful for nonavior. Quite likely to grant further benefits to me or another person who could already fly as well if they were to drink the potion, meaning it would never be useless.
Cons: 90-point Path. Unknown if it would require an actual potion to work (apparently a possibility). If it did, it's possible that the recipe would need to be independently discovered and made for the Skill to be of any use, and in which case the Skill itself would be somewhat superfluous as it would only provide *benefits* to those who could already fly instead of granting the ability all on its own.

Engineer: Aeronautics
Speculation: A crafting-type Skill that helps make flying contraptions.
Pros: Jetpacks! Airplanes! Flying machines! Quite likely to indirectly improve Flight via giving it more mechanical aid. Also has many of the benefits of Flying Potion, in that it can provide Z-axis motion to otherwise grounded individuals. *Also* helps

potentially bring various types of revolution to Joriah for good and for ill.

Cons: Unlikely to *directly* improve current Flight Skill, and it is unlikely to create any machines itself, instead just slightly improving their effectiveness and build quality when being made. Likely limited to gliders for quite some time. Also not a magical Skill, so unlikely to help with that entire swath of flying creations such as magic carpets or flying islands.

Physical Alchemist: Floatstone

Speculation: Imbue objects with or create substances that can inherently fly or float.

Pros: Flying carpets! Flying islands! Similar to Engineer, this can be used to create objects that grant the power of flight to their wielder. Could also grant functionally untethered Flight for myself, if I managed to create something that exactly canceled out my weight (further testing required). Wouldn't provide engineering knowledge, but is likely easy enough to work around with personal memories, and definitely more supernatural.

Cons: 90-point Path. Might require unusual or expensive alchemical components, or might only be temporary depending on what other Skills it keys off. Flying islands would be *stupidly* high level if even possible without an additional evolution. Once again does not directly improve Flight.

Aerialist: Improved Flight

Speculation: Flight v 2.0. Grant better maneuverability, distance, and efficiency.

Pros: Doesn't provide anything wholly new. It just brings Flight up to T2 and makes everything good about the Skill even better.

Cons: Doesn't provide anything wholly new.

Skilled Arcanist: Improved Flight like Mage or an integration into other Skill, possibly

Speculation: Some form of other-Skill integration.
Pros: Worst-case scenario likely to just be the equivalent of Aerialist, making this a low-risk experimental option. Likely to be very synergistic with one or more other Skills. Possibly allows Longstrider to function with Flight, or allows some form of Overcharged Flight, or enables Infusion with the Skill. Alternatively, might grant something wholly new akin to Mana Infusion.
Cons: If combined with only a single Skill like Overcharge, might be very difficult to level and use.

Primal Ritualist: Flight (wind)
Speculation: Change the form of Flight used, possibly to something involving winds.
Pros: Having air-based Flight is likely less precise than tether-based Flight, but not dependent on surrounding objects and other miscellaneous quirks. Likely freely able to switch between types depending on practicality.
Cons: 90-point Path. Doesn't directly improve current Flight, though *does* remove its current primary weakness (namely flight height).

Daredevil: Crash Resistance/Stunt Flying
Speculation: Some kind of aerial tight-flying bonus. Increased maneuverability, increased impact resistance, or both.
Pros: Very unlikely to be bad. Combines the best aspects of the mundane Skills into one and definitely provides a lot of potential for growth.
Cons: Survivor or Athlete are more likely to grant each possible Skill effect individually and thus more effectively and is unlikely to be a magic-boosting Skill.

Survivor: Crash Landing
Speculation: Some kind of impact-absorbing Skill. Might work with all physical attacks, knocking me back whenever hit hard enough, or just with falling damage.

Pros: Being likely to survive is always good, and not needing to
be afraid of falling is *extra* good.
Cons: Not really a Flight Skill. Also not magical.

Athlete: Flying
Speculation: Mundane aerial agility-improving Skill.
Pros: Would definitely help with precise flying maneuvers and
dodging things while in midair.
Cons: Not a magical Skill. Improvements would likely be
purely based on being able to leverage more from current Flight
capabilities.

This is so much *work,* Edwin lamented to himself. *This is actually ridiculous. Guess when I know* exactly *which Skill will evolve when I complete a Path, I get way more picky about what it is that I want out of that Skill. I'm so glad I just* can't *be this picky most of the time.*

Ugh, evolving Stamina Manipulation will be a nightmare and a half, won't it? When he realized this, he buried his head in his pillow. Not having to really worry about suffocation was very nice, and he could just keep his eyes fixed on the endless Almanac speculation as he fell asleep.

CHAPTER 9

Derailed

Okay, so there's basically three categories here, Edwin mused to himself. *There's the make-something-else-fly, the make-Flight-better, and the do-something-new-with-Flight.*

The hard part was over. Well, maybe it was more that the hard part was just *starting*, but this was just him and his own thoughts. Much better than the endless discussions of the day before. Everything remaining was just up to him and what *he* wanted. They'd all agreed on that. There were no *wrong* choices for Skill evolutions so long as you were happy.

It was without question the complete opposite of what the Empire said, what Tara and Rizzali had told him, but that wasn't much of a surprise. He was talking to Adventurers, after all, and the one thing they all had in common was they *weren't* prone to fitting in.

They disagreed about the why, though. Rillah had said it was because the only way to avoid regrets was to go with his heart. Inion had looked like she wanted to disagree on principle, but said that she liked watching him be himself, and any infringement on his Edwin-ness would interfere with her enjoyment. Lefi had the very practical argument that when adding a new tool to the toolbox, Edwin was the only one with any idea which he'd find the most useful. Yathal had of course said he needed to do whatever sounded coolest.

In other words, all their advice was basically useless. If he'd wanted to figure this out on his own, he wouldn't have asked them for advice!

Whatever.

Without question, the Paths with the most *potential* were Mystic Alchemist and Physical Alchemist. That they were also both ninety-point Paths wasn't an accident either. If he wanted to risk it, he could take Potioneer or Material Scientist for similar results, but he could also take a *bit* of a loan from his Tier 2 Skills and raise Flight up to level 70 or 75 to keep the hit from being too bad. He was definitely going to take a *long* time to get Alchemy up to level 120, and once he did, he'd have enough time to raise other Skills enough to offset a single extra level from the rest of them.

At the same time, Edwin was still hesitant. He had friends, and that was great! Or rather, he had people who were willing to spend time with him. He'd been in this situation before, and he knew how it went. Sooner or later they'd get bored, they'd move on, and Edwin would be back on his own.

He was probably wrong. He *hoped* he was wrong.

But that part of his brain just wouldn't die no matter how much he tried. It definitely didn't help that he had just been reminded that Inion only followed him around because he was interesting, Rillah was likely to run off following some shiny thing that caught her attention, and Lefi would continue shepherding Yathal and Kyni off somewhere, now that Rillah had helped draw the boy out of his shell. It was only a matter of time until they all left him, surely?

Well . . . no matter. It did mean that he shouldn't really focus too much on purely other-focused Skills. So, no Mystic Alchemist. Physical Alchemist, then? Ehhh . . . maybe.

He felt fairly safe in eliminating Athlete, Survivor, and Daredevil. They weren't very magical Paths, and magic was *always* better. After all, he was dealing with a sort of self-only telekinesis with his current Flight Skill, and that could definitely be nurtured some . . .

Ooh. Should he try and get the Physical Arcanist Path again? Would that possibly give him some sort of superior tactile telekinesis, kind of like what he had with Packing, but way stronger?

Hmm . . . probably not. It would definitely be good, but, well, maybe? Skilled Arcanist might do something like that, if it managed to tie Flight back into its parent. Physical Arcanist gave a wealth of Attributes, but he could wait on that. He needed to keep growing, and he didn't know what it would take to re-unlock the Path.

Primal Ritualist definitely had potential as well, but that potential was essentially tangential to Flight as it stood already. He'd need to relearn how to fly completely from scratch and figure out a whole new set of limitations.

Of course, that would mean more time spent with Rillah, a part of his brain whispered, and he didn't entirely have the heart to crush it. Still, it was probably *not* that useful. It *would* predilect him toward a different type of magic, but he preferred his current track. Besides, Primal Ritualist was *absurdly* broad and could give him some very . . . suboptimal possibilities. Maybe it would allow him to cast a Flight-type spell, or maybe it would let him transform into a bird. Powerful, sure, but not worth the ninety points on such a risk.

That left Assassin, Engineer, Physical Alchemist, Aerialist, and Skilled Arcanist.

Engineer he could eliminate, he felt. He could figure out flying machines easily enough if he tried, and it wasn't very magical. Assassin went next, for similar reasons. Stealth may have been *tremendously* useful, but if he was planning on using *high explosives* as his weapon of choice, stealth was *not* the right tactic for him. Also, it wasn't magical.

That brought Edwin down to what he kind of anticipated all along. Physical Alchemist, Aerialist, and Skilled Arcanist.

Did he want to double down on his alchemy, giving him even more potential in that regard and opening a literal new dimension for his creations? Did he want to become an even better flier? Or did he want to try and branch out into a novel but related ability? Each Path typified one of his options.

Who was *he?* Was he a crafter? A specialist? A generalist?

Could he trust his companions? Edwin wanted to say yes, he wanted to yell at the little voice in the back of his head saying they were only here temporarily. But there was just a little bit of unknown.

Besides, he rationalized, *Physical Alchemist would probably be way better for Tier 3. And there might be so many complications in actually making any stuff. If I can make it with alchemy, I'll be able to make it with Alchemy one day.*

Yeah. It didn't have anything to do with his trust. Physical Alchemist just wasn't as good of a choice as his other options. Sure, it gave him new possibilities, but he was already planning on bringing Alchemy to level *120*, and he had other Skills that already supported it. Any more was just overkill, clearly.

So, Aerialist or Skilled Arcanist?

Aerialist was the safe option. It was his most predictable option out of probably *all* of them. No muss, no fuss, just a quick way to capitalize on what he already had and get stronger faster. Skilled Arcanist, on the other hand, was a risk. He didn't know *what* he would get, but it would probably be good. At worst, it would just improve his Flight similar to how Aerialist would.

It was that old joke about taking risks, but in reverse. "You can either get this boat, *or* you could take your chance at a mystery prize, which could be anything! Even a boat!"

Of course, it might not be that generally useful. There was always that possibility. Boring and safe, or fun and risky? A thought flickered across his mind. Did he want to stay with what was known, what was safe, or did he want to discover something new?

Well, it might have been his time with Rillah talking, but there was only ever one answer to that question.

Further testing required.

Mana 33→37

You have completed the Skilled Arcanist Path!

You continue to grasp the endless possibilities of magic, and as you keep following this path, your strength and power grow in surprising and potent ways. With knowledge in one hand, and magic in the other, all will be in your grasp, and even the furthest target will be but a step away.

Alchemist-Errant
You may evolve your Flight Skill into the Unbound Tether Skill!
Accept Evolution? Y/N

Wait, what? If that was what he thought it was, it was better than he could have even imagined? Fully free flight? Yes, *please*.

Unbound Tether
A bit of a long shot, but I'm sure you'll be hooked.
Attach your tether to anything.
Strength increases with level.

Well, *that* was promising. *Anything?* That sounded absolutely *fantastic*. It also meant that there was probably a lot unsaid in the Skill box, not that that was anything new.

"Hey, guys!" Edwin rushed out of his room, nearly running into the halfling . . . what was her name again?

Honored Senior Mundanity Assistant
Pierash (SheraithPierash)
The housekeeper for Sheraith's wizard tower, under Rillah when I
met her. Slightly snippy at times but mostly agreeable.

"Ah, sorry!" He acted more on instinct than conscious choice, activating Flight and somersaulting over the startled woman and her basket of food.

"Children," she admonished, as Edwin drifted over her, "always fluttering around. Honestly."

Polyglot whispered there was some nuance he was missing, and she clearly expected him to catch onto some kind of wordplay because when he didn't respond, she muttered something under her breath and continued down the hall.

Edwin mentally shrugged, then turned and flew in the opposite direction. Lefi would already be up; Edwin had yet to sleep in past the guy even when he woke up at dawn, and it was *well* into midmorning by now after his deliberations on what Path to complete. Rillah would likely be awake as well, doing her wind-magic stuff up at the top of the tower.

He found Inion and Lefi talking in their favorite side room. It was one of the few rooms without glaringly ostentatious decor everywhere while still being large enough to accommodate all the furniture they'd gathered for their purposes. One wall was occupied by a massive fireplace, already lit and radiating heat though the room. Through some magic—literally, the entire tower *radiated* the stuff—it never made the room feel too hot, and Edwin didn't know where the smoke went given its lack of chimney.

Apparently a centuries-old tower that had many powerful mages in residence had a bunch of magical conveniences. Who'd've thunk it.

Edwin dropped onto his couch. "Good morning," he greeted the pair. They'd stopped talking when he'd arrived, but Edwin had caught some snatches about . . . a net? He wasn't sure, but it didn't matter and they clearly didn't want to talk about it in front of him.

"What are you doing here?"

"Um . . . saying good morning?" Edwin wasn't entirely sure how to respond to such a blatant sign that Inion didn't want him around.

"No, no. You never come here this early in the morning, you're always off in your workshop or flying."

"Oh, well . . ." Edwin shrugged. "I settled on a Path, and now I've got a new Skill to test out. Figured I shouldn't try it inside, but I'd also rather not explain it all to you later, so I wanted to try it with you guys around. But I can leave and do it on my own if you'd prefer that?"

"Nonsense! A new Skill, particularly such an intriguing one, deserves full investigation! Come along, friend Inion, let us learn of Edwin's new abilities!"

Edwin's first impression of Unbound Tether was that it was . . . a touch disappointing, honestly.

Well, perhaps more "underwhelming." The Skill's *potential* was definitely there, but at level 1 it unsurprisingly left much to be desired. Activating it bore many resemblances to Flight, and by default, the tether would attach to the ground beneath his feet. However, he could very much aim it wherever he pleased, so long as he had a direct line of sight and could accurately conceptualize what he was aiming for.

With the exception of "the ground," it was an object-by-object targeting system, so Edwin couldn't just target *half* of Lefi's sword; it was all or nothing. However, unlike what the description led him to believe, he retained his Flight limitations. He could attach his tether to any-thing, sure, but the omnidirectional mobility of Flight didn't kick in until he was within 6.36 meters of it.

What he *could* do, however, was either push or pull on the tether to try and bring himself closer or farther away from his target. It wasn't very strong—from what he could tell, it only exerted about eight new-tons of force. It was enough for him to go slightly higher with his Flight, or jump slightly farther, but that was about it.

Hmm. Well, he had speculated it might key off his other Skills, so maybe there was something more impressive before it grew in level?

Longstrider worked predictably. Some testing showed that he could jump *marginally* higher when pushing against the ground, but just barely. It made sense, by pushing against the ground it functionally reduced gravity and correspondingly allowed him to jump higher.

It actually *did* pair decently with Flight, much to his surprise. Although at level 2 it didn't provide *much* flexibility, he could aug-ment his own mana expenditure with the Skill's force, letting him fly just a bit higher and faster in exchange for the third law of motion applying.

Overcharge *felt* synergistic, but Edwin couldn't really tell what it actually did. Further testing was required.

Mana Infusion, though, was far and away the winner. He found that he could charge the Skill to build up . . . tension, really. It felt like compressing a massive spring, and releasing it had a similar sensation, giving him a massive boost in initial energy.

He could only use it on surfaces he was touching, but that felt less like an inherent limitation and more like something he could overcome with practice. Overall, he could get somewhere between a six and eight times boost when fully charged, but doing so took a full minute to prepare.

It didn't even really allow him to tether off anything for Flight. Sure, he could *target* a solitary leaf stubbornly clinging onto a mostly bare bush, but because his new Skill obeyed the laws of motion, he couldn't use it for proper Flight. Trying just ripped off the leaf, and further tests showed that pebbles fled from him or flew to his hand . . .

Edwin's eyes got very, very wide.

Eight newtons may not be a lot for him, no. But for a pebble? Or a bullet?

"Did I just get a railgun?" he whispered to himself.

Eight newtons meant that every second a one-kilo object was pushed, it would accelerate by eight meters per second. For Edwin, who probably weighed somewhere between sixty to seventy kilos, that meant he would accelerate by about .1 meters per second every second. But if he had a pebble, then that would be . . . much, much faster.

When it was at level 1, eight newtons of force on something that weighed say 10 grams would accelerate it by 800 meters per second squared. After a single second, it would be going faster than *Mach 2*. If he Infused the Skill for its full minute, that was *Mach 20*.

Assuming that at *some* point the Skill grew strong enough to completely cancel out Edwin's weight, which seemed reasonable given its ostensible purpose, that would be Mach *2,000* when fully Infused. Wasn't that getting somewhere close to c?

Edwin's breath caught in his throat. There was no way that was right, surely? He had to have made a mistake somewhere. There was no way he could be hitting *relativistic speeds*, surely? What was the speed of light again?

Right, yes. C was just shy of three hundred million meters per second, Mach 2k was "just" six hundred thousand meters per second . . . of acceleration, every single second.

Yeah, no, that wasn't any less terrifying. He'd be getting firsthand experience with *general relativity* at higher levels. There had to be a catch. Right? He didn't want to imagine the idea that *anyone* should be able to single-handedly raise everyday pebbles to supercollider levels of speed.

"Edwin, are you all right? You look pale. Is something wrong with your Skill?" Lefi asked.

"I'm . . . probably fine," he squeaked out. "I just . . . need to test something."

I really hope that this fails. Okay, that's not entirely true. I kind of want it to work because the amount of stuff I could do with it, but definitely don't want it to be that powerful. But if this does *work even a little bit . . . sheesh,* he thought. *Railgun with literally* anything *. . . What's a good semivolatile* *explosive? Nitroglycerin? To whatever System moderators there are out there deciding how Skills work, please, please let me have a nitroglycerin railgun. But not a relativistic railgun. Just give me something unreasonably powerful but that remains firmly in the bounds of Newtonian physics.*

"Stand back," he warned. "This might be dangerous."

He *was* telekinetic now, so he didn't bother picking up a pebble from the ground, instead letting his tether snap one to his hand. He intentionally didn't pull as hard as he could just in case he was right, but it still jumped into his grasp in less than a second. Not a great sign.

Edwin quickly cast his mind through Mathematics to try and figure out how much he *could* get out of his pebble if it were to slam into the giant rock that the tower was made out of. He was about, oh, ten meters away, and it weighed maybe fifty grams? Ten-ish newtons, ten meters, and a twentieth of a kilo? At an acceleration of 200 m/s^2, it would be going up to sixty-five-ish meters per second by the time it struck, that would be, what, two hundred joules? That was something like twice the energy of a speeding baseball, so definitely beyond what a random human could normally throw, but it should be all right. Definitely wouldn't break the stone tower at least.

He pinched the rock between his fingers, sighted his target, and let fly. The pebble sped off in an almost straight line, *crack*ing into the tower's base and either bouncing off or shattering so fast Edwin wasn't able to keep up with its motion.

He frowned. He wasn't entirely sure why, but it didn't feel quite right. Casting his gaze around for a larger rock, Edwin spotted a fist-sized stone only slightly embedded in the dirt near the tower's wall and he summoned it to his grip. Numeracy informed him it was about a kilo, and he repeated the test with the larger stone.

A bit over one second later, it, too, crashed into the rock wall, breaking into a few fragments and cascading to the ground. Edwin nodded to himself. When compared to something heavier, it was clear what problem the smaller stone suffered from. It felt "slippery" in comparison, the Skill not finding adequate purchase on the tiny object.

Edwin breathed a sigh of relief. It was both good and disappointing to know that he hadn't been handed a railgun . . . unless Infusion changed that?

* * *

Some testing later, it was fairly apparent that Infusion suffered from some pretty harsh limits when applied to, again, anything too much under a kilo. It took Edwin half a minute to maximally Infuse his tether when applying to a half-kilo rock, and pebbles correspondingly less time.

Some more messing around gave him better numbers—and a few more levels in the Skill, bringing him up to level 7 overall. The force he could exert grew . . . really fast, and he was worried about what it would look like when he hit level 30 or 60 or beyond in the Skill. But that was future-Edwin's problem or blessing.

For now, he needed to explain to some very worried-looking companions what exactly he'd been doing for the last twenty minutes.

"Okay, so I was just making sure I couldn't accidentally destroy the world."

"You *what?*"

"Calm down, calm down! I can't. So my new Skill can let me accelerate objects other than myself, and you see, the energy of a projectile is based *way* more off its velocity than its mass, whereas how fast I can accelerate stuff is *strongly* based on its mass . . ."

His companions seemed to *mostly* understand Edwin's concerns by the time he was done explaining things, though he didn't go too in-depth as to what would happen if he accelerated a rock to 90 percent the speed of light. Just that it would be bad.

He planned to experiment more with his newfound railgun later, but while he still had the attention of his companions, Edwin figured it made more sense to test the other uses of his Skill.

It took a bit of practice to get the timing right, but eventually Edwin got to the point where he could reliably jump, use Infused Longstrider, apply Unbound Tether, and get the boost from Infused Unbound Tether simultaneously, launching him nearly fifty meters into the air.

Discovering *that* had promptly earned him another level in Longstrider, but he wasn't keen to find out how much that had increased his vertical range. It might have only taken a minute per jump to fully set up, but after coming out of his miniature warp drive so far off the ground that Numeracy was barely able to tell him how high he was . . . it wasn't an experience he was keen to repeat any time soon.

At least he didn't have to worry about his Flight tether breaking anymore! If he used Unbound Tether on an object that could support his normal Flight, the moment he got within his six-and-a-half-meter range he could use the full functionality of his original Skill.

There would be many more experiments in the coming weeks, of course, figuring out the exact limitations, but Edwin was *quite* happy with what essentially amounted to push/pull telekinesis.

He also wanted to kick himself. In his haste to get his *new Skill*, he'd completely blanked on his plan to unlock the Artisan Path and use it to try and unlock Dexterity. He meant to do it, he *should* have done it, but he'd just . . . forgotten. He'd gotten too focused and missed the bigger picture.

At least he didn't lose out on *too* much. Without the boosts from completing further Paths, Attributes didn't do that much, and Skilled Arcanist was unlikely to have granted many physical Attribute points.

Well, he'd have another chance once he finished with his *actual* newest Skill and got ready to evolve it. He'd just . . . need to not forget again.

Stamina Manipulation
Raise your hand if you need help with that.
Manipulate your personal stamina.
Increased flow per level.

It didn't do anything obvious. Well, that wasn't strictly true. Edwin found after getting the Skill that he *was* able to vaguely direct his Stamina to do stuff inside his body, sloshing around like something somewhere between Oobleck and molasses. Unfortunately, he didn't have any idea how to leverage the presence or absence of his Stamina to useful ends. He wasn't even entirely able to block Overcharge with just his Skill. He could make some progress, yes, but it seemed that Health played the larger part in preventing the mana from suffusing his entire body.

Well, he had time. Mana Manipulation had been an absolute pain to level and figure out how to use, but Edwin had other things that he could work on. Justified or not, he was kind of annoyed with being the weakest person around, and he was going to *change* that.

A marble of phosphorus jetted through the air, speeding up with every passing second. The moment it was about to hit the boulder Edwin was aiming at, he flexed his Firestarting.

BANG!

Okay, so that was about a foot in diameter, and Bomb Throwing didn't activate for it.

Edwin made a note in Almanac and summoned the next sphere of phosphorus to his hand.

It followed its predecessor's arc almost perfectly—while Edwin's Throwing Weapons Skill didn't *fully* cover "shooting with a telekinetic railgun" in its effects by default, Edwin could still mostly trigger it by making a throwing motion with his arm.

BOOM!

Okay, a meter and a half in diameter. Bomb Throwing *did* activate that time. But what was the difference?

Further testing required.

"Still no luck." Edwin sighed. "I've yet to find any consistent thread between when Bomb Throwing is able or unable to activate. There's not even consistency between when I make the ammo, or on testing rounds. Sometimes, it'll trigger every time, others it never will. Others it'll be a mix. Rillah thinks it might be something to do with what's magically recognized as a bomb, but I don't know what that might look like."

"Oh yes, I'm sure that *she* would know," Inion snarked.

"Okay, come on. What's your problem with Rillah? And don't tell me it's her dropping me, that was months ago. This constant sniping is *much* more recent than that."

"I don't like her."

"Well, *that* much is obvious. But why? Why can't you two go five minutes without making some sort of jab at the other?"

"She's too friendly, too nice."

"Oh, really? You *sure* you're not jealous of the fact I'm spending so much time with her?"

"I told you before, I don't care."

"You say that, but then any time you're in the same room together you're snapping at each other! It feels like I have to *justify* the time I spend with her whenever she comes up, like I can't just have *friends*."

"Of course you can have *friends*."

"Oh, just not with her?"

"No!"

"Look, I don't know what you're looking for," Edwin exasperatedly replied. "She told me about a bunch of her Skills!"

"Oh, *did* she now? How many does *she* have?"

"Well," Edwin hesitated, "I suppose she didn't *actually* tell me that many of her Skills yet, but she was willing to!"

"So why *didn't* she?"

"I just wasn't feeling up to it then, and then I didn't feel up to it later, I guess."

"She's persuaded you to give it up, then? Clearly, she doesn't want you to realize what she's doing to you with them."

"Rillah isn't using Skills on me!" he snapped. "Other than the ones I ask her to. I'd know it! I just like her, all right? She's nice and understanding, unlike *some* people I know."

"Oh, you think I'm not understanding?"

"You're arguing with me over whether or not I'm allowed to have a *friend*, so, yes, I would say you are not understanding!"

"You can have friends! What about Fissath?"

"Oh, sure, let's talk about Fissath! Here's an idea. Why can't you just keep your nose out of my friendships? I'm my own person, I'm not just 'your human' you know. It's my choice, not *yours*, who I spend my time with!"

Inion seemed to recognize that raising her voice wasn't doing anything, so she appropriated a more sedate tone. "*She* is obviously using a Skill on you, you just can't see it. Do you really think that you could see very subtle manipulation Skills with your second-tier Skill?"

"I'd notice it," he defended himself. "I've noticed it before. She's *only* used Calming Touch on me, and even that's rare!"

"Exactly! You *know* she can use mental Skills and you know that she *does*. You have no idea what she's doing to make you trust her."

"Yeah, well, maybe it's because she's the first human—or close enough to one—I've met that's actually my age who's willing to spend time with me for a *very long time*. It's perfectly reasonable that I want to spend time with her. I don't know why you have to be so *paranoid*."

"It's not paranoia! You spend a lot of time with her, you know that she uses mental Skills on you, and you've opened up to her far faster than you ever did with me."

"Oh, so it *is* about you then. Well, I'll have you know that I'm not an *idiot*, and of course I'd be slow to trust a fey. And yes, sure, *you're* all right, but can you really blame me for not believing that you genuinely didn't wish me any harm when the first thing you ever said to me was about blood sacrifices?"

"You'd just *given* me one, and it was an *explicit request* to *never* do so!"

"Not the point. Besides, what if I just want to try and *be* more trusting, then? It's not like Rillah's given me any reason to *not* do so."

"Other than *dropping* you and using Skills on you."

"Other than dropping me—by accident—sure. But I'm not going to not try to befriend someone just because they let me down *once*."

"It was *not* just once . . ."

Edwin struggled to hold on to the smooth river rock as he continued to charge Unbound Tether. Force continued and continued to build the longer Edwin held it back, but he was determined to not let go. In other circumstances, he probably wouldn't have had a choice, but while Athletics may not have been quite *as* potent as some of his more specialized Skills, it still had an impressive effect on his strength.

He was *positive* that he wouldn't have enough grip strength to hold on to the stone without the Skill. *With* it, though, it was a struggle, but a manageable one.

Eventually, he hit his cap, and Edwin tried to gently release the supercharged rock. Unfortunately, as soon as he began to soften his iron grip on the stone, it wrenched its way to freedom, snapping his fingers back and flying straight ahead. It collided with the rotten tree stump Edwin was using as a target, causing the wood to explode into a cloud of splinters.

Even as he grinned at the result, he still waved his hand to try and dissipate the sting permeating his fingers. If he was going to make this a regular part of his attack routine, he seriously needed to figure out a better launch method. Maybe between his palms? He certainly wouldn't mind being able to fire off artillery-grade attacks with just a little bit of setup.

It *was* a little annoying to have his cannon be made practically irrelevant by a new Skill, but it *was* rather impractical to begin with, and Edwin had learned a fair bit while making it, so it wasn't a complete loss.

Plus, he'd gotten the Artillerist Path from it, and it was *definitely* on his shortlist for what he'd want to try and evolve Unbound Tether with when the time came. If the Skill was this potent of a weapon when completely incidental to the Skill's use, what might it look like if it were the *focus*? Definitely not a loss in that case, either.

The System was nice in that way. There was very little that was actually *pointless*. Well, in science nothing was pointless. Null results were still results! Though they *were* rather boring back on Earth, here they were just as likely to grant a level as some brand-new, earthshaking revelation. Okay, the latter would *probably* grant more rewards than the discovery that rocks did not in fact fall to the ceiling when exposed to electricity, but the sentiment remained.

Sometimes, an avenue of research was just made redundant. That wasn't a problem, you still learned something. You still *discovered* something, your understanding of the world around you going just that much deeper.

Though if he *was* going to try shooting a projectile from his hands after charging it up for an extended period of time, there was *definitely* something he needed to try.

He looked over at where Lefi was standing, the Adventurer assessing the sort of damage Edwin had done to the trees and stumps he'd been using for target practice. Yeah . . . no. He wasn't going to embarrass himself around other people, doubly so when Rillah was also around . . . somewhere.

He'd try it later. When there weren't any spectators, *then* he could indulge in all his geekish fantasies.

Edwin still thought it, the next time he was charging up for a two-handed shot, and he couldn't stop a bit of a grin creeping across his face as he did so.

KAMEHAME—

Level Up!
Skill Points 963→988 (Average level: 51)
Alchemy Level 93→94
Bomb Throwing Level 56→57
Flight Level 59→60
Longstrider Level 48→50
Mana Infusion Level 90→91
Numeracy Level 48→49
Outsider's Almanac Level 135→136
Ritual Intuition Level 46→47
Skillful Assessment Level 49→50
Stamina Manipulation Level 1→3
Unbound Tether Level 1→11
Watchful Rest Level 37→38

Name
Edwin Maxlin
Age
2
Race
Extraplanar Human
Class
Alchemist-Errant
Attributes
Health 25
Impact 7
Mana 37
Perception 19
Stamina 30
Skills

Alchemical

Alchemy 94, Alchemical Analysis 40, Refining 36, Alchemical Dismantling 46, Sapper's Apparatus 60

(Purify: 75)

Magical

Basic Thermokinesis 32, Fey's Caress 43, Ritual Intuition 47, Mana Infusion 91, Unbound Tether 11

(Flight: 60), (Basic Mana Sense: 82), (Basic Mana Manipulation: 9)

Physical

Overcharge 27, Longstrider 50, Fresh Air 44

Stamina Manipulation 3, (Athletics: 81), (Breathing: 76), (Flexibility: 74), (Nutrition: 73), (Packing: 92), (Seeing: 72), (Sleeping: 73), (Survival: 76), (Walking: 74)

Mental

Numeracy 49, Prototyping 40, Anatomy 43, Polyglot: 70, Memory 65

(Language: 36), (Mathematics: 74), (Research: 50), (Visualization: 80)

Combat

Bomb Throwing 57, Adaptive Defense 42

(Throwing Weapons: 48)

Utility

Outsider's Almanac 136, Watchful Rest 38, Skillful Assessment 50, Arcadian Elixir 35, Improbable Arsenal 39

(Firestarting: 94), (Improvisation: 14), (Status: 22), (Identify: 80), (First Aid: 82), (Harvesting: 76), (Construction: 77)

Paths

Skill Points: 988

Combat

Assassin 0/60, Bomber 0/60, Giant Slayer 0/60, Heedless Hunter 0/60, Hunter 0/30, Killer 0/30, Titan Slayer 0/90, Warrior 0/60, Way of the Empty Hand 0/60, Trapper 0/60, Artillerist 0/60, Sapper 0/60

Alchemy

Alchemical Medic 0/60, Demolitionist 0/60, Makeshift Alchemist 0/60, Potioneer 0/60, Practical Alchemist 0/60, Mystic Alchemist 0/90

Science

Chemist 0/60, Experimenter 0/60, Researcher 0/60, Purifier 0/30, Scientific Revolutionary 0/90, Scientist 0/60, Engineer 0/60, Physicist 0/60, Mathematician 0/60, Material Scientist 0/60

Magic

Aerialist 0/60, Fey Friend 0/60, Feybound 0/60, Feycaller 0/60, Mage 0/60, Magical Gardener 0/60, Micro-Biomancer 0/90, Primal Constructor 0/90, Primal Ritualist 0/90, Realm Traveler 0/120, Fey Supplicant 0/60, Feykind 0/90, Attuner 0/30, Schooled Mage 0/90

Mental

Dedicated Student 0/60, Lecturer 0/30, Scholar 0/60, Unbowed 0/90, Canny 0/60, Steady Mind 0/60, Mentalist 0/60

System

Almanac Administrator 0/60, Forerunner 0/60, Outsider's Almanac Specialist 0/90, Pioneer 0/60, Skill Researcher 0/60, System Scholar 0/60

Trophy

Blackstone Conqueror 0/60, Deepwoods Panther-Hunter 0/60, Stonehide Vanquisher 0/60, Titan Spider-Slayer 0/60

Career

Brickmaker 0/30, Butcher 0/30, Diver 0/30, Gardener 0/30, Lumberjack 0/60, Merchant 0/30, Potter 0/30, Scribe 0/30, Woodsman 0/30

Physical

Ascetic 0/60, Daredevil 0/60, Physical Alchemist 0/90, Survivor 0/60, Physical Laborer 0/30, Athlete 0/60

Traveling

Escapee 0/30, Exile 0/30, Traveler 0/30, World Traveler 0/60

Medical

Field Medic 0/60, Medic 0/30, Steadfast Medic 0/60, Medical Lecturer 0/60

Misc

Arsonist 0/60, Autopyromaniac 0/60, Burglar 0/60, Child 0/12, Expert 0/60, Imperial Ally 0/60, Novice 0/12, Pyromaniac 0/30, Razer of the Ruined Tower 0/60, Rebel 0/30, Slave 0/12, Trainee 0/60, Traitor 0/60, Brushed by Power 0/60, Lirasian Citizen 0/30, Royal Advisor 0/60, Favored by Power 0/90, Insomniac 0/30, Sleepless Disciple 0/60, Student of Power 0/60

Completed Paths

CharLimitCanttalkmuchNocluewhathappenedDidmybesttohelpyouli, Mage, Skilled Arcanist, Physical Alchemist, Bomber, Linguist, Beginner, Warrior, Path Less Traveled, Athlete, Scout, Unkillable, Superior Alchemist, Adventurer, Explorer, Outsider, Skill Researcher, Wanderer, Alchemical Warrior, Novice Pyromancer, Novice Ritualist, Alchemist, Physicist, Engineer, Physical Arcanist, Biologist, Practical Alchemist, Fey Scion, Feytouched, Skilled Arcanist

CHAPTER 10

Unafrayed

Edwin carefully Infused the water he poured out, the mana connecting to and binding with the liquid while it made its way through many tubes and pipes. It was far more complicated than strictly necessary for his mana to properly "sink in" and associate with the water, but it did make an excellent obstacle course for his control.

He'd already gotten to the point where he could pretty reliably keep his grip for as long as he needed, but he wasn't able to keep the Infused water separate from a larger mass. As soon as the two liquids touched, they'd instantly mix and dilute his Infusion. The only way he could avoid it was by maintaining two separate Infusions while they combined, but even that resulted in an almost homogeneous mixture of the two instances.

Right now, he was trying something different. At the end of the tubes wasn't another pool of water, but instead what he'd settled on calling "alchemist's fire," firevine sap concentrated and Refined into incredible flammability. It was even more flammable than white phosphorus, but thankfully it didn't burn quite as hot or as fast. It didn't mix well with water, but that was what he was trying to counteract.

Water fed into the sealed vial, and Edwin carefully expanded the container at about the same rate as water was being fed in. It wasn't perfect, having frequently found himself either stopped up or being sucked into a vacuum, but he was improving.

Inside the vial, Edwin felt his mana coil and try to mix with the intense fire magic present in the oil, but the two just slid off like, well, oil and water. But that was all right. He'd experienced that problem before, and he was pretty sure he knew how to deal with it.

It would have looked very boring to any observers, but Edwin found himself embroiled in his attempts, trying to first break down the larger clumps of fire into smaller bubbles. He squeezed, fighting past the resistance, and felt satisfaction as a bonfire burst into campfires. Then, he hunted down each and every campfire, turning them into cooking fires. Then he hunted them down again, breaking cooking fires into Bunsen burners.

Just what he needed.

Bit by bit, Edwin took his Infused water, a veritable ocean amid the countless tiny fires it surrounded like stars in the night sky, and fed it, trickle by trickle, into the Bunsen burners. In theory, he could probably use much larger quantities of mana, but that was harder to control. But at these scales, he could combine the fire and the water into, well, boiling water. At least in theory.

In practice, his sloppy attempts to merge the two types of magic was exceptionally wasteful. By the time he opened his eyes to the world again, night had fallen and all he had to show for his efforts was a hot water bottle, just slightly warmer than was comfortable.

He still grinned. His proof of concept was a *resounding* success.

The temperature dropped precipitously as the days came and went. It didn't really slow Edwin down, since he and Lefi just moved their training indoors; the entry hall *alone* was larger than most Earth gymnasiums.

Edwin didn't venture outside much at all. Why would he? There was nothing that really incentivized him to. There was plenty of food to be had within the tower, part of Rillah's compensation, and he didn't have any particular materials he wanted to get. Quite a few alchemical materials passed through the city, yes, but most weren't for sale before being shipped off to Panastalis via merchant caravans. Those few which *were* available were all absurdly expensive for materials that Edwin didn't think he could make much use of anyway.

Scarlet fern was predominantly just an anticoagulant, willow bark wasn't even *magical*, seagrass was tempting but seriously overpriced here, and none of the things he actually wanted—fulgurite, abysite, and unicorn horn chief among them—were available.

So he stayed in the tower's grounds. What few times he ventured into the streets, Edwin was usually subject to at least a little bit of harassment or whispers from commoners and guards, but nothing ever really came out of it. He couldn't say he even minded that much; at least they said what they actually thought about him and he didn't really expect anything more. He was, if anything, more annoyed at their casual derision of Rillah the "daywasr"—he still didn't know *exactly* what it meant, but he felt he had a decent idea—because he *knew* she didn't deserve it. But he still kept himself under control.

He could always just fly if he preferred to avoid them anyway.

Edwin jumped off the wall, Longstrider turning the world around him into a blur. Unbound Tether may not have let him fly, not yet, but he could *jump* so far. Ridiculously so, in fact. With just a running start, Edwin could jump nearly seven meters. Adding Unbound Tether got him to ten meters.

If he added Longstrider . . .

Well, he wasn't actually sure. Every single time he'd tried it, it ended the same way: Edwin face-planting into a wall or tree or *something* and being knocked out of the jump. He'd yet to find anywhere with enough space for him to actually check, especially without leaving the city, which he didn't really want to do . . . not for any *real* reason, he just didn't feel like it. But his jump was at least a hundred meters if not twice that. Even if he didn't use Unbound Tether beyond its initial charge, he still cleared a hundred, which was more than enough to send him from the tower to the city streets.

So now he just jumped around inside, which had significantly more space. Kicking off the wall didn't give him quite as much distance as he could with a run—while still more than the fifty meters Numeracy reached, Edwin estimated it was "only" sixty meters before Longstrider wore off.

The Skill had some interplay oddities, but it usually seemed like it didn't care how long Edwin's jump actually was, just how long it "should" be. He couldn't jump from a higher place and get more distance that way, because he always broke out of the Skill either at the same altitude he started at, or when he "landed" with his feet or Flight. That only applied when he was long jumping, though. When high jumping, it ended at the top of his arc. How the Skill could tell which Edwin was doing, he didn't know, but it worked out well enough.

The world to his sides came back into focus as Longstrider wore off, and Edwin fought back the stomach-dropping terror of free fall while he plummeted toward the stone floor below. He'd been getting better, at least! Unbound Tether helped him stay somewhat in control of his fall, which was a major factor in his current comfort, he knew.

Less than a second later, he got close enough to the hall's floor for Flight to kick in, and he lowered himself to the floor. A bit of math to account for the time spent arcing through the air, and . . .

"Sixty-two meters. Nice."

"Marvelous!" Lefi blurred into being next to Edwin, the man needing only a single step for his Longstrider to carry him the same distance. "You truly are growing fantastically with your Skills!"

Edwin gave a small smile. "Yeah. It's satisfying. I'm betting that'll be in the next obstacle course?"

"Oh, but of course!"

"Well, I *finally* found out what's taking so long," Rillah vented as she dropped into her favorite chair.

Edwin held up a finger. "Just a minute, let me finish this."

Conscious of his limited time, he quickly sped through his remaining tests. He hadn't really *expected* to succeed in his quest to synthesize ammonia simply by creating a mana "lightning potion" and imbuing water with it, but he would have felt really stupid if it *could* work and he just never tried it.

What was slightly more disappointing, though, was the complete lack of *any* change in the water. He'd hoped to get at least a little gaseous hydrogen, but if there was any, it was less than Alchemical Analysis could pick up. It was probably an issue with his imagined lightning potion, because it was definitely outside of his normal wheelhouse and he didn't know how to properly make it. Maybe he needed to figure out how to "brew" a lightning potion-spell first?

He tucked the beaker away in his bag. "What's up? You just had your weekly meeting with the politicians, right?"

Rillah threw her head back, leaning well into the chair. "Yuuup. I overheard a coupla nobles scheming in the corner. Turns out, they *have* a couple replacements for me, both well-known mages back in the capital, but they're each trying to ensure *they* get the Sheraith mage position. Lots of backstabbing and posturing, and the end result means neither's likely to get here soon."

"Okay, but if you know that they have options, but it's just political shenanigans that you're still stuck here, can't you leave with a clear conscience? Let them figure out their own mess."

She shook her head. "Unfortunately no. It would still be abandoning an official position, and that carries many, many penalties."

"Like what?"

"It's about a level ten Wanted List infraction, among others. I don't want to avoid cities, I love seeing them too much! Oh, remind me to take you to Farport at some point. That's the most beautiful city on the continent."

"Oh, uh . . . sure! I was planning on heading there at some point myself."

Wait, so when Rillah said that she wanted to take him to Farport at some point, did that mean that she didn't mind his presence? Did it mean she just wanted some company? Why not ask Lefi? Did she just want to stay in Edwin's good graces because she thought he'd help her get to Vis'Daric?

"Wonderful! Who knows when that will be, though." She sighed. "That's why I can't leave. I nor the nobles are happy now, but I can't leave without repercussions, and they can't chase me away without suffering the worst of winter. So here I am, stuck in one place for longer than I've been for *years*."

"Politics," Edwin summarized, "is the absolute worst."

"Politics," she agreed.

A thought flitted across Edwin's mind. "Well . . . what would happen if you suddenly weren't needed?"

"Oh?" Rillah sat up in attention. "What do you mean?"

"Well, I'm just imagining that we somehow figure out some automated system that does your job for you. You basically just need to supply wind magic, right?"

"It's slightly more complicated than that, but broadly speaking, yes. It's not *hard*."

"Yeah. So if I somehow figured out some way to create a wind magic supply or whatever . . ."

"How would you do that?"

"I don't have a clue. Something to do with my alchemy or magic, I'm sure. Maybe I'll finally dip into Alchemy Essentia properly? But I'm more curious what the repercussions of it would be if I *did* manage to replace your job with a self-sustaining magical artifact."

"Well," she said, "the pair currently jostling for the mage appointment would be *really* mad for one. The nobles might be happy or they might be furious, depending on if they like having a dedicated *city* weather mage, or just want to keep the wind walls up. I'd be free from my obligation, and no matter how much Kos'vilista and Finnas want to complain, it would satisfy my duty of enchantment maintenance 'until such a time a replacement is established.' It wouldn't help my reputation if I were to suddenly dance away, and I'd expect to both be accused of wasting time when there was a perfectly viable alternative and abandoning the city when I was needed like the faithless Adventurer I am."

"That doesn't . . . sound very fun. Other than the 'making the candidates mad' part—that sounds amazing."

"Bah, what do I care? They have short memories, and I've spent enough time in Sheraith to keep me happy for *years*. It'd annoy the people I want to annoy, and not affect the everyday people! You should do it." Rillah smiled at him. "I'd love it."

Edwin wrenched his emotions in check and gave a small smile back. "I mean . . . I can *try*, but like I said, I don't know where I'd even start. I can't make any promises, that's for sure. It'll just be something I keep an eye out for, see if I can't come up with anything. More of an idle thought than anything."

Despite telling Rillah that he wasn't going to dedicate too much time to making a wind magic accumulator, Edwin kept finding himself drifting toward the idea. He didn't *think* that it was a Skill affecting his thoughts, but that idea did tie into a lot of his projects.

After all, it would definitely require the use of magic, it would probably deal with alchemy in some way, and it would certainly require the use of enchanting. Ammonia production was beyond his grasp for the moment, and that barred a *lot* of modern chemistry from his grasp. Infused phosphorus served as an adequate explosive, and Unbound Tether as a decent projectile weapon. He didn't really *need* more conventional weapons yet. Training? Yes. But he had plenty of *tools*.

What he really needed to explore was *proper* alchemy, and what better project than a wind magic accumulator or maker? While atmospheric mana wasn't *abundant* this far from the Verdant, the tower's top room did have a fair bit present. If he could tap into it, then . . . Well, he could make Rillah happy, get a Path or two and some Skill levels, and, best of all, learn more about magic!

He wasn't having much luck, naturally, but it was an interesting problem.

What more could he want?

Edwin jumped, attaching his tether to the central pillar Lefi had constructed. The Adventurer apparently had some Skill called Temporary Structure Conjuration he hadn't been using before that made vaguely metallic, mirrorlike objects. Under Skillful Examination, it was reminiscent of but not quite identical to Apparatus, and Lefi was able to make much larger objects much quicker than Edwin could manage with his own trophy Skill.

Edwin had firmly locked all his feelings of inadequacy about there being yet *another* thing that Lefi could do better than him away in a deep, dark corner of his mind and instead just enjoyed the obstacle course.

He jumped off the edge, using the force that Unbound Tether could provide to swing himself back around, landing on the floor below. Immediately, he had to duck under a low ceiling, then use Longstrider to clear a gap. Below him, Lefi was making more of the course in *real time*; just as fast as Edwin could complete it, more was made and pushed up before vanishing back into Skill light.

It was a ludicrous display of power, but Edwin *wasn't thinking about that*. Instead, he raised himself into the air with Flight and leveraged himself through a tiny gap. He could have done the entire course airborne, of course, but that would defeat the purpose of learning how to integrate all his Skills into his muscle memory.

By filtering his mana through Unbound Tether, Edwin found that he could create a different form of magic; namely, movement magic. It was interesting, as he could mix it with his fire spell-potion to get a combination of movement *and* fire. If he used that mana as the basis of a Firestarting Infusion, he could make a bit of a weak blowtorch for the thirty seconds or so it took before that mana ran dry.

Truly, an earth-shattering discovery. Edwin was still superexcited when he got it to work, though. Finally, his mana was *doing stuff!*

Unbound Tether could combine with Flight in interesting ways. It *definitely* increased the amount of force Edwin could apply when airborne for one, but also just made his flight a little . . . springier.

He could deliver an *awesome* dropkick, that was certain. It was even enough to knock *Lefi* off-balance.

. . . so long as the Adventurer wasn't expecting it. And wasn't on solid footing.

Still, Edwin was *really* pleased to find that he could legitimately knock Lefi back a bit even *not* from ambush. All it took was a one-kilo stone, fully charged and with about ten meters of acceleration. Three kilojoules of energy may not have been enough to *injure* the guy, but it could disorient him.

Edwin decided to take his victories where he could.

Okay, so molai might work if I could refine it. Edwin tapped his mouth with his apparatite stirring stick. *I just need to figure out how to get to it without it just eating my Refined mana.*

Molai really was one of the unsung heroes of his garden, and he was really glad it grew so well in his greenhouse. So long as it had even a little sunlight, if he watered it with Infused water and kept it planted in Infused soil, it flourished. Once the flowers were picked, it stopped directly consuming mana for energy, but it did keep absorbing ambient magic and then holding on to it. If he overloaded it, all the mana would release in a flood, and if the molai was fresh enough, it could *keep* gathering mana afterward.

The only problem was its perishability. He hadn't had any problems with his potions having shelf lives yet, but if he wanted to make a true solution to Sheraith's mage problems, Edwin would need something whose efficacy dropped dramatically every few days, and so far as he was able to tell, his Refined creations basically fit his requirements.

If he was right, Refined molai would be a sort of mana accumulator and battery, pulling in mana from the surroundings, filling up and then needing only the tiniest of triggers to dump everything it had in seconds. After that, he'd just need a filter and some sort of conductor, to get wind mana, and *only* wind mana, from his Refined molai into the tower's enchantments.

Hmm . . .

"Great! Now faster."

Edwin groaned, picking himself up off the ground with Flight as he settled back onto his aching legs. His attempts to master Stamina Manipulation were . . . mixed, to say the least. Half the time, his trials didn't seem to do much of anything. The other half of the time, it definitely felt like he was working with *less* stamina than normal.

Edwin looked up at the looming spiral staircase above him, dreading what came next.

"Come on now, let's get to it!"

With a deep breath and with burning calves, he started running up the massive staircase *nearly* to the top once again.

At least the way back down was easy enough, if far, far too fast.

Motion mana Infused into water created a bit of a circular current in his bowl, apparently. It was too weak to accomplish much work, but Edwin did enjoy watching the leaf he'd dropped in it spin around and around and around . . .

It had been *way* harder than he had anticipated to actually get the tiny amount of preattuned magic through Mana Infusion. The Skill tended to overwrite any "flavors" of magic he tried to include, and in the end he had needed to Infuse the water *first*, and only *then* run the mana in the water through his pseudo-physical alchemical processes to turn it into motion mana.

The results *were* rather mesmerizing, at least.

Oh hey, when did that start showing I was two? Edwin wondered, blearily looking at his Status. It wasn't really his birthday, but it was close enough and meant he'd had a birthday at some point. He vaguely wondered what must have been happening back on Earth, but he quashed that thought before it could get any real foothold in his thoughts. He was *not* going there.

Edwin jumped off the wall, pushing off with all his might. He flew and flew . . . sixty-four meters. He was improving.

Practice makes perfect. He pushed more mana into his alchemical equipment, ignoring the phantom muscle pains. That wasn't real, he could push through it.

Just a bit more, then he could give Refining molai another go. He needed to test it, see if it would serve as a mana accumulator. He needed to . . .

Sunrise.

Jump. Run. Climb. Fly. Step.

Throw. Shoot. Push. Pull.

Mix. Infuse. Brew.

Study. Trace.

Food.

Sunset.

Practice makes perfect.

Sunrise.

Jump. Run. Climb. Fly. Step.

Throw. Shoot. Push. Pull.

Mix. Infuse. Brew.

Study. Trace.

Food.

Sunset.

The days started to blur together.

Sunrise.

Jump. Run. Climb. Fly. Step.

Throw. Shoot. Push. Pull.

Mix. Infuse. Brew.

Study. Trace.

Food.

Sunset.

Sunrise, jump, shoot, mix, study, sunset. Practice makes perfect.

Sunrise. Run, push, Infuse, trace, sunset.

Sunrise. Fly—

Fly.

Fly.

"Edwin, you look awful."

"What?" He blinked at the noise. "Oh, hey, Rillah. What's up?"

"Your magic just sounds *terrible*."

"Oh, thanks. That makes me feel so good."

"When was the last time you took a break?"

"Hmm . . ." He stopped to think. "What counts as a break? I'll take days off training with Lefi, spend a bit more time in the lab instead."

"A day off. No training with Lefi, no working on alchemy, nothing."

"When I unlocked Unbound Tether and was figuring that out?"

"Edwin, this isn't good for you."

"I'm fine," he promised. "Honestly, you should have seen me during exams back home."

"Exams?"

"Oh, right, you wouldn't . . ." He waved her off. "Never mind. I just have a lot on my plate is all. I need to do better."

"Better at *what?*"

"I-I still need to stay in shape, use my Skills with more fluidity." Edwin yawned slightly, looking over his to-do list. "I need to get better at magic, and investigate alchemy. I *still* need to figure out how to synthesize ammonia, but I'm more trying to Refine molai to get some wind mana synthesis . . ."

"Edwin. You can't do that if you're working yourself to the bone all the time. I've barely seen you. Do you know when was the last time you went flying?"

"I'm flying right now! Oh, you mean outside? Well, I don't know, when was it?"

"Nearly a month ago, Edwin. Which was also when you last took a day off."

"Oh, well. That's not too bad, I guess? I need to keep working, it's important."

"Edwin"—Rillah's voice stopped him in his tracks—"no, you don't. You're ruining yourself, and it's not important."

"Of course it's important! I have so much to do I couldn't possibly get it all done in my lifetime, I don't have days to waste!"

"A day spent doing things you enjoy is never wasted. Come down from there."

"But—"

"Down."

Edwin's Skill broke, and he suddenly found himself tumbling from the air, easily caught by Rillah, who set him on his feet.

"What? You can do that?"

"You're magically exhausted, Edwin. It's like pushing over someone without Stamina. All it takes is a little tap, and poof."

"You can get magically exhausted? But I never run out of mana."

"That's not . . ." She sighed. "You have Stamina, right? Right. Can you get physically exhausted, if you spend too many days pushing yourself, even if you never collapse the day of?"

"Um, no, actually. I think Sleeping prevents that. Is magic not the same?"

"I think the results speak for themselves."

"Fine." Edwin reluctantly agreed. "Fair enough. So then . . . what?"

"Come on." She tugged his arm. "You need a day off. What's the point of working to survive so hard if you don't live a little?"

"He's *fine*," Inion insisted. "He's worked harder for longer.

"It is only by truly pushing one's self, going past one's own limits, that you can truly excel, truly level!"

"He's wearing out his pinions!" Rillah countered. "Just look at his magic! His *Skills* are haggard."

"And? Did Edwin say that he needed time off, or is that what you're pushing *onto* him?"

"Oh, what, are you annoyed that your happy little human pet might not be in perfect agreement with you?"

Edwin interrupted the two. "Hey, hey, there's no reason to argue. It was Rillah's idea, but I don't disagree. She's got a point, my magic is *really* sore. Come on, Inion, I know that you must get that."

"Do you want to take a day not doing anything, Edwin? Can you really do that? When did you last truly not do *anything*? Even when you worked with the Guild, your days off you still worked on all kinds of stuff!"

"Well, it's been actual months if not *years* since I had a proper day off, which kind of indicates that I *should* have one. It's like Rillah said, what am I doing all this for if I don't just take some time off every once in a while.

"Like, come on, since I evolved Flight I've barely even been *outside* because it's no longer technically training related. Just let me have a *day*."

"Hmm. Make it two," Rillah commented.

"Oh? Why's that?"

"You'll see tomorrow."

"*Two* days off from training? You can't be *serious*."

"Look, I don't know what you have against me relaxing, Inion, but I *know* that you appreciate your days off. Why can't I get them too?"

"Can you genuinely go two days without so much as thinking about how you'll make your . . . whatever it is now? *Without* trying to figure out if you can direct the way that iron rusts with your magic?"

Hmm. Now that she mentioned that, wasn't iron oxide of some form a useful catalyst in the production of ammonia? He did have a fair bit of practice with molecular-level mana Infusion, after all. Maybe if he Infused the iron and then exposed it to some . . . hmm. How could he Infuse air?

Maybe he could do his Packing trick again, thinking of it all as a cohesive whole and also something he was touching? If he were to do that, maybe it would make sense to just use Flight?

Oh! Or he could ask Rillah if she could provide some wind mana. Her abilities were distinctly chillier these days, but there was still a decent core of wind hidden in there somewhere. That was also without her using any Skills to further adjust the attunement.

Edwin opened his mouth to ask her, then remembered he was supposed to be taking time off and closed it again soundlessly.

"You actually can't turn it off, can you?" Rillah sighed.

"I . . . don't *think* I can, no." Edwin looked sheepish. "Did Lefi hit me with some Skill again?"

"Lefi?" Rillah asked.

"'Twas not I, little snowbird!"

"Inion?"

She shrugged. "I think it's *her*. Nothing more than usual from me."

Edwin raised an eyebrow at that. "*Inion.*"

"What? Muse's Token does a lot of stuff. Sparks creativity and helps you level."

Ah, that would do it. Normally, Edwin was distracted by anything and everything and so making any kind of progress on anything basically amounted to waiting and hoping his brain decided to cooperate, but Inion had apparently managed to keep Edwin's scatterbrained focus in accordance with their Deal, meaning he just . . . not that he couldn't *do* anything else, just that his focus would always land on something productive.

Edwin honestly couldn't say that he *minded* most of the time; the effect was exactly what he had wanted for a long time, after all. He probably hadn't even noticed its effects consciously, just had his attention gently nudged from time to time.

He still glared at the fey. "Would it kill you to tell me this sort of thing *before* I worked myself to death?"

"It didn't stop you from taking breaks in Panastalis," Inion pointed out. "You'll be fine."

"Maybe it had some strange interaction with one of Lefi's Skills, then?" Edwin speculated. "It wouldn't be the first time."

"I know not of any Skills I might have which would change the nature of the lady fey's Skill."

Rillah stared at Lefi.

"What? 'Tis true!"

"Technically."

"Hmm?" Edwin asked. "I'm missing something here."

"It is nothing you need concern yourself with!"

"I mean, it clearly *is*," he retorted sharply. "What are you doing to me?"

Edwin did his best to ignore the pointed looks he *knew* Inion must be giving him right now. It was . . . it was different! He knew that Rillah wouldn't be doing anything untoward with her Skills, not when she was showing *actual* concern for his well-being! She was trustworthy; why did Inion have to be so insistent on pulling away the *one person* who actually seemed interested in him as a *person*?

"Nothing, nothing at all! Certainly nothing beyond the standard Skill-growth abilities I possess, and . . ."

"And?"

"I do possess a Skill that aids others in the strength of their Skills, in a manner of speaking."

Edwin glared at the man. "Well, *that* would do it. Have you been using that on me? I'm going to have to redo *so* many tests. Ugh. Why couldn't you have told me about this?"

"Oh, oh no! I have been certain to exclude you from the effects in all your tests and experiments."

"And training?" Edwin sighed.

"Yes, and your training."

"Could you, I don't know, use that on me when I'm trying to make stuff with Alchemy or whatever?"

"Alas, it does not work in that manner, I fear."

"Well, then how *does* it work?"

"You need not worry about such things!" Lefi clapped Edwin on the shoulder in reassurance, but he just turned and looked at Rillah.

"How true is it?"

"Excuse me!" Lefi said in false offense.

Rillah smirked. "Close enough, at least as far as you need worry about. The old man's picky about his secrets. Come on, let's get you some time to relax."

It had been a little while since Rillah had played her flute around Edwin. Oh sure, he knew that she played it a lot, the music was audible from essentially everywhere in the tower, but it was always muffled and didn't benefit as strongly from whatever Skills she had, and what literal magic she wove into the notes.

It was *transcendent*. There was something about magic and music that just *worked*, apparently, because the last time he'd felt so engrossed had been nearly a year and a half prior, when Inion had sang Obairlann into existence. If only the two of them got along, Edwin was certain that their combined musical talents would be utterly *divine*.

Not, of course, that either of them were that far from that benchmark on their own. Edwin couldn't help but sit enraptured as Rillah played her flute. The notes alone told of far-off lands and marvelous sights to be seen, of thrilling adventures and magical locales. The low notes of deep caves, the delicate tunes of grassy hills and endless plains, the majestic and bustling trade cities along the coast all wove together.

He never returned to his room that night, instead drifting off in his chair, mind and spirit joyous at the relief slumber provided.

Edwin woke up to a gentle caress along the side of his face.

He sat straight up, Watchful Rest having granted him slight forewarning to a presence. "Good morning, there."

"Oh, hey, Rillah." He stretched. "Good morning. Something wrong?"

"No, nothing at all. In fact, it snowed a lot last night, and Lefi and Yathal are already outside. What do you say we ambush them with some snowballs?"

Ooh, a snow day. Some things transcended dimensions, it seemed. This . . . might be *very* fun.

CHAPTER 11

Snowledge Is Power

Yathal was in *love* with the white blanket as it coated the landscape, clinging to the side of the stone tower and burying the massive boulder that was its first several floors. He and Kyni were busy running around, diving into drifts heedless of the cold. Lefi stood nearby in essentially his normal clothing, scooping snow together for what looked like a massive snowball.

Looking at the pair with Skillful Assessment, it looked like the Stalwart Protector—Kynigos had completed a few Paths over the intervening months, changing his Class away from Stalwart *Defender*—had a dark gray Skill wrapped around his boy. It looked quite structurally similar to the Skill he would flare whenever Yathal was about to be injured, and with context it was easy enough to figure out what it did.

"No winter clothing?" Edwin asked Rillah. "I mean, yes, I know why *you* don't have any, but what's up with Lefi?"

"Similar situation," she said cheerfully. "Makes sense to have environmental-protection Skills when you're an Adventurer. It was his suggestion I even take Unweathered Form to begin with, as having a dedicated Skill makes things *so* much easier."

Edwin nodded in agreement. His clothing was thicker than it had been in the summer, of course, but not by *that* much. He could already feel Adaptive Defense at play, cutting winter's bite away from disrupting him. Before long, the chill he felt should mostly fade, and he glanced over at Rillah, fighting back a small double take.

"Oh, hey, your eyes finally changed," he noted. "I know you said it would happen as the season shifted, but I wasn't expecting it."

Edwin's eyes momentarily went wide as he realized his mistake. "Not that I doubted you or anything!" he backpedaled. "It's just different seeing it with, well, my own eyes."

Rillah raised an eyebrow, blue eye piercing straight through Edwin's own gaze, amber firmly skeptical.

"Look, I'm really tired and exhausted. That's why I'm taking your advice and not doing anything today instead of, I don't know, figuring out if I can use snow in my magical training."

Hmm. That would actually be interesting. He could fairly readily mix mana at this point, so long as he was using his equipment and water, and while he hadn't really tried making anything actually useful, he could probably get some interesting practice by attempting to mix yet hold separate snow and water, maybe making a more wet snow?

He'd need to . . . use his mana to somehow hold the snow in-state and prevent it from melting, while also mingling them? It probably would be good practice for him doing anything but homogeneously mixing his types of mana; he really should . . .

"Ow!" Edwin rubbed his head where Rillah had smacked him. It wasn't a very hard smack, but it was more the surprise he was protesting.

"Knock it off!"

"What?"

"No working today. You need to have fun."

"But it *is* fun," he half-heartedly complained. But he couldn't *really* disagree. "So, oh, wise mage, what should I avoid?"

"Skills only!"

"Hmm?"

"No freecasting practice until tomorrow." She waved her finger in his face. "Yesterday was good, but you still need more time to recover. You can use your mage Skills, but no alchemy or anything until *tomorrow*, got it?"

He rolled his eyes but acquiesced. How was he supposed to refuse?

"So"—glancing over to where Lefi was preoccupied, a conspiratorial grin crept onto Edwin's face—"you mentioned a snowball assault?"

The attack was swift and brutal. Edwin had assembled a full array of weapons to use, compacted and throwing weapons to the last. To his left, Rillah had her own armory of significantly larger munitions, each at minimum the size of Edwin's head.

With a faint *whoosh*, snowy wings twice her arm span sprang from the Dancer's back, and she jetted into the air in almost perfect silence. Behind her trailed an arsenal, a veritable avalanche of ammunition falling in reverse.

No words were spoken, none were needed. Between his hands, Edwin held the largest of his weapons, charging it as fast as he could manage. It hummed silently with power, the sensation of motion trying to rip it from his hands before it was properly ready.

They'd need this first attack to go off perfectly if they were to stand a chance. If their target wasn't neutralized, he'd retaliate in full force and *neither* of them would withstand that. Fortunately, Lefi seemed somehow oblivious to the impending doom hanging over his head, and Edwin let a small smile play across his face.

Then it was time, and he unleashed *hail*.

Well, technically snow. But then the pun didn't work.

Lefi vanished into a cloud, then a mound of white, as a frankly inordinate amount of snow crashed into the man all at once.

Edwin knew better than to celebrate, though. He was proven correct when the temporary hill simply vanished, exploding out in every direction.

"Oho! So it is treachery then! Such vile, honorless foes I face, attacking me whilst my attention lay elsewhere!"

Edwin was barely able to dodge the barrage of loose snow flying at him, but some two years of training had done wonders for his agility and reflexes.

He dropped to the ground, using Unbound Tether to help him bounce off the ground, ending his motion hovering just above the snow cover, but behind a tiny protrusion from the ground. The wall of snow passed over him harmlessly, and Edwin got a clear look at the situation once more.

Lefi stood next to a giant mound of snow, atop which were a dog and his boy coated in a thin layer of fresh snow. Above him, Rillah hovered, untouched by the Adventurer's retaliation just as much as Edwin. Instead, a ring of snow orbited lazily around her.

"You fiend!" she called back, laughing. "You would be so reckless as to attack a bystander in your assault? For shame!"

"The little snowbird seeks to challenge me? It would not matter if all the armies of the Empire were to stand with you, for here I am mighty, you are mere pretenders to this throne of ice!"

"Not so long as we stand firm together!" Edwin hopped in on the fun. "We have you surrounded and outnumbered. If you surrender now, we may show leniency!"

The day seemed to darken as Lefi responded, gesticulating dramatically, hands sweeping for effect. "I see not the armies, I see not the soldiers standing shield to shield, flying claw to head, stretching from here unto the horizon. Where is your army, for I can still see the sun above me, feel the ground before me, hear the breeze blow around me. Return when the winds fall silent before your might, when the sky flees in terror, when the stones upon which you stand retreat at your command, and only *then* you might stand a chance against my strength!"

"Nice speech! How long did it take you to come up with that one?" Edwin shot back.

"Less time than your life yet possesses." Lefi gave a smile colder than the ice he stood upon.

Then the war *truly* began.

One by one, Edwin summoned his premade snowballs to his hands, Adaptive Defense working at full tilt as he grasped the first freezing projectile with his bare fingers. Throwing Weapons guided his hand as he drew back and threw, sending the ball flying off at Lefi. He didn't even need to look, twisting in such a way and grazing the side of Edwin's snowball in such a way it collided with a hastily constructed pair thrown by Yathal.

Naturally, Edwin's snowball utterly demolished the sloppy work of the kid, and it carried on until it collided with the snowbank Yathal, now astride Kyni, was at the top of. By then, Edwin had his next two balls in hand, and both arced through the air toward Lefi, timed to hit the man at the same time as Rillah's next assault.

The small ring of snow around Rillah had shaped itself into dozens of snowballs still orbiting the mage, and with a small melody on her flute, she spun them faster and faster until they were nothing but a blur.

The impromptu show came to a sudden close, and with her final note they began to pelt Lefi where he stood. New snowballs were apparently being created in abundance, given how long the attack was going on, but the man was preoccupied with defense there, swatting snowball after snowball out of the air or punching straight through them, filling the air with drifting snowflakes.

Edwin took the chance to empty out his remaining stock of snowballs, Lefi being so preoccupied with the rapid-fire aerial assault he didn't have much of a chance to dodge many of the projectiles Edwin was throwing, especially with all of them being so uncannily on target.

It was also nice seeing that Lefi had *some* limits, even if they were "unable to withstand a four-on-one snowball assault while clearly not taking it seriously," as the Adventurer kept staying on the defensive as long as Rillah continued her assault.

Unfortunately, for whatever reason, she wasn't able to maintain the attack indefinitely. Lefi in turn grabbed the last snowball launched at him out of the air and returned it to Rillah *hard*, colliding with one of her wings hard enough—and with a medley of Skills to back it up—to completely collapse the Skill's manifestation.

As Rillah spiraled down to the ground, Lefi blurred into action, assembling an absolutely *gigantic* snowball, at least twice as big as Edwin, from the ground around him. Strangely, it didn't seem to deplete the blanket of snow from around the man, but Edwin knew *full well* that snow-creation shenanigans were going on. In any case, before Rillah could properly recover from the attack, she was practically buried under a pile of wet snow, her cry of protest muffled underneath the new drift.

At that, Lefi no longer needed to stay on the defense. There was a low thrum in the air, and a sweeping Skill blanketed the ground around him. Then, the deluge began, and made Rillah's efforts look inferior to even Yathal's output. Hundreds if not thousands of snowballs were made and thrown every second, Lefi *literally* blurring as he moved. Even then, Edwin noticed some sort of Splitting Arrows Skill at play, turning each of the dozens of snowballs into dozens upon dozens.

Edwin fell to his knees, covering his face to avoid the assault. There was no way to dodge a veritable blizzard of snowballs, no way to block or deflect the hundreds of projectiles striking him every second, not out in the open with so little cover.

So he just needed to make himself some.

While most of his basic Skills went largely unused these days, seventy-six levels in Harvesting paid off in a big way, as a swipe of Edwin's hand across the ground produced a mound of snow in front of him. A second of work later established the beginnings of a snow fort, but even with seventy-seven levels in Construction, he didn't think for an instant that Lefi couldn't demolish, in the blink of an eye, everything that Edwin had made.

So he just needed to make more and stronger fortifications.

Every sweep of his arm scooped up more snow from his surround-ings, and a second pass piled and compacted it into his fortifications, thickening and expanding his protections into a solid wall of ice. Yes, apparatite might make for better defense, but even if it wouldn't be cheating the implied rules of engagement to use something other than snow, the Skill was far too slow to really be useful.

He sheltered behind his wall, until the rhythmic pitter-patter of snowballs fell away and Edwin could safely look out to assess the situation.

Yathal and Kyni had not been idle. The boy was atop his copper-tan steed, and they charged bravely into the fray. Snowballs burst against Kyni's hide, not even slowing the dog down while his rider pelted Lefi with (wildly inaccurate) snowballs.

Edwin wasn't sure where the snowballs were *kept*, and he thought that Kyni might have been making them as needed until the pair stopped, Yathal slid off "his" dog's back and started packing more while his loyal partner blocked the barrage with his body. It looked for a moment that Lefi might be stymied, but then he began to angle his throws to arc over the dog's body. Kynigos activated some Skill to block more of his boy's body, but while effective at stopping Lefi from hitting Yathal, it also precluded the reverse.

"Foolish Adventurers!" Lefi gloated as he paused, hands outstretched and feet planted a shoulder length apart. "Did you truly believe you stood any chance against me?"

"Oh, I knew I never had any hope! But she did!" Edwin yelled back, pointing behind Lefi.

To the Adventurer's credit, he neither dropped everything he was doing nor wholly dismissed the claim, only looking away for a brief moment. As he turned back after seeing nothing, Lefi opened his mouth for some response just in time for Edwin's snowball to slam into the side of the man's head. The hard-packed snow simply disintegrated on the contact, leaving only a tiny trace behind, like throwing against a stone wall.

Edwin raised an eyebrow. "So how much are you holding back?" he cordially asked. There was no way they'd managed to land a hit on Lefi if he was going full tilt, Edwin knew that much.

"I need use but a fraction of my potential to crush all of you beneath my snow-covered heel! I shall rule you all with an icy fist!" Lefi replied and scooped up a new snowball from the ground around him.

He had definitely changed tactics. Where before, Lefi was prioritizing quantity over all else, he now favored quality. Each snowball was perfectly aimed and devastatingly fast, as well as absolutely laden with a full rainbow medley of Skills.

Some, Edwin recognized as Skill-nullifying effects like the one that had broken Rillah's wing. Others were more like Training Combat, which Edwin had extensive experience with from sparring, to lessen the damage inflicted. Edwin had no clue about what one last Skill did until it struck his snow-wall and flared, blasting a massive chunk of material like it exploded.

Edwin's eyes widened. He wondered if *he* could get that Skill. He could probably get *some* use out of it. Though on second thought, he was probably better off just focusing on blowing things up the *normal* way.

Fortunately, the structure-destroying Skill didn't affect—if Edwin were to guess—anything alive, so while the snowballs hit with an absolutely *insane* amount of force and sent him staggering, it didn't feel like he'd get anything worse than a mild bruise at *most*. It still stung, so he kept sheltering while figuring out some kind of strategy.

He popped his head up only to be met with a snowball to his face, blinding him temporarily until he cleared out the debris covering his eyes. The next time he snuck a peek, it looked like Lefi was busy sniping Yathal and Kyni. As Edwin watched, one projectile caught Yathal in his chest and actually sent the boy *flying*, albeit only a few feet. Sheesh. His next snowball hit Kyni and sent the dog tumbling through the snow as well.

The pup recovered quickly enough, powder snow covering his coat, and with an ear flopped back, dashed over to where Yathal had sunk onto a bit of loose snow and began to dig. Then Lefi turned back around, and Edwin had to bunker down behind his wall and hope that it held.

Rillah was still buried underneath her mound of snow. Hopefully she'd break out soon, they were losing *badly* without her.

Hmm.

Edwin waited a few moments to let Lefi change his focus back to the duo and jumped up. Apparently, his motion had drawn the man's attention, and he was immediately faced with a snowball headed his way. Fortunately, that was exactly what Edwin had anticipated, and he pulled on Unbound Tether as much as possible to push the snowball back toward Lefi.

Just as the Skill connected, Lefi's Skill-breaking effect flared and shattered Edwin's tether, letting the snowball carry on unimpeded.

Right. I should have expected that, Edwin realized as he dodged out of the projectile's way. Okay, next plan then.

He tugged at an intact snowball some distance behind him with his tether. While all of Lefi's active effects on the former projectile seemed to have dissipated, it was still a really solid snowball, certainly sufficient for this.

The tiny ball accelerated under nearly a hundred newtons of force—or more like twenty N thanks to its light mass—jetting toward Edwin's outstretched hand. As it neared, Edwin brought the hand he was using his Skill through forward in a whipping motion, trying to switch from attracting to repelling his weapon at just the right moment to have a massive length of momentum buildup.

Edwin mistimed it by a split second, and it veered far off to the side, and Edwin ate a snowball as punishment for his focus on dodging lapsing. As he recovered from being knocked sprawling, he saw a figure emerge from the snow, slipping into his tiny fortress.

Rillah was a mess. Her normal neat braid had come mostly loose and was sticking every which way, soaking wet in some places and full of snow in others.

"How's that Idyllic Form working out for you?" he teased.

Rillah stuck her tongue out at him. "It's not *all-powerful*," she countered quietly.

"Ah, of course. Fear the wet snow, I see, for it does more than skydiving."

She rolled her eyes. "We'll talk about that later. How's it going?"

"Well . . ." Edwin floated just over the ground to his shelter. It was *not* designed for two people, and he found himself *very* close to Rillah as they talked. Her breath didn't have any distinct smell but was warm as it blew across his face, and her eyes . . .

Nope . . . He dragged his brain back into cooperation. He wasn't going to let stupid *emotions* potentially mess up the most promising potential friendship he had on Joriah.

"Well," he lamely repeated, realizing he'd spent too long in thought, "not great. Without you drawing his attention, he's able to focus *way* too much on either me or on Yathal and Kynigos. Every one of his snowballs has *loads* of Skills packed into it, or he unleashes hundreds every second. I've got no idea how we can beat him."

"Foolish Adventurers!" Lefi's voice bellowed. "You thought you could defeat me, yet you cower in fear at my very presence! Truly, none of you can withstand my might."

"Actually, hmm. What Skill were you using to create all those snowballs earlier?" Edwin asked, tuning out Lefi's continued boasting.

"Winter's Flurry, coupled with some of my wind Skills. Winter's Flurry can make a snowstorm, but then I can compact them into snowballs."

"Okay then. Nothing that allows you to multiply shots taken, like what Lefi's doing?" Rillah shook her head. "Pity. Okay then . . . Hmm. You said that your fire magic is stronger in the winter?"

"More than in the autumn, but ice is still my strongest. Why, what are you thinking?"

"What kinds of fire Skills do you have? Anything that's persistent, that might be able to melt snow?"

In response, she summoned an amber flame to her hand, the same color as her eye. It was oddly alluring, the way that it flickered and danced, he could stare at it for hours . . . Huh, what was burning? Well, obviously it wasn't a *requirement*, Edwin could conjure fire that just licked from his hand without consuming anything but mana, but that still had the *appearance* of fire burning his hand. But with Rillah, the fire just appeared, in midair. It looked different and strange, like a massive, invisible candle sat right in front of him. It radiated an almost uncomfortable amount of heat, so it should be sufficient.

Edwin frowned as he looked at the metaphysical parts of the fire. "I see three Skills in that. One is *definitely* a mental Skill. Care to explain?" Edwin flinched as a snowball whizzed right past his head. "Actually, remind me later when it's calmer. How much control do you have over it?"

In response, Rillah allowed another flame to sprout from her hand, then each of the two hovering fires stretched out into long snakes. "Pretty good," she answered.

"Awesome. Here's the plan."

Edwin turned into a veritable blur as he unleashed his charged tether, jumping a good ten meters into the air in the blink of an eye. Naturally, his action attracted snowballs from Lefi, but that was exactly what they were hoping for. As he began to fall, Edwin reached out and attached his tether to Lefi himself, pulling as hard as he could.

One hundred newtons wasn't a *lot*. It was more or less the equivalent of holding something that was about twenty pounds, and Edwin knew that no matter how much force he could push Lefi with, it wouldn't be enough to knock the guy off-balance, not for someone with Packing.

But if you suddenly found yourself twenty pounds *lighter*? That was significantly harder to cope with.

Edwin managed to catch Lefi just as he was midthrow, and the sudden shift in his personal gravity sent him stumbling, tripping over his own feet for just long enough to let Rillah make her move.

A half-dozen fire snakes burst forth from where she was hiding, flying toward Lefi and encircling him with fire. The Adventurer's next snowball obviously tried to cancel out the Skill at play, practically glowing with whatever anti-Skill effect he was relying on, but the combined heat of the veritable fire tornado managed to just *barely* disrupt the Skills carried within the snowballs before they could in turn dissipate the magic.

That was the most iffy part of the whole plan, and Edwin mentally cheered. Clearly, using the Skill took some amount of time and effort, and given the way the Skill structure had looked inside the projectiles Lefi had thrown, he got the impression there was some limit to the kinds of projectiles it could be paired with.

And as it turned out, a slushball, melting from the moment it started its flight, *wasn't* a valid target. Did that imply that Lefi had snowball-specific Skills? No, wait. Focus.

Edwin landed back on the ground and looked on at the scene with pride. Yes, they'd escalated the snowball fight *well* past sane limits, but Lefi was now mostly toothless, unable to throw any snowballs through the bonfire between them. Of course, that might imply that he was similarly untouchable, but Edwin disabused that notion quickly. He once again took advantage of Basic Thermokinesis's insulating properties to chuck a snowball right through the fiery barrier, where it caught Lefi by surprise and splattered all over the man's head.

The fire faded away, Rillah panting from the exertion but looking radiant at her accomplishment. In a ten-foot radius around Lefi, the ground was bare of snow, winter grass hardily standing up to the heat and cold alike.

It didn't stay empty for long though. Edwin was able to keep Lefi off-balance for a few moments by rapidly pushing and pulling on the Adventurer with his tether, just long enough for Rillah to flex her remaining magical prowess and catapult the *entire hill* of snow Yathal and Kyni had been on directly atop Lefi.

It took the golden-haired man almost five minutes to dig himself out, only to be greeted by a hail of snowballs from the victorious trio, and a mound of snow from a triumphant Kynigos.

It was barely noon.

They kept playing, but naturally toned it down after that. Edwin honestly wasn't sure if the gardens would *survive* another incident like that.

It was a good day.

The fire roared and crackled, billowing heat into their little room. It had been a very long and tiring day, and while Edwin technically still had enough *physical* energy to run a marathon, he was *mentally* exhausted. Their snowball fight had continued on for hours, but even once that was done they kept playing in the snow.

Yathal said that it was the best thing *ever*, and while there weren't any kids running around in the higher-Class part of Sheraith, Edwin couldn't help but imagine the awe anybody Yathal's age would feel had they been a fly on the wall for their war. There was somehow *more* snow when they finished than when they started, but given how much snow conjuration had been going on Edwin wasn't that surprised.

Inion had even joined in at one point, after they'd switched into less violent activities. While they found out that apparatite didn't *normally* make a good sled material, Edwin was able to manipulate the substance with a bit of guidance from Lefi into flexing under extreme pressure, making it more like a plastic than glass.

That was definitely something he'd need to investigate in the future, but Edwin could already imagine some of the possible applications. Maybe he could make some sort of fiberglass-like insulation? Further testing required.

It did annoy him a bit that Lefi was somehow able to understand Edwin's Skill better than *he* did, but he figured that Lefi must have some sort of ability akin to Skillful Assessment. Just . . . way more detailed and sensitive. It was *fine*. So they'd raced around on crystal sleds, magically creating a massive hill to race down, even making a few jumps.

If he were back on Earth still, Edwin would have never dared to go over a jump with a sled. But now that he could *fly*, the risks involved were seriously diminished and he could be reckless without risk. Well, he was still cautious, but he didn't need to be as worried about crashes. He was at full Health besides; he probably wouldn't even be *able* to break his neck in a collision.

They went sledding, they made snowmen—Lefi's was a veritable *statue*, a twenty-foot-tall representation of himself, though Inion one-upped even him by making an ice sculpture that was outright *super-natural*, a glistening representation of her home spring, with ice that was animated as though it were still liquid.

Now, they were indoors, piled around a blazing fire. Inion and Lefi were amicably chatting off to the side, boasting about their respective Skills with icy art. Yathal was drooped over Kyni, chest rising and falling rhythmically as he dozed.

Rillah and Edwin, meanwhile, were playing a game that was essentially a combination of Go and Chinese Checkers, maneuvering different-colored stones around a circular board to try and capture spaces. Edwin was still figuring out how to play exactly, meaning Rillah was absolutely *destroying* him, but they were still more closely matched than either of them and Lefi, who had an actual Skill for the game.

The entire scene made Edwin's heart ache. He loved this so, so much. Having at least casual friends, just hanging around and playing games? It was amazing. But a part of him stayed reserved, unable to commit, unable to fully enjoy it.

It was stupid, he knew. Immensely so. This was almost everything he had wanted, wasn't it? Except not *really*. His friends were more so allies of convenience. He wasn't sure why Lefi stuck around, but who knew why extroverts did anything? It probably had something to do with his existence as an Outsider, possibly spurred on by a bit of guilt.

Inion . . . he mentally sighed as he studied the fey. Was it even accurate to say that fey *could* have friends? Edwin honestly wasn't sure. But she didn't really feel like a *friend*, though he didn't know if that was better or worse.

And then there was Rillah. He liked her, he really did. She was easy to talk to and enjoyable to be around. His time with her was *fantastic*. His mask around her was remarkably easy to keep up, and other than Earth there weren't any secrets he really needed to keep from her. He didn't think there were any Skills at play making him more comfortable around her, but he could worry about that another day. He didn't want to ruin this experience.

"Your turn," she prompted, and Edwin dragged his attention back to the game. She'd hopped one of her stones over one of his, leaving her in the right position to capture two of his pieces next turn. He moved a stone to block her, only realizing when she smiled triumphantly that he'd fallen into a trap, and Rillah used her next turn to capture *six* of his, putting him in a very precarious position.

Edwin narrowed his eyes in focus, trying to escape her clutches.

He lost, of course. But the game was fun, he did *really* enjoy spending time with them, and the day was very, very nice.

So why wasn't he *happy*? He should be. He was objectively in a great position, socially speaking. He had more people around him and willing to work with him than he'd *ever* had before—he should be happy. But he couldn't beat it into his own emotions that he ought to be happy.

Was it . . . was it because he didn't feel safe around any of them, not really? It was an interesting hypothesis and fit moderately well with his observations. If he dropped his mask, expressed his worries to Rillah, he didn't know if she'd stay, or take them seriously. She definitely would just think he was being a drag, if nothing else. Lefi was a complete wildcard, and Inion . . .

Edwin sighed. Inion, at least, wouldn't leave. But it would still be awkward, and she would probably think he was just being a downer, and he didn't want that.

He curled up on his bed. Why did he have to be so ridiculous? They'd be fine.

Maybe.

Did he really want to risk it, though?

He sighed again.

Further testing required, I suppose.

Level Up!
Skill Points 988→1028 (Average level: 53)
Adaptive Defense Level 42→45

Alchemical Analysis Level 40→41

Alchemical Dismantling Level 46→49

Alchemy Level 94→95

Arcadian Elixir Level 35→36

Basic Thermokinesis Level 32→36

Bomb Throwing Level 57→58

Fresh Air Level 44→45

Improbable Arsenal Level 39→42

Longstrider Level 50→52

Memory Level 65→66

Numeracy Level 49→50

Prototyping Level 40→41

Refining Level 36→37

Ritual Intuition Level 47→50

Sapper's Apparatus Level 60→62

Skillful Assessment Level 50→51

Stamina Manipulation Level 3→4

Unbound Tether Level 11→19

Watchful Rest Level 38→40

CHAPTER 12

Heating Up

Edwin had always preferred warmth to cold, and so while Adaptive Defense did a great job of keeping him from utterly *freezing*, or even getting too cold, he really would prefer that he had superwarm, super-comfortable underclothes.

Yes, he could get something made of wool. Yes, he could have gotten clothes already made supernaturally warm via Skills. But those were the *boring* options. Edwin wanted to try and add the warming properties himself, and he needed something absorbent to test out his potion. It was all a part of solving the mana-accumulation problem, after all. He could make potions, sure, but could he make something using his potions that had magical properties?

It was perfect practice for more advanced things, after all.

Edwin ended up getting two new undershirts, both perfectly fitted to him, pure white, and apparently made out of something called "wheatspin," a surprisingly soft fabric considering it was made of discarded wheat stalks later spun into thread.

The tailor he had bought it from had boasted that his were the softest wheatspin garments in the city, that he alone had the Skills needed to take the normally coarse and stiff fabric and make it actually wearable. While somewhat skeptical, the price the man gave was about in the range that Rillah had told Edwin he should expect for the shirts, so he shrugged and bought them anyway.

When he asked her later, Rillah confirmed that what the man had said was more or less true, though certainly exaggerated. Wheatspin was a common fabric at all levels of society. The poor wore it because it was made out of incredibly cheap material, all the way up to nobility who wore it as a statement showing off how Skilled their personal tailors were. That the man Edwin had visited was open to the public meant that he wasn't good enough to be privately contracted, but that by no means made him *bad*. The fabric was still as soft as anything he could remember from Earth, almost silk-smooth but somehow with a very different texture.

It was a curious dichotomy, but not especially relevant for his current task.

Namely, how did you light a shirt on fire without burning it up or using flames?

He had practice from his hot-water experiment, sure, but that was different. There, he was just allowing the two elements to combine in a natural course of action. The flame went out because the water extinguished it, but it was heated in turn. More fire, and it would have produced more steam than water.

Unfortunately, cloth—particularly wheatspin—was *flammable*, and just shoving the Refined concentrated firevine sap he called alchemist's fire into it was a surefire way to burn his practice shirt to ash. Hmm. What about if he tried to filter his personal Infusion again? It had worked well with his little whirlpool jar when he Infused motion into water, why not heat? Of course, he'd only been able to get his Imbuement to stay permanent in *water*, but that wasn't too much of an obstacle.

Edwin closed his eyes and conjured his mana Visualization Skill. Okay, he had a source, a series of filters, and a variety of other tubes, pipes, alembics, and other glassware that didn't technically do anything but were nonetheless synonymous with alchemy thanks to fantasy media.

Once he had a clear image in his mind, he spent a minute assembling a match for it in reality, fastening different premade sections together with freshly conjured apparatite bindings. Once it was all assembled, Edwin added his two primary ingredients into the mix—distilled water and alchemist's fire.

In theory he might be able to do this with nothing but magic, but he used the liquids nonetheless. Both because they psychologically reassured him that he was doing something physical, and because they also triggered Alchemy and gave him an extra ninety-odd Skill levels of experience and power. Plus, if this worked he'd have an actual, physical result and not just mana practice.

Carefully gripping his water reservoir, Edwin slowly Infused the liquid, making sure he kept control over the mana inside. With his other hand, he Infused not the *alchemist's fire*—doing so didn't work well, as a few small explosions testified—but more tried to overlay the liquid with his mana. As he did so, he pulled on Basic Thermokinesis to tune his Infusion toward fire. It was a weird sensation, but one he was slowly getting better at.

Fortunately, for all that it was ready to burst into flames at a moment's notice, alchemist's fire wasn't a high explosive and still required air to burn. So, keeping it in a sealed container was enough to keep it as a liquid, even as he mixed it with Infused water.

Between his greater experience and additional confidence that came from working with this kind of alchemy, Edwin was able to create a steaming bottle of water with just a few minutes of work. It wouldn't get hotter or colder, he knew, but if he left it out it *would* evaporate and waste his work.

Success, it would seem, and one that was decidedly better than his last attempt at creating perpetually heated water. Edwin released his tight grip on his Infusion while he assessed the result. Now all he needed was to Refine it, mix it with molai, and turn it into a proper dye.

A tiny star lit on his finger as he began.

When Edwin was done Refining, he was left with a reddish-gold liquid that was exactly the same temperature. Interesting. He would have thought that concentrating it would have made it warmer. What was the difference, then? He knew it had to have done *something*, but what exactly that *was* . . .

Further testing required, he thought as he set a small measure off to the side.

The bulk of his Refined hot water went into his cauldron, and guided by Alchemy, he mixed crushed molai alongside some glowleaf as a stabilizer, brewing it until the entire liquid was illuminated in reddish light. He filtered out the solids remaining from his molai and glowleaf and tried to dye one of his new shirts.

He didn't exactly know *how* to dye, but that was a small matter. It was just soaking it, wringing it out, rinsing it, and repeating. How complicated could it *really* be? Yes, yes, it could be very complicated, but it didn't *need* to be.

After several washes, Edwin let his shirt hang up to dry, watching it gently steam.

A few hours later, he grinned when he returned to find his shirt an interesting faintly red color. It looked like it turned out well, and he eagerly reached out to feel his new eternally warm shirt . . .

Edwin frowned. It felt no different from before. Clearly, he was doing something wrong. Further testing . . . actually, he might not *need* to test this. There were people with way more experience than him in magical matters.

"Oh, so your *lady friend* couldn't help you?"

Edwin sighed. "No, Inion. Rillah doesn't have any experience with making magical items. Something to do with storms not being containable."

"What makes you think *I* can help you then?"

"You made Obairlann," he pointed out. "That was pretty magical."

"That's not *really* the same."

"Can you help me or not? I came to you because I thought you might be able to provide *some* kind of new insight."

"Oh, not talking to me just for fun?"

"Considering you find some way to snipe at Rillah every time we talk, no. I'm on good terms with as many people as I have fingers on this entire planet, and if I wanted to hear people bad-mouth one of them I'd just wander around the city."

"You're making a mistake with her," she cautioned.

"I don't care."

"She's manipulating you."

"And you *aren't*?"

"Not like she is."

"*I. Don't. Care.* All communication is manipulation, and *whatever* Rillah is doing is something that I *enjoy*. If it's magical compulsion, so be it. I don't think she means me any harm with it. And at this point? That's all I care about."

Inion didn't have a response to that.

Edwin said, "Can you help me or not?"

"I *can*."

"Will you? Look, if we don't have some topic that we can focus on while we chat, we're just going to fall into another argument about Rillah."

"I *do not* like that woman."

"I know. Trust me, *I know.* And I wish I knew how to help reassure you. But that's also not something I want to talk about right now. So . . . magical stuff?"

Inion finally seemed to concede. "I wouldn't *describe* myself as much of an enchanter, but I know I can *definitely* give you some information."

Edwin gave her a warm smile. "Thanks, Inion. Really, just having anything to build off is enough at this point. I can figure out the details myself, but I have no *clue* what I'm doing."

"Let me see what you've tried so far."

"Okay, so this was when . . ." Edwin gave a quick rundown.

"I see." Inion nodded. "So your *first* problem is just what you were enchanting."

"Oh, so I do need to directly apply my magic to the cloth, not just dye it then?"

"Yes, but *no*. You made the potion . . . probably fine, I can't speak to that. But you just used it *as* a dye, without doing anything to then make the cloth *itself* more magical."

"So all the magic stayed in the dye, and when that dried out, it changed the composition . . ."

"Ending all your work, yes."

"Okay," Edwin said, nodding absently. "So what? Do I— I don't know. I knew I was doing something wrong, but that only helps so much."

"That's something I *can* help with. Fey bind themselves to a location or an object, and *we're* changed accordingly, but so too is our *Bind*, ya?"

"So . . . what?"

"I'm *getting* there. What if *you* were to do something similar? You have a comparable ability, don't you?"

"Fey's Caress?" he asked, confused. "But the Skill said that I take on properties of it? Yeah. 'Bind yourself to a touched material, gaining some of its properties.' What does that have to do with enchanting, though?"

"It's a *binding*, it goes *both* ways. Remember when I bound myself to you?"

Edwin nodded, rubbing his forearm. "It is hard to forget. But I thought that was because you actually bound yourself to me while I was water, and then because of magical *stuff*, you could then keep the binding to me even afterward? What does that have to do with enchanting? Are you saying I might be able to give some sort of enchantment to myself?"

"Close enough. I doubt you could make *yourself* magical, your own inherent mana would fight it off once the Skill subsided. But you still *brought about* lasting magical change to both my pond and the Rhothos River with the Skill, yes?"

"You mean like how I took you from your pond and put you in the river?"

"Ya!"

"Wasn't that because of your ritual thing? And because that's your ability?"

"Ya! Ya, it was. Magic is complicated, much more than your science—"

Edwin scowled half-heartedly.

"—but the same idea still applies. If you bind yourself first to something magical, then hold the magic while you bind to something else, you might be able to directly transfer the magic from the one to the other."

"How do I do *that*?" he complained. "So far as I know it's only physical attributes that I copy."

"I don't know! Oh, don't look at me like that. It's your Skill, I don't know that much about it."

"Well, *you're* no help. 'Oh, Edwin. I'm a great and wise fey who can help you with your magic. But I dunno how to actually help you *do it*.' Honestly, at least Rillah's up-front with me when she doesn't know something," he teased.

"I've told you before, I'm no *magi*," she countered. "All *I* know is that I see some similarities between how *your* Skills work and some enchanting. I've never *actually* enchanted something; all I can do is follow a few rituals I know."

"Hmm," he mused. "It is a pity that you don't get along with Rillah, it would be interesting to see both of you working together with your musical magics. I won't ask you to try, it's just . . . well, a pity. How *do* your rituals work, anyway?"

"They're instinctive. It's like asking you how you *breathe*, or how your heart beats. You may know the answer, but that's because it's something you've tried to *learn*. I just never did . . ."

They stayed there for a while, talking about all sorts of things. It got tense at times, but they made it work. Edwin breathed a sigh of relief. He might not know how to reconcile the two women, but at least he didn't have to choose between them yet.

He had *two whole people* willing to put up with him, and he wasn't about to let that go any time soon.

It *itched*.

Of all the possible outcomes, Edwin had to admit, *itching* was not one he had anticipated. He'd followed Inion's advice, trying to Caress his Refined materials. For whatever reason, it didn't work, at least at first; he could copy the mundane aspects of the substance, but any mana stubbornly refused to be drawn or copied (whichever it was) into his hand.

Following a hunch and some trial and error, Edwin found that he needed to activate Overcharge at the same time as Fey's Caress if he wanted to absorb any magical properties. His Overcharge pauldron got a fair amount of use, keeping the magic confined to his arm. At this rate, he'd need to make more of the potion he used in that soon.

But, of course, absorbing magic itched. It was only a little bit while Overcharge was active, but if he let that Skill lapse while he maintained the magic, it was easily ten times worse.

It took a colossal amount of will for Edwin to actually take a good look at what was going on. So far as he could tell with his arcanoception, Overcharge drew mana from his Infusion, which these days began at his fingertips. If there was another source of mana available *right there*, they got mixed together.

Otherwise, Edwin's personal mana blocked anything foreign from entering. It was an interesting revelation, and he needed to see how flexible those limits were at some point.

In any case, his personal magic wasn't strong enough to force the foreign mana held in place by Fey's Caress *out* of his body, and that seemed to be where the itching came from.

Once he released Fey's Caress, though, it was definitely strong enough, and all the absorbed magic leaked out rapidly. If he combined that with Mana Infusion, he could even co-opt some of that mana and shove it into his target object.

It seemed perfect for what he wanted, honestly. Edwin looked at his shirt—as it turned out, washing out the fabric also got rid of most of the color—and mentally prepared himself with a curt nod and a deep breath.

Right hand into the bowl of water, check. Activate Overcharge and Fey's Caress on the water at the same time?

Check.

Mana flooded into his arm, but Edwin wasn't going to take any longer than he had to. The moment he felt Overcharge hit saturation, he pulled his hand-shaped water out of its bowl and laid it onto the fabric. It absorbed a bit of his hand, but it shouldn't do much more than leave his skin slightly sore and raw for a bit, like a rope burn.

Overcharge lasted just under thirty seconds, and if he timed his Infusion and cut off Caress at the same time the Skill ended, he had the best chance of making this work.

Check.

The collapsing Skills sought to offload mana wherever it could find, and fortunately there was another Skill right there, ready to channel as much mana as it was provided, albeit slowly. Happily, the action seemed to reduce the severity of Overcharge on his arm, as the mana wasn't left to wreak additional havoc on his biology.

Was that a potential way to reduce the Overcharge backlash in the future, maybe? Something to investigate.

That was irrelevant for right now, though; first he needed to see how the shirt fared.

Initially things looked promising. The shirt was definitely Infused, and even was the right temperature. It triggered his mana sense, too, reminiscent of a hot spring and . . . the sensation was already fading in favor of just becoming normal Infused fabric. What? Why was it fading? Mana Infusion pretty much didn't wear off so far as he knew, so why was this *fading*?

Within just a couple of hours, the inherent heat he felt from the shirt had almost entirely faded, despite the shirt still being magical. What was going on?

Repeating the experiment led to the same results, so it wasn't just a fluke. Hmm . . .

He'd come back to this later, he decided. Clearly, this was even more complicated than he'd initially thought.

Edwin's arguments with Inion kept floating back to the forefront of his mind, much to his annoyance. He'd definitely know if someone was using mental Skills on him, wouldn't he? He definitely would. Adaptive Defense would be tuned in that direction, surely? It was almost custom-tailored to trying to fight that kind of long-term insidious but harmful effect.

It would definitely work, so why was he even worrying about it? Inion was just jealous, he was sure. He could confront Rillah about it, maybe that would help. But . . . what would he *do*? Did he *want* to know if she was influencing him? He was happy the way things were.

Despite what he'd told Inion, Edwin *did* care whether or not his feelings for Rillah were genuine, or enforced on him by some external Skill. Of course, whether there was any practical difference was debatable, but if Rillah was using a Skill on him and saying she wasn't, that didn't bode well for her plans with him.

He was just being paranoid, though, he was sure. Rillah wouldn't . . . well, okay. He needed to remove what he felt that Rillah would or

wouldn't do from the situation. He didn't know her *that* well. Just looking at this objectively. He could do that.

Edwin set down his tools and pulled out a chair, dropping into it
and closing his eyes in thought. He dealt with unknown phenomena all
the time, this was no different.

> **Observation: He was very attached to Rillah, was willing to go
> out of his way to help her out, spent a lot of time with her, and
> generally trusted her.**
> **Hypothesis 1: Rillah was using some kind of mental compulsion
> Skill on him.**
> **Hypothesis 2: Edwin was just genuinely that lonely and starved
> for human contact.**
> **Evidence in favor of Hypothesis 1: Immediate fondness for
> Rillah, confirmed presence of one or more mind-affecting Skills
> in her repertoire, noted fixation on trying to help her, defending
> her against Inion, Inion's suspicions.**
> **Evidence against Hypothesis 1: No activation of Adaptive
> Defense, no obvious Skill effects active so far as Skillful
> Assessment can see.**
> **Evidence in favor of Hypothesis 2: He *did* really like Rillah. She
> was nice and willing to talk to him, willing to take him along
> on outings and intentionally make sure to include him in stuff.
> She made sure that he took breaks and took care of himself, and
> she stood up for his need of breaks. He was *keenly* interested in
> getting to know her better . . .**

In whatever form that may take, he admitted to himself, though he
was more looking for a *friend* rather than a romantic partner . . . not
that he'd really *decline* that either.

Other than with Inion, a part of him whispered, which he didn't
really have a good response for. Well, no, he did, and it was that just
physical intimacy wasn't what he *really* wanted and was what Inion was
most likely to teasingly ask him about. He'd also never taken her up on
her offers, so who even knew how serious they were?

Anyway, he was getting distracted.

Evidence against Hypothesis 2: Inordinate fixation on Rillah beyond what normal interest might dictate confirmed presence of one or more mind-affecting Skills in her repertoire and a known willingness to use them . . .

Edwin frowned. He couldn't really think of that much evidence against his second hypothesis, but that didn't mean it was true. Particularly for something like this, where it was the validity of his own perceptions that was in question. What was he really doing, anyway? He had found a person he liked, and now he was spending time with and trying to help out said friend as much as he was really capable. There wasn't anything *unnatural* about that . . . right?

Even *if* he was being excessive, that didn't mean Rillah was stepping out of line. Heck, maybe this was just how he normally would act in the stressed situation of trying to impress someone he liked; it wasn't like he had *that* much experience in that regard. At most, maybe Rillah was just trying to help him along with any Skills she might have, or maybe they were just passive or harmless. Heck, that was probably worthy of its own hypothesis come to think of it. So . . .

Hypothesis 3: Rillah has some level of passive/socially acceptable Skill that she is using and is encouraging him in his pursuit of companionship.
Evidence for Hypothesis 3: Matches with what she's doing with Yathal, encouraging him to be more confident in himself, all evidence with Hypothesis 2 applied, but with reasonable courses of action magnified.
Evidence against Hypothesis 3: Lefi and Inion most likely have similar Skills, and his feelings toward them were remarkably different from how he felt about Rillah. Inion would likely recognize that was what happened and be able to explain it.

Besides, how would he react in either situation? If it turned out that Rillah wasn't using any Skills on him, and his behavior was just the result of his own nature, then he'd obviously want to keep doing what he was doing. He didn't have any real reason to *stop* what he was doing;

her request—not that it even really was one—aligned with his personal research anyway, and it was as good a goal as any.

That also complicated things if she *was* influencing his mind with Skills. Some amount would definitely just be socially acceptable, he was sure . . . though he should probably *ask* that of Lefi, instead of just assuming they were considered all right, shouldn't he? Anyway, if she was influencing him in that way, it didn't *invalidate* his reasons for helping her out. He might ask her to not use them anymore, but what difference would it make? Well, he'd have to reevaluate his priorities when his mind was unaffected, that much was certain, but he didn't anticipate his logic really changing. And once again, it might signal whether or not she was truly benevolent, or just pretending.

I really, really *should just talk to her*, Edwin thought. *It would solve all of this so nicely.*

He really, really should. Communication was *absolutely* key to any kind of relationship. But he also didn't want to lose what he already had, however that might happen. Who knew how Rillah would take being confronted about social Skills? He definitely didn't want to say anything about his feelings, in case that might make her treat him differently.

Talking was the smart thing to do. He should do it. Right now, he should hop off his chair, head downstairs and find Rillah, then talk to her about his concerns and find out her side of the story.

He should do it.

It was exactly the right move in this situation.

. . .

It would resolve this entire situation.

It was the reasonable, emotionally mature thing to do.

. . .

. . . He couldn't do it. He just *couldn't*.

He couldn't take the chance of messing up one of his few friendships, and for what anyway? If she didn't like him and was just using him, she didn't exactly need a Skill for that, she would just have to ask. He liked *being helpful*, and hers was an intriguing problem besides. Learning how to enchant wouldn't hurt and would definitely be helpful for him going forward. It wasn't like she was asking him to do anything seriously inconvenient, nothing that he would later regret. Maybe he'd be able to ask her more about her social Skills and try and suss out some information that way.

Edwin sighed. To make himself feel better, more certain in his status as *not* just a mind-controlled puppet in the claws of someone only pretending to tolerate him, he wouldn't do any more enchanting work today. He'd . . .

Well, he'd figure something else out.

Stamina was a bit of a strange Attribute, Edwin noted. Well, all Attributes were strange in their own way, but Stamina was his current focus so its peculiarities were the most obvious. He could feel it swell and fade with every breath he took, sweeping through his body and carrying with it nutrients and carting off waste to be disposed of.

It honestly seemed like a bit of a magical enhancement or even *replacement* of his circulatory system, and Edwin idly wondered if with an insanely high level of Stamina his blood might be almost entirely redundant. As he studied it, though, it also just made everything he did . . . easier. It was subtle, definitely, but once he spotted it, it was obvious and made a lot of sense. After all, Stamina seemed to increase his physical energy, and while some of that could be explained away by nutrient transportation, there was still a finite amount of energy that Edwin had available in his body at any given time.

However, Stamina largely seemed to bypass that, and once Edwin went looking, he noted that the Attribute helped with *all* motion in his body. His muscles were saturated with Stamina, and every time he contracted them, it served to make the action smoother and easier. It didn't make him any *better*, it just made him tire out slower and recover faster. Unlike Health, it didn't seem to be exhausted per se (or if it was, it was incredibly minute), he was just constrained by his normal human limits.

Which was *stupid*. He had magic! He had superhuman resilience and a ton of different supernatural Skills! He wanted to leap tall buildings in a . . . well, okay, he could do that. But not because of Stamina! He was clearly missing *something* with his Stamina Manipulation Skill, because all he'd figured out how to do was move around some of the Attribute, and while he thought it was likely that his efforts were making things easier, whatever benefits it was providing were minuscule. He most certainly wasn't doing anything close to what he could do with mana.

. . . Whatever.

He'd figure it out eventually, and for now he was just going to keep poking around the Skill and leveling it. And so he sat, not *quite* meditating as he tried to grab on to his Stamina. If his Mana Manipulation was like trying to fill a bathtub with a spoon, this felt like picking up sand wearing oven mitts—the dexterity just wasn't there. So he tried to push instead of pull. Pushing into one arm, then the other. To his legs, into his lungs. Each time he did so, there was perhaps the *slightest* benefit to his motions, but so slight they might well have just been a placebo.

Eventually he settled into a bit of a rhythm. Since the Attribute already pulsed with his breaths, Edwin settled more deeply into a breathing routine and just tried to . . . enhance what was already there.

With every breath out, he pushed Stamina into his limbs. Every time he breathed in, he pushed it back to his torso and head. In, and out. In, and out. At some point, he tried moving his mana in unison, just to see if anything would happen.

There wasn't any obvious change in efficacy, no Path, no new Skill offered, no sparkling lights, but it felt right, so he kept doing it while he mused. Health, Mana, and Stamina were the normal "resources" in games and the like, sure, but why would they be *here*? Alongside Perception, Dexterity, Speed . . . what was the common thread, why were they all Attributes? What made Attributes different *from* Skills anyway? It wasn't like there weren't passive Skills, and heck, Edwin's Walking functioned in a way *really* similar to how Stamina reinforced his entire body. There clearly was something going on there, but what? It also really made him question how much Stamina normal people had, and how unlocking an Attribute influenced things.

Well, Mana, Stamina, and Health all gave Edwin what felt like pools of energy. Magical, Physical, and . . . Life? Life force. Hmm. He was starting to understand why the alchemists of Panastalis developed a humorlike model of the body, that's what those Attributes more or less *were*, weren't they?

He'd been thinking of Mana as the overtly supernatural of the three, because what it did had *no* analogue to how things "should" work, but that was flatly false. Here, he'd encountered creatures that used magic just as they might use their physical bodies to defend themselves or hunt. Mana was *undoubtedly* a fundamental part of the world—and he really needed to stop thinking about how things "should" work because that was just incorrect. But maybe he should look at the other Attributes like that as well? He could do supernatural things with Mana but not Stamina. Was he unintentionally constraining himself? How did all this fit in with it seeming like everyone had some amount of Health and Stamina at least?

He breathed out, his Stamina and Mana flowing to his extremities, then back in, and the Attributes ebbed back to his lungs and intermingling with the fresh air.

Was that the secret? "There is no spoon, only your imagination is holding you back?" Could he do all kinds of crazy superhuman stunts with Stamina, make his own magelike Skills? He didn't know he *couldn't*, after all. Why shouldn't he be able to fly with Stamina, phase through solid objects? It might be crazily complicated, but the System could help him out there surely. All he needed was the tools.

Edwin waited with bated breath for a Skill or Path unlock, but nothing showed up. No easy answers here, it would seem.

Well, that was no matter.

He'd just figure it out himself.

CHAPTER 13

Out of the Way

While his failures in enchanting his shirt had definitely pushed off that project slightly in favor of his other training and practice, it was ultimately too interesting of a goal, too fascinating to truly put aside completely.

Edwin had eventually figured that perhaps he was trying to take on too large of a project at once. Cloth and wheatspin were fairly complex, very inhomogeneous materials already awash with Skills and who knew what else. There were just way too many variables at play to give any kind of meaningful results.

So he was simplifying. He knew he could Infuse rocks, he did it all the time. While water was still the only substance he could meaningfully induce any amount of permanent magical change in with just filtered Infusions, his Alchemy Skill was telling him that it was decidedly possible with other things, he just needed to, well, figure it out. If he could figure out how to change the property of a pebble, he could then extrapolate into a shirt . . . hopefully. That was the idea, but it was proving difficult.

Failure was important. You could frequently learn *way* more from something that you failed on than something you succeeded with. Failure frequently led to the biggest innovations in human history.

That was what he was trying to tell himself anyway.

Edwin glowered at his latest failure to Caress magic into a rock. It felt like, well, like trying to shove water into a rock without increasing the size of the rock. Unlike most of his Infusions, it felt disconnected from his *actual* Mana Infusion Skill. Maybe because this was more along the lines of proper Alchemy Essentia, changing the fundamental nature of his materials? If his normal Mana Infusion was like dissolving solvents into water, his current efforts were more akin to heating up or cooling the water, maybe? Or perhaps more just changing the solvent. Though that didn't quite work *either*, hmm.

He was also having to revise his theory for why he couldn't Infuse his Skills like Basic Thermokinesis and Flight to them already being Infused as part of their basic state of being. It made sense; he knew that improving his mana throughput helped with his Flight range, so perhaps all his fundamental magical Skills could benefit his nonfundamental ones? A bit like how Purify worked with Fresh Air.

As for why he *needed* to revise his theory in the first place, it was because he came across yet another instance of breaking his apparent "can't use the same Skill twice simultaneously" limitation. Namely, he figured out how he could *Refine* two things at the same time.

It was all thanks to his magic practice. Not only could he get his initial Refined mana prepared *way* faster and easier by imagining it as a distillation process, he could now keep a hold on two separate mana beads simultaneously. He had to distill them separately, sure, but that was barely even a challenge. It all added together to Edwin feeling fairly confident in his ability to selectively Refine an aspect of a given object to what he wanted.

He was even able to figure out what was up with his Refined heated water! He was essentially Refining its temperature, not in such a way that it increased its heat, but more just made its heat capacity infinite. While he could still influence the temperature of un-Refined heated water—especially increasing the temperature to boil it off—nothing in his toolkit was able to so much as budge Refined heated water from its natural temperature of 61.3 Celsius. Basic Thermokinesis, burying it in snow, and a blazing fire all failed.

The only things that *did* work were Rillah bringing a significant amount of her ice magic to bear and diluting the Refined liquid in a bunch of water. Edwin wasn't sure if the latter *really* counted, though, because boiling off all the water it had been mixed into allowed him to recover almost all the Refined heated water from the bottom of his bowl, still at 61.3 degrees.

He couldn't help but grin. He'd made something that was *flatly* impossible and an inherently magical substance. Sure, he'd done that sort of thing before with his fulgurite and abysite glasses, but it felt different knowing he could make more pretty much whenever he wanted. Firevine was tricky to grow, sure, but he had an absolutely *massive* stockpile of its sap and wood so he wasn't too worried about running out.

It also gave him something of an idea. He'd been having no luck just shoving magic in, it kept leaking out, but what if he took *out* stuff to make space for what he was trying to add? It made sense in the way that only a semifrazzled brain could properly imagine, but it fit vaguely the sorts of nonsense he would expect from magic. It was a bit like trying to scrawl a modification for lab procedure over the former instructions. While both sets were present, whatever metaphysical trait-reader was responsible for translating magical aspects into physical measurements would get confused and go with what looked like the default. Just like how trying to write in a lab book with pencil wouldn't get many people to follow different procedures.

However, if you *erased* the original instructions and then wrote *replacement* text, then they'd be way more likely to actually follow instructions! In theory. Assuming . . . anyway, that wasn't relevant.

Best of all, he already had a substance that was essentially Refined temperature. Now all he needed to do was figure out what little magical part of a rock told it it was supposed to be room temperature, rip it out, and replace it with something else!

Of course, rocks didn't have an inherent temperature. With some poking and prodding with Refining Edwin *had* been able to find something that was perhaps more accurately described as magical heat capacity. Some experimentation had shown that a Refinement of it had *seriously* increased how long it took him to heat up the remaining sand with Basic Thermokinesis, and even Infused Firestarting needed a fair bit of work before it would heat up the former stone.

It didn't seem to meaningfully impact *mundane* heat capacity, but Edwin's tools to measure that were decidedly limited, and he needed to focus anyway! He had a task, he was sticking to it.

He had still been having trouble with everything he Refined turning to dust (unless it was "inherently" a liquid, a distinction Edwin hadn't been able to fully nail down yet), but a few days . . . weeks . . . of practice had solved that, too.

He'd just needed to be way more selective with his targets. Refining inherently tried to grab all the magical traits of his target and render them down into *just* whatever he was selecting for, which included structure.

Edwin wasn't entirely sure how changing a magical Attribute of a substance messed with its physical makeup, but that was *another* question for later. He *could* actually Refine "structure," in which case he was left with a sort of strange, crumbly clay as strength and toughness were reduced that nonetheless looked *more* like the original rock.

It took a long, long time to figure out how he could target specific aspects for *removal* instead of *enhancement*, but he managed it in the end by comparing his mana to *aerogel*, of all things.

"Aerogel?" Lefi, unsurprisingly, hadn't heard of the stuff and it was kind of important for Edwin's alchemy "lessons" with the guy, so he found himself in a bit of an impromptu lecture.

"Okay, so do you know what gelatin is?"

"Gelatin? Bone pudding?"

"Uh . . . probably. I think you get it from bone, anyway. So, gelatin is this strange sort of semisolid substance, yeah? Where it's not exactly liquid but it's also really jiggly and not a rigid solid. So that's a colloid, a suspension of one type of matter in another. In this case, it's a bunch of liquid, namely water, in a sort of spongelike solid structure.

"So, somewhere along the line people obviously started wondering about what would happen if you somehow took the water *out*. Now, if you are familiar with gelatin—bone pudding, whatever—you know that you can't just boil the water out, it just makes the structure collapse and get all over the place . . . basically, it ruins the structure. Well, that's only true under normal conditions. There's this thing called an autoclave, and that's basically what this is meant to be." Edwin indicated a sealed apparatite box connected to his tubing.

"So an autoclave is pretty much an oven that can go up to *really* high temperatures and is completely sealed, usually at really high pressures. Remember what I was saying about pressure and temperature influencing a substance's boiling point?"

"Aha! I see. So you— How does such a thing work?"

"Well, an autoclave can heat up the gelatin until the water in the structure is both liquid *and* gas at the same time, more or less. It's complicated, but that doesn't really matter right now. What matters is that an autoclave can, in the right circumstances, take the water out of gelatin and leave behind just the sort of spongy, dry framework around it. There's actually a *bunch* of substances like that, but aerogel is what you get if you make silicon gel—think gelatin but made with different stuff—and then take out all the liquid. That just leaves this *really* light stuff that's incredibly cool, superb at insulation, all that sort of thing."

"I see." Lefi didn't sound very confident.

"Anyway, the important thing is that I was able to picture the structural mana of the rock as gelatin, with the kind of mana I want to remove as the water. Then . . ."

It *had* taken quite a bit of time, but Edwin had been able to make a sort-of autoclave for mana, submerging the pebble in a huge pile of Refined dust of whatever it was he wanted to remove and then turning up the external forces and leaning on Alchemical Dismantling until the stone and its bed lost cohesion, with the magical structure of the rock getting really loose and allowing the chosen property to mix freely with the powder it sat in.

Once it was in that state, all he needed to do was remove the pebble from its dust bed—if he didn't, the end result absorbed additional Refined powder and ended up strengthened instead—which was still easier said than done. Introducing any other mana to the situation destabilized it all and created some very *weird* results, and touching it with his bare fingers was *completely* out of the question. Anything *without* mana was flooded with active autoclave-like mana and usually burned to a crisp.

In the end, Edwin devised a setup where the pebble sat directly atop a sieve in a bowl, then was buried in Refined dust. When it was time to remove the dust, he just lowered the bowl and allowed the powder to fall through the holes in his mesh, draining away. A few small shakes later, and the pebble was left almost completely free of that particular magical aspect.

He could even reuse the dust! If anything, each practice run he did *increased* the amount he had unless he did something wrong, but it was utterly minuscule.

In any case, removing the— He needed a word for it. Trait, maybe? Trait worked. Once he removed the heat capacity trait from the stone— which resulted in an oddly temperature-neutral substance, though only when magic was involved—he *thought* it would be easy to add in the heated water's temperature trait.

It decidedly was *not*. By removing the stone from his "mana auto-clave," it settled into its new form and once again became impervious to trait manipulation. This time, though, it didn't have any way for Edwin to leverage open the trait he wanted to edit.

It was a bit like trying to swap two blocks from the bottom of a block tower. Removing a foundational block would make the entire thing at the very least close up, at most make the entire thing collapse. Unless of course, there was some kind of secondary support holding up the tower to leave space for the replacement when it was added.

. . . or something like that, anyway.

Edwin could do some *seriously* awesome potential stuff with that. Unfortunately, the coolest ones—like magical transparency from mana-cast glass or mana absorption from molai—interfered with *his* magic enough that he couldn't actually make the autoclave work. Anything else was hampered by the fact his current trait manipulation *only* affected magical properties . . . except for when it didn't, like when he removed strength and his pebble crumbled at the slightest touch. He hoped that he could further explore or outright overcome that limitation eventu-ally, but well, one thing at a time. He *always* had things to explore, and not enough time in his entire life to explore it all.

He made a mental note to ask Lefi about immortality Skills. The guy looked *sixteen* but was apparently closer to a hundred, so he was bound to have one.

In any case, if Edwin wanted to transfer properties, he'd need to fig-ure out how to do it all in one step. The problem was, to get his mana autoclave—his manaclave?—to work properly, he had to have it be an entirely closed system. Even a simple apparatite stick, poking around to move the pebble, interrupted the process. Further complicating the whole mess was that until the autoclave seal was broken, the trait *remained*. But breaking the seal by dropping the powder away also would resolidify its traits. He couldn't even do some clever trick with piling powders together thanks to the second trait-material being *liquid*.

In other words, he needed to figure out some way to directly replace one type of mana with another type of mana. In particular, he needed something for when he couldn't mix the two substances, couldn't move his pebble around, and all in less than a fraction of a second.

It seemed like an impossible problem.

Edwin couldn't help but grin.

This was *perfect*.

Edwin sat on the ground, giving his legs a break after completing Lefi's latest obstacle course, trying (and failing—seriously, would it kill the System to give him a Skill that was easy to use? Okay, other than almost all his Skills come to think of it) to use Stamina Manipulation to fight against the soreness in his legs.

"So, Lefi," he started, getting the man's attention, "how do immortality Skills work? I talked with Rizzali—my Registrar—about them at one point, but I want to get your opinion on them. I figure you'd know a lot about that sort of thing? I'm guessing you have one, from what I've heard."

"You would be correct! I do indeed know much about those Skills. I know much about all Skills, after all."

"Yeah . . . yeah. Anyway, what sorts of things come about from the Skills? Rizzali said that just the basic Immortality was a trap . . . no advancement, or something?"

"Ah, of course! Immortality is indeed the most classic immortality Skill, hence the name, but it is far from optimal for most."

Edwin patiently waited for Lefi to finish his grandstanding.

"You see, Immortality has a very simple effect and method of leveling: every level you possess in it extends your death by old age for a single year, and it levels at the same rate! It does not prevent you from aging, however, and of course if you are no longer capable of leveling it, such as if it evolves, you lose its protections."

"Wait, so you'd just get really old from it, too? What if you were young when you got it, would you just sort of waste the extra levels? And why does evolving it make it worse? Couldn't you get something that would give you much the same benefits, just better because it was evolved or whatever?"

"It adds years upon your life, you understand. If you possessed sixty years of life ahead of you when you obtained the Skill, you would continue to have sixty years upon its evolution. As for evolving into a superior form, it is certainly possible," he agreed. "And some of the better immortality Skills can be obtained in such a manner. However, it is usually also possible to gain said Skills *without* taking the apparently useless Immortality Skill. After all, if you find yourself with a stronger form of immorality later, the original Skill no longer provides you with much in the way of benefit, you see?"

"So it still makes you get really old and is kind of pointless once you get a better Skill? I guess it makes sense why that would be considered inoptimal. But still, *immortality*. Couldn't you, I don't know, get a Skill that keeps you young without making you immortal?"

"Youthful Appearance and Youthful Vigor are what you are thinking of, and they can be obtained via a number of appearance-based and physical Skills, respectively."

"But they still aren't the best?" Edwin guessed.

"Indeed not. Age Resistance is the best Skill for retaining your youth, and although it provides not true immortality, it most certainly *can* provide a longer life than most would feasibly require."

"Slows down but never stops?"

"Indeed."

"Well, all right, then. So Immortality makes you age but not die, and Age Resistance slows down your aging. Can you combine them?"

"Such an accomplishment would indeed be quite the feat and would leave one largely untouched by the passage of ages."

"But not perfectly, and nobody's accomplished it?"

"Edwin, you must understand that most of these Skills have but one or two recorded holders. There is much we do not know of them.

I have never met the individual who has earned both Immortality and Age Resistance, but your speculation is not without merit."

"That's fair, I suppose. Do you think that I could get Age Resistance?"

"Your Adaptive Defense is a promising candidate for such a Skill, yes, though I would advise you not become too invested in the idea as of yet. You must understand that immortality Skills are very rare, particularly before Tier 5."

"But you got one at Tier 2?"

Lefi didn't respond.

Edwin sighed. "Well, what about an elixir of life, or waters of youth, or something? It's a classic pursuit of alchemy, is there anything like that?"

"I have never heard of such a thing existing, though I am certain one could. Indeed, it is not impossible you would create such a potion or be granted a Skill with such an effect. However, be aware that no immortality—save perhaps that of Emperor Xares himself—is perfect."

"Is that *known*, or just speculation?"

"Nothing with the System is known save that it can do all."

"In other words—" he started.

"Further testing required?" Lefi cut in, beaming with a mischievous smile.

"Oy! That's my line!"

Edwin's stomach was tied in knots. It wasn't technically a tricky subject but it was undeniably one that *could* go wrong, particularly if he wasn't careful. But he'd been on a bit of a roll with getting conversations out of the way, hopefully that momentum would keep him going?

"So . . . Your fire Skills? I remember noting them during our snow day, and I'm still curious. Why was there a *mental* Skill involved in that?"

Rillah chuckled. "Aw, is that all? Why the serious face then?"

Edwin shrugged and tried to school his expression into a more neutral configuration, to unknown success. "Just, other stuff," he half-heartedly responded. "Nothing to worry about."

"If you say so," she kidded. "So what didya wanna talk about?" She flopped over on her chair, stretching in a way that *was* rather appealing . . .

Focus, Edwin. That's not why you're here.

"Your fire Skill?" he asked incredulously. "Like, I literally just said as, ah, you meant beyond that. So talk to me, I don't know the right questions to ask."

"Paths, too, or just the Skills?"

"I'll record the Paths later, I think," Edwin decided. "When I'm trying to fill out the Almanac entries on them."

"Playing Registrar, are we now?"

"I mean, there's no real reason *not* to. I've got a Skill that works really well for that sort of thing, after all. And more data is never a bad thing. Anyway, what do you have?"

"Well, my basic fire Skill was Spark." Rillah pulled up a flame in her hand. "That helped me conjure fire really easily.

"Then that went to Dancing Flame." A wave of her hand directed the flame away from her hand, flickering merrily as it flew around her as she summoned another over her palm. "Which let me move my flames around as well as conjure more. Fire Snake turned it into a proper attack, so I can make all these fiery ropes and stuff, which deal more direct damage.

"But my *favorite* is my newest. Mesmeric Flare." A mental Skill wrapped around the fires as they stretched out with use of Fire Snake, and the colors of the flame began to deepen and shimmer, scintillating and luminescent. It demanded attention, and Edwin could scarcely fight it as the room grew more and more filled with the beautiful flames . . .

Adaptive Defense poked his attention, and the prompt was enough to get him to break free of the fascination.

"That's *potent*," he remarked. "I've been pretty good at resisting mental Skills in the past, but that one is *tricky*. Very beautiful though."

"It is, isn't it?" she agreed. "It definitely helps, you know? Mental Skills always work better when they just reinforce what you already want to do."

Edwin mutely nodded, looking at the curtains of fire before him. It looked almost like the aurora borealis, just right in front of him and somehow even *more* spectacular. "I suppose it's easy to get distracted by something so eye-catching, isn't it?"

"Yep! Even being immune to my own Skill's fascination doesn't keep me from loving to stare at the colors. It's definitely my best mental Skill."

Here's the perfect opportunity! Edwin mentally screamed. *I can bring up whether she's trying to charm me as just a part of the conversation. It wouldn't even be awkward!*

But do I want to know? another part of him questioned. *I don't want to lose a potential . . . friend.*

Of course I do! Knowledge, knowledge, knowledge! Ask her already!

"Your most potent? What else do you have, then?"

"Why, *Edwin*. You're being so *forward* today."

"Oh, come on," he said. "I thought you said we were past all that nonsense."

"I like it," she finished with finality.

"Oh. Yeah?" Edwin unsteadily answered. "Um, what do you have then?"

She glanced around, pretending to be furtive. "Well, other than Mesmeric Flare, the direct charm Skills I have are—"

"Direct charm Skills?" Edwin asked, then shook his head. "Wait, sorry. Continue."

"Well, Idyllic Form, among others, isn't exactly a charm Skill, but it certainly *helps* the others. Those would be, oh, Charm, Good Impression, Calming Touch, and Allure." She laughed slightly. "Turns out, the Charm Skill gives charmlike evolutions. Then I have, oh, let's see, Inspiring Speech, Memorable Night, Worthy of Notice, and Mesmeric Flare."

"Is that a lot?" Edwin asked. "It seems like a lot."

"Oh, well, it depends on who you ask. Most nobles have at least two base charm Skills, and I have one. Of course, most people have *no* basic charm Skills unless they're a merchant or performer, who have *lots*. Of course, I've definitely been *called* a bard before and it's not entirely inaccurate!" She laughed.

"But all your others?"

"Are the latest evolutions of other Skills."

"What does Allure do?" he asked.

"Why, Edwin!"

He sighed. "Are you trying to inure me to your shocked and-or scandalized reaction by using it so much or something?"

She didn't respond, and Edwin blinked. "Wait, *are* you?"

"Here, are you ready for Allure? I don't use it a lot of the time, so prepare yourself."

"Um, when you ask it like that, I'm not . . ."

Edwin trailed off as his brain was fully preoccupied with looking at Rillah. She was *gorgeous*. Gentle eyes, a slender but athletic frame, unblemished and smooth skin, clothing that accentuated her body without directly being immodest. Luxurious and immaculate hair, tied back in a way that only served to show she needed no intricate work to be the absolutely most beautiful woman Edwin had ever seen. He tried to speak, to say something about it, something about feelings, anything for her, but his tongue refused to respond. He tried to get up, to reach out and stroke her arm, but he couldn't do *anything*, his entire being affixed to simply staring at her, taking in the sights as much as he possibly could . . .

The Skill switched off.

"Gah!" It felt like his brain was plunged into freezing water, and his thoughts short-circuited once more, this time in the opposite direction, as a million different considerations rushed into his head, pulling him every which way. How Rillah looked wasn't *exactly* the last thing on his mind, but it certainly jumped back to a normal level of priority.

"That was unpleasant," Edwin admitted once he had his internal monologue in order, rubbing his temples. "And way stronger than I was expecting."

"Unpleasant? That's new," she asked. "Why?"

"Um, it's . . ."

Edwin's brain was still somewhat scattered, but he tried to pull his thoughts together to respond. "I *very* rarely am ever focused on only a single thing at a time, and I've never had all my brain forcibly shunted to a single train of thought. Then just sort of in general, it's kind of awkward . . ." he trailed off. "Yeah. Anyway, that was really strong. Normally I can distract myself, but that was . . . wow."

He shook his head, getting it mostly clear. "What made it so strong, do you think? I've been able to resist mental Skills before."

"What were they like?"

"Well, I had to deal with an order I was compulsively forced to obey, avoid responding to someone commanding me to talk, and . . . I think Inion did something at some point."

"Ah, so mostly compulsions?"

"I guess so? Oh, you think it has to do with your Skills being more around attention than actual commands? I could see it"—he rubbed his forehead—"though I should probably try to train myself to break out of it. But also, you said you don't use it much. How's it so strong if you never use it?"

"Well, it's still improved by my other Skills and my Charisma," she explained. "And because we're sitting here where it's just you and me, this is the best-case scenario for the Skill's use."

"You know, I idly tried to get a social Skill some time ago. Never pushed *that* hard, but nothing ever came of it."

"Lotsa people don't, and they do just fine. You could definitely stand to get a bargaining Skill, though." She winked at him.

Edwin rolled his eyes. "Never had any luck, unfortunately."

"Anyway, my turn! I wanna ask some questions about your Skills!"

"I still have . . . eh, I'll ask them later. Sure, ask away."

"So your cooking Skill, what's it like?"

"Arcadian Elixir? Well, it's . . ."

It had been a while since he'd been out and about, Edwin realized, and it had been a good *month* since his last proper day off in the snowball fight. He knew the reasons *why* he didn't like leaving the tower, but it would still be good for him.

It had snowed last night, and the glistening white was a marvel to behold, but he couldn't help but wonder what sorts of things were out in the city. Stretching his legs a bit would be good for him, he decided. He also should make sure he didn't take too much money—he didn't want to invite thieves—but he definitely *should* take at least a smoke bomb and a few fireball pellets.

Oh, and he should let Inion know that he'd be out and about. Just in case something happened.

Day on the town, here he came.

CHAPTER 14

A Day Off the Town

The streets were surprisingly clear, Edwin reflected, considering how much snow they'd been getting regularly. While the overcast sky ensured that a few snowflakes still were drifting to rest along the street, the textured stone itself was almost completely bare of snow that might serve as some kind of a hindrance. There weren't any obvious candidates for where all the snow might have gone, either. It definitely felt like Skill nonsense. Perhaps because this was a nicer district of the city, there was more regular road maintenance?

As he wandered around, it certainly *seemed* to be the case. As the streets became less massive stone blocks and more cobblestone, the piles of snow alongside the side of the road grew dramatically, to the point where some *houses* were almost completely buried in slightly dirty snow.

He even got to see one of the street cleaners! A human man dressed in relatively light and plain clothes held what looked like a combination of snow shovel and hoe, the blade perpendicular to the shaft.

To clear the street, the man set the blade next to the pile of snow on the road and then just *pushed*. Snow flew in every direction, mostly straight but much off to the sides, increasing the barriers by several inches at a minimum. Then, work done, he walked the hundred feet or so to where the snow had receded and carried on.

It was quite the sight to see, but Edwin didn't stick around for that long before moving on.

Humans, he noted, were largely bundled up as might be expected, wearing thick woolen jackets and scarves. Half of them wore wool mittens, and most wore some kind of hat as well, which made Edwin feel rather out of place in his standard traveling getup. He *had* gloves, sure, but they were decidedly work gloves and not *that* warm. His fingers weren't cold, anyway, and he had a small bottle of heated water if he *did* end up feeling cold at some point.

Fortunately, what did help him feel less out of place was that the avior he saw were wearing largely the same clothes they always did— namely, not much and usually either decidedly workmanlike or ostentatious with very little in the middle. He supposed it made sense if they had some kind of winter down and made a note to ask Lefi . . . and checking his note reminded him he *still* hadn't figured out what made Bomb Throwing trigger or not.

Well, next time he needed a break from his trait transference problem, he could work on that, he supposed.

"Oh, look, it's the *daywasr*'s toy!" a voice heckled.

Edwin looked up, seeing a young avior—a Treetop Hunter— perched on a nearby roof, but he shrugged and carried on. If he stopped every time he heard an insult, he'd spend more time responding to them than actually carrying on with his day. People didn't like him, that was hardly a surprise.

"Hey! I was talking to you!"

"You were?" Edwin shot back. "I'm sorry, you clearly have the wrong person."

A flap of his wings brought the avior face-to-face with Edwin, razor-sharp beak inches from his nose. The intimidation factor was definitely lessened by the fact he was at least a head and a half shorter, though. His feather was still very strong, poking into Edwin's chest just hard enough to be uncomfortable.

"I don't think I do now. I've watched you go in and out of that tower thinkin' like you own the place?"

It was kind of hilarious how the kid thought he was intimidating, like Edwin didn't *live* with three of possibly the strongest individuals in the city and regularly trained with all of them.

"You may want to work on your Mind Reading Skill," Edwin casually countered. "I think it's being influenced by something else . . . Personal Fantasy, maybe?"

"What?" The boy seemed confused.

"Look"—Edwin put on a false smile and sounded "reassuring" as he lightly rested his hand on the avior's shoulder—"I'm sure that the local Registrar might be able to help you out if you just asked. I'm sure they knew what they were doing when they assigned you some sort of delusion-based Skill. Or did you get that on your own?"

"You *Adventurer*—" the boy started, trying to shrug Edwin's hand away, but he held firm, tightly gripping the base of the wing even as pressure started to build.

"Correct. Now, get out of my face and leave me alone."

"I won't stand to be bossed around by *scum* like you."

"Oh, is there anything else you wanted to talk about? I'll give you, oh, how about a minute, before you leave?"

"Do you seriously think you have any level of control over *my* actions? You're *scum*, worthless to your communities and a bane upon the Empire and everything it stands for. You're disgraceful, and your little bitch in the tower is, too, you know that? Soon the tower's *rightful* owners will come around and then we'll see how smug you are . . ."

There didn't seem to be any useful information present, so Edwin tuned out the annoying voice and concentrated on his magic instead. Could he maybe make this go any faster, somehow? It didn't seem like the little angry ball of feathers noticed Edwin's ever-tightening grip, but that worked out fine for him.

Numeracy buzzed, letting Edwin know how long had passed.

"Minute's up. Bye."

"You still think you can—"

"It wasn't a request." Edwin released his grip on the Hunter and Unbound Tether simultaneously, the pent-up energy from the charged Skill sending the avior absolutely *flying*. He didn't rag doll too much, and once Edwin stopped pushing him, the arrogant teen did manage to catch himself and swooped away on stiff wings.

Edwin looked around the street. It hadn't been *busy* exactly, but now it was mostly deserted. Nobody had wanted to stick around, apparently. Ah well. He would check out the docks. Yeah. He'd flown *over* them a bunch of times, but it was almost always *way* above them. The one time he'd actually been *there*, he'd been distracted by Inion, and he was curious what the lifeblood of the city was really like.

As he walked, he enjoyed marveling at the city's sights. The snowbanks were everywhere, and his Skills let him see much more than normal. Skillful Assessment showed the nigh-invisible forms of alley cats stalking across the snow, Numeracy informed him of a bank of snow that was about to collapse—he danced out of the way before it could strike him—and Basic Mana Sense lit up here and there, picking up on hints of icy wind mana from the tower carried with the breeze.

Winter really was beautiful, he reflected. Without the cold bothering him, without his nose, ears, and fingers freezing, he could properly enjoy the majesty of undisturbed snowdrifts, and the quaint novelty of seeing a proper pseudomedieval city blanketed in white.

The docks were closed for the season, and while practically deserted by comparison, they were still rather busy. The sounds of a smithy echoed through the streets along with the distant barking of a dog, a hint of fresh bread was carried on the breeze, and the crowds of people scarcely looked up as they bustled about their day.

There were, of course, the frequent displays of superhuman prowess—the man carrying a crate bigger than he was like it weighed nothing, the crier making his voice heard about . . . something to do with boats, it didn't matter to Edwin, in a way that sounded like he was standing directly in front of every single person, and a halfling woman casually leaping from a second-story *door* to the streets below.

Along this street, it was clear that a significant amount of effort was put into making it look presentable, similar to the higher-Class neighborhoods like where the tower was located. However, even just looking down the alleyways unveiled where the quality of housing diminished, the walls damaged; paint chipped and peeling, wood cracked and splintered.

Meanwhile, the river itself was mostly frozen over. It wasn't *completely*—water was still flowing near the center—but the docks themselves were encased in ice. While most of the boats that otherwise would be fishing or carrying goods had either left the city for the season or had been pulled out of the water, a few ships still remained.

One, Edwin noted with interest, was surrounded by a bit of unfrozen water and was *inundated* with Skills of all forms. He wandered over that way to take a closer look at the vessel, noting an unusual lack of sails. Though perhaps they had just been taken in for the season? In all respects, the boat was crafted masterfully without so much as a single splinter out of place. Although he didn't know *exactly* how to tell, it seemed to exude understated competence from the serpent-headed bow to the dark, straight-grained wood of its body.

That was without even getting into the *Skills* inundating every inch of the craft. Now that he was looking, Edwin definitely saw several similar Skills imbuing the other boats he could see, but this one seemed to have them *all*. From the netlike weaving of Efficient Space to something reminiscent of Basic Thermokinesis, and another that was an inverted Firestarting? Ah, probably a fire-suppressing Skill. Very neat.

After a few minutes of admiring the boat's Skills, Edwin lost interest and wandered off downstream. While subtle alongside the waterfront, it was clear that this was much more of the *working* end of the port. Nets and ropes smelling strongly of fish cluttered the local scents just as surely as the stone walkway, weather-worn buildings creaked underneath the winter winds and groaned under their snowy burden.

There were still some ships in the water, but they definitely seemed to be on the rattier end of things. Some even looked as though it was only the river's thick layer of ice that was keeping them afloat, but most had very few Skills working on them. It was just *neglected*.

The people, too, matched the idea. Clothing was less fine, the people looked more haggard. A figure lay on the ground in an alleyway he passed, the Fairweather Fisher still *alive* but perhaps for not much longer.

A part of Edwin said he should try to help these people, but it was solidly vetoed. Getting involved in other people's problems was very much *not* what he wanted to do. While he could sympathize somewhat with their plight, it also wasn't his problem. He didn't *not* care, but he also couldn't *actually* care, not if he wanted to remain sane and actually able to take care of *himself.*

There didn't seem to be much more of interest—or at least the *right* kind of interesting—farther downstream, so Edwin decided to backtrack before he either got mugged or pulled into some pointless hassle.

Without the distractions of the city to slow him down on his return trip, Edwin skimmed just off the ground with Flight, only really paying any attention to obstacles in his path. Thus, it took only a few minutes before he'd fully made it back to where he started.

He didn't *really* feel like heading back to the tower quite yet, and he was kind of curious as to whether upstream the buildings and boats would be nicer. Besides, he had—and *still* had, he'd checked after leaving the semislums—his smoke bombs and a few fireballs; he'd be fine.

It definitely became apparent that everything became nicer as he explored this half of the waterfront, more and more large buildings elegantly sculpted into veritable works of art. There were no nets and ropes cluttering *these* streets, no. In their place were elegantly crafted individual piers and works of art, many more guards and far fewer people. Oh, there still *were* people, of course, but not as many as had previously been around.

More boats were still in the river up here, almost all of them with Skills similar to the ones he'd seen downstream that kept the water around them at an above-freezing temperature, but this time they were *significantly* gaudier.

Fancy carvings and gildings, luxurious paints, mental Skills—his practice with Rillah's Mesmeric Flare was paying off it would seem, and while he was still hopeless against *her*, the boats weren't nearly so powerful a distraction—and even hints of *magic.* There might not have been very many, but sheer presence and size more than accounted for that difference. One even looked to be made of a single stone, some massive boulder shaped and quarried into the form of a luxury barge.

Some had workers, too. One boat had a woodcarver actively detailing the side; others had a few humans and halflings running around with fine materials, though with almost no sounds of construction in the area, it was impossible to tell what they were doing. "Outlaws and troublemakers"—the voice resonated from the air behind and above Edwin, and he turned around to see an avior with steel-gray feathers descend to the street below him—"do not belong here, and yet you are both and remain."

Sentinel of the Distant Flow

Edwin looked around. "I'm not? Well, guess I'll head back then." He shrugged. "You might want to put up a sign."

He held back a wince. That sounded way worse than he had been hoping for, and the Sentinel clearly agreed. In the blink of an eye, Edwin found himself slammed against the closest wall, held a few inches off the ground by the avior's wing.

"It dares mock me?"

"Honestly . . ." Edwin tried to get loose, fighting back his rising panic. Okay, he had a smoke bomb within reach of his left hand, and he could also tether himself a fireball and detonate that. He hadn't tested what it would do to him point-blank but he was at . . . mostly full Health, after that wall slam, and he'd probably be fine. "I have no clue who you are. I don't think we've ever met."

"Know your betters."

Edwin felt himself flying through the air, but many, *many* hours of practice helped him catch himself, and with a twist of Flight, he landed feetfirst on the ground and *not* on the river.

"You know, this really isn't helpful," Edwin pointed out. "Also, I'm pretty sure I should be calling the guards around now?"

"Scum will forever be unaided and your actions today have proven you to be such."

"Again, you keep saying these sorts of things but I don't actually know who *you* are, so . . ."

There was pressure at the front of his chest, and Edwin looked down to see a feather sticking out of it. That wasn't good, though he wasn't really bleeding? The attack definitely took a good chunk of Health, but he stayed tethered to the ground with Flight as he pulled the feather out and slipped it in his pocket.

"I am the only authority you need to concern yourself with, *Adventurer*. It is by my will you remain alive and—"

Edwin decided enough was enough and that he ought to take Lefi's advice to heart. He didn't stick around to hear the end of the avior's rant, instead breaking a smoke bomb. As the world around him turned *completely* white, he triggered Longstrider and stepped away, the world blurring into one mess of white.

"You go *nowhere*," the voice hissed, and Edwin felt his collar yanked back. Longstrider shattered around him, leaving him just on the edge of his cloud of smoke and right next to a *very cross* raptor.

Edwin's eyebrow raised. That was pretty impressive, and he definitely should probably start taking this seriously it would seem. Even *Lefi* didn't seem to be able to pull Edwin *out* of Longstrider, just move stuff in his way.

"What is it that you want?" Edwin sighed. "I'm in a good mood, you know? Or at least I was, and this is supposed to be my day off. Oh! Are you the dad of that one kid who was bothering me earlier or something?"

"Oh, the *Adventurer* says it has a day off. How amusing. As though its every day spent here isn't a worthless waste of perfectly good food while providing nothing in return. Quite the little leech, isn't it? Attacking *actual* citizens and then pretending it isn't gliding on broken wings."

"Okay, first off: I do a *lot* of actually useful stuff and am perfectly capable of paying my own way. But other than that . . . Sorry? Not for taking care of myself, mind you, the guy had it coming. But I'm sure that if you have problems with my existence I can ask Rillah for advice on being unobtrusive."

"Oh yes, *her*. I know all about your compatriot and her worthless quackery. Though at least *she* knows her place."

"Look, are you ever going to tell me who you are?" Edwin mentally evaluated what direction he would be best off to flee toward. He held a smoke bomb behind his back, ready to detonate it at a moment's notice and run off. "I'm still under the assumption you're just the dad of that hooligan who tried to harass me earlier. And you seriously need to step up your intimidation game, because this . . . yeah, it isn't doing much."

"I ought to throw you from this city and forbid your return. You and all your kind."

"Okay." Edwin shrugged. "I'm pretty sure Rillah would be *thrilled* to be allowed to go. Though maybe you should wait for spring? Not sure how far we'd get in this weather before we had to turn around for some reason."

"You refuse to take this seriously?"

Edwin leveled a flat glare. "Look, if you're just going to do all this empty posturing and bluster, no, I'm not going to take this any more seriously than you seem to. Like, you keep saying all these things which just . . . I can't really seem to understand how a real, breathing person could say it with a straight face. Start from the beginning, because I'm *pretty sure* that being an Adventurer still means I get the legal protections of a Citizen, and I see a couple of guards coming this way."

"They will not aid you against me."

Edwin's response spilled out in exasperation. "Look, you can say these sorts of vaguely ominous-sounding threats all you want, but the fact of the matter is that without knowing anything about who you are or what sorts of things you're trying to threaten me with, it's just *not effective* and makes you sound like you're just trying to mess with my head. Like, yes, that's a very neat trick, grabbing me midstride and all, but unless I have context for that, all it means is that you have some sort of fun Skill that I haven't seen before. Specific ultimatums, not this uncertain mess."

There was a moment where the avior seemed decidedly confused, and Edwin took it as a win. Then he opened his beak again. "Very well. I am Imperial Enforcer Finnas Eshrais Reffiel. You will face justice for your numerous crimes, and the guards will not prevent that from happening."

Well, at least Edwin knew he was dealing with now.

"See? Much better. You've established your credibility as a threat, giving me a . . . more concrete thing to look out for, and now I actually know what I'm dealing with." Edwin found himself surprisingly calm, and *definitely* more sarcastic than was probably healthy. He didn't *think* Lefi was empowering him at the moment . . . maybe.

"It's an improvement, but you still need to work a bit on the specificity. For example, what crimes? What would justice look like?" he asked. "After all, I did all your stuff. Paid the gate entry fee—at the *merchant's* rate, I'll have you know—have been staying pretty much out of everyone's way, and I've even been helping take care of the weather tower or whatever you call it."

Edwin paused to think. "*Is* this *actually* about the little kid who kept heckling me?" he said as realization dawned on him. "I did my best to not hurt him, just sort of . . . shoo him away."

"As though you have any right to lay a finger upon a proper *Citizen*, Outlaw."

"Okay, getting better." Edwin wasn't nearly as calm as he was letting on, but he kept his fear from showing. There was no sense in letting the Enforcer know his little intimidation was succeeding, after all. Who knew that emotional repression might have practical applications?

"But if you really want to go all out, you should really make sure that you signal both that you know who I am and what I've done, that you don't care, and you're going to mess me up regardless. Something like, I don't know, 'Edwin Maxlin, Ally of the Empire or not, you have crossed me for the last time, now you will be exiled' or something like that."

"Edwin Maxlin?"

"Oh, have you heard of me?"

". . . Yes," Finnas growled, eyes flashing with some Identify-related Skill.

"Even better! Then you can mix in a few personal barbs, really paint a vivid picture of *everything* going on."

In lieu of replying, the avior backhanded (backwinged?) Edwin right in his face, sending his neck cracking back painfully but predominantly launching him through the air over the river.

. . . Well, shoot. That wasn't what he had wanted.

Edwin righted himself with Unbound Tether and brought Flight into play, hovering above the ice. Meanwhile, the Enforcer was nowhere to be seen.

Huh. Apparently his name-drop and reminder of his status worked better than he'd anticipated! It *was* a bit strange that his identity hadn't shown up on Identify for an Enforcer, but maybe that didn't always work or something like that. There were many reasons he might not have checked anything beyond Edwin's status as an Adventurer, ranging from simple forgetfulness and overconfidence to . . . well, there was probably something else but he couldn't think what that might have been.

Edwin breathed a sigh of relief as a torrent of delayed emotions began assaulting his mind now that the immediate danger had passed.

Well, at least it looked like he'd been given a free pass to remain in the city. Or perhaps the Enforcer would be back before long with backup? Who knew. Edwin was in one piece, mostly unharmed, and not *that* worn out.

He exhaled a long breath. It was *close* to an unmitigated disaster and could have gone much worse very easily. He knew that a day on the town likely wouldn't go *great*, but he hadn't expected it to go *this* badly. He should have just stayed in the tower; at least there people *pretended* to like him.

Honored Senior Mundanity Assistant Pierash greeted Edwin when he slunk in through the door, the too-large eyes of a halfling able to present a very convincing semiskeptical expression.

"Well, aren't you just a right mess. Did you try to swim down the waterfall?"

"What? I don't look that bad, do I?"

"A few injuries, and I know you have Health from all your yammering about the place. That any of it stuck means it woulda been bad. Not much of a mess, but a mess all the same."

Edwin sighed. "It's fine, I think. Why does everyone hate Adventurers *so much*?" he vaguely groused.

"Oh, lots of reasons."

"Is there *anyone* who isn't likely to spit at me when I pass them on the street, or anywhere where it's not common? Like seriously, from day one of being in the Empire it's been nothing but thinly veiled insults about me at *best*, open hostility at worst. Like, come on. Why even have Adventurers if everyone hates them so much? Oh, thank you." He accepted a mug of hot cider with a nod, sipping at the beverage.

"Oh, well, I imagine most folks won't be bothering you about what your Skills are. But they can't well tell you that when they see you now, can they? Those all who remember when there were no Adventurers are still pretty common and definitely louder. Just be glad they have to treat you as good as they do, or ye'd never be allowed in a city."

"Good?" Edwin incredulously raised an eyebrow. "I had to deal with some Hunter who randomly started to insult me and Rillah and get *very* up close and personal; then when I shoved him away and went about my day, the *Enforcer* came out to personally try and bully me. That's *good?*"

"Well, what do you know about your kind?"

"You mean Adventurers?" Edwin clarified. "Uh, what do you mean? Like their history?"

"For almost all of history until recently, if you weren't under Management you were an Outlaw. You proved you didn't want your community, they didn't want you. Then . . . oh, about a hundred and twenty years ago, Xares decided that they might still be *allowed* in society in exchange for but the barest lip service to tradition and law."

"And law isn't public opinion," Edwin summarized. "But why all the hate? Adventurers are just . . . harmless. So what if they don't follow one single law?"

"Where did you grow up?"

"A really, really long way from here."

"What was your home like with outsiders?"

"Ou— Oh, like foreigners, you mean? I mean . . . depends on who you asked, I suppose. For me and my circles it generally didn't matter."

"There were those who just hated foreigners, though, yes? Those who thought nothing good can come from beyond their own home?"

"I always thought it was a bit overblown . . . but yeah, I guess so."

"That's what Adventurers are, but *proven.*"

"Proven? What do you mean?"

"Adventurers are those who we *thought* were our kin, who respected our traditions and customs, then decided to throw it all away. They *are* foreigners disguised as proper citizens. They share not our values and have decided wholeheartedly that they are not like us, not *of* us. That their former kin are but dust. They rejected their citizenship; it is only fitting that they are rejected in *turn.*"

"It sounds like you don't like Adventurers either?"

"Of course I don't. They're immoral, rash, reckless individuals who seek only their own glorification at the expense of all others."

"But?"

"But that doesn't justify being awful *to* them, nor does it justify treating those who had no say over their condition in such a horrid manner. We're better than that." She sniffed. "And that describes most of you in residence, other than that hound's boy. Even with him, his parents clearly failed to raise him properly, if he'd trust a *dog* over his Registrar."

"I guess?" A thought crossed Edwin's mind. "You're aware of our plan, right?"

"To create a contraption that will remove the need for a resident mage? I am."

"Doesn't it annoy you or whatever?"

"Why might it? *I* have no desire to ensure that another stiff-feathered noble roosts here, and I certainly love seeing the ingenuity of mages. That it ruffles the feathers of the governor and Enforcer Finnas only helps my approval."

"Won't it mess up your . . . thing, though? Like, if there's nobody here, what will happen to you?"

"Oh, I imagine I'll stay here. My Charter is with the city itself; they can't remove me from the tower, and not having a mage in residence makes my life far simpler."

"That's good, I suppose. I wouldn't want to ruin your life by accident."

"Perfectly all right, young man. Now, you seem to be finished with that cider. Are you planning to hold on to that mug all night or shall I deal with it?"

"Huh? Oh, right. You can take it, I guess."

"Excellent. I believe the lady is in your sitting parlor, run along now."

"Oh, thanks . . ." Edwin didn't know how to address the halfling so just sort of awkwardly trailed off as he watched her vanish around the corner.

He wrenched his mind away from that particular gaffe before it could start to dwell on the mistake, and with just three strides he found himself at the doors of their primary sitting room. He took a brief moment totally not about pushing off human contact to admire the intricately painted carvings covering so much of the door before pushing his way inside and tossing his jacket to the side.

True to what he'd been anticipating, Rillah was lounging near the fireplace, quietly playing her flute. At his entrance, though, she looked up and stopped playing, the unearthly tunes fading into echoes.

"Edwin! Wow, what happened, you're a mess."

"Oh, come on, it's like *one* bruise!" he protested, to no avail.

"Nuh-uh, I'm not hearing it. What happened?"

He took a deep breath and settled in for another recap of his day. At least he had someone nice to talk to now.

Level Up!

Skill Points 1028→1091 (Average level: 55; Min level: 24)

Adaptive Defense Level 45→48

Alchemical Analysis Level 41→44

Alchemical Dismantling Level 49→53

Anatomy Level 43→44

Arcadian Elixir Level 36→37

Basic Thermokinesis Level 36→40

Bomb Throwing Level 58→60

Fey's Caress Level 43→46

Fresh Air Level 45→46

Longstrider Level 52→54

Memory Level 66→67

Numeracy Level 50→54

Outsider's Almanac Level 136→137

Overcharge Level 27→30

Prototyping Level 41→44

Refining Level 37→40

Ritual Intuition Level 50→52

Sapper's Apparatus Level 62→65

Skillful Assessment Level 50→52

Stamina Manipulation Level 4→12

Unbound Tether Level 19→24

Watchful Rest Level 40→44

CHAPTER 15

Rillah' Interestin'

Edwin bonelessly sank into the couch in pure bliss. He hadn't even realized just how tense and sore he'd been after his altercation with the "law" until Rillah had pointed it out and then *fixed* it, giving him the greatest shoulder massage he'd ever felt.

. . . it might have also been the *only* massage he'd ever had, come to think of it, but it was still borderline magical if not *actually* supernatural.

"That was so, *so* nice," he admitted. "Was that a Skill, or just practice?"

"I'm not Lefi," Rillah said with a laugh, "but Heightened Sensations definitely helps with this sort of thing. Makes it all so much more fun."

She traced a Skill-laden finger along his arm, and he shivered at the feeling of pleasure it brought along with it.

"Could have fooled me," Edwin groaned. He tried and failed to sit up before he called on Flight, grabbing his shirt with Unbound Tether. He didn't pull it on immediately, instead looking dejectedly at the small hole at the center of its chest and corresponding bloodstain. "Guess I need to see Lefi about this."

"Nah, toss it this way."

"You've got Mending?"

"Of course! It's *so* useful, how could I not?"

Edwin thought for a moment about whether that was some kind of dig against him, but then decided it *probably* wasn't intended to be one. "Okay, I suppose. Can you do his whole . . . instant-fix trick?"

"Not quite, but I wish I could. It's just far too high-level of an effect for Repairing, but . . ." Rillah slipped his shirt on, and the fabric almost seemed to *ripple* for a moment. Its colors shifted before settling in a turquoise color and cut that fit much better on her than on Edwin. "Whoops! I can fix that."

With a bit of focus, Edwin watched as several Skills flowed throughout his shirt, restoring it to its proper shape and green color. She slipped off the outer garment—Edwin wasn't able to not stare, even though all she was doing was undressing to her *normal* level of clothing—and tossed it back to him.

"What was that?" The hole and staining were completely gone, and the shirt thankfully fit him just as well as it had before in addition to being perfectly clean.

"Oh, Custom Fit. It makes anything I use always benefit from the effects of my Skills, as well as a few other perks."

Very convenient. He approved.

"Well, thanks. I think I could stand to relax a bit, though, and I'm a bit peckish so I'm going to make myself some dinner. I'll be back soon."

"Ooh, you cook? You any good at it?"

"Did this somehow never come up before now?" Edwin raised an eyebrow. "I guess I'm a decent cook, though a bit out of practice, I have a Skill that makes everything I make *super*tasty; we're just not sure if it's addictive."

"Is your food that good?"

"Well, I've got a Skill. Actually, haven't we talked about it?" he asked, but Rillah shook her head.

"Not that I remember."

"I could have *sworn*. Anyway, Arcadian Elixir improves the nutrition and taste of foods and other edible stuff I make, but it makes everything else taste *significantly* worse, and we don't really have any way to tell if that's the result of the Skill just being that *good*, or it's actively making other stuff taste bad."

"Oh, that's fine! I have a Skill for that!"

"Wait, what?"

"Well, *yeah*. How am I supposed to try *everything* if I can be waylaid by trying the wrong thing? Refreshed Tastes and Cleanse Palate *both* get rid of poisons, alcohol, and even addictive Skills really easily."

"Alcohol is just a type of poison," Edwin felt compelled to point out. "But neat? Do I *want* to know how you have two Skills dedicated to that?"

"I eat a lot of different stuff, try lots of foods. I don't recommend most kinds of dirt, but there *are* places where it's rather tasty."

"Ooookay, I guess. I'll make stuff for you as well, I suppose. You don't happen to have any other Skills that might be useful for me to know about?"

"Oh, come on, Edwin"—she jostled his shoulder—"isn't it way more exciting this way? Learning about me as you go along, getting little bits about my capabilities and talents as we travel together?"

"Okay, first off, yes, that may arguably be more fun, and I definitely would like to travel with you and learn . . . never mind. Anyway! I'm also in the business of *not dying*, and being able to do things in a way that's reasonable and practical. Knowing the full scope of what you can do is *useful*. Look at just now! If I had known you had these poison-cleansing Skills earlier, then I could have wrapped up this whole question ages ago.

"Besides, you know my Skills, so why can't I know all of yours? I thought that you were going to tell me about them at some point anyway."

"I will! And I *am*, you just haven't been asking often enough. You've been way too busy with your alchemy and enchanting to talk to little old me."

"You *know* why I'm doing that. If you want me to not work on *your* replacement machine, just let me know and I'll, I don't know, work on something else on my research list. But I digress. I want to know what all your Skills are, so just give me *something*."

"After dinner, then. We can talk while we eat."

Edwin sighed. "Fine. I won't bother you for a little while as I'm cooking, then."

*　*　*

It being the middle of winter meant the tower's kitchen, cellar, and panty didn't have access to *that* much variety, but it still had a decent amount of preserved foods, and Edwin returned not much later with two empanada-like beef pastries. Basic Thermokinesis made cooking *seriously* easy, as there was no preheating or anything required. There was a bit of nuance to it, of course, to make it not taste like he cooked it in a microwave, but he'd had practice.

"It's good! Does your Alchemy Skill help you make food?"

"It does, actually. It mostly lets me know the right temperature to use, when something's cooked, that kind of stuff, but I'm not entirely sure if that's just general practice I've gotten from potion-making or not. It's definitely not as effective compared to doing *actual* alchemy, but it still counts a bit."

"Well, it's good. Well-done, too, not just the Skill flavoring things."

"You can tell the difference?"

"No, but I can guess."

She finished her food with just a couple more bites and nodded. "The Skill was also good. It's about . . . oh, worth maybe two midlevel Skills? Definitely puts it a bit below Skilled cooks but for a single Skill that's . . . really good. Especially since it has other effects, and it's only midlevel itself."

"How . . . how do you know all this stuff?"

"Oh, lots and lots of food," she said. "Five high-level musical Skills is good enough to serve as entertainment in any tavern and most courts, and that comes with a meal made by someone who knows what they're doing. It's always a great time."

"And the verdict? Is it addictive? Does it make other food taste worse?"

"One minute." Rillah sprang to her feet and dashed out of the room.

While she was away, Edwin took the opportunity to start to update his Arcadian Elixir's Almanac entry with the comparisons to other flavor-related Skills.

"Yep," Rillah nodded as she sat back down, chewing on a piece of bread.

"Whoa, that startled me. Sorry, what?"

"Your Skill. It makes other stuff taste worse."

"It does? Dang it. Any idea by how much?"

"Eh, about the same as it increases? As I'm sure you're familiar with, a good cook will make everything *way* better, so even with the penalty, their stuff will still be better than a Skill-less cook could make."

"That does line up with what I've seen, I suppose."

Edwin went on, "I guess that means I'm not cooking for most people, then. Inion, myself, and now you are the only people I'm comfortable using it on."

She cocked her head in curiosity.

"Well, *I'll* never be without it as an option, so no matter how strong it gets I can always just make my own food. Inion is basically immune to it, because it apparently just tastes like food from her home. Then you . . . you *can* get rid of it, right?"

Rillah looked off to the side for a moment, and a light blue Skill ignited at her mouth, sweeping through her entire body in an instant. She took another bite out of her bread and nodded. "That did it, yeah."

"Okay, yeah. You, Inion, and myself. Anyone else, I don't want to subject them to that."

"How's it going to work for you when you want to eat something you didn't make? I promise you, you're missing out if you just eat your own stuff."

"I'm trying to figure out some kind of spice I can put on food I eat that might help trick the Skill into thinking 'I' made the food . . . it's a work in progress, and not a terribly high priority one. Anyway! I have questions."

He mentally clicked a pen and pulled up her Almanac entry. "Tell me about yourself."

Name

Seasonal Dancer of Whimsy

Rillah (no last name?) (AdventurerRillah)

Bard (really good fluter player)

Adventurer Mage and Wanderer (fond of traveling; has Skill-based wings and can fly; likes dancing)

Age

About 24 years old

Race
Half-elf

Attributes
Charisma
Dexterity
Health
Intelligence
Mana
Perception
Seasonal Mana
Speed
Stamina

Skills
Magical
Autumnal Gust, Updraft, Harvesting Winds, Cutting Gale
Basic Isochronal Magic, Isochronal Magic, Greater Isochronal
Magic, Mantle of the Seasons
Chilling Grasp, Chill, Ice Manipulation, Winter's Flurry
Spark, Dancing Flame, Fire Snake, Mesmeric Flare
Unweathered Form, Greater Unweathered Form, Idyllic
Appearance, Mercurial Shape
Vivacious Caress, Bountiful Energy, Enhanced Stamina, Energetic
Wellspring

Physical
Breathing, Deep Breath, Smelling, Read the Air
Dancing, Eternal Dance, Delicate Steps, Meandering Steps
Drinking, Pouring, Bottomless Flask, Endless [Carrying Cellar]
(Note: This is apparently a thing on Joriah, a portable spatially
expanded room full of alcohol.)
Eating, Diverse Palate, Refreshed Tastes, Cleanse Self
Flexibility, Seasonal Shift, Mystic Anatomy, Gusting Wings
Flying, Dancing Wings, Powerful Flight

Mental

Hearing, Perfect Pitch, Natural Tune, Song of the Wild
Reflexes, Quick-Witted, Pause for Thought, Worthy of Notice
Seeing, Eye for Novelty, Mana Sight, Detailed Mana Sight

Combat

Spearmanship, Spear-Dancing, Sidestepping, Fluttering Steps

Social/Musical

Charm, Good Impression, Calming Touch, Allure
Language, Polyglot, Clarity of Intent, Inspiring Speech
Music, Flute-playing, Flute of the Ancient Hollow, Melodious
Focus
Sense Motive, Discern Lie, Between the Words, Social Savvy

Utility

Bedplay, Self-Control, Heightened Sensations, Memorable Night
Cooking, Greater Cooking, Advanced Cooking, Harvest Feast
Identify, Common Knowledge, Wanderer's Guide, Musician's Ear
Repairing, Passive Maintenance, Greater Passive Maintenance,
Custom Fit
Status, Status Log, Travelogue, Atlas
Weaving, Tailoring, Hardy Clothing, Twirling Dance

Magery

Has mana that ebbs and flows with the seasons. In spring, this
predominantly is life/rain-related; in summer, fire; in autumn, wind;
and in winter, ice. Her strongest element always corresponds to the
current season, and her second strongest depends on how far into the
season it is. Early season, it's whichever season just ended. Midseason,
it's the season *opposite* (such as summer during midwinter), and near
the end of the season, it's the season just about to start.
She never loses full access to all of one mana type, but near the
solstices and equinoxes the off-season elements (summer and

winter in spring and autumn) become all but unusable save for minor uses (like starting a fire in fall, or a faint breeze in summer) Her Visualization is that of a storm which fades in intensity with overuse and can summon *lightning* by freecasting.

Personal notes

Really nice, seems to care a lot about me. She definitely makes an effort to ensure I'm included whenever feasible, is definitely actively trying to get me more comfortable around people— probably at Lefi's (LefiForolova) request.

Unknown how she would react to more personal questions, or how much she *actually* likes me versus is just trying to reassure me. Unknown how trustworthy she is for sensitive conversation. Unknown how available she is for generally doing stuff.

"That's quite the note-taking Skill you have there."

"Well, it cost a fortune and is nearly level 140, so I'd *hope* so. I'm also *so* glad I can tag multiword phrases these days. Makes the Skill list so much easier. Anyway, I have questions."

She grinned. "Ask away."

"Okay, so putting aside the fact I'll want to try and catalog the details of all these Skills at some point, such as the Path you used and all that—"

"Oh? You really are a junior Registrar-aspirant, aren't you?"

Edwin raised a finger, ready to rebut her claim, then he thought better about it and retracted his point. "Maybe. I more just want to . . . well no, that's basically what a Registrar does. Basically I just want to learn how Skills interact and what the logic beneath different Paths are. So yeah, what Registrars do. Someday, I want to be able to perfectly predict what I'll get from a Path, just like they mostly can."

"But what about the joy of discovery, of not knowing what you'll get?"

"Oh, come on. You *can't* tell me you got all these Skills just by taking what sounded the most fun."

She shrugged. "Pretty much, actually, other than the ones I got as a kid or with Lefi."

"Well . . . I like to be a bit more prepared, I guess. I need to *know*."

"I could have guessed from you evolving Flight."

Edwin paused, trying to parse whether or not he should feel complimented, insulted, both, or neither.

"I'm just going to move past that. . . . What the heck do your Isochronal Magic Skills do, and why do you have three of them? Yes, I know they're evolutions, but . . . yeah."

I feel like I'm giving an interview. Ugh, I don't like this.

"It's my magic Skill. You know, sort of like how you have your Mana Infusion? It's what helps me actually *use* magic easily. Basic helps me channel more mana. The normal version helps me channel it with more *detail*, and Greater makes it *stronger*. Brighter flames for the same effort, that kind of thing. It's kinda tricky to explain.

"Mantle of the Seasons"—she forestalled his next question—"makes the magic for whatever season I'm currently in even stronger."

"I thought that was something that was just part of how your mana worked?"

"It is! The Skill magnifies it."

"Huh, okay then. What does Read the Air do?"

"Oh, that lets me get a general sense of what's going to happen. Like when something exciting is imminent, or if there's festivities happening nearby."

"How does that work?"

"Intuition."

"Fair enough. And you don't have Walking?"

She shook her head. "Walking is boring. Dancing is better in *every* way."

He raised an eyebrow.

"I have better footwork than most guards do thanks to that Skill, I'll have you know."

"Sure you do. But what about if you want to, oh, I don't know, *walk* somewhere?"

"Eternal Dance. I just have the order mixed up, so what actually matters comes first, and it applies to my *whole body*, even if I'm *flying*."

"Point," he conceded. "I know I'd like my Flight to be easier or work with Longstrider."

His eyes skimmed over the list. "I don't want to bore you . . ."

"Edwin, it's fine. You had a stressful day, talking is a great way to unwind."

"Yeah, but I feel like I'm interrogating you and I don't want that."

"Would you rather me regale you with stories of my every Skill and how I've used it? I have a lot of stories."

Edwin thought for a second. "Maybe one day, that would be nice. It just seems like a great way to get distracted."

"Oh, getting distracted?" Rillah flashed an impish grin and summoned a prismatic tongue of fire to her hand.

Edwin's attention was immediately consumed by the Mesmeric Flare, watching its brilliant colors dance and intertwine with such magnificent depth, the scintillating light hypnotically attractive . . .

He shook his head and closed his eyes. "How'd I do?"

"Not bad. Not as fast as you've been before, but still under a minute."

Edwin opened his eyes again, and his gaze was once more drawn to the dancing fire, but already being in the right mindset (and with Adaptive Defense already in the right state) kept him from being sucked in for more than a few seconds.

"I'll take it, I guess. And your 'Carrying Cellar,' which is apparently a thing? Some spatial expansion Skill that also reduces the weight for what you carry?"

"Yeah. I'm really happy with that. It was originally *only* useful for drinks, but Custom Fit made it now work with anything. It's amazing, and packing became *so* much easier since I got it."

There seemed to be an obvious problem with that. "What happens if you hand something affected by it off?"

"So long as I carry my bags more than anyone else does, it works just fine. If I don't wear it at all for a long time, then it'll also wear off, but Passive Maintenance basically means that will never happen, so I don't have to worry about it. It's way better than Packing because it's no struggle at all."

"Oh yeah, Packing." Edwin frowned. "How come you don't have that?"

"I couldn't get it."

"You couldn't?"

She shook her head. "It's my elf half, I think. Easier to blame him, anyway. I might be able to get it, but why bother? It all turned out just fine, so it's perfectly all right."

"Huh. Okay. What about your Flexibility stuff, then?"

"That makes it easier to use spells *on* me, plus some other stuff. With my Updraft, even before I got my wings I could use it to fly into the air a bit like your Unbound Tether Skill."

"Neat. And Gusting Wings . . ."

"Are my wings, yes. That was quite the trophy to get those."

"You'll have to tell me about it sometime. Worthy of Notice?"

"Oh, jumping ahead a bit now?"

"It seemed . . . noteworthy."

Rillah shot a playful look his way, but Edwin just smiled. "It lets me always see what the most interesting thing nearby is."

"How does it determine what the most interesting thing is?"

"Usually, whatever is the most immediately impactful to me. The barkeeper in a tavern, or maybe a cool Adventurer, but usually just whatever has the most potential around it. Great for learning new stuff!"

"I bet. Is it literally a metagaming Skill?" Edwin muttered.

"A what Skill?"

"Right, you could hear that. Just a . . . well, what Lefi would call a Quest sense."

She chuckled. "You know what? That's not too far off."

"So can you . . . what, use it to find just the right book in a library for what you want to do?"

She nodded.

"Lucky."

"That's me!"

Edwin rolled his eyes. "You only have one combat Skill? Why's that?"

"Well, I'm not a warrior or hunter. I fly away from problems, and the only reason I even have that one is because Lefi *insisted* I get it way back when."

"Yeah, that doesn't look like you took it in a really combat-oriented direction, did you?" he mused. "Are those dancing-related?"

"They can be."

Edwin's eyes skimmed down the Skill list. "Is your Flute of the Ancient Hollow a trophy Skill?"

In response, she held out her hand, and a brown-green Skill stretched into existence, materializing the simple yet elegant flute.

"May I?" he asked. Rillah nodded and handed him the woodwind.

It was so perfect if he hadn't *known* it was a Skill, he might well have guessed it if not for how *real* it felt. He could see the wood grain making up its stock, feel its weight pressing into his hand, two turquoise stones embossed into the wood, the two fabric bands near its end silky smooth and with a vague, indistinct pattern. The wood itself near the mouth of the flute had some sort of intricate pattern carved into it, though he couldn't tell what it *was*.

"What does it do?"

"Ah, now that *is* my secret."

Edwin raised an eyebrow as Rillah reclaimed her instrument.

"A girl needs *some* tricks, you know. And this . . ."—she ran her hands lovingly over the wooden body—"this is one of them."

"Can I ask what Melodious Focus does, then?"

"Oh, that helps me use spells and Skills through music. Edwin, your eyebrow is trying to escape."

He scowled, bringing his errant eyebrow under control, before turning back to his list.

"Apparently you should be doing the cooking?" Edwin joked. "That's what, four Skills?"

"Hey, none of them are flavor-based. Honestly, most of them aren't that useful for me. Diverse Palate already lets me eat a lot of stuff that I otherwise couldn't, Advanced Cooking just makes it edible for *other* people. Harvest Feast is magical and annoying to level, but lets me make this absolutely *enormous* meal during autumn with the help of my magical Skills, and it has lots of really cool effects, but I missed my chance to use it this year because I was stuck *here*."

She sighed. "But it's all right. I've had fun with you, Lefi, Yathal, and Kyni, which wouldn't have happened in the same way without me being here."

Edwin smiled. "You're too nice."

"It's true!"

"Anyway, moving on . . . You have *Bedplay*?"

"I know, I'm such a stereotype."

"What?"

"In my defense, it was *very* worth the Skill."

"No, the *stereotype*."

"Oh, that Adventurers have a Skill for *everything* you could ever want? Including everything in bed?"

"Ah," Edwin felt his face flush slightly, "I get it."

"Now, it's not the *worst* stereotype to have, and a lot of people are jealous of it because of how rarely the Registrars grant it. But *Adventurers* don't have to worry about that, do we? So, the rumor goes, we have Skills for—"

"I said I get it!"

Rillah chuckled. "Where did you think my nickname came from? Now, it *is* a rather clever pun, I'll give them that, but it's more than just that."

"What nickname?"

"Oh, come on, there's no way you've never heard anyone call me *daywasr*. Especially not from what you said happened *today*."

"Polyglot doesn't translate it for me," he replied.

She frowned. "What level is it for you?

"Ahh . . . seventyish?"

"It should definitely translate for you by then. *Keiach*, that's more than I got *my* Polyglot to, you should be able to understand everything so long as they stick to one language at a time." She paused and narrowed her eyes. "Hmm. You know, I don't think I've ever heard you curse. Edwin, do you ever swear?"

"Um, no?"

"How uncomfortable does swearing make you?"

"I mean, I'm *used* to it, but I usually just try to tune it out."

Rillah started laughing uproariously.

"Oh, come on, what is it?"

She brought her laughter down to a chuckle. "Xares above, that's hilarious. I've never heard of someone *handicapping their Polyglot* to not translate any foul language before. Oh, this could be so much fun.

"Anyway, *daywasr* comes from 'weather' and a fairly derogatory term for 'whore.' Hence . . ." She gestured at herself, still trying to get her merriment under control.

It took Edwin a moment to properly parse the words, untranslating them until he caught the original pronunciation. Weather in the local language was apparently "*dayser*" and whore was "*wasr.*" As much as he disapproved of the insult . . . he had to admit it *was* rather well done.

"You done laughing?"

"Yep, I am. Oh, that's hilarious."

"Happy to be of amusement. What do Travelogue and Atlas do?"

"Travelogue includes places I go on my Status Log, and Atlas gives me a unique System display about information for places I visit."

"What do you mean?"

"Well, for cities that usually includes the name and Class of the most notable people. Here, that's Enforcer Finnas and the governor, but also Lefi, now that he's in town, plus a handful of others. It saves me so much trouble, when I can just immediately see if I have someone to avoid in a city I go to, let me tell you."

"Who do *you* need to avoid? Former lovers?"

"*Maybe.*"

Edwin smirked. "Well, that does sound useful. What about Wanderer's Guide and Musician's Ear? Are those similar things?"

She nodded. "Wanderer's Guide is a bit like Atlas, but gives more historical information. Usually a bit boring, and Musician's Ear lets me Identify sounds. There's nothing better for learning new songs, I'll tell you that much."

"What about animal cries?"

"That, too."

"Huh, neat. And then I suppose Twirling Dance lets you . . . actually, I don't know. I'm kind of impressed you got Weaving to evolve into a dancing Skill, though."

"Oh, that's actually a bit of a combat Skill. If I use some scarves . . . which are around here somewhere, I know, it helps me tie up people."

"Huh. How'd you get that?"

"Well, I was wondering what Grappler would do to Hardy Clothing. It was my last Skill to evolve that tier."

"Was it worth it?"

"Well"—she grinned—"it has its uses."

Edwin nodded absently. "And your Attributes?"

"What about them?"

"Intelligence. Does that . . ."

"Yes, it makes me smarter."

"How does that work?"

"It helps me with recall, pattern recognition, thinking speed, mental Skill management, and how many distinct *things* I can keep in my mind at one time."

"Huh, neat. That actually sounds really useful."

"It is."

"What about Seasonal Mana? How is it different from just normal Mana?"

"Well, it's more *my* mana. Everything I do will be more seasonal, stronger, easier to use, *and* it helps with some of the same stuff as Mana. You know, the size of my storm, how strong the storm is, that kind of thing."

"But don't you have Skills for that?"

"Oh sure, just like I have social Skills but also Charisma. They aren't exclusive, and the Attribute has all the effects of those Skills plus more and is easier to use besides."

"Makes sense. So then jumping back a bit, how does Worthy of Note differ from Eye for Novelty?"

"Well, you see . . ."

Edwin gritted his teeth in concentration. It had already been a bit of a stretch to get his potion mana to *make* an autoclave, but he'd done it by Visualizing his mana going *through* an autoclave and mimicking the internal conditions of being superheated yet unable to boil. Then by replicating that sensation within a closed container, Edwin had found it mimicked the effects slightly. He was trying to come up with an easier method, but he hadn't had much luck yet.

All that to say, maintaining a single manaclave was hard enough. But maintaining *two*? It was straining the limits of what he could actually hold on to at one time. To compensate, he'd made both as small as possible, but that carried its own difficulties.

In front of him sat a moderately complex Apparatus, a sealed sphere of the crystal-like solid Skill held several feet off his workbench and sealed entirely within a *second* apparatite container maintaining its own manaclave at the same strength as the first container.

Underneath the first container, a grate set at an angle led into a small bowl filled with his Refined heated water. When he would release the first manaclave, the pebble would fall and roll down the grate into the water, while the powder it had been surrounded by would fall through the grate for collection.

Once the pebble had adequately absorbed its new trait, he would release the seal on the outer manaclave, and hopefully everything worked well.

At first Edwin had just tried to just set the pebble on a shelf of sorts and only dissolve that, but doing so dissolved his manaclave. He felt like it had to do with his perception of what was going on. After all, the manaclave *was* basically just a free-form spell of his, albeit a simple one, and he needed what essentially amounted to training wheels to get his magic to do anything. Maybe one day, he could do this sort of thing with *no* setup, but one step at a time.

This *should* work, he felt. The stone's base trait would be dissolved away in the inner autoclave, and then removed when it was released. However, it would stay under the same conditions at all times so it would never settle into a new state. It would go from normal, to empty but supported, to filled with its new trait.

Speaking of which . . .

Edwin felt the stone's heat capacity trait finish disassociating. Removing the stone from the powder (or the other way around) would remove the trait as well at this point, and Edwin did just that, dissolving the tiny sphere it had been held in.

Edwin's left hand immediately started cramping up as its magical burden was released, but he couldn't tend to it yet.

He watched the pebble bounce just as he had predicted with Prototype, once, twice . . . and roll. It dropped into the liquid perfectly with barely a splash, and the powder all collected in its bowl beneath the grate.

All according to plan.

A few bubbles seeped out from the stone as it sat, absorbing heated water. It only took about a minute for it to stop, but Edwin let it sit for a bit longer despite the increasing strain of maintaining the manaclave.

Eventually, Edwin released his hold over the manaclave and dissolved the apparatite cap keeping the system sealed. While there wasn't *technically* any heat involved in the process, it still radiated something strongly approximating high temperatures, no doubt a side effect of Edwin's spell.

He fished out the pebble from where it sat, dropping it in cold water. Edwin retrieved the stone after a minute sitting in its third and final location. While it was chilly for a moment after he pulled it out . . .

It was warming up. He'd done it! He had made a rock inherently a higher temperature than it should have been! He let out a quiet cheer, not wanting to disturb anyone or attract too much attention and glanced at his notifications, feeling like he already knew what he'd find there.

Congratulations! By successfully imbuing the magical attributes of one substance into another, you have unlocked the Essential Alchemist Path!

Edwin grinned. Complete and total success, it would seem. Now, to figure out all the ways to do this *better*.

Level Up!
Skill Points 1091→1112 (Average level: 56)
Alchemical Dismantling Level 53→54
Alchemy Level 95→96
Anatomy Level 44→45
Arcadian Elixir Level 37→39
Basic Thermokinesis Level 40→41
Mana Infusion Level 91→92
Memory Level 67→68
Numeracy Level 54→55
Outsider's Almanac Level 137→138
Polyglot Level 70→71
Refining Level 40→43

Ritual Intuition Level 52→53
Sapper's Apparatus Level 65→66
Skillful Assessment Level 52→53
Stamina Manipulation Level 12→14
Unbound Tether Level 24→26

CHAPTER 16

Alloying Insight

"Are you . . . Are you *freaking kidding me?*" Edwin didn't swear, but that part of him was being *heavily* tested with his newest finding. "No! No, that's not . . ."

Rillah dropped down right next to him. "What's up?"

"Gah! What the heck, Rillah! What was that for?" He frowned, glancing upward. "Were you . . . were you on the *ceiling?*"

"I was close to it."

"What were you doing there? No, how *long* were you there?"

"Oh, not long at all. I came when you called and decided to surprise you."

"Well, I suppose you succeeded there. Wait. I didn't call you?"

"You called for me? Are you all right, Edwin?" Lefi burst into the room almost right on cue.

"No . . . I . . . no, never mind." Edwin sighed. "I was just testing out Bomb Throwing."

"Did you manage to figure out . . . whatever you were testing about it?"

"You mean my testing to figure out why the Skill triggers really unpredictably? Yeah, I did."

"Marvelous!" Lefi cheered, moving closer to clap Edwin on the shoulder, which Edwin didn't dodge.

"You did? Congratulations!" Rillah wrapped him in a quick hug, which he enjoyed *immensely* before he caught himself. It was still too short, though.

Inion appeared from somewhere, seemingly materializing in the few inches between Edwin and Rillah after they disconnected. "What happened?" she asked breathlessly, which made Edwin mentally frown. What had brought *everyone* here so quickly?

"Oh, come on, I wasn't *that* loud!" Edwin complained. "Why did all three of you decide to come visit me at the exact same time?"

"We heard—" Rillah started, only to be cut off.

"There were *many* explosions from this room for *hours*, followed by sudden relative quiet and shouting," Inion interjected. "*I* wanted to make sure you were all right."

". . . Okay, that's fair," he conceded. "I always forget how loud they are because Adaptive Defense helps make up for everything my earplugs don't cover."

"What happened, then?" Inion asked.

"Well, I just told Rillah and Lefi, but I was experimenting with Bomb Throwing and I finally figured out what makes the Skill trigger."

"Oh, you did? Good job!" she congratulated him.

"Yeah, well, if I could explain my findings to people . . ."

"Just go ahead and tell us," Rillah added, "or we'll be here all day."

"It might be easier if I show you," Edwin said. A quick tug on Unbound Tether summoned an Infused Phosphorus pellet to his hand, and he showed it to his spectators. "See this? This is a fire pellet. When ignited, the pellet expands into a fireball."

Edwin held the pellet between his fingers and *pushed* with his tether, sending the projectile hurtling toward the open window. As it passed over the windowsill, he twisted his hand to help trigger Firestarting.

WHOMP!

The fireball enveloped most of the windowsill, momentarily blocking the view outside with white-orange flames. Then, it subsided into white smoke and some drifting flakes of black phosphorus slowly settling into place.

"See? No Bomb Throwing activation, because it wasn't a bomb and I didn't throw it." Lefi looked like he was about to ask something but

Edwin preempted it. "Wait just a minute still. Next I want to show you what happens when I throw a fireball *bomb*," he explained, holding up an identical object to what he'd just used.

He once again pinched the bomb between his fingers and pushed it with his tether. As before, he twisted his hand as it flew through the windowsill—though this time he waited until *after* it was mostly outside.

BANG!

The fireball was largely made of white flames, but the accompanying shock wave was unmistakable. From experience, he knew the fireball was about three meters in radius, from the base explosion's one, and it completely blanketed the exterior.

"It's exactly what I think it is," Edwin explained.

Rillah frowned. "So what's the difference?"

"No, no. I mean, it's *literally* what I think it is. If I perceive something as a bomb, it'll trigger the Skill. If I think of it as something else—like as a pellet—it won't. If I don't think of *anything*, well . . . I still need to do some more tests, but I think it's the same as when I consider my projectile an 'explosive,' namely that it sometimes triggers and sometimes doesn't. While I still need to do a bit of testing"—he shot a glare at Inion, who looked *very* ready to try and take words out of his mouth—"I'm pretty sure it then depends on if I've ever thought of myself as making a bomb somewhere previously. Now, there does seem to be a lower limit to what counts as a bomb—I can't make a rock explode no matter how much I try—but I still need to figure out the exact criteria."

"So then it does respond to how you think of it? Is that so surprising?" Lefi asked.

"Well, no. I actually tested it, back when I was first experimenting, because that seemed like a very magic-y thing for it to trigger on. However, I think I messed up the experiment because I didn't realize it's whatever is *most* recently thought about the object, and it's supersensitive. I had to really, really focus to figure it out, absolutely *no* wandering thoughts."

"Aw, that must have been torture," Rillah said. "Guess I should have been here. It would have been way more fun!"

"Oh, why, so you could distract him?" Inion asked sarcastically.

"Yup! There's gotta be some point where my Skill just occupies all his spare attention and keeps his mind from wandering. It would be fun!"

"Oh, so *you* think you know what would be good for him? I'll have you know that—"

"That . . . actually sounds like it might be useful," Edwin cut in. "We should probably experiment with that at some point, yeah?"

"Most excellent!" Lefi was clearly eager to go back to whatever he was doing before he ran to check in on Edwin—that was actually quite nice, now that Edwin thought about it. All three of them cared enough to see that he was all right . . . or, he supposed, it might be that they came in the hopes that he'd blown himself up at long last.

He chose to interpret it as the former.

Bill was *such* a good pony. Despite being stuck in an outbuilding somewhere between a stable and a barn for several months, he seemed perfectly content to just stay indoors, particularly as the weather was so cold.

When Edwin had asked Lefi, because of *course* he knew about horses, the Adventurer had said it was one of the Skills most good beastmasters and trainers encouraged their beasts to take. Stabling (or Kenneling, for creatures such as dogs) allowed them to not get restless in relatively enclosed spaces and require very little exercise to stay healthy.

Edwin felt moderately confident that he could identify which Skill was doing so, even. A faint brown aura surrounded and flowed around Bill's body while he was in the stable, interacting with a similar-looking Skill that permeated the stables. While Anatomy was more focused on humans, giving the horse a physical checkup still fed into the intuitive knowledge the Skill granted him, and so far as Edwin could tell, the pony was doing just fine.

"You make this too easy, you know that?" he told his horse, stroking his mane.

In response, Bill shook his head, neighing slightly before nuzzling toward Edwin's side pocket.

"Little rascal." Edwin withdrew for a moment, pulling out a carrot from the suspicious pouch and handing it off to the uncomplaining animal.

He spent a little more time with Bill, brushing his fur, but that was about it. Edwin had other things to take care of, after all.

The solstice was coming up soon, according to Rillah. It was one of four days in the year where she was all but totally cut off from all types of mana except for the one associated with the season she was in, but the power of that one type of mana was correspondingly *massive*. However, it meant that she would be totally incapable of doing her job—which required more wind mana than she could realistically call upon—and even wouldn't be able to use most of the tower's enchantments.

A single day wouldn't do much, of course, but in general she'd be *almost* incapable of using the tower's magic for about a week before and afterward, until she could call upon more than the smallest mote of wind mana without totally exhausting herself.

While there was no way that Edwin would have anything ready by that point that could actually *do* anything useful, it was a bit of a reminder that grumpy Enforcers or not, he *did* have a project to work on. While his foray into Alchemy Essentia was interesting, he couldn't help but feel like he'd drifted slightly off course from his original primary goal of replacing Rillah. In a good way! She was decidedly irreplaceable in lots of other ways.

Edwin had never managed to imbue his new shirt with warmth, unfortunately. He found himself unable to Refine the traits he wanted to get out of the process, as even when he Infused the garment (or any other cloth for that matter), it didn't seem to have the same mana structure he'd found inside of magical substances like stone or metal. Maybe because it was so full of Skills, and that was a sort of not-magic that didn't really interact with Refining.

He probably should have checked that first, honestly.

It was arguably wasted time, but it wasn't *really*, because now he knew how to perform some form of Alchemy Essentia, so he didn't mind one bit. Actually, now that he'd done the procedure so many times between his practice runs and the actually important ones, he felt he might be able to start branching out slightly . . .

Anyway. He should talk more about the weather.

His basic design for his mana accumulator hadn't changed much from its initial inception. It still consisted of three parts. First was the gatherer itself, which would scoop up the ambient wind mana and deliver it to the storage, the second part of the device. The final part was the injector itself, whatever he'd use to take mana from the storage and feed it into the enchantments.

Fortunately, the tower seemed to be adaptable enough that so long as he provided *enough* magic to it, it could take care of itself. Whoever made the tower was *really* impressive, to make such a critical job into the mage's equivalent of turning a hand crank. That just left Edwin with the challenge of actually *making* the accumulator.

He was imagining some sort of mana structure, a funnel made of something repulsive to wind mana. Then, some kind of filter—made *of* wind mana, perhaps?—that would block everything but that single type of mana, and then it would feed into the storage?

Prototyping sadly didn't work with magic. Levels in the Skill had practically been flying in comparison to how much he used it, though he wasn't entirely sure why. Regardless, while it did allow him to simulate an entire alchemy set, perfect for Apparatus, it didn't give him any information on how to influence mana. Maybe after his next tier-up.

The storage was still key. Depending on what he was able to make, that would influence both parts 1 and 3, because he didn't know how to get mana *into* or *out* of it yet. Molai was the obvious candidate, yes, but there were still so many issues that trying to use the flower might present that Edwin didn't know about.

Well, it had been some time since he had last tried to refine molai.

Perhaps his manaclave would help in that regard? If he could some-how set up the situation where he could extract the mana-absorption trait from the dried petals? Well, no. That would require him to Refine the petals first and *then* he could manipulate them with his manaclave.

It was a pity he couldn't Refine the flower petals while they were in the manaclave, because the loosened magical bonds between the different traits might help him in his endeavor, but even with addi-tional practice, if he tried adding any mana to the setup besides what he needed for the device to function, it would all unravel.

Perhaps he could do it bit by bit? The main problem with trying to Refine molai, after all, was that the plant would absorb all his mana before he could actually Refine it. So, the primary issue was how *long* it would take to get any kind of meaningful results. A half a petal of molai would produce almost *no* dust or liquid, but if he could *use* what little he had in his manaclave, he could then speed up the process somewhat by directly extracting the desired property from what he had.

Or maybe, Edwin realized, his Visualization Skill would help? If he could somehow make an acidlike manifestation of his mana, would that help eat away at the molai? He'd tried combining Refine with his Visualization, of course, but concentrating his mana was still really slow and yielded really tiny amounts of workable mana. He hadn't tried using an *acid*, but it was conceptually similar to how his manaclave functioned, so maybe?

It could work. He'd have to give it a try, probably also with really tiny amounts of molai so as to successfully overload its absorptive effects. Edwin nodded to himself. It was worth a try, if nothing else.

It wasn't easy, of course. Nothing ever was, when it came to mana, but after a few days brainstorming different configurations to synthesize acid, Edwin had a breakthrough.

Because of how many things boiling water could already dissolve, he started with that, but then turned down the temperature, while still keeping the dissolution at full strength. To do *that*, he had to make a virtual manaclave separating out the different components of his magic *within his own magic*, then pull out the temperature of the water, imagine purifying the resultant dissolving water, and only *then* did he have the right kind of vaguely acidic mana he'd need.

Even thinking about it after the fact made Edwin's head hurt, and without Inion's and Rillah's guidance for stretching his visualization, and how to layer his visualizations for more complex results, he would have never managed it. As it stood, he used *every last level* he had in Visualization and definitely felt the limitations he *did* have. It was a lot. But he could do it!

Trial seven. Using five milligrams of crushed molai petal and thirty seconds of mana channeling, he narrated to Almanac.

With his not-boiling acid potion-mana (a thought that made his whole setup feel even more ridiculous) on hand, Edwin triggered Refining. In his mental image of his mana, he had a hearty supply of acid, but then he fed it over a Bunsen burner burning a Refining flame—pure white and almost painful to look at—and boiled off what was left of the . . . nonboiling water.

Mana didn't always make a lot of sense, apparently. What mattered to his visualization was apparently that he'd made something close enough to an acid that he could then treat it as though it *were* one. He hoped that one day he'd be able to apply it to more things, but one step at a time.

In any case, by the time Refining was done with its preparations, he had just a tiny amount, just a few millimeter-equivalent-size drops of concentrated Refining mana acid. He'd already prepared his target molai with more on standby, and there was nothing more he could do.

With a deep breath, he allowed the mana to drip onto the molai.

Instantly, half of what he'd brought was just *gone*. The dried and crushed petals absorbed it like a sponge, cutting off his connection to the mana. Then, it overloaded, dumping similar but disconnected mana into the mixture and almost disrupting his attempt.

This was as far as his previous trials had gotten—the molai absorbing and discharging his mana until he had nothing left under his control. This time, though, he felt the corrosive nature of his "acid" at play. The molai had released its mana *really* easily, the instant it reached saturation. That was probably a good sign?

He'd need to rely a lot on Alchemy for this, he could already tell, and possibly just have to figure out what he did *after* the fact. It pained him, but if it was the optimal way to go about things?

Well, he'd make it work.

He felt the mana structure of the molai unravel beneath his fingertips. Doing it like this damaged it somewhat, but he could make do. He didn't need it to be *that* strong, after all, he was more after the effect and if the final substance didn't hold on to mana as tightly . . . that was almost a benefit.

Bit by bit he broke down the little molai he had, and as soon as the tiny pile was deconstructed, he added another dried petal. He didn't know *what* trait he was Refining, but that wasn't really an issue.

It wasn't the first time he'd tried adding in additional Refining substance to an ongoing Refinement, but it wasn't any easier than the first time he tried. The fresh molai scooped up a hefty amount of his Refining mana, but enough fortunately remained that he could keep the reaction going, and with just a bit of a mental twist, the molai began to dissolve.

Nearly an hour and a half later, Edwin came out of his Refining trance, completely mentally exhausted. Even his *magic* felt tired, having spent so long trying to corral larger and larger amounts of disconnected mana.

The results were well worth it, though. A large pile of white dust sat before him, practically radiating possibility, and flickering with magic. One moment, it felt like nothing, the next moment like a dry wind, followed by a gushing spring or a brilliant light, then a raging fire and . . .

Huh. What had he created?

With a bit of trepidation, he pushed a tiny bit of mana, just free-casting, a single drop of neutral potion-mana dripping onto the pile of molai.

Instantly, the flickering sensations Ritual Intuition fed him vanished, replaced by a steady sensation of typeless mana emanating from the substance, as though it were his exact shade of personal magic.

Edwin grinned. Well, you never knew what you might find. He'd wanted storage, but it looked like he'd found his filter. He cut off the trickle of mana he was feeding the pile, and the flicker returned immediately.

Interesting. No retention whatsoever?

A bit of testing later, he'd developed a working theory for what he had on hand and noted it in his Almanac log.

Results: Success! Hypothesis for resulting material: Standard Refined Molai seems to have excellent mana-emission and mana-absorption properties, though only of a single type at a time—defined by contiguous mass.

It might be able to work as a conductor, but it *definitely* would work as a filter. Weird that *that* was the default result for Refining Molai, but maybe it had to do with his methodology? Further testing required.

With his initial plans for molai usage somewhat scrapped, Edwin found himself in the position of needing to find a new mana storage device

. . . or did he? He'd revised his plans to try and simplify them a fair amount: instead, he'd plug the filter directly into the ritual circle. All that he would need for *that* was a substance that was easily workable and mana-conductive.

He *was* in a port, and while the alchemical options available were really sparse, surely he could find *something* that conducted mana. Heck, it was built into the tower, the lines etched into the floor. While he hadn't yet figured out what element they were *mainly* made of, he knew it wasn't iron, gold, silver, or copper. The latter two *were* included, just in relatively small quantities, but there was some element present; he just didn't know *what* it was.

It was the weakness of Alchemical Analysis, he realized. If he hadn't been able to label a substance in another object, he wasn't going to find out what it was. For all he knew, the lines might have been made of mostly pure titanium. Or maybe platinum. Heck, it might have been a completely new element not found on Earth.

How that might work . . . he had no idea, unless it was either seriously radioactive or the laws of physics and chemistry had been edited to make more room on the periodic table. He might be able to test that, actually? He'd look into it later.

Some playing around with Alchemical Analysis had also revealed that he could determine species! Namely, it told him that Rillah was 50 percent Human, 50 percent some unknown species (which he promptly labeled as elven). There was probably some clever way to use that new capability, but he didn't know *what* use that might be. Maybe as a way to identify if people were related, perhaps he could tag people based on heritage instead of just species, but that wasn't *too* generally useful except as a way to help him avoid putting his foot in his mouth.

(Interestingly, it also revealed that Lefi wasn't 100 percent human, only about 90 percent, but what the remaining 12-ish percent was remained a mystery that the Adventurer himself remained frustratingly unhelpful in cracking.)

Anyway.

Perhaps he could *make* something that was conductive to mana? Perhaps he could work with copper. It had decent electrical conductivity, perhaps he could edit that in some way to make it *magical* conductivity?

If he could refine out the *electrical* conductivity of copper and replace that with a *mana* conductive trait?

While he couldn't ignore the filtering trait of molai, it *was* technically conductive in that it could decidedly hold mana while also not keeping the mana trapped. It was definitely close enough to at least *try*, and Alchemy whispered that it might just work.

Sounded like a plan to him. Also, he might need to reevaluate his habit of ignoring Alchemy's baseless information when doing exploratory research. He needed to find the weird patterns before he could understand them, after all.

It took a *really* long time to Refine metals. Like molai, they had a really high mana capacity, but fortunately, unlike the annoying flower, Edwin retained his connection the entire time and so didn't have to resort to any particularly fancy tricks to render down Refined materials. It just took power and time. Lots, and lots, of time.

It felt a bit like corrosion, to Refine copper. Edwin could feel his mana, acting like an acid, slowly dissolve the metal one atom at a time. It stole away nuclei and electrons one at a time, snatching them from their established crystal structure and binding them to mana itself.

Did Infusion have something to do with bonds or electrons? Perhaps Refining worked by interrupting intramolecular bonds somehow, reducing it to a powder? He hadn't encountered any Refining products that ended up as a gas, but that didn't mean they didn't exist.

Still, by cannibalizing a pile of ves he eventually assembled a decent amount of copper, which he then Refined into a faintly green pile of Refined dust. In theory, it should be a superconductor, but Edwin didn't really have any way to test it.

It still served as an excellent trait-solvent, though.

Edwin had redesigned his manaclave a few times, with the latest iteration being a single apparatite sphere he could just rotate to move his sample from one trait-powder to the second. It was tricky making sure that the powders wouldn't mix, but he got it without *too* much difficulty. That the powders were physical was a decent boon, as it meant he could rely heavily on apparatite *everything*.

He triumphantly loaded up the device, ran through the procedure, and . . .

Nothing.

Well, that was disappointing. A bit of prodding showed that he *did* successfully remove conductivity from copper, but there hadn't been any change in the mana conductivity. He shouldn't be that surprised, though; he didn't have *that* much experience with Essentia and this was a bigger change than the native temperature of an object.

Annoyingly, his normal cheat of asking Rillah or Lefi what the substance Identified as didn't work, as it only ever came back as "alchemical copper." Apparently custom-made, brand-new totally novel altered variations of a metal didn't count as "common knowledge" or something. Truly, life was fantastically unfair.

He kept most of the failures for later testing.

The solstice had come and gone to no particular fanfare in the tower. The weather had been mild, Rillah used very little wind mana, and the days marched on. Outside there had been some celebration going on near the shortest day of the year, but after how his *last* trek into the city had gone, Edwin was more than happy to stay inside and mess around with his potion set.

Edwin wished he could say he gained some clever insight over the next few weeks and his dozens of Essentia experiments, but honestly all he was gaining was sheer *practice*. The levels he earned in Alchemy were helpful, sure, but what he primarily refined was his own technique, and the ways he could tweak his manaclave's function to more effectively swap traits. He hadn't had any luck in directly editing a substance's natural traits, so he was stuck swapping similar ones between substances.

The only real change he'd encountered with his copper-editing experiments was mixing in a bit of Refined copper dust with his Refined molai dust. He also found that for this kind of trial, the margins for success versus failure was measured in *milliseconds*. His copper had to go essentially straight from dissolution to replacement, and that was only possible *because* it didn't matter if copper got mixed in with the molai.

Those two discoveries were actually *related*, but that was beside the point. Because of the massive difference in densities between the two substances, he could separate them again later, but it added even *more* time onto an already time-consuming procedure. Heck, starting his manaclave already took nearly half an hour thanks to the volume of mana needed in its use.

This time, though, Edwin knew it. He'd succeed totally, and the copper wouldn't glow but do nothing else; it wouldn't just make all the mana he tried to pour into it just skate right along the surface; it wouldn't suffer any of the many unique failures he'd experienced over dozens of experiments.

This one would work, he could feel it.

The workbench in front of him held a single crystal ball, suspended off the table by apparatite supports. The crystal ball was far from clear or even solid, and held in its center was a tiny bowl, just barely larger than the copper disk—formed from half a dozen ves beaten into a uniform mass—it held. A faintly green-tinted copper powder completely enveloped the disk, and a large pile of white dust was mounded at the bottom of the sphere.

Edwin took a deep breath and pulled on his mana. He fed it through Basic Thermokinesis flame and the Unbound Tether press, through a Refining crucible and ignited in Bomb Throwing. It was lit on fire with Firestarting and filtered through Fey's Caress. Over time, the combined pressure and heat was imbued into his mana, and it was in turn fed into the crystal sphere.

If Edwin had his eyes open, he would have seen a slightly reddish glow begin to suffuse the manaclave, but Ritual Intuition told him everything he needed to know. Alchemical Dismantling was at full work, gently coaxing the copper to magically melt and mix with the copper it was surrounded by. Bit by bit, the metal complied, its structure weakening under extreme conditions.

Then, complete collapse. The copper's conductivity disassociated, and the copper dust it was buried in shifted and flowed.

Edwin flipped the contraption upside down with a sharp shake, sending white and copper powder flying into the air, mixing and combining around the copper disc. He could feel the magical aspects of the molai mixing with the familiarity of the copper . . . and then it settled into a single pile, flowing smoothly into the copper disc.

With a triumphant grin, Edwin unsealed the container as he allowed the manaclave to dissipate. The air inside hissed as the pressure was released, and the firelike mana blasted out like actual hot air.

With what basically amounted to apparatite chopsticks, Edwin delicately fished out the copper disc at the center of all this. Was it glimmering slightly? This was a big moment; all that was left was to drip a bit of his basic mana against the coin and see if it conducted it properly. With bated breath, he summoned a drop of mana at his fingertip and let it fall . . .

. . . where it promptly splashed against the metal's exterior with minimal absorption, the disc apparently no more mana conductive than normal unmodified copper.

Dang it. He hadn't mixed the copper and molai enough, it seemed. Or maybe he'd used too *much* molai? Should he try introducing just a bit of magic to the familiar conductivity, instead of the other way around?

. . . Okay, maybe *next* time he'd succeed. He had a good feeling about this one!

Level Up!

Skill Points 1112→1142 (Avg level: 57)

Adaptive Defense Level 48→49

Alchemical Analysis Level 44→47

Alchemical Dismantling Level 54→55

Alchemy Level 96→98

Anatomy Level 45→47

Basic Thermokinesis Level 41→44

Bomb Throwing Level 60→62

Improbable Arsenal Level 42→43

Outsider's Almanac Level 138→139

Prototyping Level 44→45

Refining Level 43→46

Ritual Intuition Level 53→54

Sapper's Apparatus Level 66→67

Stamina Manipulation Level 14→19

Unbound Tether Level 26→29

CHAPTER 17

A Mana on a Mission

Though it was tricky, Edwin *was* eventually able to properly give copper the mana-conducting properties he'd been aiming for. It was quite the ordeal, with significant amounts of trial and error, where each experiment had a tremendous amount of cleanup. At least copper and molai had drastically different densities even when Refined, so it wasn't too hard to separate them out.

After so long, he couldn't help but feel satisfied watching—sensing, rather—his drops of mana soaking into the metal on contact, then radiating out again over the course of a few seconds. During that whole process, it became impermeable to other types of mana, just like the Refined molai it was based on.

Now the only problem was making sure it would only *ever* accept wind mana. While he thought of several ways he might be able to accomplish that, most of them still required a mage to keep a battery topped up. For obvious reasons, that wasn't an acceptable compromise. Instead, he needed to make a self-sustaining filter.

The next step . . .

The next step would truly test his resolve and Skills, he knew.

He read through every Almanac note that he had from both the *Zosiman Grimoire* and his time in Panastalis alike, and all of it had led to a single, horrifying conclusion.

He could do this. Attuning an object to a type of magic was a well-documented field, and copper was especially easy. It probably wouldn't even be *that* technically challenging.

He'd just . . . need to use Panastalin alchemy techniques.

Naturally, given the fact he'd never successfully completed a single potion using the directions their tradition had created, this also presented a bit of a problem. However, he felt that with just a few tweaks to the procedure, he could *make* it compatible with his own brand of alchemy.

The theory was simple: he'd take some of his filter-copper and attune it to wind mana *permanently*, by essentially alloying it to a substance that was itself air-attuned.

. . . except it wasn't actually an alloy despite using one in construction, and what he was using for attunement was just the air *itself*, or at least condensed air mana and . . . Well, it was complicated.

Condensing air mana was *in theory* relatively straightforward. He'd had a *lot* of practice making a manaclave at this point, after all, and a condenser was kind of just the reverse of that. Of course, because making something hot was much easier than making it cold, especially when using Basic Thermokinesis as a base, it was nowhere near as nice and neat as it should have been.

If his mana were a *gas*, this would be so much simpler. Then he could just create a mana-heat pump and make a mana-refrigerator. Manafrigerator. Manerator. Manainator. Manarefrigeratorinator.

Refrigerators worked by taking a gas and almost squeezing heat out of it, putting it under immense pressure. Charles's Law did as Charles's Law did, raising the temperature of the compressed gas, and then thermodynamics did as thermodynamics did and let that heat bleed out of the system. That way, when the pressure was released, the gas expanded back to a larger volume, and heat would be pulled back into the system, cooling its surroundings.

If you had the right setup, you could make sure all the heat was dumped into the air *away* from where the cooling was happening, and that gave you a heat pump, the basis for refrigeration, air-conditioning, and efficient heating units.

Unless . . .

Well, his mana *did* behave like a liquid most of the time. Perhaps he could set up a heat pump . . . mana pump. Yeah, he liked that way more than manarefrigeratorinator. If he set up a mana pump based on a liquid, it might still work; he'd just need to pull a vacuum around a drop of liquid . . . which he totally could do with Apparatus, actually. Huh, yeah. That might actually work. It might not be as effective, though . . . but what about if he used a liquid that was *just* shy of being able to boil? Or that boiled at room temperature?

His potion-mana *was* flexible in that regard—he'd made it both flammable and nonflammable at different times when trying to make his manaclave—so a liquid with a high heat capacity that boiled at just barely above room temperature would be an excellent refrigerant . . . probably.

Actually, come to think of it, weren't there liquid refrigerants? Memory pulled pentane to mind, as it boiled at about 35 Celsius, but he couldn't remember if it was actually a *good* refrigerant.

It was a pity he couldn't exactly synthesize the mana equivalents of *specific* chemicals with his Visualization Skill yet, but he might get there one day. For now . . . well, he could definitely Visualize a potion that heatlessly boiled and bubbled within its container. That would work for his purposes, he felt.

Now, he just needed to *do* it.

"You know what I don't get?"

Inion looked up. "I have genuinely no idea what you're talking about."

"Well, with this"—Edwin indicated the partially assembled refrigerator—"mana is this weird thing that doesn't seem to care about pretty much any laws of physics, but it can be manipulated like it's a gas."

"It's your visualization."

"What?"

"Your science stuff, and alchemy? Ya, you act as though it's a 'thing' in the world, and it behaves like it should."

"Wait, it applies to mana that *isn't* mine?"

"How did you think artifacts work?"

"Like magic items, artifacts? I mean, I guess I assumed they were a trophy Skill or something, or the result of a Skill like Mana Infusion."

He shrugged. "I don't think I've ever seen a properly enchanted item that might not just be the result of a Skill . . . no wait, Lefi has a magical tooth necklace, but it might still just be a Skill. But . . . well, actually, I suppose this is a magical item, isn't it?"

"Look at my little alchemist, all grown up and making artifacts," she teased.

Edwin grinned cheekily. "I'm glad you're proud of me, *Mom*. You know, for someone who claims to not know anything about magic, you sure seem to have a lot of experience with it."

"Comes with age, if you'd respect your elders."

"Elders? Forget respect, you belong in a *museum*."

"Oh, now *I'm* supposed to go in the museum, Mister I'm-Not-from-This-World?"

"At least I'd have company."

"Oh, *believe me,* you'll . . ."

Because nothing involving magic was easy, it took Edwin nearly two days of work before he managed to properly Visualize a mana pump that actually worked the way it was supposed to. Even then, it took a *ton* more work before he got it working at the proper scales. He could at least make it somewhat easier on himself by making a crystal apparatus to mirror his mana manipulation.

Of course, since he wasn't actually using any liquids or the like for this experiment, it all looked empty to the eye, but he could feel just how brimming with mana the entire contraption was. A tightly wound coil of hollow apparatite encircled a funnel and corresponding pipe. In theory, air—and air mana—would be cooled by the mana pump, condense along the surface, and run down into a waiting collection jar.

Working with so much "lab" hardware reminded him a bit of his research, actually, which in turn idly made him wonder how people back on Earth must have been getting on without him. It *had* been a couple years now, after all. It was just . . . it was just . . .

Edwin stopped and set down the apparatite pipe he was working with. He closed his eyes, clenching his hand into a fist as he took a deep, deep breath. He breathed out into his hands as he reached up to wipe away some of the wetness around his eyes. He was fine. He was here, he was happy *enough*. At least as happy as he'd been back on Earth, anyway. He was doing his dream job, he had people who tolerated him, he *could do this*.

He was fine.

He was *fine*.

He dried his hands with Basic Thermokinesis and picked up the pipe he was working with, holding it in place while he slowly summoned the connecting piece that would hold it in place. It was important that this was a completely airtight seal, because while it wasn't *technically* effective in holding in energy, his mana *wasn't* energy, was it? It was a potion. In this case, a near-boiling potion, but a potion nonetheless. So airtight seals would *definitely* help keep his potions in place.

Edwin had found that he was able to manipulate far more mana than his extremely restrictive Basic Mana Manipulation strictly allowed for, but only in very specific circumstances, among which this counted. After all, he saw mana as a potion, as an actual *thing* that could be manipulated. That was why this should work. If he did this with a physical setup, he'd be basically making liquid nitrogen and oxygen, probably with a fair amount of ice . . . condensing a snippet of the entire atmosphere.

How else would you condense atmospheric mana?

Finally, he got the contraption set up in its entirety. On one side, a reservoir with *plenty* of surface area awaited being filled by refrigerant mana. It was in turn connected to a set of tubes and pipes that snaked around the entrance to his collections flask, which it would pull heat from. Then, all that would work together to condense atmospheric mana and let it drip onto a specially prepared molai flower that he was using as a makeshift battery for this experiment.

To keep the pressure differential up, and thus allow for actual transmission of heat, two valves were attached to the entrance and exit of the reservoir, and at the entrance of the reservoir (where mana would flow after completing the full course of pipes) he combined a ball-bearing one-way valve with a tesla one-way valve to, well, only allow mana one way through the piping.

His role in the entire setup was serving as the vacuum pump, pushing mana from the tubing through the valves and back into the reservoir, repressurizing the gas into a liquid and squeezing "heat" out of the mana through a combination of spatial expansion and contraction (thanks to Improbable Arsenal) and raw mana "muscle."

He double-checked all his connections, ensured that everything was in working order.

He triple-checked everything to make sure nothing was out of place.

He let loose the valves, letting the mana vaporize, felt it draw in heat from its surroundings, and started repressurizing mana as fast as he could manage, shoving that accumulated heat back into the reservoir.

Nothing happened.

Hmm.

It didn't seem to be a problem with his theory—he could definitely feel "heat" being pushed out of the reservoir, and his vacuum pump setup was working about as well as he could hope.

Well, maybe if he—

Crack.

That *probably* wasn't good. Still, it could be worse.

Hiss.

At least it didn't explode?

Three design iterations later, Edwin finally had something that should work. Instead of trying to condense air as it passed through an open-topped container, he had a closed and sealed vessel, which he had filled with air while expanded with Improbable Arsenal. When he dismissed that Skill, it of course put the gas under pressure—about seven atmospheres if his math was right.

He wasn't *sure* that putting the air under pressure would make that much of a difference, but considering he was Visualizing air mana as behaving like actual air, higher pressure should result in a higher dew point for the mana.

The core mechanism of the pump remained intact, but it had a few key differences, mostly centered around the actual cooling side.

The most obvious difference was that it was made out of copper. While the apparatite pipes *technically* worked, and were really easy for him to make, they didn't have the greatest thermal conductivity as well as not always being able to withstand the intense temperatures and pressures when made superthin, breaking relatively easy and wrecking a lot of hard work.

He'd thought that it shouldn't make a difference because there was no *actual* temperature or pressure manipulation going on, just magical equivalents like when working with his manaclave, but it seemed as though he'd been mistaken for some reason. Maybe this was just too many levels of abstraction from his *actual* mana that he was directly controlling? Something to test in the future.

Edwin also made a note to himself to, once he left Sheraith, really, *really* delve deeply into what the "loosened limits" of Sapper's Apparatus did at such a high level. It was entirely possible he could get something superstrong and superconductive if only he knew how, but copper was easy enough for now. To make his tubing, all he needed to do was create a *mold* out of apparatite, and pray that it didn't shatter from the thermal shock of melted copper being poured into it—though apparently Lefi had a Skill for that, because of *course* he did.

With the copper tubing thus formed, it was simple enough to substitute it into Edwin's existing design, but instead of being wrapped around the outside of his container, he'd made it into a protruding shape from the *top* of his container. He wasn't *actually* sure if it made a difference in terms of how effective the condenser was, but it at least removed a layer of insulation and was, critically, *easier to make*. It also should drip directly onto his molai blossom as well, which was a bonus.

Moment of truth.

Edwin filled the reservoir with refrigerant-mana, and he could immediately feel the volatile "potion" begin to boil. That was put to a quick stop when he pressurized the container, but it came back with a vengeance as he opened the exit valve.

It really was kind of impressive, the amount of force he was able to put his mana under. To do this for real, he'd need a really strong air pump and chemical refrigerants he didn't even know how to *start* trying to synthesize. But here he was, able to compress a refrigerant "by hand" and manually run an entire mana pump. His Skills definitely helped, but he felt rather proud of himself nonetheless. He supposed that this was what his mana *was* really good at. He couldn't use it directly most of the time, but he *could* use it as a lever for even more impressive feats.

Speaking of impressive feats.

Within just a few minutes, he felt a buildup of air mana along the copper heat sink. It slowly coalesced, shining brightly to his arcano-ception and feeling like so much air, so much wind compressed into a shining drop of mana. It felt like gentle breezes and violent hurricanes, vicious tornadoes and encouraging updrafts, the gentle warmth of a summer evening and the charged atmosphere of a thunderstorm. It carried a depth that was well past what Edwin had anticipated but was absolutely *perfect* for what he needed.

He looked on with wonder as the miniature atmosphere condensed, collecting into a single drop of natural potionlike mana at the end of his copper condenser and falling with a satisfying *drip* onto the waiting petals of the molai beneath it.

The flower greedily slurped up the mana, and the process started anew.

Edwin held in his whoop of triumph. It was working! Actually, truly working! He had spent . . . so long on this stupid little contraption, but this was proof! He could work with atmospheric mana like it was a physical substance, even if only in limited circumstances. He could make what he needed for his mana accumulator, he . . .

Another drop of air mana fell into the molai, vanishing without a trace. To work properly, the molai would need to be *almost* at satura-tion, and when it was filling in at the rate of one drop per minute at most . . .

. . . He'd be at this for hours.

I really should update my level-up window, Edwin mused, play-ing with the notification as he lay in bed that night. He'd initially included the "average level" in his pop-up to help reassure him he was getting closer and closer to his goal back when he was trying to hit Tier 2, but it didn't really measure his progress toward the next tier anymore. After all, he was at *least* waiting until Alchemy hit level 120 so he could get the Alchemy Specialist Path and possibly even beyond that, if he decided he wanted to take more 90-point Paths this time around.

Because Specialist Paths *were* 90 points, that was two right away that he definitely wanted to take. Then after that, he'd absolutely need Essential Alchemist, and he wanted to take Realm Traveler this tier. Oh! Scientific Revolutionary as well, and of course Material Scientist. Then Physicist and Schooled Mage—he hoped that one might help Prototyping and his Visualization interact in some way—and . . .

No, bad Edwin.

He wanted *all* the Paths. All of them. Oh, right, he also needed to earn the Artisan Path to get Dexterity, and probably take Scholar at some point because it was likely to unlock Intelligence. Oh, but what did he want to evolve Stamina Manipulation with?

Cough.

Right, right. He'd cross that bridge when he got there. He just wanted all the Paths; was that really so bad? But to get all the Paths, he'd need to know how many he could afford . . .

Edwin flexed his Status Skill, removing the "average level" marker he usually kept up, replacing it with the level of Stamina Manipulation, Alchemy, and how many 60-point Paths he could afford with his current Skill Point total.

Oh, should he subtract sixty from that to account for what he'd evolve Stamina Manipulation with? That might be a good idea.

Oh, and—

Keep it simple. No subtractions, no fancy business.

He couldn't help but grumble at himself slightly, but he *did* eventually keep the setup relatively straightforward.

Level Up!
Skill Points 1142→1147
(Alchemy: 99; Stamina Manipulation: 19; 13/25 60-point Paths)

Yeah, that would work just fine. His Alchemy might nearly be breaking into the triple digits, but he knew better than to think it meant he'd have an *easy* time getting it to 120. He'd been leveling the Skill *blazingly* fast by his normal standards, at nearly one level a week at times, but that was because he was diving headlong into the wonders of Alchemy Essentia for the first time.

Well . . . he had time. He hadn't *fully* decided what he would do when they left Sheraith, but hopefully Lefi and Rillah would be traveling together toward the coast. That way, he'd be able to keep traveling with them while he went to get abysite and visit Farport.

That was a problem for another day. Future-Edwin could deal with that when he was older and wiser. Current-Edwin really ought to *get to sleep*. He idly wondered if blue "light" from System text had the same impact on brains as blue light normally did, in that it caused it to wake up slightly.

Maybe not? So far as he could tell, System messages were entirely hallucinatory, with no physical or optical component. Pulling up a System message should then be the equivalent of imagining a blue sky, right? Not that it would really matter, not when he could consciously activate his Sleeping Skill and make himself fall asleep in an instant.

He was getting distracted again.

Okay, no more messing around, he needed his rest.

Sleeping.

It was time. After *days* of experimentation and *hours* of constant work, Edwin had finally managed to saturate his molai blossom with enough atmospheric air mana to attune his filter-copper to the local air magic.

He'd tried a few related experiments with Rillah's wind mana to get some practice, so he knew he wasn't going to waste the precious atmospheric mana to some stupid mistake. So long as he followed his notes and his Alchemy Skill, it would all go fine.

He couldn't use Rillah's personal mana for his actual experiment for a few reasons, most notably that it didn't actually *match* atmospheric mana all that well. It was permeated from top to bottom with the sensations of motion and change, and while good enough for the tower's enchantments to accept it as a power source—they could accept *anything*—using it as the filter for his mana accumulator would result in almost *no* mana actually being accumulated.

He'd checked.

Extensively.

At least the filter-copper was reusable—the attunement process involved flushing out all lingering traces of mana, anyway, which included all previous attunements. He could even reclaim the gold used . . . but he was getting ahead of himself.

Before him, an apparatite sphere rested over a powerful but tiny flame, and within rested his ingot of filtered copper. In turn, his molai flower sat atop the copper ingot, covered ever so gently by a small disc of gold leaf, draping over the petals like a stiff cloth. The entire contraption was at as good of a vacuum he could pull, which was actually pretty impressive these days, to prevent the blossom from catching on fire as he heated it all to absurd temperatures. Wilting was fine, but burning was *not*.

Lefi had been kind enough to provide him with the needed coins, not that Edwin needed that much—about one gram of gold was enough for the gilding, which was in turn about a sixth of a penny-sized grai. His half-kilo of copper came from about fifty ves Refined into being proper filters, and then melted together.

Ah, gold-based economies. It made acquiring precious metals *so easy*.

Edwin's entire setup was apparently leaning fairly heavily into Alchemy Essentia, which wasn't nearly as intimidating as it had once seemed. It was all about changing the structure of a substance, and while it wasn't quite the same as chemical bonds, it wasn't entirely different, either. While the more advanced forms of the discipline were the equivalent of editing atomic nuclei, this was *far* simpler and, crucially, *possible* at his current skill level (and Skill level).

Because gold and copper were so alchemically similar to each other (both of them being colored metals with similar melting points and in the same column of the periodic table, which Edwin felt was important even if it wasn't listed in *Zosiman*), when they alloyed there was a brief moment where the magical structure of the copper loosened to allow ingress to the gold and its magical structure, of the sort he could induce in his manaclave. However, unlike with his manaclave, there were no traits being removed, just the synthesis of preexisting ones.

By placing the molai between the gold and copper, he was including the flower in that reaction, sensitizing the gold to another type of mana, and when the metals mixed, the gold would carry with it just enough wind mana to replace its normal purity. In Panastalin terms, he was creating a potion with copper as the base, gold as the primary, and molai as the tuner.

It would work even better if the flower was *gilded*, but Edwin was sure that his setup was sufficient for his purposes, and it didn't involve risking his molai blossom in yet *another* fiddly alchemical reaction that could burn up all his hard work in an instant if he messed up.

There was more going on, and he was *determined* to figure out what, but for now the reaction had shown that it *worked*, and that was ultimately what mattered at the moment.

Edwin kept stoking the flames as he waited for the gold to melt. He was very glad that apparatite just *didn't* melt and was borderline immune to damage from temperature. It definitely became more *brittle* with extreme heat or cold whether magical or mundane, but it never shattered or melted so long as he didn't expose it to too much thermal shock. For this, he was using a magnesium fire and slowly lowering his apparatus into the crucible.

After his experiment was suspended five centimeters above the fire for a few minutes, Edwin sensed the change moments before it happened, and he quickly wrapped the entire system in a thin layer of mana to help isolate it. He barely finished when the gold leaf began to melt, completely enveloping the dried, shriveled molai flower.

He could feel there was still atmospheric mana trapped in the remnant, whatever property of the flower that made it so good at absorbing magic still holding true even as it was heated to unreasonable temperatures. But, as the gold melted over it and, a few moments later, the copper began to melt and mix, he felt a brief flash of intense magic.

It faded away almost instantly, but left behind a faint sense of . . . potential. An endless sky, shapeless but full of possibility. Edwin released his mana isolation grip on the system, and the liquid metal immediately turned almost invisible against the normal air's mana.

Success.

In an effort to maximize the surface area of his newly finished copper, Edwin once again enlisted Lefi's aid in metalworking to beat his ingot of copper into as thin a sheet as possible. By the end of it, he had a disc nearly as thin as paper and about a meter and a half in diameter. That was good, but still not sufficient. A copper circle did a lot to *block* wind, after all, not harness it, so Edwin then found himself using Construction and Alchemical Dismantling to cut and shape the metal into approximately the shape of a fan, then reinforced it with some apparatite and copper supports.

It all went . . . surprisingly well. It was just mechanical cuts and fastening and the like, which while not something he had a *ton* of experience in was far simpler than the alchemical problems he normally found himself dealing with.

He even had Rillah test it, having her unleash a relatively anemic gust of wind at the contraption. While the amount of wind mana was low, the fan worked admirably as it spun on its mount. With every rotation, more wind mana was allowed to pass through and the more the fan picked up. Because the density of atmospheric mana was higher in the air than in the copper, it was drawn into the metal and radiated out closer to the floor, where it could then be absorbed into the tower's enchantment. The enchantment was actually pretty impressive, or so Edwin felt, because of just how readily it absorbed any kind of air or wind mana to power itself, like an eternally dry mana sponge . . . if the sponge was then used to run a hydroelectric power plant.

Edwin couldn't help but feel that the mechanical side of *his* creation worked *great*, at least once he *liberally* cheated with magic, both in the Skill sense—using Prototyping for perhaps the first time in the context it was meant for and leaning on well-used Construction techniques—and in the alchemy sense.

He might not have had slipstone, that magical mortar variety that had basically *no* friction—though he probably could have made more lime if he had really tried—but Infused sand still acted pretty much like a superfluid, meaning it made for an almost perfect grease once he had it properly contained. Everything that should spin did, and everything that shouldn't, didn't. Because of how much he was using Sapper's Apparatus, it looked more crystalline than metal, but he didn't really see that as much of an *issue*, particularly when it let him explore his more creative side when decorating the supports.

That everything went so well on the *mechanical* side of things just made his failures on the magical part of the device all the more frustrating. It wasn't even a true failure in any particular area, either; all the individual components of the device worked just fine. The "windmill" filtered atmospheric mana and transmitted it to a copper wire running to the floor, the filter-copper successfully radiated mana . . . it just wasn't radiating *enough* in the relevant section, so the enchantments stayed underpowered.

What Edwin eventually diagnosed was that there just wasn't a *reason* for the copper to radiate mana preferentially near the floor over any other surface—and it had a *lot* of surface area. He'd need some way to keep the relative mana density lower near the enchantments, which would create a bit of a vacuum and thus radiate more mana in the appropriate area.

Refining was no help, still. The solution was bound to be in molai, but the flower continued to eat all the mana he sent its way unless it was specifically corrosive—and in that case, the mana storage trait was ruined, rendering it useless for this.

Ultimately, classic alchemy came to the rescue. Molai still worked just fine in potions and everything that *didn't* involve Refining, and if his Alchemy Skill was good at determining how he could use Refining, it was *fantastic* at potions. It only took a few tweaks to his overcharge-barrier potion to bring it back to mana-sensitive, and by adding a few touches of Refined copper and ground glowleaf, sealing it all in with a rousing boil, he created a slightly luminescent, milky-white potion held within an apparatite crystal custom-made to fit into the gaps between his mana engine and the corresponding section of the enchantment.

Personally, Edwin couldn't help but feel particularly satisfied with his ability to take a potion meant to temporarily inhibit mana from running rampant through his body and turning it into a mana sink that was actually useful in real life!

It was always such a fun feeling.

Edwin was amused at how much the final device had in common with his initial prototype. He had his copper turbine as the wind mana accumulator and filter, the potion as his storage, and then a small container meant to aid in the transfer. When the wind blew, the minuscule amounts of mana it carried with it would be blown across the fan and absorbed. It would then be carried through the copper and absorbed into the molai potion. Once the potion hit saturation, it overloaded and emptied completely, charging up the enchantment. Then the cycle would start anew.

Edwin allowed the system to run a few cycles, wind blowing through the open top of the tower as the turbine spun to face the wind. As the air's speed increased, so, too, did the rate of charge and discharge. The enchantment was accepting the new source of mana, no problem; there weren't any creaks and groans.

He stepped back, put his hands on his hips, and looked with satisfaction at his creation.

Success.

Congratulations! For imbuing a substance with an elemental affinity you have unlocked the Elemental Alchemist Path!
Congratulations! For fashioning a useful device primarily out of metal you have unlocked the Metalworker Path!
Congratulations! For completing a lengthy, complex, personal project utilizing your own Skills you have unlocked the Artisan Path!
Congratulations! For creating a complex magical device combining multiple disciplines you have unlocked the Artificer Path!
Congratulations! By crafting a mana accumulator you have unlocked the Mana Harvester Path!

Level Up!
Skill Points 1142→1156
(Alchemy: 100; Stamina Manipulation: 21; 13/25 60-point Paths)
Alchemical Analysis Level 47→48
Alchemical Dismantling Level 55→56
Alchemy Level 98→100
Improbable Arsenal Level 43→44

Prototyping Level 45→48
Refining Level 46→49
Ritual Intuition Level 54→56
Sapper's Apparatus Level 67→68
Stamina Manipulation Level 19→21
Unbound Tether Level 29→30

Name
Edwin Maxlin
Age
2
Race
Extraplanar Human
Class
Alchemist-Errant
Attributes
Health 25
Impact 7
Mana 37
Perception 19
Stamina 30
Skills
Alchemical
Alchemy 100, Alchemical Analysis 48, Refining 46, Alchemical
Dismantling 56, Sapper's Apparatus 68
(Purify: 75)
Magical
Basic Thermokinesis 44, Fey's Caress 46, Ritual Intuition 56,
Mana Infusion 92, Unbound Tether 30
(Flight 60), (Basic Mana Sense: 82), (Basic Mana Manipulation:
9)
Physical
Overcharge 30, Longstrider 54, Fresh Air 46
Stamina Manipulation 21, (Athletics: 81), (Breathing: 76),
(Flexibility: 74), (Nutrition: 73), (Packing: 92), (Seeing: 72),
(Sleeping: 73), (Survival: 76), (Walking: 74)

Mental

Numeracy 55, Prototyping 48, Anatomy 47, Polyglot 71, Memory 68

(Language: 36), (Mathematics: 74), (Research: 50), (Visualization: 80)

Combat

Bomb Throwing 62, Adaptive Defense 49

(Throwing Weapons: 48)

Utility

Outsider's Almanac 139, Watchful Rest 44, Skillful Assessment 53, Arcadian Elixir 39, Improbable Arsenal 44

(Firestarting: 94), (Improvisation: 14), (Status: 22), (Identify: 80), (First Aid: 82), (Harvesting: 76), (Construction: 77)

Paths

Skill Points: 1156

13 60-point Paths, 12 30-point Paths

Combat

Assassin 0/60, Bomber 0/60, Giant Slayer 0/60, Heedless Hunter 0/60, Hunter 0/30, Killer 0/30, Titan Slayer 0/90, Warrior 0/60, Way of the Empty Hand 0/60, Trapper 0/60, Artillerist 0/60, Sapper 0/60

Alchemy

Alchemical Medic 0/60, Demolitionist 0/60, Makeshift Alchemist 0/60, Potioneer 0/60, Practical Alchemist 0/60, Mystic Alchemist 0/90, Essential Alchemist 0/90, Elemental Alchemist 0/60

Science

Chemist 0/60, Experimenter 0/60, Researcher 0/60, Purifier 0/30, Scientific Revolutionary 0/90, Scientist 0/60, Engineer 0/60, Physicist 0/60, Mathematician 0/60, Material Scientist 0/60

Magic

Aerialist 0/60, Fey Friend 0/60, Feybound 0/60, Feycaller 0/60, Mage 0/60, Magical Gardener 0/60, Micro-Biomancer 0/90, Primal Constructor 0/90, Primal Ritualist 0/90, Realm Traveler 0/120, Fey Supplicant 0/60, Feykind 0/90, Attuner 0/30, Schooled Mage 0/90, Mana Harvester 0/60

Mental

Dedicated Student 0/60, Lecturer 0/30, Unbowed 0/90, Canny 0/60, Steady Mind 0/60, Mentalist 0/60

System

Almanac Administrator 0/60, Forerunner 0/60, Outsider's Almanac Specialist 0/90, Pioneer 0/60, Skill Researcher 0/60, System Scholar 0/60

Trophy

Blackstone Conqueror 0/60, Deepwoods Panther-Hunter 0/60, Stonehide Vanquisher 0/60, Titan Spider-Slayer 0/60

Attribute

Artisan 0/60, Scholar 0/60

Career

Brickmaker 0/30, Butcher 0/30, Diver 0/30, Gardener 0/30, Lumberjack 0/60, Merchant 0/30, Potter 0/30, Scribe 0/30, Woodsman 0/30, Metalworker 0/30, Artificer 0/90

Physical

Ascetic 0/60, Daredevil 0/60, Physical Alchemist 0/90, Survivor 0/60, Physical Laborer 0/30, Athlete 0/60

Traveling

Escapee 0/30, Exile 0/30, Traveler 0/30, World Traveler 0/60

Medical

Field Medic 0/60, Medic 0/30, Steadfast Medic 0/60, Medical Lecturer 0/60

Misc

Arsonist 0/60, Autopyromaniac 0/60, Burglar 0/60, Child 0/12, Expert 0/60, Imperial Ally 0/60, Novice 0/12, Pyromaniac 0/30, Razer of the Ruined Tower 0/60, Rebel 0/30, Slave 0/12, Trainee 0/60, Traitor 0/60, Brushed by Power 0/60, Lirasian Citizen 0/30, Royal Advisor 0/60, Favored by Power 0/90, Insomniac 0/30, Sleepless Disciple 0/60, Student of Power 0/60

Completed Paths

CharLimitCanttalkmuchNocluewhathappenedDidmybesttohelpyouli, Mage, Skilled Arcanist, Physical Alchemist, Bomber, Linguist, Beginner, Warrior, Path Less Traveled, Athlete, Scout, Unkillable,

Superior Alchemist, Adventurer, Explorer, Outsider,
Skill Researcher, Wanderer, Alchemical Warrior, Novice
Pyromancer, Novice Ritualist, Alchemist, Physicist, Engineer,
Physical Arcanist, Biologist, Practical Alchemist, Fey Scion,
Feytouched, Skilled Arcanist

CHAPTER 18

Conversensational

"You got it working?" Rillah perked up from her slouched position by the fire.

"Well, you don't have to sound so surprised, but yes. Now, I want to keep an eye on it for a couple weeks just to make sure no problems pop up, mind you, but it *should* be fine."

"That's amazing! I had no clue you were that good with crafting."

"Have you obtained any new fascinating Skills then?" Lefi asked.

"Um . . ." Edwin flicked through his notifications. "Not that I can see. Oh, huh, I got Potion-making and Coppersmithing. No, I don't see anything *too* noteworthy. Oh yeah, that does remind me."

He waved his hand through the notification, dismissing it. "I got the Artisan Path from that."

"Marvelous! I recall that was one of your current endeavors?"

"Yeah. I got it for completing a 'lengthy, complex, personal project utilizing my own Skills.' I hadn't thought about it like that, but it does make sense."

"Did you get any other fun Paths?"

"Well . . ." Edwin read off his other Path notifications—they'd been dismissed, of course, but recording it all in Almanac was basically second nature at this point.

"Interesting. You continue to find Paths that I have never encountered or even heard of," Lefi mused.

"They definitely *sound* fun."

"Indeed. I suspect your Mana Harvester Path may in fact be a Trophy Path," the Adventurer noted. "It certainly sounds akin to one, though it is strange that you would obtain one for such an impersonal project. Usually such are gained upon forging one's self a spectacular suit of armor, or a generational sword, perhaps even a ship."

Edwin shrugged. "Don't look at me, you're the System expert. Anyway, the accumulator. It should work fine, especially if all those Paths mean anything, but I just want to make *sure* and it's not quite good enough weather for leaving anyway."

"How long will it last?" Rillah asked.

"I'm not sure. I'll be *shocked* if it lasts more than a few years without maintenance; the wheels will probably get jammed up, and it's not impossible that the potion might be broken. But if that doesn't happen . . . I mean, most of the thing's properties are inherent to the materials, and I don't think the traits I modified and added will *ever* fade. I'll probably see if Pierash is interested in learning how to take care of it, because it would *not* be hard. She wouldn't even have to grease the thing, with how much sand I stuffed in there."

"So what I'm hearing is that I get a vacation?"

"I mean, you'll still need to stick around for a bit in case I need you for something, but yeah, your daily chores should now be automated."

"Sweet! Hmm, whatever shall I do."

"Play your flute," Lefi and Edwin answered in unison.

"And probably dance," Edwin added.

"Alternatively she might decide to fly around," Lefi countered.

"Well, *that's* a given. How's your Powerful Flight going, by the way?"

"Fifty-seven. If I got some help from Lefi, I might get it before leaving Sheraith," she pointedly said.

"Sorry, little snowbird, you know there's not much I can aid you with for that Skill."

"Yeah, I *know* but that doesn't change that I want you to," she pouted. "Not that I want— Never mind."

"So, anyway, what's the plan? Leave early spring? That's what, three weeks away?" Edwin asked.

"Indeed!" Lefi said.

"And the plan?"

"I have a new quest to embark upon! While the young ones have learned much, they still have far to go, but they must return home to truly appreciate all they've learned and face the evils therein."

"Are there *actually* evils hiding back at their home?"

"I have learned it is best to not bet against such a thing."

"Fair enough. Rillah?"

"Don't know yet. We'll see where the wind goes."

"What of you, Edwin? Do you plan to venture with us still, or where does thy adventure take you?"

"Eh, toward the coast, maybe? I need to look into it more. But first," he said, breathing a sigh of relief, "I'm going to take a few days off—no goal or research, just playing around with my Skills. Then? I don't know, maybe I'll put some more work in on my greenhouse."

"Ooh, do you want to play catch with Unbound Tether?"

"You know what? Sure, that does sound fun. Lead the way."

"So where *has* Yathal been, anyway? It feels like I haven't seen him for a month."

"You've barely seen *me* for a month, why would you see the kid?" Inion asked.

"Well, I don't know. It just seems like I would have heard him or something during all that. Also I'm *sorry*, I just got so wrapped up in everything that I just couldn't see you that much."

"You're free to spend your time however you like. You doing your alchemy is *so* fun to watch."

"You weren't even *there* most of the time."

"Pah, like I'd need *that*."

"Kind of creepy, but okay. Anyway, I take it 'however I like' doesn't include being with Rillah?"

"She's not good for you."

"You *don't* get to choose how I spend my time, you know. That is my decision and my decision alone."

"*I'm* just trying to *save* you, and you're too blind to see it. It's for your *own good*."

"No." Edwin put his foot down. "We're not getting into this again right now. Beyond the fact that *nothing* good has ever come from the phrase 'doing this for your own good,' I wanted this to be a nice, relaxing chat with you about what's been going on during my time in the lab."

"Well, fine, if you *insist*."

"I do. So what has Yathal been up to?"

"Well, you know, since he got Polyglot a couple weeks ago he's been all *over* the place. Kyni's been keeping him safe but I've run along with him a few times as well, and he's been running with the local kids. Really energetic, you know?"

"I'm sure. Well, at least he's been quiet most of the time."

Inion laughed.

"What?"

She shook her head, not answering.

"What? Oh come on, don't give me that. He isn't *that* loud these days, is he?"

"Just you wait and see."

"You're still planning to wait until the day we leave for you to let the city know about the accumulator?" Edwin snagged the boulder they were playing catch with out of the air, pushing Packing to its limits as he returned it to the flying girl.

Rillah nodded. "That way, they can't come up with reasons why it wouldn't count or try to break it."

"They wouldn't do that, would they? Ah, who am I kidding. They totally would. That wouldn't mean you'd have to come back, would it?"

She shook her head. "I was to help 'until another has assumed your duty,' which the accumulator *definitely* counts for. If they then break the directive, well, that's just their problem. It's not something I need to worry about. You aren't worried about it, are you?"

Edwin waved his hand. "Ah, not *especially*. It was a fun project, but I'm still just giving it away. What happens to it beyond that I don't care about *that* much. Like, don't get me wrong, it would be very cool if something I made stayed in active use for years and years to come, but it's also not why I made it. I made it to free you of your responsibility and because I *wanted* to. It was fantastic practice, for sure, but I also can think of a dozen ways I could improve it.

"So sure, if they smash it to bits, I'll be somewhat sad but I'll *cope*, and it's not my problem. I try not to be sentimental about stuff for all that I fail. Also, the System helps with that. I got my payment in Paths and Skill levels, and even if it's broken, who cares? Same reason I don't get bitter about the time I spent making my cannon when Unbound Tether basically makes it redundant."

While Unbound Tether wasn't even *close* to strong enough to toss around the boulder they were using, it was a *really* effective way for both of them to train while having fun. Multitasking!

"You had fun making it and that's what matters?"

"Sure. I learned a lot and found the experience valuable. The stuff associated with it, who cares?"

Rillah raised an eyebrow and prompted him to continue with a giant rock, as she caught, spun, and returned the stone from her position above him.

". . . Also I made peace with the idea that stuff I make might become *immediately* invalidated back when I made a cannon, then promptly got a Skill that turns me into a railgun."

"You *sure* you made peace with the idea? Because I've seen your wagon these days."

"Okay, so I *know* I still have the whole thing strapped to the roof, but it's a *lot* of apparatite. I don't know when it might become useful again."

"Can't you just make it all up again?"

"I mean, yeah, but there's hundreds of kilos of the stuff in that construct; it would take me *hours* to conjure that much."

"Oh, because it's so much easier to repurpose parts from a cannon for whatever little piece you may want?"

"Look, can we talk about something else?" Edwin grunted slightly as he caught the stone, Packing pushed in a new way. Huh. Was that a twinge of Stamina usage? Something to look into later. "Like . . . how are you going to keep them from immediately pulling you back like they did initially?"

"Oh, that? Have you ever paid your service tax?"

"My what? No, I can't say that I have."

"Well, it's this thing the Empire does where instead of just *paying* the tax collector, Adventurers can be recruited into a situation where they're needed."

"You know, I think I *have* heard of that, actually, but the Enforcer who talked to me said that because I'm an Ally I actually have to do it or something, because most of the time Adventurers ran?"

"Oh yeah, it's always possible to run. It's almost expected sometimes, but they're marked as tax evaders in that province. Nobody *really* cares about it because of how minor it is to the Wanted List, something like level forty. But the Enforcer here is no fun and would hunt me down anyways."

"Doesn't surprise me. I'll just need to remember to hide from future Enforcers, if I stand a chance of being waylaid for half a year suddenly if I don't."

"But you, hiding from the Enforcers? Now *that's* something to imagine."

"Hey, I'll have you know I'm *excellent* at hiding from people. I spent *months* in Panastalis and never once met the rival alchemist to my sponsor, and I only met the Alchemy Guild's guildmaster when she sought me out. I assure you, that was *not* an accident."

"Oh, please, there's no way you're better at that than *I* am, and I can never go more than a few days before I'm noticed by what feels like everyone in the province."

"Well, maybe if *someone* didn't have a half-dozen 'hey look at me' Skills, they wouldn't have to deal with so much attention."

"It's not *half a dozen*," she protested, though her complaint was off-set slightly by the massive rock she was holding above her head while flying on massive snow-covered wings made of budding flowers.

"Oh, you're right, it's eight? But I was dodging attention even *before* I had the option of hiding away and not interacting with people. You, on the other hand, go around acting as a bard wearing flashy clothing and an eye-catching Class."

She shook her head, flicking her hand in dismissal.

"You know I'm right," Edwin teased, returning the rock.

"I don't know anything about what you're talking about. So have you decided what you're going to do yet?" she asked, quickly changing the topic.

"No, not really." Edwin sighed. "Well, okay, that's not actually true. I have a whole list of what I want to do, I just don't know what to do next, and I don't want to be a drag if I go with you guys."

"You won't be a boulder! Come with us!" she offered again. "It'll be way more fun."

"What did you end up deciding on? Or are you still planning to follow where the winds blow?"

"Well, I think I'm wanting to head to Rhothos and actually visit my mum this time. I was getting close but didn't quite make it before I was called to Sheraith, so I'll be heading there along with Lefi, Yathal, and Kynigos. Now that the kid's a little less shy and the pup has more experience on his paws, they might make a decent guard pair a few years from now."

"What's so special about Rhothos, anyway? Like it's clearly the center of a lot of activity, but why?"

"Lots and *lots* of food, and more recently an agreeable Enforcer. It's a great place for us. There's other places that are also good, but I'm partial because it's home."

"Fair enough. I *might* join you. I don't know."

"Why's that?"

"I just have other things I need to do and that I want to do. I have alchemical ingredients to get, experiments to run, people and places to visit. And they're all toward the coast."

"You don't have *anything* you need inland?"

"I mean, I guess I could try and get my payment from Panastalis for services rendered and I really should check in with my Registrar."

"Great! You can get that done, then! Come on, you know you'll enjoy it."

"It's just so *little*. That's two tasks among so very many I'm trying to deal with. I'm just not sure if it's a good use of my time."

Other than for the people, his brain whispered. *They don't actually want me around, they're just trying to make me think that they care so that when I leave them, I'll remember them fondly.*

"Come on! You'll enjoy it."

"I-I still need to think about it more."

The air inside Edwin's greenhouse was hot and humid as he cut a few molai flowers for harvest, as well as trimming back the more bushlike plants to properly encourage their growth. To his left, Inion summoned a bit of water, chatting as they tended to his garden.

It was really only thanks to her that Edwin's garden was turning out as well as it was. The crystal pots, filled with soil taken from the Verdant, were exceptionally thirsty for mana. While Edwin *could* take care of them on his own, other than if he tried to grow talsanenris, they wouldn't flourish nearly so much. Instead, the fey's combination of waterlike mana, natural gifts as a nature spirit, and relevant Skills all combined to make Edwin's greenhouse as good if not a *better* environment for magical plant growth as the Verdant itself.

"Edwin, stop being ridiculous. You don't need them."

He raised an eyebrow. "I thought you approved of me being with other people, and that you liked Lefi."

"Oh, they're fine, but you don't need them."

"Of course not! I don't need anybody, not really. But I like them, I like working with them just like I enjoy working with *you*. You don't *need* to be here, but here you are anyway."

"You came up with a way to grow plants easily year-round! What, was I supposed to stay far away?"

"You know, I'm still surprised you'd never encountered a greenhouse before I made this one. Like sure, you—"

"I was *asleep* for several millennia, of *course* I'm not completely aware of what's new in architecture."

"Like sure, you were asleep for ages," Edwin finished. "And they didn't have widespread glass back then, but you didn't have this kind of thing back in Arcadia or whatever?"

"No."

"Why, though? But that doesn't mean you have to help me take *care* of it to have the ability to enjoy it. No, I don't really care about whatever you're planning to say to countermand me, you didn't *need* to, but you clearly wanted to."

"You do lots of things you don't like."

"Yeah," he flatly replied, "like going for years without any friends. I definitely didn't like *that*. I don't really care what your latest excuse for why you don't like Rillah is—I know that you dislike her—but I'm not going to pass up a chance for an actual human *friend* just because you dislike her smile."

"You don't know what she's doing to you!"

"Well, what *is* she doing to me then?"

Inion looked away sheepishly.

"Yeah, that's what I thought. If you don't have any *actual* things you can say about Rillah, just don't even bother. Pass me the watering can, would you?"

Inion handed the teapotlike creation over, and Edwin accepted it with a nod, pouring about half of it out around the base of his molai.

"I'm going to go with them," Edwin decided.

"What? You can't do that! You have plans, things to do!"

"Yeah, and you being so insistent that I *not* go is making me suspicious. Besides, all the stuff I want to see isn't time-dependent, and sticking with Lefi helps my Skills level anyway."

"It's *not* why I'm here."

"Well, then, why *are* you here? I'm being interesting. Isn't *that* what you wanted?" he snapped. "I'm not your little lapdog for you to order around, to come, sit, lie down, and roll over at your command. You wanted something interesting? This is me being interesting, deal with it or leave."

"Maybe I *will.*"

"I won't stop you! I have other people I can be with!"

"They won't stick around like *I* will. They'll leave you when you need them most."

"Oh, like potentially haring off because I'm traveling with a person they didn't like?"

Inion stayed tellingly quiet as she snatched a handful of mulched talsanenris branches, spreading it around the firevine shoot she was tending to.

Silence fell in the greenhouse for several minutes before Edwin broke it. "I don't want to leave you, you know. But I *will* if you make me. I know that you're trying to look out for me, which I *do* appreciate, and I know I wouldn't even be alive right now without your help. But I think you're looking for something that just isn't there, and I can't help but wonder if you're not that different from me, just without realizing it."

"Like *you*? I just don't see what ya mean."

"I'm awful with people, and because I *know* I'm bad with people I overcompensate for that and make myself annoying in *other* ways. I second-guess myself constantly, say stupid things, and otherwise drive people away in so many different ways because I can't figure out what people *do* like. Yes, I know that about myself. I've spent years trapped in my own head, I'm aware of my prison even if I can't figure out how to escape.

"I think you might just be doing something similar, just without realizing it. You don't want to lose me as—" Edwin cut himself off before he finished his thought, *lose me as your plaything.*

Then he went on, "Lose me to Rillah, so you're jumping at every shadow and trying to find some reason why I can't go with her."

"I told you before, I'm *not jealous.*"

Edwin raised an eyebrow but didn't say anything right away.

He pulled out a particularly tenacious weed from his talsanenris pot. "I don't want to choose between the two of you, you know. I'm not limited to only a single friend, and if I could I'd have both of you. It's only *your* insistence that keeps me from spending time with both of you at the same time."

"As soon as that *woman* stops *manipulating* you I'll tolerate her."

"All communication is manipulation," Edwin replied. "Especially here, where it seems like any random person I meet might have some sort of social Skill. And don't you go pretending that you aren't *constantly* trying to manipulate me yourself. At least *Rillah's* manipulation seems to be for my benefit. And again, if she *is* manipulating me, I'm still not sure I really care? It's like . . . like I've been falling for a really long time, and now I'm *not*. It doesn't make a difference for me if it's because I hit something solid, or because something caught me and is just holding me in place. All I care is that I'm not *falling*."

"You're not used to Skills. If you had more exposure to people, more time spent getting yourself used to dealing with Charisma and even normal social Skills, then you wouldn't be nearly so obsessed with her."

"I'm not— I'm not *obsessed* with her."

"She's the first person you haven't tried to dismiss as irrelevant."

"That's not *entirely* true. I know she's just being nice to me as a favor to Lefi. I just hope, I just *hope* that's not the *only* reason."

"Ya."

"Oh, come on, I don't try— I don't— She's not a true friend. She's a potential one for sure, but . . ."

"Then *stop obsessing over her*."

"No," Edwin shook his head. "*No.* That's not what— I don't want to give up."

He set his pruning dagger off to the side, trying to gather his thoughts.

"You'll find other people who aren't trying to manipulate you!"

"No. I won't. Look at me. I'm an alchemist from another world, a mage and with the eyes of everyone up to Emperor Xares himself on me. Simply saying my name was enough to get an aggressive Enforcer to back down. I'm a literal and figurative gold mine, I'll never find someone who wants to befriend me *just* because of who I am as a person; there will always be some aspect of what I can do for them that will play a part of their calculation."

"Seems cynical."

"Well, then I guess I'm a cynic, but I don't believe it wouldn't enter into someone's considerations at the very least. Rillah's not using me just for what I can make, after all."

Inion raised an eyebrow. "You just spent two months making something just to make sure she didn't have to do her job."

"That's different. Somehow. I don't know how. It just feels different to me."

"Ya, because she has *Skills*."

"What will make you happy, Inion? Me never having friends other than *you*? Is that it? Because that's *not* happening." Edwin had finished with his work in the greenhouse, but he leaned against an invisible wall as he watched the fey float cross-legged in front of him. "*Everyone* in this world has Skills. Am I supposed to just dismiss them all?"

Inion's face was unusually readable, Edwin getting the distinct impression she was trying to come up with some suitable compromise. So the only logical conclusion was she was putting on a deliberate show and he needed to come up with a solution before she could "find" one.

"Look, I'm slow to make friends. I'll . . . you know what? I have a kind of test or something that lets me know if she's actually interested in *me*, like I want to be the case, or is just trying to manipulate me for . . ." He paused. "Actually, what *do* you think she's trying to manipulate me for?"

"As though you *didn't* spend the last *two months* working on something for her? Like I *just said.*"

"Well, okay. But you thought she was manipulating me even before I had any idea about that, or before she even knew I *could* do that."

"Bah, you're a *mage.* They don't *need* a reason to see why digging your creek into their river would be good. You being an alchemist and an Outsider just makes that *clearer.*"

"Oh, like you, then?"

"That's uncalled for!"

"Oh, is it then? I used to have a test for how I'd be able to tell who was actually interested in being my friend, I'll have you know, and . . ."

Edwin's mind finally caught up with his mouth, and he trailed off. Wow. He hadn't been expecting to think of that today. Or ever, really. It had been what, five years? Six? Not since he had started college, not since.

"And what? Edwin, what happened?"

"Nothing, nothing. I'm fine. Don't worry about me," he brushed her off. "It doesn't matter."

"Well, okay, so long as you're able to hold yourself together."

And you never passed it, he mentally finished.

At least their conversation passed on to more pleasant content after that.

"So I'm also leaving additional storage crystals there." Edwin pointed out the chest in the corner of the room. "That way if the one in the accumulator breaks, you have replacements. Now, Alchemy is telling me they should last a *really* long time if they aren't intentionally broken, probably on the order of decades, so it shouldn't be often you need to do anything with those. You'll know that it's the crystal that's acting up if this indicator here stops pulsing. Now granted, it'll stop pulsing if any of the other steps are broken instead, so make sure you check the other spots as well."

Edwin was really proud of himself for getting the indicators working. They were redundant for him, yes, but he'd managed to make a glowleaf solution that *only* glowed when exposed to magic, and from there he was able to tune the sensitivity up and down until it suited his purposes. He wasn't entirely sure how they worked, but well, in all honesty it wasn't *as* important that he fully understood everything he was doing. It was a nice goal, but it was just *so* infeasible for some of the cooler things.

He'd hit level *100* in Alchemy, after all, and while it seemed like comprehension was important for leveling the Skill, actually benefiting from it was more along the lines of utilizing the instinctive knowledge it gave him. So he'd had to loosen his normal guidelines a bit. Make the crazy device first, figure out how it works later.

Honestly it would probably be advice he could stand to integrate into more parts of his life, but that wasn't relevant yet.

"So long as it stays lit, it shines bright?"

"Uh, sure." Pierash, the halfling assistant, was fond of odd turns of phrase that never seemed to *quite* translate properly, but Edwin could generally get a decent idea of what she meant. He explained further, "The lights themselves I'm pretty sure will last *ages*, but if you can somehow pick up a mana-sensing Skill, then you'd just be able to sense the different parts yourself."

"Oh, I'm not some two-bit Outlaw like you seem to think I am, nor am I a fool. Even if I *could* get that kinna Skill why would I be such an *Outlaw?*"

"Right. You know, I spend so much time with Adventurers I kind of forget that most people are only allowed twelve Skills. Anyway, is everything making sense so far?"

"Polish the turbine but the other stuff's fine, make sure to leave the sand in when cleaning it—"

"But not when it's in the wrong places like—"

"Yeah, not when it's in the wrong places like between parts that aren't joints," she interrupted him back. "I'm *well aware*."

"Heh. Well, sorry, I'm just not used to people actually listening to me, I guess."

"So it would seem."

"Anyway, yeah. Do you think it'll hold?" Edwin asked.

"Ah, well, that's a tricky question now. It'll certainly cover all of what the tower's for if it can even do half what you think it does. It'll just be those once-a-decade storms when they already go and need some extra help, but from my experience, it should be quite sufficient otherwise."

"Um, thanks?" Edwin awkwardly said. "Any questions? Or does it all make sense?"

"I think I can figure it out. It's part of the tower now, and thus is a part of my domain."

"You have Skills for that?"

"Oh, but of course."

"Huh. I mean I *guess,* anyway. If you think of any concerns before we head out, let me know."

"That will be on the morn, yes?"

"Yeah. That's when Rillah's letting them know about this thing, and we want to get out of here before the political fallout comes crashing down around us. It's a good thing she's on board, because I would *not* have thought of that in time."

"Yes, well, it will be a relief to see that furry menace leave at last."

"What?"

"Fur gets everywhere! And what's worse, that mongrel has Skills that fight against my own in an effort to make *more* of a mess. No, I will be quite happy once he no longer is here to sully up the furniture."

"Hmm, fair enough, I guess I didn't really think of it that way."

"Of course you didn't! You wanderers never settle down long enough to understand the pain of maintaining a place like this."

"Sorry?"

"You should be! Bah, kids these days."

"So, anyway, if you don't have any more questions for me I'm going to go finish packing." Edwin awkwardly fled, throwing himself down the massive staircase.

Tomorrow would be a big day, after all, and there was always so much to do.

Level Up!
Skill Points 1156→1162
(Alchemy: 100; Stamina Manipulation: 23; 13/25 60-point
Paths)
Improbable Arsenal Level 44→45
Polyglot Level 71→72
Sapper's Apparatus Level 68→69
Stamina Manipulation Level 21→23
Watchful Rest Level 44→45

CHAPTER 19

A Rapid Giveaway

The tower was pure chaos.

Well, it was honestly rather organized, but at the moment it *felt* chaotic. Edwin hadn't properly appreciated just how much *stuff* he'd gotten during his stay until he actually needed to put it all in one place. Most of it was alchemical products, including a *lot* of failed experiments and by-products of successful ones. A lot of it was apparatite, but the stuff didn't go bad and it was still clean, so there was no need to dismiss it now only for him to summon it again later.

Of course, because of the insane volume of stuff that he had, Edwin had found himself in the position of needing a few more chests and crates to store it all in. Improbable Arsenal had actually gotten to the point where most cheap bags and other containers were actually *less* effective than his own Skill. Granted, a ten-times expansion was far from the biggest he'd seen, but he also didn't really feel like spending one of his few remaining grai on a wooden box with a hundred-times expansion.

He'd briefly toyed with the idea that he might be able to make a business out of applying Improbable Arsenal to premade boxes and selling the then-larger containers, but it didn't work for a few reasons. The primary reason was that over long periods of time, the Skill *did* fade. The mana he Infused into the container gradually bled out into the surroundings, the Skill weakened, and it all faded. It took a few months, he'd found, so he could easily fleece people if he wanted, but he *didn't* want to. Why bother? He was an *alchemist*, he could make health potions, he remembered how to make porcelain, he was already a gold-printing machine if he decided to get rich at any point.

The one thing that *didn't* seem to lose potency was his apparatite, if he used Improbable Arsenal *while* conjuring the crystal. While it meant he *did* have options for long-term constructions beyond just refreshing the Skill every so often, it was too fragile to be useful storage for most people and he didn't really want to sell it anyway.

In any case, for his personal use he could pretty easily make crystal boxes and vials for his substances, then buy a few wooden boxes and chests without any spatial expansion for just a few ves (they had apparently been made by an apprentice, not that you'd know it from the quality of their woodwork) and expand them himself.

It still took *ages* to pack everything away properly. Part of that was admittedly because Edwin also wanted to sort his stuff while he was at it, but it also was just really time-consuming to take down his entire lab and greenhouse, then relocate their materials and contents into his wagon. The potted plants returned to their shelves and were reattached, drying racks relocated to the ceiling; some local plants had been dug up while wintering and needed their own places to be stored. While Sheraith didn't have any known overtly magical plants, it *did* have a few with mundane uses, and it didn't *hurt* to take a few saplings from the garden.

All the chaos involved just made it more embarrassing when Rillah showed up fully packed in a single bag, a leather satchel not much larger than Edwin's two hands.

"Really?" Edwin hefted the bag, feeling that it barely weighed twenty pounds. The satchel was crafted out of fine leather, a scroll of parchment rolled up at the bottom and held securely in place below the main pouch by a pair of metal clasps.

"What? I like it."

He peeked inside her sack and couldn't help but do a double take. "What the *heck* is your Skill's level?"

"Oh, Endless Carrying Cellar? Just level forty or so."

"That's the level *my* Skill is at, but this has to be three times as strong. *How?*"

She smiled. "It's a good Skill. *And* it's helped by a lot of my other Skills."

"It's bound to be. Sheesh, I wish it lasted more than a day or two on its own. I could *use* that much space."

"You have an entire *cart*."

"And I'm trying to bring an entire lab with me. What's your point?"

"Nothing, I suppose. Is there somewhere I should put this? It's all a bit messy."

"Huh? Oh, right. Just hang it on one of the outside hooks, I'd say. You off to your meeting?"

"No, not quite yet. Their court is in session, but it's not my time to report until closer to noon."

"How does that all work, anyway? I don't think I ever asked."

"I think you might have at one point, but it's not really worth remembering. A couple dozen nobles sit at this big desk, with the governor at the center, and they ask me a couple questions while trying to make themselves sound impressive. It could be done in six minutes if they actually stayed on topic, but there's just *so much* posturing it might take an hour."

"Better you than me." That comment earned a playful swat from her. "Good luck. See you on the other side."

"Where are you off to?"

"Now that you reminded me, I should check that Lefi's stuff will fit in the wagon. I bet he'll be happy to not have to carry it all, but . . . well, he probably has his own spatial expansion Skill, doesn't he?"

Rillah just shrugged as they turned in opposite directions.

Lefi did *not* have a Skill of his own for spatial expansion, a fact that Edwin felt very momentarily proud of as a single area in which he was actually better than the omnicompetent Adventurer. Then, of course, Lefi had to go and lift Edwin's entire cart with a single hand and carry it outside when they were trying to get it around the obstacles in the stable. Edwin could have *probably* done that, thanks to Packing, but it wouldn't have been anywhere near as effortless.

At least everything found its place in the end, and other than a brief scuffle involving Yathal having somehow misplaced his *shoe*—and how it ended up on the roof of the tower he could only wonder at—it was blessedly uneventful. All that was left now was to actually leave the city, and they'd be free once more.

Edwin had all but forgotten how impressive the Sheraith gate was. The twin *waterfalls*, he reminded himself, as the mistake of past-Edwin thinking they were rainbows came slamming into the forefront of his mind, framed the massive doorway perfectly, allowing a trickle of people in and out.

A gnome with the color palette of a sunset scrambled past the cart, darting between the comparative giants surrounding him before effortlessly scaling the interior wall on unseen handholds, slipping into the gatehouse above.

With a bit of closer inspection, Edwin realized that the waterfalls weren't painted; they genuinely were blue. And also granite. He suspected Skill shenanigans, though without closer examination he couldn't see if Skillful Assessment would give any insight into if the Skill was still present.

At least the way *out* of the city should be a lot quicker than when they came in. He just hoped Lefi would get his weapons back without any issue.

Almanac told Edwin that the "Experienced Lirasian Gatekeeper" was apparently present when he came into the city, as was the Junior Gate Guard functioning as his assistant, not that Edwin remembered either of them.

"I see your 'month or two' turned into half a year, Adventurer."

"Indeed! It was not intended, but the snows came early this year."

"You shouldn't have been here when they came, but that is *decidedly* not my problem."

The man turned and said something to his assistant that Polyglot seemed to be blocked from understanding. It wasn't a very *good* block— Edwin could have easily overpowered the effect just by trying to listen in, but why bother? It might make them mad if they detected it, and it *probably* wasn't important if their body language was anything to go by. True to form, they waved Lefi and Yathal through just a moment later, and it was Edwin's turn.

"Good riddance, I see."

"Look, I didn't get into any trouble other than what found *me*," he defended himself.

"Yeah, yeah. Don't really care. Get along."

"So I had some weapons to pick up?"

It took a fair bit of wrangling, but Edwin eventually managed to retrieve, among other things, no less than seven daggers, *six* swords ranging from a foot long to as tall as Edwin himself, five gold-colored flails, four different shields, three short tridents, two halberds . . .

And a full sash of throwing knives, his internal monologue sang.

"I don't know *why* you need this many weapons"—Edwin leveled a stare at Lefi—"or how you could possibly use them all, but seriously *what the heck.*"

"One must always be prepared!"

"Five! You have *five* flails, and they're *all* made out of brass. *Why.* And also *how.* Where do you *keep* all these when they aren't piled in the carriage? I *know* you don't have a Skill for it, you just told me you didn't!"

Inion emerged from where she was hiding in the back of the wagon, slipping next to Edwin. He gave her a quick smile as she brushed against him, distracting him from his complaints against Lefi.

"I hope it wasn't too cramped?" He was glad that Inion had in the end decided to come along, but shoving her in a barrel of water to smuggle her past the gates probably wasn't the most comfortable.

She shook her head. "It was just fine. Now hop off. I'll drive today."

"Really?" He raised an eyebrow. "Today was my day."

"Bill and I have an *understanding.* I'll take care of it, now *shoo.*"

"Okay? It'll be nice to stretch my legs, I guess."

Edwin hopped off the wagon, trying to figure out what Inion's game was today, but after a few moments without success, he turned back to keep talking with Lefi. Unsurprisingly, the Adventurer had already moved to speak more with Yathal, leaving Edwin behind.

Ah well, he could appreciate just being on the road as much as anyone, and while his muscles had atrophied after several months of less than constant use—his training had *definitely* fallen off a fair bit, particularly toward the end—his Skills and Stamina had not, so he wasn't suffering too much from just walking. It gave him the chance to appreciate the sights, and he could always fly if his legs *ever* got sore.

The fields, so full of ready-to-harvest crops when they entered the city, were now barren dirt save for a few opportunistic weeds popping up here and there. The road still carried a few traces of the recent cold, a couple snowdrifts piled at the edge just off the stonework. The air was as clean as anything Edwin had ever experienced, carrying with it the scent of recent rain, and the faint trills of birdsong were just barely audible over the clatter of the wagon.

It was a nice day.

An hour after they'd left the city, Kynigos barked something to his boy, who perked up immediately.

"Huh? Oh!" Yathal started spinning around, searching the area for something.

Curious, Edwin decided to see what it was the boy was looking for. Within seconds, he spotted Rillah's figure about a kilometer back, her face beaming as she looped and dove through the air, her wings the color of frosted grass.

"Oh, hey, Rillah got out," Edwin said when he noted the distant figure.

"Aw, man, I wanted to see her first!" Yathal complained.

"Maybe next time, when you get Seeing to a higher level."

"We gonna stop and wait for her?"

"Nah." Edwin shook his head. "Look at the rate she's going, she'll catch up before too long. Although . . ."

He thought for a moment before a grin snuck across his face. While level 30 in Unbound Tether was just *barely* too weak to fully lift himself up—he estimated he could output about seven hundred newtons of force at this point, which could cut his effective gravity nearly in fourth—Rillah *was* a bit lighter than Edwin, and he could toss her around with relative ease if she wasn't fighting back. He hadn't tried this recently, but perhaps he ought to give her a bit of "help" catching up?

Though Unbound Tether couldn't hit the *moon*, a mere kilometer was *well* within its range.

He mentally reached out with his Skill, attached it to the tiny figure and *pulled*. Far off, Rillah jerked slightly as gravity suddenly seemed to shift around her. Then she adjusted and tucked her wings in for a dive. While she was *well* out of range for Numeracy, Mathematics came in and saved the day. Assuming she was about 55 kilos, Edwin should be accelerating her at about 11 meters per second per second, so then when combined with gravity speeding her up by around 10 meters per second per second she was experiencing about a forty-five-degree angle dive by flying straight forward and a combined acceleration of about 16 meters a second. That would total something like 70 meters a second at terminal velocity? He wasn't sure how her wings interacted with it . . . Further testing required.

It took about thirty seconds for the speeding figure to finally reach them, but as she got close enough Edwin cut off his Skill—he didn't *actually* want to be hit by her, after all. While potentially amusing, being struck by someone flying at 250 kilometers per hour would *not* be good for his continued health.

He needn't have worried overmuch, as Rillah swept her wings out on approach, bleeding off massive amounts of speed in seconds and gliding to a stop right in front of him.

"Edwin!" she complained, playfully swatting his shoulder as her wings faded away.

He just laughed. "What? I wanted to give you a hand."

"Mm. Fine. But a little warning next time?"

"And how, may I ask, would I give you a warning when you're that far out, exactly?"

"Well, you *could* . . ." She trailed off. "Okay, you win *this* round. I'll forgive you. *If* you do it again later."

He chuckled. "Deal. You know, I think my Skill is strong enough to properly lift you now. I'm probably a bit heavier than you and I'm *almost* there when not too geared up."

"Speaking of gear . . ."

"We had to toss your bag inside when we went through inspection. Second chest on the left."

"Thanks." Rillah ducked inside, slipping past Inion. The fey pretended to not notice her, but the slender girl had no issue slipping past the fey regardless.

She reemerged a couple seconds later with her bag slung over her shoulder and was still adjusting it as she nimbly hopped onto the road and stepped up to walk—eh, she was more dancing then walking—beside him.

"So, how'd it—" Edwin started, but found he was already drowned out by the booming voice of the last member of their little Adventurers' party.

"You rejoin us at long last! Did your quest conclude admirably?"

Rillah's smile grew slightly wider as she nodded in recollection. "Oh *yeah*. You should have seen their faces, Lefi. So I was standing there like during any of the other boring meetings, and they were talking about how despite their best efforts they still hadn't gotten an adequate replacement, yadda yadda, and the whole time I'm trying to not just straight-up yawn just because of how boring it all is.

"Then this one real *pain*, Soraeflas, decides to puff his feathers by saying how I *clearly* can't be trusted because I said I'd have trouble come winter and spring but they hadn't had any kind of poor weather. Another noble said that it was probably just nature doing my job for me and I hadn't really been needed after all."

Edwin couldn't hold back his chortle, and Rillah smiled even wider as her eyes twinkled. "So naturally I took *great* delight in saying that no, as a matter of fact, I wasn't lying. Nor had the natural weather been incredibly calm, but he *was* right that I hadn't been needed, nor *would* I ever be needed again, and I was leaving the city right after the meeting. Now *that* set off a whole chain of amazing responses. They ranged from accusing me of being a faithless Adventurer leaving the moment I could—let's be fair, I *am*—to saying I was sabotaging their city, and it was absolute pandemonium until Governor Kos'velista brought it all under control. He demanded I explain, and I mentioned that you'd made an artifact which could replace the role of the city mage altogether, and they wouldn't have to keep trying to find anyone, since they were clearly having so much trouble."

Edwin laughed, but Yathal looked confused so he explained, "There were two nobles far, far away who were both trying to get the job, but they didn't know Rillah knew that. So when I made the spinny thing upstairs, I made it so *neither* of the nobles could get the job."

Yathal nodded in probably-not-understanding, but he at least looked less confused so Edwin returned his attention to Rillah, who had paused in her explanation.

"Their feathers spun such lovely shapes, let me tell you. There were a few screeches about shoddy craftsmanship, intentional sabotage, and undermining authority. I just blew back at them that my tax was to serve until a 'suitable replacement had been found,' which your little artifact qualified for.

"Some tried to complain that I was flying off and leaving them with something that would clearly break immediately, but they shut up when I said it had been in use for over two weeks and had stopped one storm I wouldn't have been able to prevent without it."

"Wait, it did? When was there a storm?"

"Oh, yeah. It would have been a big one. I'm surprised you didn't feel it. I promise it was there though."

"You're the weather mage," he said. "I was just making sure the machine worked, and I didn't . . . oh! Was that the day the local wind mana like *doubled* or something?"

"Week and a half ago?"

"Yep. That's actually good to know. I mean it *should* have worked but it's nice to know for sure. Sorry, you were saying?"

"Yeah! Stop interrupting!" Yathal complained.

"*Excuse me* for wanting to know how the debut of my greatest creation so far went."

"Yeah, well, you're a bluequill."

Kynigos barked something that Edwin got the distinct impression was an admonishment along the lines of "language," prompting his boy to stick his tongue out at the dog.

"Now that set off a whole new set of arguments, a lot of which aren't suitable for young ears."

"Hey! I'm almost ten! That's basically an adult."

"And what tier are you?"

"One . . ." he grumbled. "But I know if Kyni let me, then I'd get to Tier 3 quick!"

"You'll get there eventually," Rillah reassured him. "There's no need to rush it. The older you are when you become an adult, the stronger you are."

"It's true," Edwin confirmed. "I'm only Tier 2 and look how strong I am."

Well, *technically* Stamina Manipulation meant he was Tier 1, but that didn't count.

"Wha!" Yathal looked betrayed. "You're not an adult either? How come you get to be all grown-up then?"

"Because I made sure to level my Skills when I was young so I grew up big and strong. And you know Lefi's only Tier 1 too."

"*Yeah*, but he's *Lefi*. He doesn't need to be all grown-up to be awesome."

"Well, that's what my situation is too."

"Do you have a buncha Skills like him too?"

Rillah said, "I don't think *anyone* has Skills like Lefi does. Well, maybe *everyone* combined does, but he's got pretty much any Skill he's seen."

Lefi cut in. "It is simply the burden—"

"Let me guess, the burden of being *Exceptional?*"

"It is simply the burden of . . . exceptional*ism*," he conceded, sounding a bit defeated.

Edwin rolled his eyes. "Sure. I'm *certain* that's what you were about to say. You're just mad I predicted it."

"Alas, being as Exceptional as I is not an easy task, though you make a valiant effort."

Rillah smacked Lefi's shoulder. "Stop getting distracted, you lug. Now, where was I?"

"Arguments that Yathal isn't old enough to hear about," Edwin reminded.

"Right. So . . . lots of arguments. I managed to shut most of them up by saying you got Paths for it, but then they started accusing you of trying to pluck them with maintenance. It took *ages* before I could sneak a word in, but I eventually managed to say you were giving up all claim to it, it was a gift, and that you'd trained Pierash on how to keep it running for at least a decade.

"You should have seen their faces in response to *that*; ah, such a sight. The thought that a *commoner* would be taking over? It kept going after that, of course, but I managed to sneak out before it got too bad, and no Task break notification for me!"

"You know, in the abstract I'd almost feel sorry for screwing over people. But at the same time, I can't say I'm *actually* sorry for automating a superfluous task and screwing over a bunch of nobles jostling to get themselves a cushy job."

"I know! Messing with people who deserve it is so much fun."

Off to the side, Edwin noticed Inion perk up slightly, which made sense. Fey classically *loved* puncturing inflated egos and providing some comeuppance, and this story definitely qualified for both.

"So congratulations! You're now officially a nuisance."

"Why, because I gave them a nigh-priceless treasure?"

"Yep!"

Edwin laughed, a mischievous smile creeping across his face at the thought. He had a notification pending from the looks of it, and he curiously pulled it up.

Congratulations! For giving away an expensive artifact with no expectation of repayment you have unlocked the Philanthropist Path!

That was . . . strange. Why did it only update now?

"Path?" she asked.

Edwin nodded. "Any idea why it only just now awarded it, and not when you actually let them know I was giving them the accumulator?"

She replied, "It happens sometimes."

"Yeah, but doesn't the System know everything? Why did it wait until just now? It's never had any problem awarding me a Path for something I didn't know I had done before."

Rillah just said, "Who knows?"

"Hmm. Hey, Lefi!"

* * *

Lefi didn't know, either, but he *did* have several stories of him in a similar situation—earning a Path well past the actual actions taken to unlock it, when he found out that it had occurred. At the same time, he *also* had stories about him learning about events that happened nearby, but he had neither heard nor seen.

Proximity, perhaps? Was everyone's System individual and they couldn't share information, so it could only read what should be earned based on the individual's perceptions, or they were close enough? But then how would Skills like Common Knowledge work? Or just in general, Skills that provided information to the individual that they didn't have before.

Come to think of it, did Common Knowledge actually call upon some form of crowdsourced knowledge repository, or did it draw on some kind of objective truth behind the System? Edwin had dismissed it as likely just being the former, but if it was based on the same kind of knowledge as his Alchemy did, maybe he *was* missing out on something really useful.

Clearly, the answer is to just stick with Rillah, who has lots of Skills like that and can fill in all my gaps of knowledge . . .

His eyes drifted toward Rillah, who had paused her dance to talk to Yathal about something. He didn't hear their exchange, but her giggle was unmissable and almost brought a smile to Edwin's face all on its own.

Yeah, if she'll have me.

It would be nice to have a friend. It would be oh so nice. Ideally— Well, *ideally* Rillah would sometime soon pass his test for friendship, and he could do *something*. He wasn't sure what. Be more forward? That would be awkward, but odds were good that by the time she passed the test—assuming it *ever* happened—he'd be much more comfortable about being honest around her. Not that she was uncomfortable now, but . . .

He shook his head, and his fingers idly reached for a string bracelet that hadn't been on his wrist for *years*. As Rillah started playing her flute once again, Edwin's mind couldn't help but wander back slightly to a time before he fell and—

No. He was *not* going into that now. It was thinking about Earth as *well* as already-painful memories. This was a *good* day. He wasn't allowed to feel bad.

Edwin did keep half an eye out in hopes that Rillah or Inion had noticed his lapse into sadness, but no such luck. He was absolutely awful with emotions, he knew. For both his own and those of others, his strategy essentially amounted to "ignore it and hope it goes away," which he *knew* wasn't conducive to making friends.

He also didn't know how to *fix* that, though. Even on the off chance he *did* recognize when someone had an emotion, he wasn't able to muster up the social courage to do anything about it other than provide slightly awkward advice. So it was kind of hypocritical of him to hope that anyone else might be any better in regard to *him*.

Then again, it was really only a test to see if someone actually cared about him and his emotions or they were just pretending or being polite, so he could definitely pass the test with other people. Noticing when someone was feeling bad, then actually trying to find out what was wrong with them—even pushing past a light dismissal—that was definitely within the realm of possibility.

Right? He wasn't being unreasonable, surely.

All it would take was someone just pushing a *bit*, when he was feeling sad, not just telling him to "cheer up," but actually trying to find out why he was sad and not settling for an empty platitude or two. Rillah was inquisitive and empathetic, so surely she'd be able to figure that out if she tried.

Until then, he'd just *wait*, apparently.

Wait and hope.

That was no call to be sad *now*, though. The sun was shining, the air was clear, and he was on the road again for the first time in what had to have been six months. He was just a level or two from true, nigh-limitless flight, and he had quite fun traveling partners, each doing their own thing.

Rillah was playing a phenomenal, upbeat tune to which Yathal was loudly singing lyrics both off-key and off-beat. Kynigos scrambled ahead, chasing a bird off from where it had perched on the road ahead of them. Despite a heroic leap from Kynigos, the bird he was chasing got away, and the dog landed in a heap. Then he picked himself up, shook himself out, and promptly started running after the next bird. Lefi's laughter boomed out at the scene, and even Inion smiled.

Edwin grinned.

What a great day.

ABOUT THE AUTHOR

Kaleb England, also known as NorskDaedalus, is an author who loves to integrate magic and science to tell interesting stories. England holds a bachelor's degree in physics.